The Best
AMERICAN
SHORT
STORIES
1986

The Best
AMERICAN
SHORT
STORIES
1986

Selected from
U.S. and Canadian Magazines
by RAYMOND CARVER
with SHANNON RAVENEL

With an Introduction by Raymond Carver

HOUGHTON MIFFLIN COMPANY BOSTON 1986

Shannon Ravenel is grateful to Allison Bell, who gave
valuable consultation on science fiction and science fantasy.

ISSN 0067-6233
ISBN 0-395-38399-4
ISBN 0-395-38398-6 (pbk.)

Printed in the United States of America

Q 10 9 8 7 6 5 4 3 2 1

Contents

Publisher's Note

The *Best American Short Stories* series was started in 1915 under the editorship of Edward J. O'Brien. Its title reflects the optimism of a time when people assumed that an objective "best" could be identified, even in fields not measurable in physical terms.

Martha Foley took over as editor of the series in 1942. With her husband, Whit Burnett, she had edited *Story* magazine since 1931, and in later years she taught creative writing at Columbia School of Journalism. When Miss Foley died in 1977, at the age of eighty, she was at work on what would have been her thirty-seventh volume of *The Best American Short Stories*.

Beginning with the 1978 edition, Houghton Mifflin introduced a new editorial arrangement for the anthology. Inviting a different writer or critic to edit each new annual volume would provide a variety of viewpoints to enliven the series and broaden its scope. *Best American Short Stories* has thus become a series of informed but differing opinions that gains credibility from its very diversity.

Also beginning with the 1978 volume, the guest editors have worked with the annual editor, Shannon Ravenel, who during each calendar year reads as many qualifying short stories as she can get hold of, makes a preliminary selection of 120 stories for the guest editor's consideration, and selects the "100 Other Distinguished Short Stories of the Year," a listing that has always been an important feature of these volumes.

The stories chosen for this year's anthology were originally published in magazines issued between January 1985 and January 1986. The qualifications for selection are: (1) original publication in nationally distributed American or Canadian periodicals; (2) publication in English by writers who are American or Canadian; and (3) publication *as* short stories (novel excerpts are not knowingly considered by the editors). A list of the magazines consulted by Ms. Ravenel appears at the back of this volume. Other publications wishing to make sure that their contributors are considered for the series should include Ms. Ravenel on their subscription list (P.O. Box 3176, University City, Missouri 63130).

Introduction

THE NEXT BEST THING to writing your own short story is to read someone else's short story. And when you read and reread, as I did, 120 of them back to back in a fairly short span of time (January 25 to February 25), you come away able to draw a few conclusions. The most obvious is that clearly there are a great many stories being written these days, and generally the quality is good — in some cases even exceptional. (There are plenty of stories that aren't so good, by both "known" and "unknown" writers, but why talk about these? So what if there are? So what? We do what we can.) I want to remark on the good stories I read and say why I think they're good and why I chose the twenty I did. But first a few words about the selection process itself.

Shannon Ravenel, who has been the annual editor for this series since 1977, read 1,811 short stories from 165 different periodicals — a big increase over previous years, she tells me. From her reading she sent 120 for my consideration. As editor, my job was to pick twenty stories for inclusion. But I had liberty in making my selections: I didn't have to take all or, conceivably, any of the 120 that arrived one morning by Express Mail — an event that brought conflicting emotions, as they say, on my part. For one thing, I was writing a story of my own, and I was nearly finished with it. Of course I wanted to go on without interruption. (As usual, when working on a story, this one felt like the best I'd ever write. I was loath to turn my attention from it to the 120 others that waited for some sign from me.) But I was also more than a little interested in knowing just which 120 stories I now had in my possession. I leafed through the stories then and there, and while I didn't read any of them that day, or even the next, I noted the names of the authors, some of whom were friends or acquaintances, others belonging to writers I knew by name only, or by name *and* some prior work. But, happily, most of the stories were by writers I didn't know, writers I'd never heard of — unknowns, as they're called, and as they indeed are to the world at large. The magazines the stories had come from were nearly as diverse and as numerous as the writers. I say *nearly*. Stories from *The New Yorker* predominated, and this is as it should be. *The New Yorker* not only publishes good stories — on occasion wonderful stories — but, by virtue of the fact that they publish every week, fifty-two weeks a year, they bring out more fiction than any other magazine in the country. I took three stories that had first appeared in that magazine. The other magazines I selected from are represented with one story each.

In November 1984, when I was invited to serve as this year's editor, I made plans to begin my own list of "best" come January 1985. And in the course of my reading last year I came across a dozen or so that I liked exceedingly well, stories that excited me enough to put them aside for a later reading. (In the final analysis, being excited by a story is the only acceptable criterion for including it in a collection of this kind, or for publishing the story in a magazine in the first place.) I kept these stories in a folder with the intention of rereading them this January or February, when I knew I would be looking at the other 120. And most often, in 1985, when I read something I liked, something that stirred me enough to put it by for later, I wondered — a stray thought — if I'd see that same story turn up in Shannon Ravenel's choices.

Well, there was some duplication. A few of the stories I'd flagged were among those she sent along. But most of the stories I'd noted were not, for whatever reasons, included among those 120. In any event, I had liberty, as I've said, to take what I wanted from her selections, as well as include what I wanted from my own reading. (I could, I suppose, if I'd been willful, or out of my mind, have selected twenty stories entirely of my own choosing, had none of the stories she sent pleased me.) Now —

and this is the last set of figures, just about, that you'll hear on the matter — the breakdown went as follows: of the 120 stories I received in the mail, I selected twelve, all beauties, for inclusion. I found eight other beauties from my own reading.

I'd like to make claims for these twenty as being *the* best stories published in the United States and Canada in 1985. But since I know there will be some people who won't agree with this and since I know, too, that another editor would have chosen differently, with possibly two or three notable exceptions, I'd better say instead that I believe these twenty are among the best stories published in 1985. And I'll go on to say the obvious: under someone else's editorship, this would be a different book with an entirely different feel and composition to it. But this is only as it should be. For no editor puts together a collection such as this without bringing to it his or her own biases and notions of what makes a good story a good story. What works in a short story? What convinces us? Why am I moved, or perturbed, by this story? Why do some stories seem good the first time around but don't hold up on rereading? (I read every story I've included here at least four times; if I found myself still interested, still *excited* by the story after I'd read it a fourth time, I figured it might be a story I wanted to see in the book.)

There were other biases at work. I lean toward realistic, "life-like" characters — that is to say, people — in realistically detailed situations. I'm drawn toward the traditional (some would call it old-fashioned) methods of storytelling: one layer of reality unfolding and giving way to another, perhaps richer layer; the gradual accretion of meaningful detail; dialogue that not only reveals something about character but advances the story. I'm not very interested, finally, in haphazard revelations, attenuated characters, stories where method or technique is all — stories, in short, where nothing much happens, or where what *does* happen merely confirms one's sour view of a world gone out of control. Too, I distrust the inflated language that some people pile on when they write fiction. I believe in the efficacy of the concrete word, be it noun or verb, as opposed to the abstract or arbitrary or slippery word — or phrase, or sentence. I tried to steer away from stories that, in my terms, didn't seem to be *written* well, stories where the words seemed to slide into one another and blur the meaning. If that happens, if the reader loses his way and his interest, for whatever reason, the story suffers and usually dies.

Abjure carelessness in writing, just as you would in life.

The present volume is not to be seen as a holding action against slipshod writing or poorly conceived and executed stories. But it does, by virtue of its contents, stand squarely against that brand of work. I believe it is safe to say that the day of the campy, or crazy, or trivial, stupidly written account of inconsequential acts that don't count for much in the world has come and gone. And we should all be grateful that is *has* passed on. I deliberately tried to pick stories that rendered, in a more or less straightforward manner, what it's like out there. I wanted the stories I selected to throw some light on what it is that makes us and keeps us, often against great odds, recognizably human.

Short stories, like houses — or cars, for that matter — should be built to last. They should also be pleasing, if not beautiful, to look at, and everything inside them should *work*. A reader searching for "experimental" or "innovative" stories won't find them here. (Along with Flannery O'Connor, I admit to being put off by something that "looks funny" on the page.) Donald Barthelme's "Basil from Her Garden" is the closest thing anyone will find to the experimental or avant-garde. But Barthelme is the exception in this, as he is in all things: his oftentimes "funny-looking" stories are properly inimitable, and this is as good a touchstone as any for picking stories you want to preserve. His stories are also, in some strange way, quite often moving, which is another touchstone.

Since I mentioned Barthelme, I'm brought to remark on a final item in the selection process. On the one hand, you have stories of the first order by some of the best, and best-known, living American and Canadian writers — which is to say, stories by some of the best writers in the English language. On the other hand, you have a few equally wonderful stories from unknown, or virtually unknown, writers. And the editor of this collection is supposed to pick twenty and no more for his book. A plethora of riches. But what if there are two "equally wonderful" stories, and finally you're making the last selection, and there's room in the book for, say, only one of those? Which story is to be included? Should the interests of the great or well-known authors be looked after over and above the interests of the lesser known? Should extraliterary considerations ever apply? Happily, I can say it never came to that, quite. In the one or two instances when it seemed headed in that direction, I picked a story of quality by an unknown writer. But finally — in every case, really — the stories I selected were, in my estimation, the best stories available, "name" and prior achievements notwithstanding.

Yet looking back, I see it's turned out that many, if not the majority, of my selections fell on younger, lesser-known writers. Jessica Neely, say. Who is she, and how does she come to write a story as beautiful as "Skin Angels"? Look at this irresistible first sentence: "In the beginning of the summer my mother memorized the role of Lady Macbeth four mornings a week and worked the late shift in Geriatrics." Or Ethan Canin. Why have I read only one short story by him before now? What is his fine story "Star Food" doing in a "city magazine" like *Chicago* — a magazine, I'm told, that doesn't plan to publish fiction any longer. And this writer David Michael Kaplan. His name rings a bell, faintly. I think so, anyway. (Maybe I'm thinking of another writer, a poet or a fiction writer who uses three names and who has a name that sounds like David Michael Kaplan.) In any event, "Doe Season" is an amazing piece of work. What a joy, what a great pleasure it was to come across this story and to be able to reprint it in the company of such other fine stories. Or take, for instance, another unknown writer, Mona Simpson, and her superb "Lawns" with *her* irresistible first sentence, "I steal." Take another writer whose work I was not familiar with, Kent Nelson. His wonderful story "Invisible Life" has to do, in part, with the new beginnings some people are always trying to make.

A further admission. I confess to not having read David Lipsky before this. Surely he's published other work. Have I been asleep and missed some stories of his, or maybe even a novel or two? I don't know. I do know I intend to pay attention from now on if I see his name over a short story. "Three Thousand Dollars" is, well, there's nothing in the book quite like it. Which is partly, but only partly, the point I'm trying to make.

James Lee Burke. Here's another writer I didn't know the first thing about. But he's written a story called "The Convict" that I'm proud to have in this collection. There's a remarkable evocation of a particular time and place at work in the story (as there is with each story I picked, which is undoubtedly one of the reasons I was attracted to begin with; a sense of place, location, *setting* being as important to me as it is). But there is the strong personal 'drama of the young narrator and his father, Will Broussard, who tells the boy, "You have to make choices in this world."

Choices. Conflict. Drama. Consequences. *Narrative.*

Christopher McIlroy. Where in the world did he come from? How does he know so much about alcohol, ranch life, *pastry,* and the dreary existence of the reservation Indians — not to mention the secrets of the human heart?

Grace Paley, of course, is Grace Paley — fundamental reading to short story readers. She has been doing inimitable work for nearly thirty years. I'm pleased to be able to include her splendid story "Telling." And Alice Munro, the distinguished Canadian short story writer. For some years she's been quietly writing some of the best short fiction in the world. "Monsieur les Deux Chapeaux" is a good example.

Are we our brothers' keepers? Before answering, read Munro's story and "The Rich Brother," an unforgettable story by Tobias Wolff. "Where is he? Where is your brother?" is the question Donald, the rich brother, has to answer at the conclusion.

And there's Ann Beattie's scrupulously written and singular story "Janus," which is given entirely in narrative.

Some of the writers whose work I was to one degree or another familiar with before I selected their stories include Joy Williams, Richard Ford, Thomas McGuane, Frank Conroy, Charles Baxter, Amy Hempel, Tess Gallagher — the last an established poet. (Fact: short stories are closer in spirit to poems than they are to novels.)

What do these writers have in common so far as the stories in this anthology are concerned?

For one thing they are, each of them, concerned with writing accurately, that is to say, thoughtfully and carefully, about recognizable men and women and children going about the sometimes ordinary business of living, which is, as we all know, not always an easy matter. And they are writing, in most cases, not just about living and getting by, but about *going on,* sometimes against the odds, sometimes even prevailing against the odds.

They are writing, in short, about things that count. What counts? Love, death, dreams, ambition, growing up, coming to terms with your own and other people's limitations. Dramas every one, and dramas played out against a larger canvas than might be apparent on first glance.

Talk about bias! I see now that each of the stories in the book has to do, in one way or another, with family, with other people, with community. "Real people" in the guise of fictional characters inhabit the stories, make decisions for good or evil (mostly good), and reach a turning point, which in some cases is a point of no return. In any case, things will never be the same for them again. The reader will find grown-up men and women in the stories — husbands, wives, fathers and mothers, sons and daughters, lovers of every stripe including one poignant father-daughter relationship (Mona Simpson's "Lawns"). The characters in the stories are people you're likely to be familiar with. If they're not kin, or your immediate neighbors, they live on a nearby street, or else in a neighboring town, or maybe even the next state over. (I'm talking about a real state now, a place on the map, not just a state of mind.) The Pima Indian reservation in Arizona, for instance. Or else northern California, the Eureka and Mendocino counties area in particular; the high tableland country around Victory, Montana; a small town in northern Vermont. Or else they live in New York, or Berkeley, or Houston, or just outside New Orleans — not such exotic places finally, when all is said and done. The people in the stories are not terribly exotic, either. We've seen them in the cities, towns, and countrysides I've just mentioned, or else on TV, talking to the news commentator, bearing witness, telling how it feels to have survived, to have come through, after the house was carried away in the flood, or the fourth-generation farm has been foreclosed on by the FHA. They are people who've been struck and altered by circumstance and who are about to turn this way or that, depending.

I'm saying the people in the stories are very much like us, in our better — and worse — moments. In "Gossip," Frank Conroy has his narrator say and, more importantly, understand, the following: "Everyone was connected in a web . . . pain was part of the web, and yet despite it, people loved one another. That's what you found out when you got older." The people in the stories make decisions, as we all do, that affect the way they will live their lives ever after. In "Communist," Richard Ford's young narrator, Les, says, "I felt the way you feel when you are on a trestle all alone and the train is coming, and you know you have to decide." He does decide, and nothing is the same for him afterward.

The train *is* coming, and we have to decide. Is this true, or is this true? "There're limits to everything, right?" says Glen, the ex-CIA man, the mother's boyfriend in the story, the goose hunter, the "communist."

Right.

In his story "All My Relations" — a title, incidentally, that could serve as an overall title for this collection — Christopher McIlroy has his rancher, Jack Oldenburg, say these words to Milton, concerning Milton's self-destructive drinking: "Drawing the line helps you. It's not easy living right. . . . The right way is always plain, though we do our best to obscure it."

In "Today Will Be a Quiet Day," the little gem of a story by Amy Hempel, the dad who is trying to raise his two precocious kids and do the right "dad" things on a rainy Sunday afternoon has this to say about a father's concerns: "You think you're safe . . . but it's thinking you're invisible because you closed your eyes." Hempel also has one of the best and simplest descriptions of happiness I've ever read: "He doubted he would ever feel — not better, but *more* than he did now."

From "Sportsmen," Thomas McGuane's fine story that takes place in the 1950s in a little town on the shore of Lake Erie, we share a strange meal with two teenagers, one of whom has suffered a broken neck in a diving accident:

> I had to feed Jimmy off the point of my Barlow knife, but we ate two big ducks for breakfast and lunch at once. . . .
> "Fork me some of that there duck meat," said Jimmy Meade in his Ohio voice.
> [Later] I wrap Jimmy's blanket up under his chin.

And in David Lipsky's "Three Thousand Dollars" there is the following little exchange:

> "I just don't want to be a burden."

"You are," she says. "But it's O.K. I mean, I'm your mother, and you're supposed to be my burden."

You see what I'm saying? I'm not sure what I'm saying, but I think I know what I'm trying to get at. Somehow, and I feel strongly about this, these twenty stories are connected, they belong together — at least to my way of thinking — and when you read them I hope you'll see what I mean.

Putting together a collection such as this lets the reader in on what it is, in the way of short stories at least, that the editor likes and holds dear to his heart. Which is fine. One of the things I feel strongly about is that while short stories often tell us things we don't know anything about — and this is good, of course — they should also, and maybe more importantly, tell us what *everybody* knows but what nobody is talking about. At least not publicly. Except for the short story writers.

Of the writers included here, Grace Paley is the one who has been at it the longest. Her first book of stories appeared in 1959. Donald Barthelme published his first book four years later, in 1963. Alice Munro, Frank Conroy, Ann Beattie, Thomas McGuane, Joy Williams — they've also been working at this trade for a while. Two writers who have come to prominence recently are Richard Ford and Tobias Wolff. I don't in the least worry about the other, newer writers. Charles Baxter. Amy Hempel. David Lipsky. Jessica Neely. David Michael Kaplan. Tess Gallagher. James Lee Burke. Mona Simpson. Christopher McIlroy. Kent Nelson. Ethan Canin. They're fine writers, each of them, and I have the feeling they're stickers as well. I think they've found the road and will keep to it.

Of course, if this collection was anything like the other *Best American* collections or like *Prize Stories: The O. Henry Awards,* odds are that many of the writers I've included would never be seen or heard from again. (If you don't believe this, go look at the table of contents of any of the major anthologies for the past several years. Open the 1976 *Best American* collection or the 1966 edition and see how many names you recognize.) The more established writers I've included will, I'm sure, go on producing work of distinction. But, as I've said, I don't plan to worry about the newer writers in this book finding their way. I have the feeling they've pretty much done that already.

Writers write, and they write, and they go on writing, in some cases long after wisdom and even common sense have told them to quit. There are always plenty of reasons — good, compelling reasons, too — for quitting, or for not writing very much or very seriously. (Writing is trouble, make no mistake, for everyone involved, and who needs trouble?) But once in a great while lightning strikes, and occasionally it strikes early in the writer's life. Sometimes it comes later, after years of work. And sometimes, most often, of course, it never happens at all. Strangely, it seems, it may hit people whose work you can't abide, an event that, when it occurs, causes you to feel there's no justice whatsoever in the world. (There isn't, more often than not.) It may hit the man or woman who is or was your friend, the one who drank too much, or not at all, who went off with someone's wife, or husband, or sister, after a party you attended together. The young writer who sat in the back of the class and never had anything to say about anything. The dunce, you thought. The writer who couldn't, not in one's wildest imaginings, make anyone's list of top ten possibilities. It happens sometimes. The dark horse. It happens, lightning, or it doesn't happen. (Naturally, it's more fun when it does happen.) But it will never, never happen to those who don't work hard at it and who don't consider the act of writing as very nearly the most important thing in their lives, right up there next to breath, and food, and shelter, and love, and God.

I hope people will read these stories for pleasure and amusement, for solace, courage — for whatever reasons people turn to literature — and will find in them something that will not just show us how we live now (though a writer could do worse than set his sights on this goal), but something else as well: a sense of union maybe, an aesthetic feeling of correctness; nothing less, really, than beauty given form and made visible in the incomparable way only short stories can do. I hope readers will find themselves interested and maybe even *moved* from time to time by what they find herein. Because if short story writing, along with the reading of short stories, doesn't have to do with any of these matters, then what is it we are all doing, what is it we are about, pray tell? And why are we gathered here?

RAYMOND CARVER

The Best
AMERICAN
SHORT
STORIES
1986

DONALD BARTHELME

Basil from Her Garden

FROM THE NEW YORKER

A — In the dream, my father was playing the piano, a Beethoven something, in a large concert hall that was filled with people. I was in the audience and I was reading a book. I suddenly realized that this was the wrong thing to do when my father was performing, so I sat up and paid attention. He was playing very well, I thought. Suddenly the conductor stopped the performance and began to sing a passage for my father, a passage that my father had evidently botched. My father listened attentively, smiling at the conductor.

Q — Does your father play? In actuality?

A — Not a note.

Q — Did the conductor resemble anyone you know?

A — He looked a bit like Althea. The same cheekbones and the same chin.

Q — Who is Althea?

A — Someone I know.

Q — What do you do, after work, in the evenings or on weekends?

A — Just ordinary things.

Q — No special interests?

A — I'm very interested in bow hunting. These new bows they have now, what they call a compound bow. Also, I'm a member of the Galapagos Society, we work for the environment, it's really a very effective —

Q — And what else?

A — Well, adultery. I would say that that's how I spend most of my free time. In adultery.

Q — You mean regular adultery.

A — Yes. Sleeping with people to whom one is not legally bound.

Q — These are women.

A — Invariably.

Q — And so that's what you do, in the evenings or on weekends.

A — I had this kind of strange experience. Today is Saturday, right? I called up this haircutter that I go to, her name is Ruth, and asked for an appointment. I needed a haircut. So she says she has openings at ten, ten-thirty, eleven, eleven-thirty, twelve, twelve-thirty — On a Saturday. Do you think the world knows something I don't know?

Q — It's possible.

A — What if she stabs me in the ear with the scissors?

Q — Unlikely, I would think.

A — Well, she's a good soul. She's had several husbands. They've all been master sergeants, in the Army. She seems to gravitate toward NCO clubs. Have you noticed all these little black bugs flying around here? I don't know where they come from.

Q — They're very small, they're like gnats.

A — They come in clouds, then they go away.

A — I sometimes think of myself as a person who, you know what I mean, could have done something else, it doesn't matter what particularly. Just something else. I saw an ad in the Sunday paper for the CIA, a recruiting ad, maybe a quarter of a page, and I suddenly thought, It might be interesting to do that. Even though I've always been opposed to the CIA, when they were trying to bring Cuba down, the stuff with Lumumba in Africa, the stuff in Central America . . . Then here is this ad, perfectly straightforward, "where your career is America's strength" or something like that, "aptitude for learning a foreign language is a plus" or something like that. I've always been good at languages, and I'm sitting there thinking about how my résumé might look to them, starting completely over in something completely new, changing the very sort of person I am, and there was an attraction, a definite attraction. Of course the

maximum age was thirty-five. I guess they want them more
malleable.

Q — So, in the evenings or on weekends —
  A — Not every night or every weekend. I mean, this depends
on the circumstances. Sometimes my wife and I go to dinner
with people, or watch television —
  Q — But in the main —
  A — It's not that often. It's once in a while.
  Q — Adultery is is a sin.
  A — It is classified as a sin, yes. Absolutely.
  Q — The Seventh Commandment says —
  A — I know what it says. I was raised on the Seventh Com-
mandment. But.
  Q — But what?
  A — The Seventh Commandment is wrong.
  Q — It's wrong?
  A — Some outfits call it the Sixth and others the Seventh. It's
wrong.
  Q — The whole Commandment?
  A — I don't know how it happened, whether it's a mistransla-
tion from the Aramaic or whatever, it may not even have been
Aramaic, I don't know, I certainly do not pretend to scholarship
in this area, but my sense of the matter is that the Seventh
Commandment is an error.
  Q — Well if that was true it would change quite a lot of things,
wouldn't it?
  A — Take the pressure off, a bit.
  Q — Have you told your wife?
  A — Yes, Grete knows.
  Q — How'd she take it?
  A — Well, she *liked* the Seventh Commandment. You could
reason that it was in her interest to support the Seventh Com-
mandment for the preservation of the family unit and this sort
of thing but to reason that way is, I would say, to take an ex-
tremely narrow view of Grete, of what she thinks. She's not
predictable. She once told me that she didn't want me, she
wanted a suite of husbands, ten or twenty —
  Q — What did you say?

A — I said, Go to it.

Q — Well, how does it make you feel? Adultery.

A — There's a certain amount of guilt attached. I feel guilty. But I feel guilty even without adultery. I exist in a morass of guilt. There's maybe a little additional wallop of guilt but I already feel so guilty that I hardly notice it.

Q — Where does all this guilt come from? The extra-adulterous guilt?

A — I keep wondering if, say, there is intelligent life on other planets, the scientists argue that something like two percent of the other planets have the conditions, the physical conditions, to support life in the way it happened here, did Christ visit each and every planet, go through the same routine, the Agony in the Garden, the Crucifixion, and so on . . . And these guys on these other planets, these life forms, maybe they look like boll weevils or something, on a much larger scale of course, were they told that they shouldn't go to bed with other attractive six-foot boll weevils arrayed in silver and gold and with little squirts of Opium behind the ears? Doesn't make sense. But of course our human understanding is imperfect.

Q — You haven't answered me. This general guilt —

A — Yes, that's the interesting thing. I hazard that it is not guilt so much as it is inadequacy. I feel that everything is being nibbled away, because I can't *get it right* —

Q — Would you like to be able to fly?

A — It's crossed my mind.

Q — Myself, I think about being just sort of a regular person, one who worries about cancer a lot, every little thing a prediction of cancer, no I don't want to go for my every-two-years checkup because what if they find something? I wonder what will kill me and when it will happen and how it will happen, and I wonder about my parents, who are still alive, and what will happen to them. This seems to me to be a proper set of things to worry about. Last things.

A — I don't think God gives a snap about adultery. This is just an opinion, of course.

Q — So how do you, how shall I put it, pursue —

A — You think about this staggering concept, the mind of

God, and then you think He's sitting around worrying about this guy and this woman at the Beechnut TraveLodge? I think not.

Q — Well He doesn't have to think about every particular instance, He just sort of laid out the general principles —

A — He also created creatures who, with a single powerful glance —

Q — The eyes burn.

A — They do.

Q — The heart leaps.

A — Like a terrapin.

Q — Stupid youth returns.

A — Like hockey sticks falling out of a long-shut closet.

Q — Do you play?

A — I did. Many years ago.

Q — Who is Althea?

A — Someone I know.

Q — We're basically talking about Althea.

A — Yes. I thought you understood that.

Q — We're not talking about wholesale —

A — Oh Lord no. Who has the strength?

Q — What's she like?

A — She's I guess you'd say a little on the boring side. To the innocent eye.

Q — She appears to be a contained, controlled person, free of raging internal fires.

A — But my eye is not innocent. To the already corrupted eye, she's —

Q — I don't want to question you too closely on this. I don't want to strain your powers of —

A — Well, no, I don't mind talking about it. It fell on me like a ton of bricks. I was walking in the park one day.

Q — Which park?

A — That big park over by —

Q — Yeah, I know the one.

A — This woman was sitting there.

Q — They sit in parks a lot, I've noticed that. Especially when they're angry. The solitary bench. Shoulders raised, legs kicking —

.

A — I've crossed both major oceans by ship — the Pacific twice, on troopships, the Atlantic once, on a passenger liner. You stand out there, at the rail, at dusk, and the sea is limitless, water in every direction, never ending, you think *water forever,* the movement of the ship seems slow but also seems inexorable, you feel you will be moving this way forever, the Pacific is about seventy million square miles, about one-third of the earth's surface, the ship might be making twenty knots, I'm eating oranges because that's all I can keep down, twelve days of it with thousands of young soldiers all around, half of them seasick —   On the Queen Mary, in tourist class, we got rather good food, there was a guy assigned to our table who had known Paderewski, the great pianist who was also prime minister of Poland, he talked about Paderewski for four days, an ocean of anecdotes —

Q — When I was first married, when I was twenty, I didn't know where the clitoris was. I didn't know there was such a thing. Shouldn't somebody have told me?

A — Perhaps your wife?

Q — Of course, she was too shy. In those days people didn't go around saying, This is the clitoris and this is what its proper function is and this is what you can do to help out. I finally found it. In a book.

A — German?

Q — Dutch.

A — A dead bear in a blue dress, face down on the kitchen floor. I trip over it, in the dark, when I get up at 2 a.m. to see if there's anything to eat in the refrigerator. It's an architectural problem, marriage. If we could live in separate houses, and visit each other when we felt particularly gay —   It would be expensive, yes. But as it is she has to endure me in all my worst manifestations, early in the morning and late at night and in the nutsy obsessed noontimes. When I wake up from my nap you don't *get* the laughing cavalier, you get a rank pigfooted belching blunderer. I knew this one guy who built a wall down the middle of his apartment. An impenetrable wall. He had a very big apartment. It worked out very well. Concrete block, basically, with fiber glass insulation on top of that and Sheetrock on top of that —

Q — What about coveting your neighbor's wife?

A — Well on one side there are no wives, strictly speaking, there are two floors and two male couples, all very nice people. On the other side, Bill and Rachel have the whole house. I like Rachel but I don't covet her. I could covet her, she's covetable, quite lovely and spirited, but in point of fact our relationship is that of neighborliness. I jump-start her car when her battery is dead, she gives me basil from her garden, she's got acres of basil, not literally acres but — Anyhow, I don't think that's much of a problem, coveting your neighbor's wife. Just speaking administratively, I don't see why there's an entire Commandment devoted to it. It's a mental exercise, coveting. To covet is not necessarily to take action.

Q — I covet my neighbor's leaf blower. It has this neat Vari-Flo deal that lets you —

A — I can see that.

Q — I am feverishly interested in these questions.

Q — Ethics has always been where my heart is.

Q — Moral precepting stings the dull mind into attentiveness.

Q — I'm only a bit depressed, only a bit.

Q — A new arrangement of ideas, based upon the best thinking, would produce a more humane moral order, which we need.

Q — Apple honey, disposed upon the sexual parts, is not an index of decadence. Decadence itself is not as bad as it's been painted.

Q — That he watched his father play the piano when his father could not play the piano and that he was reading a book while his father played the piano in a very large hall before a very large audience only means that he finds his roots, as it were, untrustworthy. The father imagined as a root. That's not unusual.

Q — As for myself, I am content with too little, I know this about myself and I do not commend myself for it and perhaps one day I shall be able to change myself into a hungrier being. Probably not.

Q — The leaf blower, for example.

A — I see Althea now and then, not often enough. We sigh together in a particular bar, it's almost always empty. She tells me about her kids and I tell her about my kids. I obey the Commandments, the sensible ones. Where they don't know what they're talking about I ignore them. I keep thinking about the story of the two old women in church listening to the priest discoursing on the dynamics of the married state. At the end of the sermon one turns to the other and says, "I wish I knew as little about it as he does."

Q — He critiques us, we critique Him. Does Grete also engage in dalliance?

A — How quaint you are. I think she has friends whom she sees now and then.

Q — How does that make you feel?

A — I wish her well.

Q — What's in your wallet?

A — The usual. Credit cards, pictures of the children, driver's license, forty dollars in cash, Amex receipts —

Q — I sometimes imagine that I am in Pest Control. I have a small white truck with a red diamond-shaped emblem on the door and a white jumpsuit with the same emblem on the breast pocket. I park the truck in front of a subscriber's neat three-hundred-thousand-dollar home, extract the silver cannister of deadly pest killer from the back of the truck, and walk up the brick sidewalk to the house's front door. Chimes ring, the door swings open, a young wife in jeans and a pink flannel shirt worn outside the jeans is standing there. "Pest Control," I say. She smiles at me, I smile back and move past her into the house, into the handsomely appointed kitchen. The cannister is suspended by a sling from my right shoulder, and, pumping the mechanism occasionally with my right hand, I point the nozzle of the hose at the baseboards and begin to spray. I spray alongside the refrigerator, alongside the gas range, under the sink, and behind the kitchen table. Next, I move to the bathrooms, pumping and spraying. The young wife is in another room, waiting for me to finish. I walk into the main sitting room and spray discreetly behind the largest pieces of furniture, an oak sideboard, a red plush Victorian couch, and along the inside of the fireplace. I do the study, spraying the Columbia Encyclopedia, he's been looking up the Seven Years' War, 1756–63, yellow highlighting there, and behind the forty-five-inch RCA television. The master bedroom requires just touches, short bursts in her closet which must avoid the two dozen pairs of shoes there and in his closet which contains six to eight long guns in canvas cases. Finally I spray the laundry room with its big white washer and dryer, and behind the folding table stacked with sheets and towels already folded. Who folds? I surmise that she folds. Unless one of the older children, pressed into service, folds. In my experience they are unlikely to fold. Maybe the au pair. Finished, I tear a properly made out receipt from my receipt book and present it to the young wife. She scribbles her name in the appropriate space and hands it back to me. The house now stinks quite palpably but I know and she knows that the stench will dissipate in two to four hours. The young wife escorts me to the door, and, in parting, pins a silver medal on my chest and kisses me on both cheeks. Pest Control!

A — Yes, one could fit in in that way. It's finally a matter, perhaps, of fit. Appropriateness. Fit in a stately or sometimes hectic dance with nonfit. What we have to worry about.

Q — It seems to me that we have quite a great deal to worry about. Does the radish worry about itself in this way? Yet the radish is a living thing. Until it's cooked.

A — Grete is made for radishes, can't get enough. I like frozen Mexican dinners, Patio, I have them for breakfast, the freezer is stacked with them —

Q — Transcendence is possible.

A — Yes.

Q — Is it possible?

A — Not out of the question.

Q — Is it really possible?

A — Yes. Believe me.

CHARLES BAXTER

Gryphon

FROM EPOCH

ON WEDNESDAY AFTERNOON, between the geography lesson on ancient Egypt's hand-operated irrigation system and an art project that involved drawing a model city next to a mountain, our fourth-grade teacher, Mr. Hibler, developed a cough. This cough began with a series of muffled throat clearings and progressed to propulsive noises contained within Mr. Hibler's closed mouth. "Listen to him," Carol Peterson whispered to me. "He's gonna blow up." Mr. Hibler's laughter — dazed and infrequent — sounded a bit like his cough, but as we worked on our model cities we would look up, thinking he was enjoying a joke, and see Mr. Hibler's face turning red, his cheeks puffed out. This was not laughter. Twice he bent over, and his loose tie, like a plumb line, hung down straight from his neck as he exploded himself into a Kleenex. He would excuse himself, then go on coughing. "I'll bet you a dime," Carol Peterson whispered, "we get a substitute tomorrow."

Carol sat at the desk in front of mine and was a bad person — when she thought no one was looking she would blow her nose on notebook paper, then crumble it up and throw it into the wastebasket — but at times of crisis she spoke the truth. I knew I'd lose the dime.

"No deal," I said.

When Mr. Hibler stood us up in formation at the door just prior to the final bell, he was almost incapable of speech. "I'm sorry, boys and girls," he said. "I seem to be coming down with something."

"I hope you feel better tomorrow, Mr. Hibler," Bobby Kryza-nowicz, the faultless brown-noser said, and I heard Carol Peter-son's evil giggle. Then Mr. Hibler opened the door and we walked out to the buses, a clique of us starting noisily to hawk and cough as soon as we thought we were a few feet beyond Mr. Hibler's earshot.

Five Oaks being a rural community, and in Michigan, the supply of substitute teachers was limited to the town's unem-ployed community college graduates, a pool of about four mothers. These ladies fluttered, provided easeful class days, and nervously covered material we had mastered weeks earlier. Therefore it was a surprise when a woman we had never seen came into the class the next day, carrying a purple purse, a checkerboard lunchbox, and a few books. She put the books on one side of Mr. Hibler's desk and the lunchbox on the other, next to the Voice of Music phonograph. Three of us in the back of the room were playing with Heever, the chameleon that lived in the terrarium and on one of the plastic drapes, when she walked in.

She clapped her hands at us. "Little boys," she said, "why are you bent over together like that?" She didn't wait for us to answer. "Are you tormenting an animal? Put it back. Please sit down at your desks. I want no cabals this time of the day." We just stared at her. "Boys," she repeated, "I asked you to sit down."

I put the chameleon in his terrarium and felt my way to my desk, never taking my eyes off the woman. With white and green chalk, she had started to draw a tree on the left side of the blackboard. She didn't look usual. Furthermore, her tree was outsized, disproportionate, for some reason.

"This room needs a tree," she said, with one line drawing the suggestion of a leaf. "A large, leafy, shady, deciduous . . . oak."

Her fine, light hair had been done up in what I would learn years later was called a chignon, and she wore gold-rimmed glasses whose lenses seemed to have the faintest blue tint. Har-old Knardahl, who sat across from me, whispered "Mars," and I nodded slowly, savoring the imminent weirdness of the day. The substitute drew another branch with an extravagant arm gesture, then turned around and said, "Good morning. I don't believe I said good morning to all you yet."

Facing us, she was no special age — an adult is an adult — but her face had two prominent lines, descending vertically from the sides of her mouth to her chin. I knew where I had seen those lines before: *Pinocchio.* They were marionette lines. "You may stare at me," she said to us, as a few more kids from the last bus came into the room, their eyes fixed on her, "for a few more seconds, until the bell rings. Then I will permit no more staring. Looking I will permit. Staring, no. It is impolite to stare, and a sign of bad breeding. You cannot make a social effort while staring."

Harold Knardahl did not glance at me, or nudge, but I heard him whisper "Mars" again, trying to get more mileage out of his single joke with the kids who had just come in.

When everyone was seated, the substitute teacher finished her tree, put down her chalk fastidiously on the phonograph, brushed her hands, and faced us. "Good morning," she said. "I am Miss Ferenczi, your teacher for the day. I am fairly new to your community, and I don't believe any of you know me. I will therefore start by telling you a story about myself."

While we settled back, she launched into her tale. She said her grandfather had been a Hungarian prince; her mother had been born in some place called Flanders, had been a pianist, and had played concerts for people Miss Ferenczi referred to as "crowned heads." She gave us a knowing look. "Grieg," she said, "the Norwegian master, wrote a concerto for piano that was," she paused, "my mother's triumph at her debut concert in London." Her eyes searched the ceiling. Our eyes followed. Nothing up there but ceiling tile. "For reasons that I shall not go into, my family's fortunes took us to Detroit, then north to dreadful Saginaw, and now here I am in Five Oaks, as your substitute teacher, for today, Thursday, October the eleventh. I believe it will be a good day: All the forecasts coincide. We shall start with your reading lesson. Take out your reading book. I believe it is called *Broad Horizons,* or something along those lines."

Jeannie Vermeesch raised her hand. Miss Ferenzi nodded at her. "Mr. Hibler always starts the day with the Pledge of Allegiance," Jeannie whined.

"Oh, does he? In that case," Miss Ferenczi said, "you must know it *very* well by now, and we certainly need not spend our time on it. No, no allegiance pledging on the premises today, by my reckoning. Not with so much sunlight coming into the room. A pledge does not suit my mood." She glanced at her watch. "Time *is* flying. Take out *Broad Horizons*."

She disappointed us by giving us an ordinary lesson, complete with vocabulary word drills, comprehension questions, and recitation. She didn't seem to care for the material, however. She sighed every few minutes and rubbed her glasses with a frilly perfumed handkerchief that she withdrew, magician style, from her left sleeve.

After reading we moved on to arithmetic. It was my favorite time of the morning, when the lazy autumn sunlight dazzled its way through ribbons of clouds past the windows on the east side of the classroom, and crept across the linoleum floor. On the playground the first group of children, the kindergartners, were running on the quack grass just beyond the monkey bars. We were doing multiplication tables. Miss Ferenczi had made John Wazny stand up at his desk in the front row. He was supposed to go through the tables of six. From where I was sitting, I could smell the Vitalis soaked into John's plastered hair. He was doing fine until he came to six times eleven and six times twelve. "Six times eleven," he said, "is sixty-eight. Six times twelve is . . ." He put his fingers to his head, quickly and secretly sniffed his fingertips, and said, "seventy-two." Then he sat down.

"Fine," Miss Ferenczi said. "Well now. That was very good."

"Miss Ferenczi!" One of the Eddy twins was waving her hand desperately in the air. "Miss Ferenczi! Miss Ferenczi!"

"Yes?"

"John said that six times eleven is sixty-eight and you said he was right!"

"*Did* I?" She gazed at the class with a jolly look breaking across her marionette's face. "Did I say that? Well, what *is* six times eleven?"

"It's sixty-six!"

She nodded. "Yes. So it is. But, and I know some people will not entirely agree with me, at some times it is sixty-eight."

"When? When is it sixty-eight?"

We were all waiting.

"In higher mathematics, which you children do not yet understand, six times eleven can be considered to be sixty-eight." She laughed through her nose. "In higher mathematics numbers are . . . more fluid. The only thing a number does is contain a certain amount of something. Think of water. A cup is not the only way to measure a certain amount of water, is it?" We were staring, shaking our heads. "You could use saucepans or thimbles. In either case, the water *would be the same.* Perhaps," she started again, "it would be better for you to think that six times eleven is sixty-eight only when I am in the room."

"Why is it sixty-eight," Mark Poole asked, "when you're in the room?"

"Because it's more interesting that way," she said, smiling very rapidly behind her blue-tinted glasses. "Besides, I'm your substitute teacher, am I not?" We all nodded. "Well, then, think of six times eleven equals sixty-eight as a substitute fact."

"A substitute fact?"

"Yes." Then she looked at us carefully. "Do you think," she asked, "that anyone is going to be hurt by a substitute fact?"

We looked back at her.

"Will the plants on the windowsill be hurt?" We glanced at them. There were sensitive plants thriving in a green plastic tray, and several wilted ferns in small clay pots. "Your dogs and cats, or your moms and dads?" She waited. "So," she concluded, "what's the problem?"

"But it's wrong," Janice Weber said, "isn't it?"

"What's your name, young lady?"

"Janice Weber."

"And you think it's wrong, Janice?"

"I was just asking."

"Well, all right. You were just asking. I think we've spent enough time on this matter by now, don't you, class? You are free to think what you like. When your teacher, Mr. Hibler, returns, six times eleven will be sixty-six again, you can rest assured. And it will be that for the rest of your lives in Five Oaks. Too bad, eh?" She raised her eyebrows and glinted herself at us. "But for now, it wasn't. So much for that. Let us go to

your assigned problems for today, as painstakingly outlined, I
see, in Mr. Hibler's lesson plan. Take out a sheet of paper and
write your names in the upper left-hand corner."

For the next half hour we did the rest of our arithmetic problems. We handed them in and went on to spelling, my worst
subject. Spelling always came before lunch. We were taking
spelling dictation and looking at the clock. "Thorough," Miss
Ferenczi said. "Boundary." She walked in the aisles between the
desks, holding the spelling book open and looking down at our
papers. "Balcony." I clutched my pencil. Somehow, the way she
said those words, they seemed foreign, Hungarian, mis-voweled
and mis-consonanted. I stared down at what I had spelled. *Bal-
conie.* I turned my pencil upside down and erased my mistake.
Balconey. That looked better, but still incorrect. I cursed the
world of spelling and tried erasing it again and saw the paper
beginning to wear away. *Balkony.* Suddenly I felt a hand on my
shoulder.

"I don't like that word either," Miss Ferenczi whispered, bent
over, her mouth near my ear. "It's ugly. My feeling is, if you
don't like a word, you don't have to use it." She straightened
up, leaving behind a slight odor of Clorets.

At lunchtime we went out to get our trays of sloppy joes,
peaches in heavy syrup, coconut cookies, and milk, and brought
them back to the classroom, where Miss Ferenczi was sitting at
the desk, eating a brown sticky thing she had unwrapped from
tightly rubber-banded wax paper. "Miss Ferenczi," I said, raising my hand. "You don't have to eat with us. You can eat with
the other teachers. There's a teachers' lounge," I ended up,
"next to the principal's office."

"No, thank you," she said. "I prefer it here."

"We've got a room monitor," I said. "Mrs. Eddy." I pointed to
where Mrs. Eddy, Joyce and Judy's mother, sat silently at the
back of the room, doing her knitting.

"That's fine," Miss Ferenczi said. "But I shall continue to eat
here, with you children. I prefer it," she repeated.

"How come?" Wayne Razmer asked without raising his hand.

"I talked with the other teachers before class this morning,"
Miss Ferenczi said, biting into her brown food. "There was a
great rattling of the words for the fewness of ideas. I didn't

care for their brand of hilarity. I don't like ditto machine
jokes."

"Oh," Wayne said.

"What's that you're eating?" Maxine Sylvester asked, twitch-
ing her nose. "Is it food?"

"It most certainly *is* food. It's a stuffed fig. I had to drive
almost down to Detroit to get it. I also bought some smoked
sturgeon. And this," she said, lifting some green leaves out of
her lunchbox, "is raw spinach, cleaned this morning before I
came out here to the Garfield-Murry school."

"Why're you eating raw spinach?" Maxine asked.

"It's good for you," Miss Ferenczi said. "More stimulating
than soda pop or smelling salts." I bit into my sloppy joe and
stared blankly out the window. An almost invisible moon was
faintly silvered in the daytime autumn sky. "As far as food is
concerned," Miss Ferenczi was saying, "you have to shuffle the
pack. Mix it up. Too many people eat . . . well, never mind."

"Miss Ferenczi," Carol Peterson said, "what are we going to
do this afternoon?"

"Well," she said, looking down at Mr. Hibler's lesson plan, "I
see that your teacher, Mr. Hibler, has you scheduled for a unit
on the Egyptians." Carol groaned. "Yessss," Miss Ferenczi continued, "that is what we will do: the Egyptians. A remarkable
people. Almost as remarkable as the Americans. But not quite."
She lowered her head, did her quick smile, and went back to
eating her spinach.

After noon recess we came back into the classroom and saw that
Miss Ferenczi had drawn a pyramid on the blackboard, close to
her oak tree. Some of us who had been playing baseball were
messing around in the back of the room, dropping the bats and
the gloves into the playground box, and I think that Ray Schont-
zeler had just slugged me when I heard Miss Ferenczi's high-
pitched voice quavering with emotion. "Boys," she said, "come
to order right this minute and take your seats. I do not wish
to waste a minute of class time. Take out your geography
books." We trudged to our desks and, still sweating, pulled
out *Distant Lands and Their People.* "Turn to page forty-two."
She waited for thirty seconds, then looked over at Kelly Mun-

ger. "Young man," she said, "why are you still fossicking in your desk?"

Kelly looked as if his foot had been stepped on. "Why am I what?"

"Why are you . . . burrowing in your desk like that?"

"I'm lookin' for the book, Miss Ferenczi."

Bobby Kryzanowicz, the faultless brown-noser who sat in the first row by choice, softly said, "His name is Kelly Munger. He can't ever find his stuff. He always does that."

"I don't care what his name is, especially after lunch," Miss Ferenczi said. *"Where is your book?"*

"I just found it." Kelly was peering into his desk and with both hands pulled at the book, shoveling along in front of it several pencils and crayons, which fell into his lap and then to the floor.

"I hate a mess," Miss Ferenczi said. "I hate a mess in a desk or a mind. It's . . . unsanitary. You wouldn't want your house at home to look like your desk at school, now, would you?" She didn't wait for an answer. "I should think not. A house at home should be as neat as human hands can make it. What were we talking about? Egypt. Page forty-two. I note from Mr. Hibler's lesson plan that you have been discussing the modes of Egyptian irrigation. Interesting, in my view, but not so interesting as what we are about to cover. The pyramids and Egyptian slave labor. A plus on one side, a minus on the other." We had our books open to page forty-two, where there was a picture of a pyramid, but Miss Ferenczi wasn't looking at the book. Instead, she was staring at some object just outside the window.

"Pyramids," Miss Ferenczi said, still looking past the window. "I want you to think about the pyramids. And what was inside. The bodies of the pharaohs, of course, and their attendant treasures. Scrolls. Perhaps," Miss Ferenczi said, with something gleeful but unsmiling in her face, "these scrolls were novels for the pharaohs, helping them to pass the time in their long voyage through the centuries. But then, I am joking." I was looking at the lines on Miss Ferenczi's face. "Pyramids," Miss Ferenczi went on, "were the respositories of special cosmic powers. The nature of a pyramid is to guide cosmic energy forces into a concentrated point. The Egyptians knew that; we have generally for-

gotten it. Did you know," she asked, walking to the side of the
room so that she was standing by the coat closet, "that George
Washington had Egyptian blood, from his grandmother? Certain features of the Constitution of the United States are notable
for their Egyptian ideas."

Without glancing down at the book, she began to talk about
the movement of souls in Egyptian religion. She said that when
people die, their souls return to Earth in the form of carpenter
ants or walnut trees, depending on how they behaved — "well
or ill" — in life. She said that the Egyptians believed that people
act the way they do because of magnetism produced by tidal
forces in the solar system, forces produced by the sun and by its
"planetary ally," Jupiter. Jupiter, she said, was a planet, as we
had been told, but had "certain properties of stars." She was
speaking very fast. She said that the Egyptians were great ex-
plorers and conquerors. She said that the greatest of all the
conquerors, Genghis Khan, had had forty horses and forty
young women killed on the site of his grave. We listened. No
one tried to stop her. "I myself have been in Egypt," she said,
"and have witnessed much dust and many brutalities." She said
that an old man in Egypt who worked for a circus had person-
ally shown her an animal in a cage, a monster, half bird and half
lion. She said that this monster was called a gryphon and that
she had heard about them but never seen them until she traveled to the outskirts of Cairo. She said that Egyptian astrono-
mers had discovered the planet Saturn, but had not seen its
rings. She said that the Egyptians were the first to discover that
dogs, when they are ill, will not drink from rivers, but wait for
rain, and hold their jaws open to catch it.

"She lies."

We were on the school bus home. I was sitting next to Carl
Whiteside, who had bad breath and a huge collection of marbles. We were arguing. Carl thought she was lying. I said she
wasn't, probably.

"I didn't believe that stuff about the bird," Carl said, "and
what she told us about the pyramids? I didn't believe that either.
She didn't know what she was talking about."

"Oh yeah?" I had liked her. She was strange. I thought I could nail him. "If she was lying," I said, "what'd she say that was a lie?"

"Six times eleven isn't sixty-eight. It isn't ever. It's sixty-six, I know for a fact."

"She said so. She admitted it. What else did she lie about?"

"I don't know," he said. "Stuff."

"What stuff?"

"Well." He swung his legs back and forth. "You ever see an animal that was half lion and half bird?" He crossed his arms. "It sounded real fakey to me."

"It could happen," I said. I had to improvise, to outrage him. "I read in this newspaper my mom bought in the IGA about this scientist, this mad scientist in the Swiss Alps, and he's been putting genes and chromosomes and stuff together in test tubes, and he combined a human being and a hamster." I waited, for effect. "It's called a humster."

"You never." Carl was staring at me, his mouth open, his terrible bad breath making its way toward me. "What newspaper was it?"

"The *National Enquirer,*" I said, "that they sell next to the cash registers." When I saw his look of recognition, I knew I had bested him. "And this mad scientist," I said, "his name was, um, Dr. Frankenbush." I realized belatedly that this name was a mistake and waited for Carl to notice its resemblance to the name of the other famous mad master of permutations, but he only sat there.

"A man and a hamster?" He was staring at me, squinting, his mouth opening in distaste. "Jeez. What'd it look like?"

When the bus reached my stop, I took off down our dirt road and ran up through the back yard, kicking the tire swing for good luck. I dropped my books on the back steps so I could hug and kiss our dog, Mr. Selby. Then I hurried inside. I could smell Brussels sprouts cooking, my unfavorite vegetable. My mother was washing other vegetables in the kitchen sink, and my baby brother was hollering in his yellow playpen on the kitchen floor.

"Hi, Mom," I said, hopping around the playpen to kiss her, "Guess what?"

"I have no idea."

"We had this substitute today, Miss Ferenczi, and I'd never seen her before, and she had all these stories and ideas and stuff."

"Well. That's good." My mother looked out the window behind the sink, her eyes on the pine woods west of our house. Her face and hairstyle always reminded other people of Betty Crocker, whose picture was framed inside a gigantic spoon on the side of the Bisquick box; to me, though, my mother's face just looked white. "Listen, Tommy," she said, "go upstairs and pick your clothes off the bathroom floor, then go outside to the shed and put the shovel and ax away that your father left outside this morning."

"She said that six times eleven was sometimes sixty-eight!" I said. "And she said she once saw a monster that was half lion and half bird." I waited. "In Egypt, she said."

"Did you hear me?" my mother asked, raising her arm to wipe her forehead with the back of her hand. "You have chores to do."

"I know," I said. "I was just telling you about the substitute."

"It's very interesting," my mother said, quickly glancing down at me, "and we can talk about it later when your father gets home. But right now you have some work to do."

"Okay, Mom." I took a cookie out of the jar on the counter and was about to go outside when I had a thought. I ran into the living room, pulled out a dictionary next to the TV stand, and opened it to the G's. *Gryphon:* "variant of griffin." *Griffin:* "a fabulous beast with the head and wings of an eagle and the body of a lion." Fabulous was right. I shouted with triumph and ran outside to put my father's tools back in their place.

Miss Ferenczi was back the next day, slightly altered. She had pulled her hair down and twisted it into pigtails, with red rubber bands holding them tight one inch from the ends. She was wearing a green blouse and pink scarf, making her difficult to look at for a full class day. This time there was no pretense of doing a reading lesson or moving on to arithmetic. As soon as the bell rang, she simply began to talk.

She talked for forty minutes straight. There seemed to be less connection between her ideas, but the ideas themselves were, as the dictionary would say, fabulous. She said she had heard of a huge jewel, in what she called the Antipodes, that was so brilliant that when the light shone into it at a certain angle it would blind whoever was looking at its center. She said that the biggest diamond in the world was cursed and had killed everyone who owned it, and that by a trick of fate it was called the Hope diamond. Diamonds are magic, she said, and this is why women wear them on their fingers, as a sign of the magic of womanhood. Men have strength, Miss Ferenczi said, but no true magic. That is why men fall in love with women but women do not fall in love with men: they just love being loved. George Washington had died because of a mistake he made about a diamond. Washington was not the first *true* President, but she did say who was. In some places in the world, she said, men and women still live in the trees and eat monkeys for breakfast. Their doctors are magicians. At the bottom of the sea are creatures thin as pancakes which have never been studied by scientists because when you take them up to the air, the fish explode.

There was not a sound in the classroom, except for Miss Ferenczi's voice, and Donna DeShano's coughing. No one even went to the bathroom.

Beethoven, she said, had not been deaf; it was a trick to make himself famous, and it worked. As she talked, Miss Ferenczi's pigtails swung back and forth. There are trees in the world, she said, that eat meat: their leaves are sticky and close up on bugs like hands. She lifted her hands and brought them together, palm to palm. Venus, which most people think is the next closest planet to the sun, is not always closer, and, besides, it is the planet of greatest mystery because of its thick cloud cover. "I know what lies underneath those clouds," Miss Ferenczi said, and waited. After the silence, she said, "Angels. Angels live under those clouds." She said that angels were not invisible to everyone and were in fact smarter than most people. They did not dress in robes as was often claimed but instead wore formal evening clothes, as if they were about to attend a concert. Often angels *do* attend concerts and sit in the aisles where, she said, most people pay no attention to them. She said the most terrible angel had the shape of the Sphinx. "There is no running away from that one," she said. She said that unquenchable fires burn

just under the surface of the earth in Ohio, and that the baby
Mozart fainted dead away in his cradle when he first heard the
sound of a trumpet. She said that someone named Narzim al
Harrardim was the greatest writer who ever lived. She said that
planets control behavior, and anyone conceived during a solar
eclipse would be born with webbed feet.

"I know you children like to hear these things," she said,
"these secrets, and that is why I am telling you all this." We
nodded. It was better than doing comprehension questions for
the readings in *Broad Horizons.*

"I will tell you one more story," she said, "and then we will
have to do arithmetic." She leaned over, and her voice grew
soft. "There is no death," she said. "You must never be afraid.
Never. That which is, cannot die. It will change into different
earthly and unearthly elements, but I know this as sure as I
stand here in front of you, and I swear it: you must not be
afraid. I have seen this truth with these eyes. I know it because
in a dream God kissed me. Here." And she pointed with her
right index finger to the side of her head, below the mouth,
where the vertical lines were carved into her skin.

Absent-mindedly we all did our arithmetic problems. At recess
the class was out on the playground, but no one was playing.
We were all standing in small groups, talking about Miss Ferenczi. We didn't know if she was crazy, or what. I looked out
beyond the playground, at the rusted cars piled in a small heap
behind a clump of sumac, and I wanted to see shapes there,
approaching me.

On the way home, Carl sat next to me again. He didn't say
much, and I didn't either. At last he turned to me. "You know
what she said about the leaves that close up on bugs?"

"Huh?"

"The leaves," Carl insisted. "The meat-eating plants. I know
it's true. I saw it on television. The leaves have this icky glue that
the plants have got smeared all over them and the insects can't
get off 'cause they're stuck. I saw it." He seemed demoralized.
"She's tellin' the truth."

"Yeah."

"You think she's seen all those angels?"

I shrugged.

"I don't think she has," Carl informed me. "I think she made that part up."

"There's a tree," I suddenly said. I was looking out the window at the farms along County Road H. I knew every barn, every broken windmill, every fence, every anhydrous ammonia tank, by heart. "There's a tree that's . . . that I've seen . . ."

"Don't you try to do it," Carl said. "You'll just sound like a jerk."

I kissed my mother. She was standing in front of the stove. "How was your day?" she asked.

"Fine."

"Did you have Miss Ferenczi again?"

"Yeah."

"Well?"

"She was fine. Mom," I asked, "can I go to my room?"

"No," she said, "not until you've gone out to the vegetable garden and picked me a few tomatoes." She glanced at the sky. "I think it's going to rain. Skedaddle and do it now. Then you come back inside and watch your brother for a few minutes while I go upstairs. I need to clean up before dinner." She looked down at me. "You're looking a little pale, Tommy." She touched the back of her hand to my forehead and I felt her diamond ring against my skin. "Do you feel all right?"

"I'm fine," I said, and went out to pick the tomatoes.

Coughing mutedly, Mr. Hibler was back the next day, slipping lozenges into his mouth when his back was turned at forty-five minute intervals and asking us how much of the prepared lesson plan Miss Ferenczi had followed. Edith Atwater took the responsibility for the class of explaining to Mr. Hibler that the substitute hadn't always done exactly what he would have done, but we had worked hard even though she talked a lot. About what? he asked. All kinds of things, Edith said. I sort of forgot. To our relief, Mr. Hibler seemed not at all interested in what Miss Ferenczi had said to fill the day. He probably thought it was woman's talk; unserious and not suited for school. It was enough that he had a pile of arithmetic problems from us to correct.

For the next month, the sumac turned a distracting red in the field, and the sun traveled toward the southern sky, so that its rays reached Mr. Hibler's Halloween display on the bulletin board in the back of the room, fading the scarecrow with a pumpkin head from orange to tan. Every three days I measured how much farther the sun had moved toward the southern horizon by making small marks with my black Crayola on the north wall, ant-sized marks only I knew were there, inching west.

And then in early December, four days after the first permanent snowfall, she appeared again in our classroom. The minute she came in the door, I felt my heart begin to pound. Once again, she was different: this time, her hair hung straight down and seemed hardly to have been combed. She hadn't brought her lunchbox with her, but she was carrying what seemed to be a small box. She greeted all of us and talked about the weather. Donna DeShano had to remind her to take her overcoat off.

When the bell to start the day finally rang, Miss Ferenczi looked out at all of us and said, "Children, I have enjoyed your company in the past, and today I am going to reward you." She held up the small box. "Do you know what this is?" She waited. "Of course you don't. It is a tarot pack."

Edith Atwater raised her hand. "What's a tarot pack, Miss Ferenczi?"

"It is used to tell fortunes," she said. "And that is what I shall do this morning. I shall tell your fortunes, as I have been taught to do."

"What's fortune?" Bobby Kryzanowicz asked.

"The future, young man. I shall tell you what your future will be. I can't do your whole future, of course. I shall have to limit myself to the five-card system, the wands, cups, swords, pentacles, and the higher arcanes. Now who wants to be first?"

There was a long silence. Then Carol Peterson raised her hand.

"All right," Miss Ferenczi said. She divided the pack into five smaller packs and walked back to Carol's desk, in front of mine. "Pick one card from each of these packs," she said. I saw that

Carol had a four of cups, a six of swords, but I couldn't see the other cards. Miss Ferenczi studied the cards on Carol's desk for a minute. "Not bad," she said. "I do not see much higher education. Probably an early marriage. Many children. There's something bleak and dreary here, but I can't tell what. Perhaps just the tasks of a housewife life. I think you'll do very well, for the most part." She smiled at Carol, a smile with a certain lack of interest. "Who wants to be next?"

Carl Whiteside raised his hand slowly.

"Yes," Miss Ferenczi said, "let's do a boy." She walked over to where Carl sat. After he picked his five cards, she gazed at them for a long time. "Travel," she said. "Much distant travel. You might go into the Army. Not too much romantic interest here. A late marriage, if at all. Squabbles. But the Sun is in your major arcana, here, yes, that's a very good card." She giggled. "Maybe a good life."

Next I raised my hand, and she told me my future. She did the same with Bobby Kryzanowicz. Kelly Munger, Edith Atwater, and Kim Foor. Then she came to Wayne Razmer. He picked his five cards, and I could see that the Death card was one of them.

"What's your name?" Miss Ferenczi asked.

"Wayne."

"Well, Wayne," she said, you will undergo a *great* metamorphosis, the greatest, before you become an adult. Your earthly element will leap away, into thin air, you sweet boy. This card, this nine of swords here, tells of suffering and desolation. And this ten of wands, well, that's certainly a heavy load."

"What about this one?" Wayne pointed to the Death card.

"That one? That one means you will die soon, my dear." She gathered up the cards. We were all looking at Wayne. "But do not fear," she said. "It's not really death, so much as change." She put the cards on Mr. Hibler's desk. "And now, let's do some arithmetic."

At lunchtime Wayne went to Mr. Faegre, the principal, and told him what Miss Ferenczi had done. During the noon recess, we saw Miss Ferenczi drive out of the parking lot in her green Rambler. I stood under the slide, listening to the other kids coasting down and landing in the little depressive bowl at the bottom. I was kicking stones and tugging at my hair right up to the moment when I saw Wayne come out to the playground. He smiled, the dead fool, and with the fingers of his right hand he was showing everyone how he had told on Miss Ferenczi.

I made my way toward Wayne, pushing myself past two girls from another class. He was watching me with his little pinhead eyes.

"You told," I shouted at him. "She was just kidding."

"She shouldn't have," he shouted back. "We were supposed to be doing arithmetic."

"She just scared you," I said. "You're a chicken. You're a chicken, Wayne. You are. Scared of a little card," I singsonged.

Wayne fell at me, his two fists hammering down on my nose. I gave him a good one in the stomach and then I tried for his head. Aiming my fist, I saw that he was crying. I slugged him.

"She was right," I yelled. "She was always right! She told the truth!" Other kids were whooping. "You were just scared, that's all!"

And then large hands pulled at us, and it was my turn to speak to Mr. Faegre.

In the afternoon Miss Ferenczi was gone, and my nose was stuffed with cotton clotted with blood, and my lip had swelled, and our class had been combined with Mrs. Mantei's sixth-grade class for a crowded afternoon science unit on insect life in ditches and swamps. I knew where Mrs. Mantei lived: she had a new house trailer just down the road from us, at the Clearwater Park. She was no mystery. Somehow she and Mr. Bodine, the other fourth-grade teacher, had managed to fit forty-five desks into the room. Kelly Munger asked if Miss Ferenczi had been arrested, and Mrs. Mantei said no, of course not. All that afternoon, until the buses came to pick us up, we learned about field crickets and two-striped grasshoppers, water bugs, cicadas, mosquitoes, flies, and moths. We learned about insects' hard outer shell, the exoskeleton, and the usual parts of the mouth, including the labrum, mandible, maxilla, and glossa. We learned about compound eyes and the four-stage metamorphosis from egg to larva to pupa to adult. We learned something, but not much, about mating. Mrs. Mantei drew, very skillfully, the internal anatomy of the grasshopper on the blackboard. We learned about the dance of the honeybee, directing other bees in the hive to pollen. We found out about which insects were pests to man, and which were not. On lined white pieces of paper we made lists of insects we might actually see, then a list of insects too small to be clearly visible, such as fleas; Mrs. Mantei said that our assignment would be to memorize these lists for the next day, when Mr. Hibler would certainly return and test us on our knowledge.

ANN BEATTIE

Janus

FROM THE NEW YORKER

THE BOWL WAS PERFECT. Perhaps it was not what you'd select if you faced a shelf of bowls, and not the sort of thing that would inevitably attract a lot of attention at a crafts fair, yet it had real presence. It was as predictably admired as a mutt who has no reason to suspect he might be funny. Just such a dog, in fact, was often brought out (and in) along with the bowl.

Andrea was a real estate agent, and when she thought that some prospective buyers might be dog lovers, she would drop off her dog at the same time she placed the bowl in the house that was up for sale. She would put a dish of water in the kitchen for Mondo, take his squeaking plastic frog out of her purse and drop it on the floor. He would pounce delightedly, just as he did everyday at home, batting around his favorite toy. The bowl usually sat on a coffee table, though recently she had displayed it on top of a pine blanket chest and on a lacquered table. It was once placed on a cherry table beneath a Bonnard still life, where it held its own.

Everyone who has purchased a house or who has wanted to sell a house must be familiar with some of the tricks used to convice a buyer that the house is quite special: a fire in the fireplace in early evening; jonquils in a pitcher on the kitchen counter, where no one ordinarily has space to put flowers; perhaps the slight aroma of spring, made by a single drop of scent vaporizing from a lamp bulb.

The wonderful thing about the bowl, Andrea thought, was that it was both subtle and noticeable — a paradox of a bowl. Its glaze was the color of cream and seemed to glow no matter what light it was placed in. There were a few bits of color in it — tiny geometric flashes — and some of these were tinged with flecks of silver. They were as mysterious as cells seen under a microscope; it was difficult not to study them, because they shimmered, flashing for a split second, and then resumed their shape. Something about the colors and their random placement suggested motion. People who liked country furniture always commented on the bowl, but then it turned out that people who felt comfortable with Biedermeier loved it just as much. But the bowl was not at all ostentatious, or even so noticeable that anyone would suspect that it had been put in place deliberately. They might notice the height of the ceiling on first entering a room, and only when their eye moved down from that, or away from the refraction of sunlight on a pale wall, would they see the bowl. Then they would go immediately to it and comment. Yet they always faltered when they tried to say something. Perhaps it was because they were in the house for a serious reason, not to notice some object.

Once, Andrea got a call from a woman who had not put in an offer on a house she had shown her. That bowl, she said — would it be possible to find out where the owners had bought that beautiful bowl? Andrea pretended that she did not know what the woman was referring to. A bowl, somewhere in the house? Oh, on a table under the window. Yes, she would ask, of course. She let a couple of days pass, then called back to say that the bowl had been a present and the people did not know where it had been purchased.

When the bowl was not being taken from house to house, it sat on Andrea's coffee table at home. She didn't keep it carefully wrapped (although she transported it that way, in a box); she kept it on the table, because she liked to see it. It was large enough so that it didn't seem fragile, or particularly vulnerable if anyone sideswiped the table or Mondo blundered into it at play. She had asked her husband to please not drop his house key in it. It was meant to be empty.

When her husband first noticed the bowl, he had peered into it and smiled briefly. He always urged her to buy things she liked. In recent years, both of them had acquired many things to make up for all the lean years when they were graduate students, but now that they had been comfortable for quite a while, the pleasure of new possessions dwindled. Her husband had pronounced the bowl "pretty," and he had turned away without picking it up to examine it. He had no more interest in the bowl than she had in his new Leica.

She was sure that the bowl brought her luck. Bids were often put in on houses where she had displayed the bowl. Sometimes the owners, who were always asked to be away or to step outside when the house was being shown, didn't even know that the bowl had been in their house. Once — she could not imagine how — she left it behind, and then she was so afraid that something might have happened to it that she rushed back to the house and sighed with relief when the woman owner opened the door. The bowl, Andrea explained — she had purchased a bowl and set it on the chest for safekeeping while she toured the house with the prospective buyers, and she . . . She felt like rushing past the frowning woman and seizing her bowl. The owner stepped aside, and it was only when Andrea ran to the chest that the lady glanced at her a little strangely. In the few seconds before Andrea picked up the bowl, she realized that the owner must have just seen that it had been perfectly placed, that the sunlight struck the bluer part of it. Her pitcher had been moved to the far side of the chest, and the bowl predominated. All the way home, Andrea wondered how she could have left the bowl behind. It was like leaving a friend at an outing — just walking off. Sometimes there were stories in the paper about families forgetting a child somewhere and driving to the next city. Andrea had only gone a mile down the road before she remembered.

In time, she dreamed of the bowl. Twice, in a waking dream — early in the morning, between sleep and a last nap before rising — she had a clear vision of it. It came into sharp focus and startled her for a moment — the same bowl she looked at every day.

She had a very profitable year selling real estate. Word spread, and she had more clients than she felt comfortable with. She had the foolish thought that if only the bowl were an animate object she could thank it. There were times when she wanted to talk to her husband about the bowl. He was a stockbroker, and sometimes told people that he was fortunate to be married to a woman who had such a fine aesthetic sense and yet could also function in the real world. They were a lot alike, really — they had agreed on that. They were both quiet people — reflective, slow to make value judgments, but almost intractable once they had come to a conclusion. They both liked details, but while ironies attracted her, he was more impatient and dismissive when matters became many sided or unclear. But they both knew this; it was the kind of thing they could talk about when they were alone in the car together, coming home from a party or after a weekend with friends. But she never talked to him about the bowl. When they were at dinner, exchanging their news of the day, or while they lay in bed at night listening to the stereo and murmuring sleepy disconnections, she was often tempted to come right out and say that she thought that the bowl in the living room, the cream-colored bowl, was responsible for her success. But she didn't say it. She couldn't begin to explain it. Sometimes in the morning, she would look at him and feel guilty that she had such a constant secret.

Could it be that she had some deeper connection with the bowl — a relationship of some kind? She corrected her thinking: how could she imagine such a thing, when she was a human being and it was a bowl? It was ridiculous. Just think of how people lived together and loved each other . . . But was that always so clear, always a relationship? She was confused by these thoughts, but they remained in her mind. There was something within her now, something real, that she never talked about.

The bowl was a mystery, even to her. It was frustrating, because her involvement with the bowl contained a steady sense of unrequited good fortune; it would have been easier to respond if some sort of demand were made in return. But that only happened in fairy tales. The bowl was just a bowl. She did not believe that for one second. What she believed was that it was something she loved.

In the past, she had sometimes talked to her husband about a new property she was about to buy or sell — confiding some clever strategy she had devised to persuade owners who seemed ready to sell. Now she stopped doing that, for all her strategies involved the bowl. She became more deliberate with the bowl, and more possessive. She put it in houses only when no one was there, and removed it when she left the house. Instead of just moving a pitcher or a dish, she would remove all the other objects from a table. She had to force herself to handle them carefully, because she didn't really care about them. She just wanted them out of sight.

She wondered how the situation would end. As with a lover, there was no exact scenario of how matters would come to a close. Anxiety became the operative force. It would be irrelevant if the lover rushed into someone else's arms, or wrote her a note and departed to another city. The horror was the possibility of the disappearance. That was what mattered.

She would get up at night and look at the bowl, It never occurred to her that she might break it. She washed and dried it without anxiety, and she moved it often, from coffee table to mahogany corner table or wherever, without fearing an accident. It was clear that she would not be the one who would do anything to the bowl. The bowl was only handled by her, set safely on one surface or another; it was not very likely that anyone would break it. A bowl was a poor conductor of electricity: it would not be hit by lightning. Yet the idea of damage persisted. She did not think beyond that — to what her life would be without the bowl. She only continued to fear that some accident would happen. Why not, in a world where people set plants where they did not belong, so that visitors touring a house would be fooled into thinking that dark corners got sunlight — a world full of tricks?

She had first seen the bowl several years earlier, at a crafts fair she had visited half in secret, with her lover. He had urged her to buy the bowl. She didn't *need* any more things, she told him. But she had been drawn to the bowl, and they had lingered near it. Then she went on to the next booth, and he came up behind her, tapping the rim against her shoulder as she ran her fingers over a wood carving. "You're still insisting that I buy that?" she said. "No," he said. "I bought it for you." He had bought her other things before this — things she liked more, at first — the child's ebony-and-turquoise ring that fitted her little finger; the wooden box, long and thin, beautifully dovetailed, that she used to hold paper clips; the soft gray sweater with a pouch pocket. It was his idea that when he could not be there to hold her hand she could hold her own — clasp her hands inside the lone pocket that stretched across the front. But in time she became more attached to the bowl than to any of his other presents. She tried to talk herself out of it. She owned other things that were more striking or valuable. It wasn't an object whose beauty jumped out at you; a lot of people must have passed it by before the two of them saw it that day.

Her lover had said that she was always too slow to know what she really loved. Why continue with her life the way it was? Why be two-faced, he asked her. He had made the first move toward her. When she would not decide in his favor, would not change her life and come to him, he asked her what made her think she could have it both ways. And then he made the last move and left. It was a decision meant to break her will, to shatter her intransigent ideas about honoring previous commitments.

Time passed. Alone in the living room at night, she often looked at the bowl sitting on the table, still and safe, unilluminated. In its way, it was perfect: the world cut in half, deep and smoothly empty. Near the rim, even in dim light, the eye moved toward one small flash of blue, a vanishing point on the horizon.

JAMES LEE BURKE

The Convict

FROM THE KENYON REVIEW

For Lyle Williams

MY FATHER WAS a popular man in New Iberia, even though his
ideas were different from most people's and his attitudes were
uncompromising. On Friday afternoons he and my mother and
I would drive down the long yellow dirt road through the sugarcane fields until it became a blacktop and followed the Bayou
Teche into town, where my father would drop my mother off
at Musemeche's Produce Market and take me with him to the
bar at the Frederic Hotel. The Frederic was a wonderful old
place with slot machines and potted palms and marble columns
in the lobby and a gleaming mahogany and brass barroom that
was cooled by long-bladed wooden fans. I always sat at a table
with a bottle of Dr. Nut and a glass of ice and watched with
fascination the drinking rituals of my father and his friends: the
warm handshakes, the pats on the shoulder, the laughter that
was genuine but never uncontrolled. In the summer, which
seemed like the only season in south Louisiana, the men wore
seersucker suits and straw hats, and the amber light in their
glasses of whiskey with ice and their Havana cigars and Pica-
yune cigarettes held between their ringed fingers made them
seem everything gentlemen and my father's friends should
be.

But sometimes I would suddenly realize that there was not
only a fundamental difference between my father and other
men but also that his presence would eventually expose that

difference, and a flaw, a deep one that existed in him or them, would surface like an aching wisdom tooth.

"Do you fellows really believe we should close the schools because of a few little Negro children?" my father said.

"My Lord, Will. We've lived one way here all our lives," one man said. He owned a restaurant in town and a farm with oil on it near Saint Martinville.

My father took the cigar out of his teeth, smiled, sipped his whiskey, and looked with his bright green eyes at the restaurant owner. My father was a real farmer, not an absentee landlord, and his skin was brown and his body straight and hard. He could pick up a washtub full of bricks and throw it over a fence.

"That's the point," he said. "We've lived among Negroes all our lives. They work in our homes, take care of our children, drive our wives on errands. Where are you going to send our own children if you close the school? Did you think of that?"

The bartender looked at the Negro porter who ran the shoe shine stand in the bar. He was bald and wore an apron and was quietly brushing a pair of shoes left him by a hotel guest.

"Alcide, go down to the corner and pick up the newspapers," the bartender said.

"Yes suh."

"It's not ever going to come to that," another man said. "Our darkies don't want it."

"It's coming, all right," my father said. His face was composed now, his eyes looking through the open wood shutters at the oak tree in the courtyard outside. "Harry Truman is integrating the army, and those Negro soldiers aren't going to come home and walk around to the back door anymore."

"Charlie, give Mr. Broussard another Manhattan," the restaurant owner said. "In fact, give everybody one. This conversation puts me in mind of the town council."

Everyone laughed, including my father, who put his cigar in his teeth and smiled good-naturedly with his hands folded on the bar. But I knew that he wasn't laughing inside, that he would finish his drink quietly, then wink at me, and we'd wave good-bye to everyone and leave their Friday afternoon good humor intact.

On the way home he didn't talk and instead pretended that

he was interested in Mother's conversation about the New Iberia ladies' book club. The sun was red on the bayou, and the cypress and oaks along the bank were a dark green in the gathering dusk. Families of Negroes were cane fishing in the shallows for goggle-eye perch and bullheads.

"Why do you drink with them, Daddy? You all always have an argument," I said.

His eyes flicked sideways at my mother.

"That's not an argument, just a gentlemen's disagreement," he said.

"I agree with him," my mother said. "Why provoke them?"

"They're good fellows. They just don't see things clearly sometimes."

My mother looked at me in the back seat, her eyes smiling so he could see them. She was beautiful when she looked like that.

"You should be aware that your father is the foremost authority in Louisiana on the subject of colored people."

"It isn't a joke, Margaret. We've kept them poor and uneducated, and we're going to have to settle accounts for it one day."

"Well, you haven't underpaid them," she said. "I don't believe there's a darkie in town you haven't lent money to."

I wished I hadn't said anything. I knew he was feeling the same pain now that he had felt in the bar. Nobody understood him — not my mother, not me, none of the men he drank with.

The air suddenly became cool, the twilight turned a yellowish green, and it started to rain. Up the blacktop we saw a blockade and men in raincoats with flashlights in their hands. They wore flat campaign hats and water was dancing on the brims. My father stopped at the blockade and rolled down the window. A state policeman leaned his head down and moved his eyes around the inside of the car.

"We got a nigger and a white convict out on the ground. Don't pick up no hitchhikers," he said.

"Where were they last seen?" my father said.

"They got loose from a prison truck just east of the four corners," he said.

We drove on in the rain. My father turned on the headlights, and I saw the anxiety in my mother's face in the glow from the dashboard.

"Will, that's only a mile from us," she said.

"They're probably gone by now or hid out under a bridge somewhere," he said.

"They must be dangerous or they wouldn't have so many police officers out," she said.

"If they were really dangerous they'd be in Angola, not riding around in a truck. Besides, I bet when we get home and turn on the radio we'll find out they're back in jail."

"I don't like it. It's like when all those Germans were here."

During the war there had been a POW camp outside New Iberia. We used to see them chopping in the sugarcane, with a big white P on their backs. Mother kept the doors locked until they were sent back to Germany. My father always said they were harmless and they wouldn't escape from their camp if they were pushed out the front door at gunpoint.

The wind was blowing hard when we got home, and leaves from the pecan orchard were scattered across the lawn. My pirogue, which was tied to a small dock on the bayou behind the house, was knocking loudly against a piling. Mother waited for my father to open the front door, even though she had her own key; then she turned on all the lights in the house and closed the curtains. She began to peel crawfish in the sink for our supper, then turned on the radio in the window as though she were bored for something to listen to. Outside, the door on the tractor shed began to bag violently in the wind. My father went to the closet for his hat and raincoat.

"Let it go, Will. It's raining too hard," she said.

"Turn on the outside light. You'll be able to see me from the window," he said.

He ran through the rain, stopped at the barn for a hammer and a wood stob, then bent over in front of the tractor shed and drove the stob securely against the door.

He walked back into the kitchen, hitting his hat against his pants leg.

"I've got to get a new latch for that door. But at least the wind won't be banging it for a while," he said.

"There was a news story on the radio about the convicts," my mother said. "They had been taken from Angola to Franklin for a trial. One of them is a murderer."

"Angola?" For the first time my father's face showed concern.

"The truck wrecked and they got out the back and later made a man cut their handcuffs."

He picked up a shelled crawfish, bit it in half, and looked out the window at the rain slanting in the light. His face was empty now.

"Well, if I was in Angola I'd try to get out, too," he said. "Do we have some beer? I can't eat crawfish without beer."

"Call the sheriff's department and ask where they think they are."

"I can't do that, Margaret. Now, let's put a stop to all this." He walked out of the kitchen, and I saw my mother's jawbone flex under the skin.

It was about three in the morning when I heard the shed door begin slamming in the wind again. A moment later I saw my father walk past my bedroom door buttoning his denim coat over his undershirt. I followed him halfway down the stairs and watched him take a flashlight from the kitchen drawer and lift the twelve-gauge pump out of the rack on the dining room wall. He saw me, then paused for a moment as though he were caught between two thoughts.

Then, "Come on down a minute, Son. I guess I didn't get that stob hammered in as well as I thought. But bolt the door behind me, will you?"

"Did you see something, Daddy?"

"No, no. I'm just taking this to satisfy your mother. Those men are probably all the way to New Orleans by now."

He turned on the outside light and went out the back door. I watched through the kitchen window as he crossed the lawn. He had the flashlight pointed in front of him, and as he approached the tractor shed he raised the shotgun and held it with one hand against his waist. He pushed the swinging door all the way back against the wall with his foot, shined the light over the tractor and the rolls of chicken wire, then stepped inside the darkness.

I could hear my own breathing as I watched the flashlight beam bounce through the cracks in the shed. Then I saw the light steady in the far corner where we hung the tools and tack. I waited for something awful to happen — the shotgun to streak fire through the boards, a pick in murderous hands to rake downwards in a tangle of harness. Instead, my father appeared in the doorway a moment later, waved the flashlight at me, then replaced the stob and pressed it into the wet earth with his boot. I unbolted the back door and went up to bed, relieved that the convicts were far away and that my father was my father, a truly brave man who kept my mother's and my world a secure place.

But he didn't go back to bed. I heard him first in the upstairs hall cabinet, then in the icebox, and finally on the back porch. I went to my window and looked down into the moonlit yard and saw him walking with the shotgun under one arm and a lunch pail and folded towels in the other.

Just at false dawn, when the mist from the marsh hung thick on the lawn and the gray light began to define the black trees along the bayou, I heard my parents arguing in the next room. Then my father snapped:

"Damn it, Margaret. The man's hurt."

Mother didn't come out of their room that morning. My father banged out the back door, was gone a half hour, then returned and cooked a breakfast of cush-cush and sausages for us.

"You want to go to a picture show today?" he said.

"I was going fishing with Tee Batist." He was a little Negro boy whose father worked for us sometimes.

"It won't be any good after all that rain. Your mother doesn't want you tracking mud in from the bank, either."

"Is something going on, Daddy?"

"Oh, Mother and I have our little discussions sometimes. It's nothing." He smiled at me over his coffee cup.

I almost always obeyed my father, but that morning I found ways to put myself among the trees on the bank of the bayou. First, I went down on the dock to empty the rainwater out of my pirogue, then I threw dirt clods at the heads of water moccasins on the far side, then I made a game of jumping from cypress root to cypress root along the water's edge without actually touching the bank, and finally I was near what I knew my father wanted me to stay away from that day: the old houseboat that had been washed up and left stranded among the oak trees in the great flood of 1927. Wild morning glories grew over the rotting deck, kids had riddled the cabin walls with .22 holes, and a slender oak had rooted in the collapsed floor and grown up through one window. Two sets of sharply etched footprints, side by side, led down from the levee to a sawed-off cypress stump that someone had used to climb up on the deck.

The air among the trees was still, humid, and dappled with broken shards of sunlight. I wished I had brought my .22, and then I wondered at my own foolishness in involving myself in something my father had been willing to lie about in order to protect me. But I had to know what he was hiding, what or who it was that would make him choose the welfare of another over my mother's anxiety and fear.

I stepped up on the cypress stump and leaned foward until I could see into the doorless cabin. There were an empty dynamite box and a half-dozen beer bottles moted with dust in one corner, and I remembered the seismograph company that had used the houseboat as a storage shack for their explosives two years before. I stepped up on the deck more bravely now, sure that I would find nothing else in the cabin than possibly a possum's nest or a squirrel's cache of acorns. Then I caw the booted pants leg in the gloom just as I smelled his odor. It was like a slap in the face — a mixture of dried sweat and blood and the sour stench of swamp mud. He was sleeping on his side, his knees drawn up before him, his green and white pinstriped uniform streaked black, his bald brown head tucked under one arm. On each wrist was a silver manacle with a short length of broken chain. Someone had slipped a narrow piece of cable through one manacle and had nailed both looped ends to an oak floor beam with a twelve-inch iron spike. In that heart-pounding moment the length of cable and the long spike leaped at my eye even more than the convict did, because both of them had come from the back of my father's pickup truck.

I wanted to run, but I was transfixed. There was a bloody tear across the front of his shirt, as though he had run through barbed wire, and even in sleep his round hard body seemed to radiate a primitive energy and power. He breathed hoarsely through his open mouth, and I could see the stumps of his teeth and the snuff stains on his soft pink gums. A deer fly hummed in the heat and settled on his forehead, and when his face twitched like a snapping rubber band I jumped backwards involuntarily. Then I felt my father's strong hands grab me like vise grips on each arm.

My father was seldom angry with me, but this time his eyes were hot and his mouth was a tight line as we walked back through the trees toward the house. Finally I heard him blow out his breath and slow his step next to me. I looked up at him and his face had gone soft again.

"You ought to listen to me, Son. I had a reason not to want you back there," he said.

"What are you going to do with him?"

"I haven't decided. I need to talk with your mother a little bit."

"What did he do to go to prison?"

"He says he robbed a laundromat. For that they gave him fifty-six years."

A few minutes later he was talking to Mother again in their room. This time the door was open, and neither one of them cared what I heard.

"You should see his back. There are whip scars on it as thick as my finger," my father said.

"You don't have an obligation to every person in the world. He's an escaped convict. He could come in here and cut our throats for all you know."

"He's a human being who happens to be a convict. They do things up in that penitentiary that ought to make every civilized man in this state ashamed."

"I won't have this, Will."

"He's going tonight. I promise. And he's no danger to us."

"You're breaking the law. Don't you know that?"

"You have to make choices in this world, and right now I choose not to be responsible for any more suffering in this man's life."

They avoided speaking to each other the rest of the day. My mother fixed lunch for us, pretended she wasn't hungry, and washed the dishes while my father and I ate at the kitchen table. I saw him looking at her back, his eyelids blinking for a moment, and just when I thought he was going to speak she dropped a pan loudly in the dish rack and walked out of the room. I hated to see them like that. But I particularly hated to see the loneliness that was in his eyes. He tried to hide it but I knew how miserable he was.

"They all respect you. Even though they argue with you, all those men look up to you," I said.

"What's that, Son?" he said, and turned his gaze away from the window. He was smiling, but his mind was still out there on the bayou and the houseboat.

"I heard some men from Layfayette talking about you in the bank. One of them said, 'Will Broussard's word is better than any damned signature on a contract.'"

"Oh, well, that's good of you to say, Son. You're a good boy."

"Daddy, it'll be over soon. He'll be gone and everything will be just the same as before."

"That's right. So how about you and I take our poles and see if we can't catch us a few goggle-eye?"

We fished until almost dinnertime, then cleaned and scraped our stringer of bluegill, goggle-eye perch, and *sacalait* in the sluice of water from the windmill. Mother had left wax-paper-covered plates of cold fried chicken and potato salad for us on the kitchen table. She listened to the radio in the living room while we ate, then picked up our dishes and washed them without ever speaking to my father. The western sky was aflame with the sunset, fireflies spun circles of light in the darkening oaks on the lawn, and at eight o'clock, when I usually listened to "Gangbusters," I heard my father get up out of his straw chair on the porch and walk around the side of the house toward the bayou.

I watched him pick up a gunny sack weighted heavily at the bottom from inside the barn door and walk through the trees and up the levee. I felt guilty when I followed him, but he hadn't taken the shotgun and he would be alone and unarmed when he freed the convict, whose odor still reached up and struck at my face. I was probably only fifty feet behind him, my face prepared to smile instantly if he turned around, but the weighted gunny sack rattled dully against his leg and he never heard me. He stepped up on the cypress stump and stooped inside the door of the houseboat cabin; then I heard the convict's voice: "What game you playing, white man?"

"I'm going to give you a choice. I'll drive you to the sheriff's office in New Iberia, or I'll cut you loose. It's up to you."

"What you doing this for?"

"Make up your mind."

"I done that when I went out the back of that truck. What you doing this for?"

I was standing behind a tree on a small rise, and I saw my father take a flashlight and a hand ax out of the gunny sack. He squatted on one knee, raised the ax over his head, and whipped it down into the floor of the cabin.

"You're on your own now. There's some canned goods and an opener in the sack, and you can have the flashlight. If you follow the levee you'll come out on a dirt road that'll lead you to a railway track. That's the Southern Pacific and it'll take you to Texas."

"Gimme the ax."

"Nope. You already have everything you're going to get."

"You got a reason you don't want the law here, ain't you? Maybe a still in that barn."

"You're a lucky man today. Don't undo it."

"What you does is your business, white man."

The convict wrapped the gunny sack around his wrist and dropped off the deck onto the ground. He looked backward with his cannonball head, then walked away through the darkening oaks that grew beside the levee. I wondered if he would make that freight train, or if he would be run to ground by dogs and state police and maybe blown apart with shotguns in a cane field before he ever got out of the parish. But mostly I wondered at the incredible behavior of my father, who had turned Mother against him and broken the law himself for a man who didn't even care enough to say thank you.

It was hot and still all day Sunday; then a thunder shower blew in from the Gulf and cooled everything off just before suppertime. The sky was violet and pink, and the cranes flying over the cypress in the marsh were touched with fire from the red sun on the horizon. I could smell the sweetness of the fields in the cooling wind and the wild four-o'clocks that grew in a gold and crimson spray by the swamp. My father said it was a perfect evening to drive down to Cypremort Point for boiled crabs. Mother didn't answer, but a moment later she said she had promised her sister to go to a motion picture in Layfayette. My father lit a cigar and looked at her directly through the flame.

"It's all right, Margaret. I don't blame you," he said.

Her face colored, and she had trouble finding her hat and her car keys before she left.

The moon was bright over the marsh that night, and I decided to walk down the road to Tee Batist's cabin and go frog gigging with him. I was on the back porch sharpening the point of my gig with a file when I saw the flashlight wink out of the trees behind the house. I ran into the living room, my heart racing, the file still in my hand, my face evidently so alarmed that my father's mouth opened when he saw me.

"He's back. He's flashing your light in the trees," I said.

"It's probably somebody running a trot line."

"It's him, Daddy."

He pressed his lips together, then folded his newspaper and set it on the table next to him.

"Lock up the house while I'm outside," he said. "If I don't come back in ten minutes, call the sheriff's office."

He walked through the dining room toward the kitchen peeling the wrapper off a fresh cigar.

"I want to go, too. I don't want to stay here by myself," I said.

"It's better that you do."

"He won't do anything if two of us are there."

"Maybe you're right," he said. He smiled and winked at me, then took the shotgun out of the wall rack.

We saw the flashlight again as soon as we stepped off the back porch. We walked past the tractor shed and the barn into the trees. The light flashed once more from the top of the levee; then it went off and I saw him outlined against the moon's reflection off the bayou. Then I heard his breathing — heated, constricted, like a cornered animal's.

"There's a roadblock just before that railway track. You didn't tell me about that," he said.

"I didn't know about it. You shouldn't have come back here," my father said.

"They run me four hours through a woods. I could hear them yelling to each other, like they was driving a deer."

His prison uniform was gone. He wore a brown short-sleeved

shirt and a pair of slacks that wouldn't button at the top. A butcher knife stuck through one of the belt loops.

"Where did you get that?" my father said.

"I taken it. What do you care? You got a bird gun there, ain't you?"

"Who did you take the clothes from?"

"I didn't bother no white people. Listen, I need to stay here two or three days. I'll work for you. There ain't no kind of work I can't do. I can make whiskey, too."

"Throw the knife in the bayou."

"What'chu talking about?"

"I said to throw it away."

"The old man I taken it from put an inch of it in my side. I don't throw it in no bayou. I ain't no threat to you, no how. I can't go nowheres else. Why I'm going to hurt you or the boy?"

"You're the murderer, aren't you? The other convict is the robber. That's right, isn't it?"

The convict's eyes narrowed. I could see his tongue on his teeth.

"In Angola that means I won't steal from you," he said.

I saw my father's jaw work. His right hand was tight on the stock of the shotgun.

"Did you kill somebody after you left here?" he said.

"I done told you, it was me they was trying to kill. All them people out there, they'd like me drug behind a car. But that don't make no never-mind, do it? You worried about some no-good nigger that put a dirk in my neck and cost me eight years."

"You get out of here," my father said.

"I ain't going nowhere. You done already broke the law. You got to help me."

"Go back to the house, Son."

I was frightened by the sound in my father's voice.

"What you doing?" the convict said.

"Do what I say. I'll be along in a minute," my father said.

"Listen, I ain't did you no harm," the convict said.

"Avery!" my father said.

I backed away through the trees, my eyes fixed on the shotgun that my father now leveled at the convict's chest. In the moonlight I could see the sweat running down the Negro's face.

"I'm throwing away the knife," he said.

"Avery, you run to the house and stay there. You hear me?"

I turned and ran through the dark, the tree limbs slapping against my face, the morning glory vines on the ground tangling around my ankles like snakes. Then I heard the twelve-gauge explode, and by the time I ran through the back screen into the house I was crying uncontrollably.

A moment later I heard my father's boot on the back step. Then he stopped, pumped the spent casing out of the breech, and walked inside with the shotgun over his shoulder and the red shells visible in the magazine. He was breathing hard, and his face was darker than I had ever seen it. I knew then that neither he, nor my mother, nor I would ever know happiness again.

He took his bottle of Four Roses out of the cabinet and poured a jelly glass half full. He drank from it, then took a cigar stub out of his shirt pocket, put it between his teeth, and leaned on his arms against the drainboard. The muscles in his back stood out as though a nail were driven between his shoulder blades. Then he seemed to realize for the first time that I was in the room.

"Hey there, little fellow. What are you carrying on about?" he said.

"You killed a man, Daddy."

"Oh no, no. I just scared him and made him run back in the marsh. But I have to call the sheriff now, and I'm not happy about what I have to tell him."

I didn't think I had ever heard more joyous words. I felt as though my breast, my head, were filled with light, that a wind had blown through my soul. I could smell the bayou on the night air, the watermelons and strawberries growing beside the barn, the endlessly youthful scent of summer itself.

Two hours later my father and mother stood on the front lawn with the sheriff and watched four mud-streaked deputies lead the convict in manacles to a squad car. The convict's arms were pulled behind him, and he smoked a cigarette with his head tilted to one side. A deputy took it out of his mouth and flipped it away just before they locked him the back of the car behind the wire screen.

"Now, tell me this again, Will. You say he was here yesterday

and you gave him some canned goods?" the sheriff said. He was
a thick-bodied man who wore blue suits, a pearl-gray Stetson,
and a fat watch in his vest pocket.

"That's right. I cleaned up the cut on his chest, and I gave
him a flashlight, too," my father said. Mother put her arm in
his.

"What was that fellow wearing when you did all this?"

"A green and white work uniform of some kind."

"Well, it must have been somebody else because I think this
man stole that shirt and pants soon as he got out of the prison
van. You probably run into one of them niggers that's been
setting traps out of season."

"I appreciate what you're trying to do, but I helped the fellow
in that car to get away."

"The same man who turned him in also helped him escape?
Who's going to believe a story like that, Will?" The sheriff
tipped his hat to my mother. "Good night, Mrs. Broussard. You
drop by and say hello to my wife when you have a chance.
Goodnight, Will. And you, too, Avery."

We walked back up on the porch as they drove down the dirt
road through the sugarcane fields. Heat lightning flickered
across the blue-black sky.

"I'm afraid you're fated to be disbelieved," Mother said, and
kissed my father on the cheek.

"It's the battered innocence in us," he said.

I didn't understand what he meant, but I didn't care, either.
Mother fixed strawberries and plums and hand-cranked ice
cream, and I fell asleep under the big fan in the living room
with the spoon still in my hand. I heard the heat thunder roll
once more, like a hard apple rattling in the bottom of a barrel,
and then die somewhere out over the Gulf. In my dream I
prayed for my mother and father, the men in the bar at the
Frederic Hotel, the sheriff and his deputies, and finally for myself and the Negro convict. Many years would pass before I
would learn that it is our collective helplessness, the frailty and
imperfection of our vision, that ennobles us and saves us from
ourselves; but that night, when I awoke while my father was
carrying me up to bed, I knew from the beat of his heart that
he and I had taken pause in our contention with the world.

ETHAN CANIN

Star Food

FROM CHICAGO

THE SUMMER I turned eighteen I disappointed both my parents
for the first time. This hadn't happened before, since what disappointed one usually pleased the other. As a child, if I played
broom hockey instead of going to school, my mother wept and
my father took me outside later to find out how many goals I
had scored. On the other hand, if I spent Saturday afternoon
on the roof of my parents' grocery store staring up at the clouds
instead of counting cracker cartons in the stockroom, my father
took me to the back to talk about work and discipline, and my
mother told me later to keep looking for things that no one else
saw.

This was her theory. My mother felt that men like Leonardo
da Vinci and Thomas Edison had simply stared long enough at
regular objects until they saw new things, and thus my looking
into the sky might someday make me a great man. She believed
I had a worldly curiosity. My father believed I wanted to avoid
stock work.

Stock work was an issue in our family, as were all the jobs that
had to be done in a grocery store. Our store was called Star
Food and above it an incandescent star revolved. Its circuits
buzzed, and its yellow points, as thick as my knees, drooped
with the slow melting of the bulb. On summer nights flying
insects flocked in clouds around it, droves of them burning on
the glass. One of my jobs was to go out on the roof, the sloping,
eaved side that looked over the western half of Arcade, Califor-

nia, and clean them off the star. At night, when their black bodies stood out against the glass, when the wind carried in the marsh smell of the New Jerusalem River, I went into the attic, crawled out the dormer window onto the peaked roof, and slid across the shingles to where the pole rose like a lightning rod into the night. I reached with a wet rag and rubbed away the June bugs and pickerel moths until the star was yellow-white and steaming from the moisture. Then I turned and looked over Arcade, across the bright avenue and my dimly lighted high school in the distance, into the low hills where oak trees grew in rows on the curbs and where girls drove to school in their own convertibles. When my father came up on the roof sometimes to talk about the store, we fixed our eyes on the red tile roofs or the small clouds of blue barbecue smoke that floated above the hills on warm evenings. While the clean bulb buzzed and flickered behind us, we talked about loss leaders or keeping the elephant-ear plums stacked in neat triangles.

The summer I disappointed my parents, though, my father talked to me about a lot of other things. He also made me look in the other direction whenever we were on the roof together, not west to the hills and their clouds of barbecue smoke, but east toward the other part of town. We crawled up one slope of the roof, then down the other so I could see beyond the back alley where wash hung on lines in the moonlight, down to the neighborhoods across Route 5. These were the neighborhoods where men sat on the curbs on weekday afternoons, where rusted, wheel-less cars lay on blocks in the yards.

"*You're* going to end up on one of those curbs," my father told me.

Usually I stared farther into the clouds when he said something like that. He and my mother argued about what I did on the roof for so many hours at a time, and I hoped that by looking closely at the amazing borders of clouds I could confuse him. My mother believed I was on the verge of discovering something atmospheric, and I was sure she told my father this, so when he came upstairs, made me look across Route 5, and talked to me about how I was going to end up there, I squinted harder at the sky.

"You don't fool me for a second," he said.

He was up on the roof with me because I had been letting someone steal from the store.

From the time we first had the star on the roof, my mother believed her only son was destined for limited fame. Limited because she thought that true vision was distilled and could not be appreciated by everybody. The first time I discovered this was shortly after the star was installed, when I spent an hour looking out over the roofs and chimneys instead of helping my father stock a shipment of dairy. It was a hot day and the milk sat on the loading dock while he searched for me in the store and in our apartment next door. When he came up and found me, his neck was red and his footfalls shook the roof joists. At my age I was still allowed certain mistakes, but I'd seen the dairy truck arrive and knew I should have been downstairs, so it surprised me later, after I'd helped unload the milk, when my mother stopped beside me as I was sprinkling the leafy vegetables with a spray bottle.

"Dade, I don't want you to let anyone keep you from what you ought to be doing."

"I'm sorry," I said. "I should have helped with the milk earlier."

"No," she said, "that's not what I mean." Then she told me her theory of limited fame while I sprayed the cabbage and lettuce with the atomizer. It was the first time I had heard her idea. The world's most famous men, she said, presidents and emperors, generals and patriots, were men of vulgar fame, men who ruled the world because their ideas were obvious and could be understood by everybody. But there was also limited fame. Newton and Galileo and Enrico Fermi were men of limited fame, and as I stood there with the atomizer in my hands my mother's eyes watered over and she told me she knew in her heart that one day I was going to be a man of limited fame. I was twelve years old.

After that day I found I could avoid a certain amount of stock work by staying up on the roof and staring into the fine layers of stratus clouds that floated above Arcade. In the *Encyclopedia Americana* I read about cirrus and cumulus and thunderheads, about inversion layers and currents like the currents at sea, and in the afternoons I went upstairs and watched. The sky was a changing thing, I found out. It was more than a blue sheet. Twirling with pollen and sunlight, it began to transform itself.

Often as I stood on the roof my father came outside and swept the sidewalk across the street. Through the telephone poles and crossed power lines he looked up at me, his broom strokes small and fierce as if he were hoeing hard ground. It irked him that my mother encouraged me to stay on the roof. He was a short man with direct habits and an understanding of how to get along in the world, and he believed that God rewarded only two things, courtesy and hard work. God did not reward looking at the sky. In the car my father acknowledged good drivers and in restaurants he left good tips. He knew the names of his customers. He never sold a rotten vegetable. He shook hands often, looked everyone in the eye, and on Friday nights when we went to the movies he made us sit in the front row of the theater. "Why should I pay to look over other people's shoulders?" he said. The movies made him talk. On the way back to the car he walked with his hands clasped behind him and greeted everyone who passed. He smiled. He mentioned the fineness of the evening as if he were the admiral or aviator we had just seen on the screen. "People like it," he said. "It's good for business." My mother was quiet, walking with her slender arms folded in front of her as if she were cold.

I liked the movies because I imagined myself doing everything the heroes did — deciding to invade at daybreak, swimming half the night against the seaward current — but whenever we left the theater I was disappointed. From the front row, life seemed like a clear set of decisions, but on the street afterward I realized that the world existed all around me and I didn't know what I wanted. The quiet of evening and the ordinariness of human voices startled me.

Sometimes on the roof, as I stared into the layers of horizon, the sounds on the street faded into this same ordinariness. One afternoon when I was standing under the star my father came outside and looked up to me. "You're in a trance," he called. I glanced down at him, then squinted back at the horizon. For a minute he waited, and then from across the street he threw a rock. He had a pitcher's arm and could have hit me if he wanted, but the rock sailed past me and clattered on the shingles. My mother came right out of the store anyway and stopped him. "I wanted him off the roof," I heard my father tell her later in the same frank voice in which he explained his position to vegetable salesmen. "If someone's throwing rocks at him he'll come down. He's no fool."

I was flattered by this, but my mother won the point and from then on I could stay up on the roof when I wanted. To appease my father I cleaned the electric star, and though he often came outside to sweep, he stopped telling me to come down. I thought about limited fame and spent a lot of time noticing the sky. When I looked closely it was a sea with waves and shifting colors, wind seams and denials of distance, and after a while I learned to look at it so that it entered my eye whole. It was blue liquid. I spent hours looking into its pale wash, looking for things, though I didn't know what. I looked for lines or sectors, the diamond shapes of daylight stars. Sometimes, silver-winged jets from the air force base across the hills turned the right way against the sun and went off like small flash bulbs on the horizon. There was nothing that struck me and stayed, though, nothing with the brilliance of white light or electric explosion that I thought came with discovery, so after a while I changed my idea of discovery. I just stood on the roof and stared. When my mother asked me, I told her that I might be seeing new things but that seeing change took time. "It's slow," I told her. "It may take years."

The first time I let her steal I chalked it up to surprise. I was working the front register when she walked in, a thin, tall woman in a plaid dress that looked wilted. She went right to the standup display of cut-price, nearly expired breads and crackers, where she took a loaf of rye from the shelf. Then she turned and looked me in the eye. We were looking into each other's eyes when she walked out the front door. Through the blue-and-white LOOK UP TO STAR FOOD sign on the window I watched her cross the street.

There were two or three other shoppers in the store, and over the tops of the potato chip packages I could see my mother's broom. My father was in back unloading chicken parts. Nobody else had seen her come in; nobody had seen her leave. I locked the cash drawer and walked to the aisle where my mother was sweeping.

"I think someone just stole."

My mother wheeled a trash receptacle when she swept, and as I stood there she closed it, put down her broom, and wiped her face with her handkerchief. "You couldn't get him?"

"It was a her."

"A lady?"

"I couldn't chase her. She came in and took a loaf of rye and left."

I had chased plenty of shoplifters before. They were kids usually, in sneakers and coats too warm for the weather, and I chased them up the aisle and out the door, then to the corner and around it while ahead of me they tried to toss whatever it was — Twinkies, freeze-pops — into the sidewalk hedges. They cried when I caught them, begged me not to tell their parents. First time, my father said, scare them real good. Second time, call the law. I took them back with me to the store, held them by the collar as we walked. Then I sat them in the straight-back chair in the stockroom and gave them a speech my father had written. It was printed on a blue index card taped to the door. "Do you know what you have done?" it began. "Do you know what it is to steal?" I learned to pause between the questions, pace the room, and check the card. "Give them time to get scared," my father said. He was expert at this. He never talked to them until he had dusted the vegetables or run a couple of women through the register. "Why should I stop my work for a kid who steals from me?" he said. When he finally came into the stockroom he moved and spoke the way policemen do at the scene of an accident. His manner was slow and deliberate. First he asked me what they had stolen. If I had recovered whatever it was, he took it and held it up to the light, turned it over in his fingers as if it were of large value. Then he opened the freezer door and led the kid inside to talk about law and punishment amid the frozen beef carcasses. He paced as he spoke, breathed clouds of vapor into the air.

In the end, though, my mother usually got him to let them

off. Once when he wouldn't, when he had called the police to pick up a third-offense boy who sat trembling in the stockroom, my mother called him to the front of the store to talk to a customer. In the stockroom we kept a key to the back door hidden under a silver samovar that belonged to my grand-mother, and when my father was in front that afternoon my mother came to the rear, took it out, and opened the back door. She leaned down to the boy's ear. "Run," she said.

The next time she came in it happened the same way. My father was at the vegetable tier, stacking avocados. My mother was in back listening to the radio. It was afternoon. I rang in a cus-tomer, then looked up while I was putting the milk cartons in the bottom of the bag and there she was. Her gray eyes were looking into mine. She had two cans of pineapple juice in her hands, and on the way out she held the door for an old woman.

That night I went up to clean the star. The air was clear. It was warm. When I finished wiping the glass I moved out over the edge of the eaves and looked into the distance where little tur-quoise squares — lighted swimming pools — stood out against the hills.

"Dade — "

It was my father's voice from behind the peak of the roof.

"Yes?"

"Come over to this side."

I mounted the shallow-pitched roof, went over the peak, and edged down the other slope to where I could see his silhouette against the lights on Route 5. He was smoking. I got up and we stood together at the edge of the shingled eaves. In front of us trucks rumbled by on the interstate, their trailers lit at the edges like the mast lights of ships.

"Look across the highway," he said.

"I am."

"What do you see?"

"Cars."

"What else?"

"Trucks."

For a while he didn't say anything. He dragged a few times

on his cigarette, then pinched off the lit end and put the rest back in the pack. A couple of motorcycles went by, a car with one headlight, a bus.

"Do you know what it's like to live in a shack?" he said.

"No."

"You don't want to end up in a place like that. And it's damn easy to do if you don't know what you want. You know how easy it is?"

"Easy," I said.

"You have to know what you want."

For years my father had been trying to teach me competence and industry. Since I was nine I had been squeeze-drying mops before returning them to the closet, double-counting change, sweeping under the lip of the vegetable bins even if the dirt there was invisible to customers. On the basis of industry, my father said, Star Food had grown from a two-aisle, one-freezer corner store to the largest grocery in Arcade. When I was eight he had bought the failing gas station next door and built additions, so that now Star Food had nine aisles, separate coolers for dairy, soda, and beer, a tiered vegetable stand, a glass-fronted butcher counter, a part-time butcher, and, under what used to be the rain roof of the failing gas station, free parking while you shopped. When I started high school we moved into the apartment next door, and at meals we discussed store improvements. Soon my father invented a grid system for easy location of foods. He stayed up one night and painted, and the next morning there was a new coordinate system on the ceiling of the store. It was a grid, A through J, 1 through 10, and for weeks there were drops of blue paint in his eyelashes.

A few days later my mother pasted up fluorescent stars among the grid squares. She knew about the real constellations and was accurate with the ones she stuck to the ceiling, even though she also knew that the aisle lights in Star Food stayed on day and night, so that her stars were going to be invisible. We saw them only once, in fact, in a blackout a few months later when they lit up in hazy clusters around the store.

"Do you know why I did it?" she asked me the night of the blackout as we stood beneath their pale light.

"No."

"Because of the idea."

She was full of ideas, and one was that I was accomplishing something on the shallow-pitched section of our roof. Sometimes she sat at the dormer window and watched me. Through the glass I could see the slender outlines of her cheekbones. "What do you see?" she asked. On warm nights she leaned over the sill and pointed out the constellations. "They are the illumination of great minds," she said.

After the woman walked out the second time I began to think a lot about what I wanted. I tried to discover what it was, and I had an idea it would come to me on the roof. In the evenings I sat up there and thought. I looked for signs. I threw pebbles down into the street and watched where they hit. I read the newspaper, and stories about ballplayers or jazz musicians began to catch my eye. When he was ten years old, Johnny Unitas strung a tire from a tree limb and spent afternoons throwing a football through it as it swung. Dizzy Gillespie played with an orchestra when he was seven. There was an emperor who ruled China at age eight. What could be said about me? He swept the dirt no one could see under the lip of the vegetable bins.

The day after the woman had walked out the second time, my mother came up on the roof while I was cleaning the star. She usually wore medium heels and stayed away from the shingled roof, but that night she came up. I had been over the glass once when I saw her coming through the dormer window, skirt hem and white shoes lit by moonlight. Most of the insects were cleaned off and steam was drifting up into the night. She came through the window, took off her shoes, and edged down the roof until she was standing next to me at the star. "It's a beautiful night," she said.

"Cool."

"Dade, when you're up here do you ever think about what is in the mind of a great man when he makes a discovery?"

The night was just making its transition from the thin sky to the thick, the air was taking on weight, and at the horizon distances were shortening. I looked out over the plain and tried to think of an answer. That day I had been thinking about a story my father occasionally told. Just before he and my mother were married he took her to the top of the hills that surround Arcade. They stood with the New Jerusalem River, western California, and the sea on their left, and Arcade on their right. My father has always planned things well, and that day as they stood in the hill pass a thunderstorm covered everything west, while Arcade, shielded by hills, was lit by the sun. He asked her which way she wanted to go. She must have realized it was a test, because she thought for a moment and then looked to the right, and when they drove down from the hills that day my father mentioned the idea of a grocery. Star Food didn't open for a year after, but that was its conception, I think, in my father's mind. That afternoon as they stood with the New Jerusalem flowing below them, the plains before them, and my mother in a cotton skirt she had made herself, I think my father must have seen right through to the end of his life.

I had been trying to see right through the end of my life, too, but these thoughts never led me in any direction. Sometimes I sat and remembered the unusual things that had happened to me. Once I had found the perfect, shed skin of a rattlesnake. My mother told my father that this indicated my potential for science. I was on the roof another time when it hailed apricot-size balls of ice on a summer afternoon. The day was hot and there was only one cloud, but as it approached from the distance it spread a shaft of darkness below it as if it had fallen through itself to the earth, and when it reached the New Jerusalem the river began throwing up spouts of water. Then it crossed onto land and I could see the hailstones denting parked cars. I went back inside the attic and watched it pass, and when I came outside again and picked up the ice balls that rolled between the corrugated roof spouts, their prickly edges melted in my fingers. In a minute they were gone. That was the rarest thing that ever happened to me. Now I waited for rare things because it seemed to me that if you traced back the lives of men you arrived at some sort of sign, rainstorm at one horizon and sunlight at the other. On the roof I waited for mine. Sometimes I thought about the woman and sometimes I looked for silhouettes in the blue shapes between the clouds.

"Your father thinks you should be thinking about the store."

"I know."

"You'll own the store some day."

There was a carpet of cirrus clouds in the distance, and we watched them as their bottom edges were gradually lit by the rising moon. My mother tilted back her head and looked up into the stars. "What beautiful names," she said. "Cassiopeia, Lyra, Aquila."

"The Big Dipper," I said.

"Dade?"

"Yes?"

"I saw the lady come in yesterday."

"I didn't chase her."

"I know."

"What do you think of that?"

"I think you're doing more important things," she said. "Dreams are more important than rye bread." She took the bobby pins from her hair and held them in her palm. "Dade, tell me the truth. What do you think about when you come up here?"

In the distance there were car lights, trees, aluminum power poles. There were several ways I could have answered.

I said, "I think I'm about to make a discovery."

After that my mother began meeting me at the bottom of the stairs when I came down from the roof. She smiled expectantly. I snapped my fingers, tapped my feet. I blinked and looked at my canvas shoe-tips. She kept smiling. I didn't like this so I tried not coming down for entire afternoons, but this only made her look more expectant. On the roof my thoughts piled into one another. I couldn't even think of something that was undiscovered. I stood and thought about the woman.

Then my mother began leaving little snacks on the sill of the dormer window. Crackers, cut apples, apricots. She arranged them in fan shapes or twirls on a plate, and after a few days I started working regular hours again. I wore my smock and checked customers through the register and went upstairs only in the evenings. I came down after my mother had gone to sleep. I was afraid the woman was coming back, but I couldn't

face my mother twice a day at the bottom of the stairs. So I
worked and looked up at the door whenever customers entered.
I did stock work when I could, stayed in back where the air was
refrigerated, but I sweated anyway. I unloaded melons, tuna
fish, cereal. I counted the cases of freeze-pops, priced the cans
of All-American ham. At the swinging door between the stockroom and the back of the store my heart went dizzy. The woman
knew something about me.

In the evenings on the roof I tried to think what it was. I saw
mysterious new clouds, odd combinations of cirrus and stratus.
How did she root me into the linoleum floor with her gray
stare? Above me on the roof the sky was simmering. It was blue
gas. I knew she was coming back.

It was raining when she did. The door opened and I felt the
wet breeze, and when I looked up she was standing with her
back to me in front of the shelves of cheese and dairy, and this
time I came out from the counter and stopped behind her. She
smelled of the rain outside.

"Look," I whispered, "why are you doing this to me?"

She didn't turn around. I moved closer. I was gathering my
words, thinking of the blue index card, when the idea of limited
fame came into my head. I stopped. How did human beings
understand each other across huge spaces except with the lowest
of ideas? I have never understood what it is about rain that
smells, but as I stood there behind the woman I suddenly realized I was smelling the inside of clouds. What was between us at
that moment was an idea we had created ourselves. When she
left with a bottle of milk in her hand I couldn't speak.

On the roof that evening I looked into the sky, out over the
plains, along the uneven horizon. I thought of the view my
father had seen when he was a young man. I wondered whether
he had imagined Star Food then. The sun was setting. The blues
and oranges were mixing into black, and in the distance windows were lighting up along the hillsides.

"Tell me what I want," I said then. I moved closer to the edge
of the eaves and repeated it. I looked down over the alley, into
the kitchens across the way, into living rooms, bedrooms, across

slate rooftops. "Tell me what I want," I called. Cars pulled in
and out of the parking lot. Big rigs rushed by on the interstate.
The air around me was as cool as water, the lighted swimming
pools like pieces of the daytime sky. An important moment
seemed to be rushing up. "Tell me what I want," I said again.

Then I heard my father open the window and come out onto
the roof. He walked down and stood next to me, the bald spot
on top of his head reflecting the streetlight. He took out a cigarette, smoked it for a while, pinched off the end. A bird fluttered around the light pole across the street. A car crossed below
us with the words JUST MARRIED on the roof.

"Look," he said, "your mother's tried to make me understand
this." He paused to put the unsmoked butt back in the pack.
"And maybe I can. You think the gal's a little down and out;
you don't want to kick her when she's down. OK, I can understand that. So I've decided something, and you want to know
what?"

He shifted his hands in his pockets and took a few steps toward the edge of the roof.

"You want to know what?"

"What?"

"I'm taking you off the hook. Your mother says you've got a
few thoughts, that maybe you're on the verge of something, so
I decided it's OK if you let the lady go if she comes in again."

"What?"

"I said it's OK if you let the gal go. You don't have to chase
her."

"You're going to let her steal?"

"No," he said. "I hired a guard."

He was there the next morning in clothes that were all dark
blue. Pants, shirt, cap, socks. He was only two or three years
older than I was. My father introduced him to me as Mr. Sellers.
"Mr. Sellers," he said, "this is Dade." He had a badge on his
chest and a ring of keys the size of a doughnut on his belt. At
the door he sat jingling them.

I didn't say much to him, and when I did my father came out
from the back and counted register receipts or stocked impulse
items near where he sat. We weren't saying anything important,

though. Mr. Sellers didn't carry a gun, only the doughnut-size key ring, so I asked him if he wished he did.

"Sure," he said.

"Would you use it?"

"If I had to."

I thought of him using his gun if he had to. His hands were thick and their backs were covered with hair. This seemed to go along with shooting somebody if he had to. My hands were thin and white and the hair on them was like the hair on a girl's cheek.

During the days he stayed by the front. He smiled at customers and held the door for them, and my father brought him sodas every hour or so. Whenever the guard smiled at a customer I thought of him trying to decide whether he was looking at the shoplifter.

And then one evening everything changed.

I was on the roof. The sun was low, throwing slanted light. From beyond the New Jerusalem and behind the hills, four air force jets appeared. They disappeared, then appeared again, silver dots trailing white tails. They climbed and cut and looped back, showing dark and light like a school of fish. When they turned against the sun their wings flashed. Between the hills and the river they dipped low onto the plain, then shot upward and toward me. One dipped, the others followed. Across the New Jerusalem they turned back and made two great circles, one inside the other, then dipped again and leveled off in my direction. The sky seemed small enough for them to fall through. I could see the double tails, then the wings and the jets. From across the river they shot straight toward the store, angling up so I could see the V-wings and camouflage and rounded bomb bays, and I covered my ears, and in a moment they were across the water and then they were above me, and as they passed over they barrel-rolled and flew upside down and showed me their black cockpit glass so that my heart came up into my mouth.

I stood there while they turned again behind me and lifted back toward the hills, trailing threads of vapor, and by the time their booms subsided I knew I wanted the woman to be caught. I had seen a sign. Suddenly the sky was water-clear. Distances moved in, houses stood out against the hills, and it seemed to me that I had turned a corner and now looked over a rain-washed street. The woman was a thief. This was a simple fact and it presented itself to me simply. I felt the world dictating its course.

I went downstairs and told my father I was ready to catch her. He looked at me, rolled the chewing gum in his cheek. "I'll be damned."

"My life is making sense," I said.

When I unloaded potato chips that night I laid the bags in the aluminum racks as if I were putting children to sleep in their beds. Dust had gathered under the lip of the vegetable bins, so I swept and mopped there and ran a wet cloth over the stalls. My father slapped me on the back a couple of times. In school once I had looked through a microscope at the tip of my own finger, and now as I looked around the store everything seemed to have been magnified in the same way. I saw cracks in the linoleum floor, speckles of color in the walls.

This kept up for a couple of days, and all the time I waited for the woman to come in. After a while it was more than just waiting; I looked forward to the day when she would return. In my eyes she would find nothing but resolve. How bright the store seemed to me then when I swept, how velvety the skins of the melons beneath the sprayer bottle. When I went up to the roof I scrubbed the star with the wet cloth and came back down. I didn't stare into the clouds and I didn't think about the woman except with the thought of catching her. I described her perfectly for the guard. Her gray eyes. Her plaid dress.

After I started working like this my mother began to go to the back room in the afternoons and listen to music. When I swept the rear I heard the melodies of operas. They came from behind the stockroom door while I waited for the woman to return, and when my mother came out she had a look about her of disappointment. Her skin was pale and smooth, as if the blood had run to deeper parts.

"Dade," she said one afternoon as I stacked tomatoes in a pyramid, "it's easy to lose your dreams."

"I'm just stacking tomatoes."

She went back to the register. I went back to stacking, and my father, who'd been patting me on the back, winking at me from behind the butcher counter, came over and helped me.

"I notice your mother's been talking to you."

"A little."

We finished the tomatoes and moved on to the lettuce.

"Look," he said, "it's better to do what you have to do, so I wouldn't spend your time worrying frontwards and backwards about everything. Your life's not so long as you think it's going to be."

We stood there rolling heads of butterball lettuce up the shallow incline of the display cart. Next to me he smelled like Aqua Velva.

"The lettuce is looking good," I said.

Then I went up to the front of the store. "I'm not sure what my dreams are," I said to my mother, "And I'm never going to discover anything. All I've ever done on the roof is look at the clouds."

Then the door opened and the woman came in. I was standing in front of the counter, hands in my pockets, my mother's eyes watering over, the guard looking out the window at a couple of girls, everything revolving around the point of calm that, in retrospect, precedes surprises. I'd been waiting for her for a week, and now she came in. I realized I never expected her. She stood looking at me, and for a few moments I looked back. Then she realized what I was up to. She turned around to leave, and when her back was to me I stepped over and grabbed her.

I've never liked fishing much, even though I used to go with my father, because the moment a fish jumps on my line a tree's length away in the water I feel as if I've suddenly lost something. I'm always disappointed and sad, but now as I held the woman beneath the shoulder I felt none of this disappointment. I felt strong and good. She was thin, and I could make out the bones and tendons in her arm. As I led her back toward the stockroom, through the bread aisle, then the potato chips that were puffed and stacked like a row of pillows, I heard my mother begin to weep behind the register. Then my father came up behind me. I didn't turn around, but I knew he was there and I knew the deliberately calm way he was walking. "I'll be back as soon as I dust the melons," he said.

I held the woman tightly under her arm but despite this she moved in a light way, and suddenly, as we paused before the stockroom door, I felt as if I were leading her onto the dance floor. This flushed me with remorse. Don't spend your whole life looking backwards and forwards, I said to myself. Know what you want. I pushed the door open and we went in. The room was dark. It smelled of my whole life. I turned on the light and sat her down in the straight-back chair, then crossed the room and stood against the door. I had spoken to many children as they sat in this chair. I had frightened them, collected the candy they had tried to hide between the cushions, and presented it to my father when he came in. Now I looked at the blue card. DO YOU KNOW WHAT YOU HAVE DONE? it said. DO YOU KNOW WHAT IT IS TO STEAL? I tried to think of what to say to the woman. She sat trembling slightly. I approached the chair and stood in front of her. She looked up at me. Her hair was gray around the roots.

"Do you want to go out the back?" I said.

She stood up and I took the key from under the silver samovar. My father would be there in a moment, so after I let her out I took my coat from the hook and followed. The evening was misty. She crossed the lot, and I hurried and came up next to her. We walked fast and stayed behind cars, and when we had gone a distance I turned and looked back. The stockroom door was closed. On the roof the star cast a pale light that whitened the aluminum-sided eaves.

It seemed we would be capable of a great communication now, but as we walked I realized I didn't know what to say to her. We went down the street without talking. The traffic was light, evening was approaching, and as we passed below some trees the streetlights suddenly came on. This moment has always amazed me. I knew the woman had seen it too, but it is always a disappointment to mention a thing like this. The streets and buildings took on their night shapes. Still we didn't say anything to each other. We kept walking beneath the pale violet of the lamps, and after a few more blocks I just stopped at one corner. She went on, crossed the street, and I lost sight of her.

I stood there until the world had rotated fully into the night, and for a while I tried to make myself aware of the spinning of the earth. Then I walked back toward the store. When they slept that night, my mother would dream of discovery and my father would dream of low-grade crooks. When I thought of this and the woman I was sad. It seemed you could never really know another person. I felt alone in the world, in the way that makes me aware of sound and temperature, as if I had just left a movie theater and stepped into an alley where a light rain was falling, and the wind was cool, and, from somewhere, other people's voices could be heard.

FRANK CONROY

Gossip

FROM ESQUIRE

IT WAS TEN O'CLOCK on a Wednesday night in 1966 when George paid the cab driver and stepped out onto the sidewalk in front of McShane's Bar and Grille. A tall, thin young man, slightly stooped, slightly pigeon-toed, with an odd narrow face, unmarked by age or worry lines, a face so smooth and youthful it seemed that life must never have touched him. His face may thus have represented, by some hidden chemistry, the power of his will, since the method he had used to deal with pain — of which he had had his full human share — was denial. He did not deny pain's existence, but only its power over him. (In this he was of course mistaken.) He was twenty-eight, intelligent, and ignorant of the forces that moved him. More than most young men he was entranced by the surface of life, not because he was shallow, but because he thought the surface might reveal some hitherto unknown (to him) route of access to the interior, to the inside of life, where he might finally become a man instead of a young man. He wanted an older face.

He felt a pleasant anticipation as he entered McShane's, a writer's hangout, where on any given night he could be sure of meeting a few friends who, like himself, were unknown artists working on faith. The camaraderie of the place was satisfying. It assuaged the sense of loneliness he felt in his marriage, a college marriage he refused to examine out of fear of what he might find. His wife refused to come to McShane's, perhaps for the same reason.

Scotch and soda in hand, George rested the small of his back against the bar and surveyed the room. He saw half a dozen people he knew, but the special friends he was to meet had not yet arrived. The Group — Ivan, the painter, Jean-Claude, the journalist for *Paris Match,* Yolande, the Eurasian model, Ted, the jazz pianist, and Bobbie, the Brazilian-American hostess. An outrageously glamorous group, whose friendship he prized deeply. At dinners, parties, and social events all over the city he'd had fun with them, more fun than he'd ever had in his life. He valued fun. It was much more to him than diversion.

"I had a weird dream, the weirdest dream."

He realized with surprise that Mary Stein, a writer of about his own age whom he knew slightly, was sitting beside him, facing the opposite direction. Her remark was addressed to him.

"What happened?" He half turned toward her while watching the front door for Ivan and the others.

"I was on the bank of a river, or like the Intracoastal Waterway or something, and . . ."

George listened abstractedly. Mary was a good writer, a working-class intellectual, not particularly pretty but decidedly sexy. Recently, she had been going out with Joshua Barnes, and George admired her courage. Barnes was a poet, blind from birth, brimming with repressed anger, and generally neurotic and difficult. She continued, now, to describe her convoluted and surreal dream, a dream of which, her tone suggested, she was slightly in awe. George half listened, and it was perhaps precisely for that reason — that he was not so much listening as monitoring the story unconsciously — that its meaning came to him complete and fully formed.

"Weird," she said when she'd finished.

The big table was ready now, and George stood up fully. "Not so weird," he said, flip, showing off. "It means you're pregnant." He started to move away, aware that she was getting up to go with him, when he glanced at her and stopped. Her knees seemed about to give way, and he quickly grabbed her elbow. Her body leaned in toward his.

"Don't tell anybody," she said quickly. "Please don't tell anybody."

"It's okay," he said, holding her. "Mary, I'm sorry, I'm very sorry."

"You can't tell anybody. I can't explain, but you . . ."

"Stop. Stop. I promise. Mary, I promise I won't breathe a word. You don't have to explain anything. I absolutely promise."

"My God."

"Come on." He led her toward a table. "We need to sit down. We need a drink."

She followed his lead and they took chairs next to each other. "What do you want?"

"What?" Still stunned, she looked at him as if she'd never seen him before.

"Scotch?"

"Brandy. A large brandy." She took a deep breath, looked down at the surface of the table, and slowly shook her head. "Jesus."

When the group came in he caught Ivan's eye and made a movement with his head to indicate the back of the restaurant. Ivan understood and swept the others along.

George stayed with Mary until, finally, she touched his arm. "I'm okay," she said. "I know you want to join them."

"Are you sure?"

On his way to the back table he unconsciously puffed his cheeks and blew out some air. He sat down with his friends.

"What was that all about?" Ivan asked.

"Nothing, nothing."

He kept his promise and told no one. For a week or so the incident would pop into his mind now and then. The strength of Mary's reaction surprised him. She would have Joshua Barnes's child, and presumably they'd get married before, or after, or perhaps never. Maybe she hadn't told Joshua. Maybe he'd get angry. Maybe his blindness was a factor. George came to see there was no way to know what might be involved.

After two or three weeks he'd forgotten the whole episode.

A year later George's book came out. Modest sales but a critical success. He was dizzy with happiness. He did not, however, feel any older. Despite years of hard work and hard drinking, he still looked, and to some extent felt, like a kid out of college.

Ivan had a show at an important gallery and sold every piece. Yolande signed a design contract with a big fashion house. Jean-

Claude's translation of a new American play was a hit in Paris, and Bobbie's invitations were more sought after than ever. All this worked to bring the group closer together, as if they needed one another to understand what was happening. In truth, they didn't understand much. They were having fun. It was that time of life for them.

When someone offered them a free house in the Caribbean for ten days, they accepted instantly. They invited two other people, who got reservations at nearby hotels — Harriet Brement, the famous playwright, a tough old woman who seemed to be amused by them, and Susan Strand, an actress from their own generation. George's wife didn't want to go.

"Listen," Ivan said. "Why do you think she came?"

"For this!" George swept an arm to indicate the great bowl of clear sky, the blue-green Caribbean. "Susan loves the sun."

"Why did you invite her, then?"

"Me? I thought *you* invited her, that night we went down to hear Ted sit in with Zoot Sims."

"It was you."

"It was? Okay. So? She understood it was a whole gang. It wasn't like . . ."

"George," Ivan interrupted, "are you going to leave her all alone in that hotel every night? While you come back here to your little room?"

George laughed. "Hey. I've never touched her. She's a pal. Anyway, I'm married."

Ivan smiled and turned to look out at the ocean. "Okay, my friend," he said gently.

George turned his back to the sun, lay down on the hot, smooth rock, and looked down at the swimming pool. Yolande and Bobbie were in the water. Jean-Claude sat on the diving board. Near the shallow end, Harriet and Susan sat at a white table under a white umbrella, sipping tall drinks. When people moved, they moved languidly. George watched through half-closed eyes, and drifted into sleep.

By the second day patterns seemed to have emerged spontaneously — at the beach by late morning, back for naps in the late afternoon, communal dinners in the big house, the casino until closing, and everyone to bed. Jean-Claude prepared the big lunch basket. Ivan — a compulsively neat man — kept the house clean. Yolande and Bobbie made splendid dinners, and George was responsible for transportation in the rented car, picking up Harriet and Susan, dropping them off, getting the groceries. They all took quiet pleasure in this effortless cooperation.

Sometimes the American staff at the casino would invite them to stay after closing. They'd drink champagne, and if they'd lost, Susan would parody their state of mind by crawling along the floor under the slot machines looking for quarters. She'd find them, too, and bring them back to George, whispering, "Here's our stake for tomorrow. We'll break these bastards yet."

One night, as he drove Susan back to her hotel, she began horsing around. It was a re-enactment, she said, of a scene she'd played in a movie. She mussed his hair, kept a line of monologue running about something from the plot he didn't understand (he'd never seen the movie), blew in his ear, and generally vamped him.

"Hey!" He laughed, pulling the car off the shoulder back onto the road. "We'll crash!" She stopped. She'd been goofing, of course, but he'd felt her power, the perfect control over her voice, her body, the tempo of events. He was simply no match for her, and he knew it.

"Let's stop," she said. "Over there, by the pier. I want to look at the water."

He pulled off the road and they got out of the car. Susan skipped ahead.

"Isn't this gorgeous?" She held her arms aloft.

Indeed it was. A warm, clear night. Stars. The lights of her hotel across the little bay shining steadily, the reflections of each point of light rocking in the black water. He stood with his back against a piling. She walked up the pier a little way, and then came back. She wore a white cotton dress and white shoes. As she joined him, he saw that she was smiling. She raised both arms and clasped her hands behind his neck. Her touch seemed almost supernaturally light.

"I understand," she said, kissing him, "that we must exercise the utmost discretion." Another soft kiss. "I can assure you," she said, pressing him gently against the piling, "that I'm good at discretion."

His hands went automatically to her hips. He was momentarily at a loss for words.

"Don't you want to?" she asked, her hands moving up to cradle the back of his head. The pupils of her brown eyes seemed enormous.

"Yes." He gathered her in. "I want to."

They made love that night in her hotel room. For the rest of their time on the island they made love every day — either in the afternoon or at night — and managed to hide it from everyone. At the beach, at dinner, at the casino, their behavior toward each other was, to all outward appearances, the same as before. George was astonished. "Are we really fooling them?" he asked one afternoon as they lay, naked and glistening, on her bed. "Or are they just letting us think that we're fooling them?"

"I think we're fooling them," she said.

He was very careful, and yet he couldn't quite believe it. Aware that he was obsessed with her, and profoundly moved by the fact that she wanted him as much as he wanted her, cleansed, lightened, and glowing as he was, he found it impossible to believe that his friends had noticed nothing.

The morning before the last day, they went to a new beach, on the far end of the island, all save Harriet, who was too hung over and chose to remain in her hotel. They explored, swam, collected shells in groups of two or three, and eventually drifted back to the picnic basket at midday.

"One more swim before lunch," Yolande said. "Anybody?"

"You're on." Susan got up from her towel.

The others watched as the two women ran into the water. Susan kicked spray on her way to the deep water, dove cleanly, and disappeared.

"Well," Ivan said. "You blew it, George. Life passes, and you let it pass."

"Tais-toi, imbécile," Jean-Claude said.

George lay down on his back and closed his eyes. There was silence.

Bobbie spoke. "Not everybody is like you, Ivan," she said.

George thought he should say something, but he felt too many conflicting emotions. Guilt, that he had fooled his friends, accompanied by satisfaction, a feeling of safety. He didn't like the satisfaction — it seemed tinged with smugness. He knew, he had known all along, that his time with Susan would end when they left the island, so it seemed both easier and better to say nothing.

The end of the sixties marked a period of great change for George — all crammed into a year or two, like the playing out of some cabalistic, mystical prophecy — and the changes frightened him profoundly. His marriage ended and he left the house with $130, no job, and little confidence that he could ever write another book. His depression was intensified by the after-effects of having gone, twice weekly, for six months, to a corrupt doctor who administered intravenous vitamin B_{12}, B complex, calcium gluconate, and methamphetamine. The Group had broken up. Jean-Claude left Yolande and returned to Paris. Ted moved to California to do movie scores. When Ivan became Yolande's lover, George knew it was all over. He left the city and moved to a small town on the east coast of Maine. After several years he married a local girl, and eked out a living doing magazine journalism by mail, and hard physical labor on the fishing boats.

In the early seventies he went to New York to interview a famous poet for a magazine. At a cocktail party in the poet's loft, he bumped into Mary and Joshua Barnes. Mary left her husband's side as soon as George entered, approaching him with an odd expression, at once dreamy and intense.

"I was told you might be here."

"You were?" he said stupidly. He wondered what was going on. Her eyes seemed locked on his.

"It was a girl, you know," she said.

For a moment he was at a loss, and then he remembered the night at McShane's. "Oh, that's wonderful," he said, and smiled. "Terrific."

Now her expression was slightly quizzical, as if he had some important knowledge and she had to find a way to get it out of him.

"My life is completely different now," he found himself saying. "I haven't been in New York for years."

"I know that." She led him over to Joshua. "Josh. It's George, visiting from the wilderness."

"Hi, Josh."

Josh turned his blind, rigid face toward the source of the sound. "The dream reader. Hello, George."

They made small talk, with Mary hovering silently, watching them. George was uncomfortable — he sensed some subtle animus in Josh, a faint pressure under the surface of the words, and he moved away as soon as he could.

The hard winter of 1978 began early in Maine. Heavy snow in November, dark skies, constant wind. George tried to write in the bedroom of the partially heated house. His wife, Kate, worked as a waitress in a local restaurant. They were $3,000 in debt — not that much for George in the old days (which seemed to him truly another life, a previous incarnation), but a great deal now.

One night he sat in the kitchen with a beer, waiting for Kate. The faucet was set to drip so the pipes wouldn't freeze, and he could see his breath in the air. She entered all in a rush, slamming the door behind her against the wind. A small woman with a sharp, mobile face that seemed to him the personification of alertness and intelligence. A lively face, full of optimism. She was fourteen years his junior. She moved quickly, slipping off boots, scarf, and her puffy down-filled jacket.

"I got an interesting phone call today," George said.

"A book review?" Stowing the boots. Getting slippers.

"No. A university in Kansas. They want me to go out there and teach a semester."

She looked up. "Teach? I thought you said you didn't want to teach." Her voice was neutral, as if she needed more information before committing herself to a response.

"That was literature. This is writing. It's because of my book. They want me to teach writing. Joshua Barnes is doing the poetry out there, and they want me to do the fiction."

"Is that possible? I mean, can people be taught?"

"I don't know."

"How much? Did they say?"

"Thirteen thousand."

"What?" She sat down, and then immediately stood up. "Thirteen thousand?" Her surprise gave way to a sudden smile. "My God. The light at the end of the tunnel. When do we go?"

It took them five days in Kate's old Volkswagen, George driving carefully through the wind and snow. All through the Northeast, the radio kept talking about the Winter of '78 in portentous tones.

"I don't see why they go on like that," Kate said, "It isn't *that* bad."

In the mountains, he began worrying about the car. The engine was worn, and even a modest grade forced him to gear down and crawl along at thirty miles an hour. They stayed in inexpensive motels, and ate roadside food. At a Howard Johnson's an elderly waitress thought Kate was his daughter, and Kate immediately began improvising dialogue for the occasion.

"Daddy, you promised," she said, embracing her role. "I did all my homework in study hall, and you promised." She was good at it. A natural actress.

"Okay," he said for the waitress's benefit. "But be back by ten P.M. or you're grounded."

At the cashier's desk, waiting to pay, he glanced at himself in the marbled-mirror wall. "Do I look that old?"

"I was all bundled up," Kate said laughing. "My head is small."

He was forty, and he suddenly realized he looked it. Graying hair, lines in his face, a bit jowly. Eight years in Maine, and he'd jumped from college kid to middle age, without the intervening stages.

George had been teaching for two weeks — seventeen graduate students in a seminar workshop. He sat in his office one morning stapling photocopied pages of Stendhal into seventeen piles when someone knocked on the door.

"Come in."

Immediately — simply by the way she entered, her carriage, her first few words — he felt he understood something about her. She was aware that she was beautiful — tall, a great fall of coppery hair, large green eyes, straight nose, generous mouth

— but her manner suggested that all that was irrelevant. She wore voluminous clothing in a slightly dated peasant style, as if to hide herself. Her small waist, perfect shoulders, and elegant neck could not, however, be hidden. She sat down and spoke directly, without hesitation, an old leather briefcase on her lap.

"I started off doing poetry," she said. "That's how I got in the program. But now I want to do prose. I've heard how you run your workshop — going line by line — and I want to transfer in." She was in her early twenties, and spoke with a very slight Canadian accent.

"Who are you working with now?"

"Joshua Barnes. He's good, but as I say, I want to do prose. I know you don't have much time," she said, opening the briefcase. (In fact he had a good deal of time.) "Could you read some of my stuff? I'll come by tomorrow if that's okay." She placed a couple of chapbooks and some manuscripts on the desk.

She was all business, this one, and just a bit pushy. Nevertheless, they were paying him to teach — a responsibility he took seriously — and she was a student, eager to work.

"Okay," he said. "Sure."

She thanked him and left, closing the door behind her.

At the end of the day he dropped in on the director of the program. "Who is this" — George looked down at one of the stories to find her name — "Joan Lavin?"

"*Ah*, yes. Joan."

George held up the papers. "This is incredibly good stuff."

"Yes. I know."

"She wants to transfer into my class."

"Entirely up to you," the director said. "I don't know much about her. She's from Ontario, I think. She's on scholarship. Very serious." He paused.

George waited, but the director would not say more.

"Well, then. I'll tell her it's okay." George said. "I understand her prose, what she's trying to do. I can save her some time."

Joan Lavin tended to be rather quiet in class, measuring her remarks on the other students' work with care. She was inevitably direct and fair-minded, eschewing intellectual games, and although George sensed a suggestion of distance between her and the others (Based on what? he wondered. The fact of her being so far ahead as a writer? Her physical beauty?), they obviously respected her. He wondered if she felt isolated, or lonely, and was immediately irritated at himself for the banality of the speculation. It was none of his business, in any case.

She wrote more material than could be covered in class and so they would meet in his office at the end of the week. Side by side at his desk, each with a copy of whatever she had written, they would work through the prose, with George doing most of the talking.

Her concentration was intense, and it quickly formed a sort of shield around her. It was almost as if, once he started talking, he was no longer really there as far as she was concerned. She would stare at the page, correlating his remarks with the written words, utterly attentive and alert, her brain working, and he might as well have been speaking to her over the telephone. If another student knocked, or there was some interruption, it was always a slight shock for them both. She could never entirely conceal her impatience at such moments — making a small sound with her tongue, tapping the surface of the desk with her knuckles, or pushing back her hair.

After assuring her of his high opinion of her as a writer, he spent week after week, month after month going after every weakness he could find in her prose, attacking from one direction after another, trying to tear the work apart in front of her eyes. She responsed by writing better and better stuff, paradoxically with more and more confidence, until it became difficult for him to find any of the weaknesses she had originally exhibited. The onus shifted, and it became necessary for him to work hard in order to keep up with her, rather than the reverse.

"Why don't you ask her over for dinner?" Kate said one night.

"Here?"

"Joan, and a couple of the other hard workers."

"Well, you know," he said, "teaching. It's probably a good idea to keep the lines drawn. Work is work, and then the personal stuff . . ." He trailed off.

Part of his reluctance came from his awareness that Joan was no longer just a student to him. Despite the fact that in their sessions they had never talked about anything but work, he was undeniably drawn to her. She was important to him, and the degree of importance was a secret that he had to keep to himself. Their relationship was based on the tacit understanding that they would remain always in their respective roles of teacher and student, and he needed her enough to want to do nothing to threaten that arrangement. Dinner, small talk, socializing were full of imponderables, and the prospect made him nervous, and so he said no.

During the last month of classes and office sessions the pace of work increased, and George was forced to set aside a short story of his own. There were increasing demands on his time and attention, and he made a conscious effort to be available, even for the weaker writers, at the same time as he met with Joan every few days.

But he began to notice a certain tension in Joan, a kind of general guardedness in class, where she spoke much less than before, and a slightly harried quality in the office meetings. She worked hard as ever, but at odd moments would seem preoccupied, as if listening for some sound just out of earshot.

"Maybe you ought to ease up a bit," he said one day in the hall outside his office. She looked up in surprise. "You've done a great deal of work," he went on. "Maybe too much. You seem tired."

She turned her face away and looked down the corridor. Students and teachers milled around. "It's not the work," she said. "I've just been here too long. I've got t get out of here."

There was an intensity to the last phrase that took him aback. "But why?"

She hesitated for a moment, and then made a small dismissive gesture. "Oh, it's nothing, really." A couple of undergraduates passed. "All of us in the program, everybody knows everybody, people don't know how good they are, who's going to make it, or get published. There's a lot of competition. It gets a little" — she paused again — "claustrophobic. Sometimes."

"Oh," he said. "Yes. Of course."

"I'll have the new story in by Friday." She walked away.

He went back in his office and sat down. He realized that when she'd said "I've got to get out of here," he'd felt a shock, a moment of panic. It worried him that he had reacted thus. It surprised him.

In the vast Student Union building, on his way to the bookstore, George made his way down the wide main hall, passing the video-game arcade (electronic rumble; explosions of quick white noise; the sound of giants marching; ironic, mocking little melodic phrases, twitters, squeaks, zaps — an electric madhouse), the cafeteria, the TV lounge, the banks of shiny vending machines. He glanced through the glass into the bowling alleys, and stopped. Only one lane was in use. George pushed through the door and stood quite still. Joshua Barnes was bowling, and his daughter Amy was keeping score, hunched over the board like some child clerk from Dickens.

On the left-hand side of the free area two standing ashtrays had been placed about ten feet apart, one near the left-hand gutter and one back near the scoring table. A taut piece of string ran between them, extending the left-hand edge of the alley. Joshua bowled in the traditional manner, except that when his backswing was complete, and his left arm came out for balance, the tips of his fingers made contact with the string. As he moved forward his hand slid along the string with astonishing delicacy, allowing him to orient himself correctly and bowl straight. He threw hard, and remained motionless at the foul line, bent over, his ear cocked for the sound of the ball rolling down the alley. As the pins crashed, he straightened up.

"The four and the seven," Amy called out, naming the pins still standing.

As the ball returned, Joshua moved to the right, picked it up as it emerged from the gate, raised it to the right side of his chin, and walked back to throw again. His movements were crisp, almost military.

He threw again, listened with intense concentration, and made a quick, impatient gesture with his shoulders as the ball thumped into the heavy back curtain.

"To the right?" he asked.

"By two inches," Amy answered, her pencil moving in her fist, her head down.

Joshua went to the gate for the ball. George backed up slowly.

He wanted to get out before Amy became aware of him. He did not want Josh to know he had watched. For a moment Josh's head turned, as if he had heard something. George slipped out.

Joan did not come to the last two classes, nor did she come to his office. He found himself reacting with a mixture of anger and sadness, and it was the very complexity of his mood that kept him from picking up the phone to call her and find out what was going on. If she didn't come, she didn't come. She had done far more work than anyone else, and perhaps she had no more to learn from him.

He concentrated on the other students and tried not to think of her. But he found himself hoping he would bump into her in the halls. He didn't.

On the last day, he and Kate packed up the Volkswagen (new clutch, overhauled engine, new tires) and stopped off at the English Department building on their way out of town.

"I'll only be a second," George said in the parking lot. "I left a couple of books in my office, and I have to turn in the key."

He checked his office, pulling out the drawers a final time, making sure nothing was left on the shelves. When he gave the key to the director's secretary, he asked, "Have you seen Joan Lavin? Is she around?"

"I don't know."

One of the typists looked up from her desk. "She was here right after lunch, picking up those flyers for her reading."

"Flyers?"

"Yes. She had thumb tacks and Scotch tape. I bet she's around the building someplace, putting them up."

He walked quickly through the halls of each floor, and worked his way down to ground level. He was about to give up when he saw her at the inner doors of one of the side entrances, taping up a mimeographed notice.

"Hey," he said. "I was looking for you."

She seemed flustered, glancing at him quickly, then pulling out tape to stick up another notice. "Hi, I guess you're off soon," she said.

"Today. This minute, in fact. The car is outside."

"Oh." She stopped. "Well, you're lucky. Where are you going?"

"Back east. Another teaching job."

She met his eye for a moment. "That's good. You're a good teacher." She turned, and they walked down the hall. At the main doors, she started taping notices, and he felt a surge of irritation. He wanted to say something to her, but he couldn't figure out what it was. He gave a little wave and went through the doors.

" 'Bye," he heard her call.

In the car, Kate folded up the road map she'd been looking at. "All set?"

"Yup." He started the engine and they drove away.

A year passed. George taught a workshop at Princeton one day a week and worked hard at his writing. Kate had signed up for courses toward accreditation as an X-ray technician. ("I like to see inside," she'd said.) When she found out she was pregnant, she increased her course load. They lived in a small walk-up near the university.

One day the mailman delivered a parcel. It contained a book-length manuscript from Joan, who asked George to read it — almost all of the stories from the workshop in Kansas were included — and tender his advice about the sequence and any style editing that seemed appropriate. A major publisher had agreed to do the book. George wrote back (to Port Townsend, Washington) with his congratulations, a couple of pages of notes, and the following request;

> . . . Can you satisfy my curiosity about something? Why were you so eager to leave the Kansas workshop? I heard you turned down a job there. And why did you drop out so abruptly toward the end of the term?

She answered quickly, thanking him for his notes, and then going on to say:

> . . . About the other stuff, it seems almost silly now, but it sure didn't at the time. It threw me. I started getting some strange vibrations from the other students, and then some anger from certain quarters,

and finally a definite feeling of having been sent to Coventry. I simply couldn't understand what was going on. It was weird. I even went
to the university shrink at one point. Finally I worked it out of Mimi
— you remember her? The southern girl who always had so many
flowers in her stories? It was gossip. There was gossip going around
that you and I were sleeping together. It sounds silly, but it made me
so mad I thought I was going to explode.

What I did was find out who Mimi heard it from. Then I went to
him, laid out the whole thing, and asked him who he'd heard it from.
It took a long time, but I was like a crazy person. Some of them didn't
want to tell me, and I had to convince them. I can't remember how
many people it was — ten or twelve, anyway — but I finally ran it to
ground. It was a girl from the poetry workshop. She cried when she
told me. Joshua Barnes had been putting the make on her, and she'd
said it wasn't right, they were student and teacher, etc. He said,
"Well, look at George and Joan." And that was where it started. I
don't know why he would say a thing like that. . . .

George wrote back:

I'm sorry you had to go through that mess. It doesn't sound silly to
me, it sounds like a nightmare. I believe I understand most of
Barnes's motivation. It had nothing to do with you, but goes back to
an incident many years ago when I interpreted a dream of his wife's.
It's complicated, but I'm sure that's where the whole thing started.

Kate was angry when he told her. "That sleazy son of a bitch!
I'd like to punch him in the mouth!"

"I was angry, too," George said, adding gravy to his meat loaf.
"But then I understood. The dream, the way he must have —"

"Fuck the dream! Fuck his motivation!" She slammed her flat
palms on the table, making everything bounce. "It's *women* that
take the shit! Look at how she had to go around, getting it out
of them, goddamn it!"

"Kate, I know you must —"

"Oh, shut up," she cried, and there were sudden tears in her
eyes. "What do you care? You're probably *flattered*, you probably
think it's *great* all those people thought you were sleeping with
her. Right? Am I right?"

Later, lying in bed, their bodies not touching, he told her
about his affair in the Caribbean, and the gossip that he had *not*

been sleeping with Susan, also that he had been faithful to *her* throughout their marriage, and that even if he were a tiny bit flattered, somewhere deep — the thoughtless reaction of some smooth-faced boy-self he would never be entirely rid of — given all that, when you looked at it, it didn't matter. What mattered was that everyone was connected in a web, that pain was part of the web, and yet despite it, people loved one another. That's what you found out when you got older, he said.

RICHARD FORD

Communist

FROM ANTAEUS

My mother once had a boyfriend named Glen Baxter. This was in 1961. We — my mother and I — were living in the little house my father had left her up the Sun River, near Victory, Montana, west of Great Falls. My mother was thirty-one at the time. I was sixteen. Glen Baxter was somewhere in the middle, between us, though I cannot be exact about it.

We were living then off the proceeds of my father's life insurance policies, with my mother doing some part-time waitressing work up in Great Falls and going to the bars in the evenings, which I know is where she met Glen Baxter. Sometimes he would come back with her and stay in her room at night, or she would call up from town and explain that she was staying with him in his little place on Lewis Street by the GN yards. She gave me his number every time, but I never called it. I think she probably thought that what she was doing was terrible, but simply couldn't help herself. I thought it was all right, though. Regular life it seemed and still does. She was young, and I knew that even then.

Glen Baxter was a Communist and liked hunting, which he talked about a lot. Pheasants. Ducks. Deer. He killed all of them, he said. He had been to Vietnam as far back as then, and when he was in our house he often talked about shooting the animals over there — monkeys and beautiful parrots — using military guns just for sport. We did not know what Vietnam was then, and Glen, when he talked about that, referred to it only as "the Far East." I think now he must've been in the CIA and been disillusioned by something he saw or found out about and had been thrown out, but that kind of thing did not matter to us. He was a tall, dark-eyed man with thick black hair, and was usually in a good humor. He had gone halfway through college in Peoria, Illinois, he said, where he grew up. But when he was around our life he worked wheat farms as a ditcher, and stayed out of work winters and in the bars drinking with women like my mother, who had work and some money. It is not an uncommon life to lead in Montana.

What I want to explain happened in November. We had not been seeing Glen Baxter for some time. Two months had gone by. My mother knew other men, but she came home most days from work and stayed inside watching television in her bedroom and drinking beers. I asked about Glen once, and she said only that she didn't know where he was, and I assumed they had had a fight and that he was gone off on a flyer back to Illinois or Massachusetts, where he said he had relatives. I'll admit that I liked him. He had something on his mind always. He was a labor man as well as a Communist, and liked to say that the country was poisoned by the rich, and strong men would need to bring it to life again, and I liked that because my father had been a labor man, which was why we had a house to live in and money coming through. It was also true that I'd had a few boxing bouts by then — just with town boys and one with an Indian from Choteau — and there were some girlfriends I knew from that. I did not like my mother being around the house so much at night, and I wished Glen Baxter would come back, or that another man would come along and entertain her somewhere else.

At two o'clock on a Saturday, Glen drove up into our yard in a car. He had had a big brown Harley-Davidson that he rode most of the year, in his black-and-red irrigators and a baseball cap turned backwards. But this time he had a car, a blue Nash Ambassador. My mother and I went out on the porch when he stopped inside the olive trees my father had planted as a shelter belt, and my mother had a look on her face of not much pleasure. It was starting to be cold in earnest by then. Snow was down already onto the Fairfield Bench, though on this day a chinook was blowing, and it could as easily have been spring, though the sky above the Divide was turning over in silver and blue clouds of winter.

"We haven't seen you in a long time, I guess," my mother said coldly.

"My little retarded sister died," Glen said, standing at the door of his old car. He was wearing his orange VFW jacket and canvas shoes we called wino shoes, something I had never seen him wear before. He seemed to be in a good humor. "We buried her in Florida near the home."

"That's a good place," my mother said in a voice that meant she was a wronged party in something.

"I want to take this boy hunting today, Aileen," Glen said. "There's snow geese down now. But we have to go right away or they'll be gone to Idaho by tomorrow."

"He doesn't care to go," my mother said.

"Yes I do," I said and looked at her.

My mother frowned at me. "Why do you?"

"Why does he need a reason?" Glen Baxter said and grinned.

"I want him to have one, that's why." She looked at me oddly. "I think Glen's drunk, Les."

"No, I'm not drinking," Glen said, which was hardly ever true. He looked at both of us, and my mother bit down on the side of her lower lip and stared at me in a way to make you think she thought something was being put over on her and she didn't like you for it. She was pretty, though when she was mad her features were sharpened and less pretty by a long way. "All right then, I don't care," she said to no one in particular. "Hunt, kill, maim. Your father did that too." She turned to go back inside.

"Why don't you come with us, Aileen?" Glen was smiling still, pleased.

"To do what?" my mother said. She stopped and pulled a package of cigarettes out of her dress pocket and put one in her mouth.

"It's worth seeing."

"See dead animals?" my mother said.

"These geese are from Sibera, Aileen," Glen said. "They're not like a lot of geese. Maybe I'll buy us dinner later. What do you say?"

"Buy what with?" my mother said. To tell the truth, I didn't know why she was so mad at him. I would've thought she'd be glad to see him. But she just suddenly seemed to hate every-thing about him.

"I've got some money," Glen said. "Let me spend it on a pretty girl tonight."

"Find one of those and you're lucky," my mother said, turning away toward the front door.

"I've already found one," Glen Baxter said. But the door slammed behind her, and he looked at me then with a look I think now was helplessness, though I could not see a way to change anything.

My mother sat in the back seat of Glen's Nash and looked out the window while we drove. My double gun was in the seat between us beside Glen's Belgian pump, which he kept loaded with five shells in case, he said, he saw something beside the road he wanted to shoot. I had hunted rabbits before, and had ground-sluiced pheasants and other birds, but I had never been on an actual hunt before, one where you drove out to some special place and did it formally. And I was excited. I had a feeling that something important was about to happen to me and that this would be a day I would always remember.

My mother did not say anything for a long time, and neither did I. We drove up through Great Falls and out the other side toward Fort Benton, which was on the benchland where wheat was grown.

"Geese mate for life," my mother said, just out of the blue, as we were driving. "I hope you know that. They're special birds."

"I know that," Glen said in the front seat. "I have every respect for them."

"So where were you for three months?" she said. "I'm only curious."

"I was in the Big Hole for a while," Glen said, "and after that I went over to Douglas, Wyoming."

"What were you planning to do there?" my mother said.

"I wanted to find a job, but it didn't work out."

"I'm going to college," she said suddenly, and this was something I had never heard about before. I turned to look at her, but she was staring out her window and wouldn't see me.

"I knew French once," Glen said. "Rose's pink. Rouge's red." He glanced at me and smiled. "I think that's a wise idea, Aileen. When are you going to start?"

"I don't want Les to think he was raised by crazy people all his life," my mother said.

"Les ought to go himself," Glen said.

"After I go, he will."

"What do you say about that, Les?" Glen said, grinning.

"He says it's just fine," my mother said.

"It's just fine," I said.

Where Glen Baxter took us was out onto the high flat prairie that was disked for wheat and had high, high mountains out to the east, with lower heartbreak hills in between. It was, I remember, a day for blues in the sky, and down in the distance we could see the small town of Floweree and the state highway running past it toward Fort Benton and the high line. We drove out on top of the prairie on a muddy dirt road fenced on both sides, until we had gone about three miles, which is where Glen stopped.

"All right," he said, looking up in the rearview mirror at my mother. "You wouldn't think there was anything here, would you?"

"*We're* here," my mother said. "You brought us here."

"You'll be glad though," Glen said, and seemed confident to me. I had looked around myself but could not see anything. No water or trees, nothing that seemed like a good place to hunt anything. Just wasted land. "There's a big lake out there, Les," Glen said. "You can't see it now from here because it's low. But the geese are there. You'll see."

"It's like the moon out here, I recognize that," my mother said, "only it's worse." She was staring out at the flat, disked wheatland as if she could actually see something in particular and wanted to know more about it. "How'd you find this place?"

"I came once on the wheat push," Glen said.

"And I'm sure the owner told you just to come back and hunt any time you like and bring anybody you wanted. Come one, come all. Is that it?"

"People shouldn't own land anyway," Glen said. "Anybody should be able to use it."

"Les, Glen's going to poach here," my mother said. "I just want you to know that, because that's a crime and the law will get you for it. If you're a man now, you're going to have to face the consequences."

"That's not true," Glen Baxter said, and looked gloomily out over the steering wheel down the muddy road toward the mountains. Though for myself I believed it was true, and didn't care. I didn't care about anything at that moment except seeing geese fly over me and shooting them down.

"Well, I'm certainly not going out there," my mother said. "I like towns better, and I already have enough trouble."

"That's okay," Glen said. "When the geese lift up you'll get to see them. That's all I wanted. Les and me'll go shoot them, won't we, Les?"

"Yes," I said, and I put my hand on my shotgun, which had been my father's and was heavy as rocks.

"Then we should go on," Glen said, "or we'll waste our light."

We got out of the car with our guns. Glen took off his canvas shoes and put on his pair of black irrigators out of the trunk. Then we crossed the barbed-wire fence and walked out into the high, tilled field toward nothing. I looked back at my mother when we were still not so far away, but I could only see the small, dark top of her head, low in the back seat of the Nash, staring out and thinking what I could not then begin to say.

On the walk toward the lake, Glen began talking to me. I had never been alone with him and knew little about him except what my mother said — that he drank too much, or other times that he was the nicest man she had ever known in the world and that someday a woman would marry him, though she didn't think it would be her. Glen told me as we walked that he wished he had finished college, but that it was too late now, that his mind was too old. He said he had liked "the Far East" very much, and that people there knew how to treat each other, and that he would go back someday but couldn't go now. He said also that he would like to live in Russia for a while and mentioned the names of people who had gone there, names I didn't know. He said it would be hard at first, because it was so different, but that pretty soon anyone would learn to like it and wouldn't want to live anywhere else, and that Russians treated Americans who came to live there like kings. There were Communists everywhere now, he said. You didn't know them, but they were there. Montana had a large number, and he was in touch with all of them. He said that Communists were always in danger and that he had to protect himself all the time. And when he said that he pulled back his VFW jacket and showed me the butt of a pistol he had stuck under his shirt against his bare skin. "There are people who want to kill me right now," he said, "and I would kill a man myself if I thought I had to." And we kept walking. Though in a while he said, "I don't think I know much about you, Les. But I'd like to. What do you like to do?"

"I like to box," I said. "My father did it. It's a good thing to know."

"I suppose you have to protect yourself too," Glen said.

"I know how to," I said.

"Do you like to watch TV?" Glen said, and smiled.

"Not much."

"I love to," Glen said. "I could watch it instead of eating if I had one."

I looked out straight ahead over the green tops of sage that grew at the edge of the disked field, hoping to see the lake Glen said was there. There was an airishness and a sweet smell that I thought might be the place we were going, but I couldn't see it. "How will we hunt these geese?" I said.

"It won't be hard," Glen said. "Most hunting isn't even hunting. It's only shooting. And that's what this will be. In Illinois you would dig holes in the ground to hide in and set out your decoys. Then the geese come to you, over and over again. But we don't have time for that here." He glanced at me. "You have to be sure the first time here."

"How do you know they're here now?" I asked. And I looked toward the Highwood Mountains twenty miles away, half in snow and half dark blue at the bottom. I could see the little town of Floweree then, looking shabby and dimly lighted in the distance. A red bar sign shone. A car moved slowly away from the scattered buildings.

"They always come November first," Glen said.

"Are we going to poach them?"

"Does it make any difference to you?" Glen asked.

"No, it doesn't."

"Well then we aren't," he said.

We walked then for a while without talking. I looked back once to see the Nash far and small in the flat distance. I couldn't see my mother, and I thought that she must've turned on the radio and gone to sleep, which she always did, letting it play all night in her bedroom. Behind the car the sun was nearing the rounded mountains southwest of us, and I knew that when the sun was gone it would be cold. I wished my mother had decided to come along with us, and I thought for a moment of how little I really knew her at all.

Glen walked with me another quarter mile, crossed another barbed-wire fence where sage was growing, then went a hundred yards through wheatgrass and spurge until the ground went up and formed a kind of long hillock bunker built by a farmer against the wind. And I realized the lake was just beyond us. I could hear the sound of a car horn blowing and a dog barking all the way down in the town, then the wind seemed to move and all I could hear then and after then were geese. So many geese, from the sound of them, though I still could not see even one. I stood and listened to the high-pitched shouting sound, a sound I had never heard so close, a sound with size to it — though it was not loud. A sound that meant great numbers and that made your chest rise and your shoulders tighten with expectancy. It was a sound to make you feel separate from it and everything else, as if you were of no importance in the grand scheme of things.

"Do you hear them singing?" Glen asked. He held his hand up to make me stand still. And we both listened. "How many do you think, Les, just hearing?"

"A hundred," I said. "More than a hundred."

"Five thousand," Glen said. "More than you can believe when you see them. Go see."

I put down my gun and on my hands and knees crawled up the earthwork through the wheatgrass and thistle until I could see down to the lake and see the geese. And they were there, like a white bandage laid on the water, wide and long and continuous, a white expanse of snow geese, seventy yards from me, on the bank, but stretching onto the lake, which was large itself

— a half mile across, with thick tules on the far side and wild plums farther and the blue mountain behind them.

"Do you see the big raft?" Glen said from below me, in a whisper.

"I see it," I said, still looking. It was such a thing to see, a view I had never seen and have not since.

"Are any on the land?" he said.

"Some are in the wheatgrass," I said, "but most are swimming."

"Good," Glen said. "They'll have to fly. But we can't wait for that now."

And I crawled backwards down the heel of land to where Glen was, and my gun. We were losing our light, and the air was purplish and cooling. I looked toward the car but couldn't see it, and I was no longer sure where it was below the lighted sky.

"Where do they fly to?" I said in a whisper, since I did not want anything to be ruined because of what I did or said. It was important to Glen to shoot the geese, and it was important to me.

"To the wheat," he said. "Or else they leave for good. I wish your mother had come, Les. Now she'll be sorry."

I could hear the geese quarreling and shouting on the lake surface. And I wondered if they knew we were here now. "She might be," I said with my heart pounding, but I didn't think she would be much.

It was a simple plan he had. I would stay behind the bunker, and he would crawl, on his belly with his gun through the wheatgrass as near to the geese as he could. Then he would simply stand up and shoot all the ones he could close up, both in the air and on the ground. And when all the others flew up, with luck some would turn toward me as they came into the wind, and then I could shoot them and turn them back to him, and he would shoot them again. He could kill ten, he said, if he was lucky, and I might kill four. It didn't seem hard.

"Don't show them your face," Glen said. "Wait till you think you can touch them, then stand up and shoot. To hesitate is lost in this."

"All right," I said. "I'll try it."

"Shoot one in the head, and then shoot another one," Glen said. "It won't be hard." He patted me on the arm and smiled. Then he took off his VFW jacket and put it on the ground, climbed up the side of the bunker, cradling his shotgun in his arms, and slid on his belly into the dry stalks of yellow grass out of my sight.

Then for the first time in that entire day I was alone. And I didn't mind it. I sat squat down in the grass, loaded my double gun, and took my other two shells out of my pocket to hold. I pushed the safety off and on to see that it was right. The wind rose a little then, scuffed the grass and made me shiver. It was not the warm chinook now, but a wind out of the north, the one geese flew away from if they could.

Then I thought about my mother in the car alone, and how much longer I would stay with her, and what it might mean to her for me to leave. And I wondered when Glen Baxter would die and if someone would kill him, or whether my mother would marry him and how I would feel about it. And though I didn't know why, it occurred to me then that Glen Baxter and I would not be friends when all was said and done, since I didn't care if he ever married my mother or didn't.

Then I thought about boxing and what my father had taught me about it. To tighten your fists hard. To strike out straight from the shoulder and never punch backing up. How to cut a punch by snapping your fist inwards, how to carry your chin low, and to step toward a man when he is falling so you can hit him again. And most important, to keep your eyes open when you are hitting in the face and causing damage, because you need to see what you're doing to encourage yourself, and because it is when you close your eyes that you stop hitting and get hurt badly. "Fly all over your man, Les," my father said. "When you see your chance, fly on him and hit him till he falls." That, I thought, would always be my attitude in things.

And then I heard the geese again, their voices in unison, louder and shouting, as if the wind had changed and put all new sounds in the cold air. And then a *boom*. And I knew Glen was in among them and had stood up to shoot. The noise of geese rose and grew worse, and my fingers burned where I held my gun too tight to the metal, and I put it down and opened my fist to make the burning stop so I could feel the trigger when the moment came. *Boom,* Glen shot again, and I heard him shuck a shell, and all the sounds out beyond the bunker seemed to be rising — the geese, the shots, the air itself going up. *Boom,* Glen shot another time, and I knew he was taking his careful time to make his shots good. And I held my gun and started to crawl up the bunker so as not to be surprised when the geese came over me and I could shoot.

From the top I saw Glen Baxter alone in the wheatgrass field, shooting at a white goose with black tips of wings that was on the ground not far from him, but trying to run and pull into the air. He shot it once more, and it fell over dead with its wings flapping.

Glen looked back at me and his face was distorted and strange. The air around him was full of white rising geese and he seemed to want them all. "Behind you, Les," he yelled at me and pointed. "They're all behind you now." I looked behind me, and there were geese in the air as far as I could see, more than I knew how many, moving so slowly, their wings wide out and working calmly and filling the air with noise, though their voices were not as loud or as shrill as I had thought they would be. And they were very close! Forty feet, some of them. The air around me vibrated and I could feel the wind from their wings and it seemed to me I could kill as many as the times I could shoot — a hundred or a thousand — and I raised my gun, put the muzzle on the head of a white goose and fired. It shuddered in the air, its wide feet sank below its belly, its wings cradled out to hold back air, and it fell straight down and landed with an awful sound, a noise a human would make, a thick, soft, *hump* noise. I looked up again and shot another goose, could hear the pellets hit its chest, but it didn't fall or even break its pattern for flying. *Boom,* Glen shot again. And then again. "Hey," I heard him shout. "Hey, hey." And there were geese flying over me, flying in line after line. I broke my gun and reloaded, and thought to myself as I did: I need confidence here, I need to be sure with this. I pointed at another goose and shot it in the head, and it fell the way the first one had, wings out, its belly down, and with the same thick noise of hitting. Then I sat down in the grass on the bunker and let geese fly over me.

By now the whole raft was in the air, all of it moving in a slow swirl above me and the lake and everywhere, finding the wind and heading out south in long wavering lines that caught the last sun and turned to silver as they gained a distance. It was a thing to see, I will tell you now. Five thousand white geese all in the air around you, making a noise like you have never heard before. And I thought to myself then: This is something I will never see again. I will never forget this. And I was right.

Glen Baxter shot twice more. One shot missed, but with the other he hit a goose flying away from him and knocked it half-falling and -flying into the empty lake not far from shore, where it began to swim as though it was fine and make its noise.

Glen stood in the stubbly grass, looking out at the goose, his gun lowered. "I didn't need to shoot that, did I, Les?"

"I don't know," I said, sitting on the little knoll of land, looking at the goose swimming in the water.

"I don't know why I shoot 'em. They're so beautiful." He looked at me.

"I don't know either," I said.

"Maybe there's nothing else to do with them." Glen stared at the goose again and shook his head. "Maybe this is exactly what they're put on earth for."

I did not know what to say because I did not know what he could mean by that, though what I felt was embarrassment at the great number of geese there were, and a dulled feeling like a hunger because the shooting had stopped and it was over for me now.

Glen began to pick up his geese, and I walked down to my two that had fallen close together and were dead. One had hit with such an impact that its stomach had split and some of its inward parts were knocked out. Though the other looked un-hurt, its soft white belly turned up like a pillow, its head and jagged bill teeth and its tiny black eyes looking as if it were alive.

"What's happened to the hunters out here?" I heard a voice speak. It was my mother, standing in her pink dress on the knoll above us, hugging her arms. She was smiling though she was cold. And I realized that I had lost all thought of her in the shooting. "Who did all this shooting? Is this your work, Les?"

"No," I said.

"Les is a hunter, though, Aileen," Glen said. "He takes his time." He was holding two white geese by their necks, one in each hand, and he was smiling. He and my mother seemed pleased.

"I see you didn't miss too many," my mother said and smiled. I could tell she admired Glen for his geese, and that she had done some thinking in the car alone. "It *was* wonderful, Glen," she said. "I've never seen anything like that. They were like snow."

"It's worth seeing once, isn't it?" Glen said. "I should've killed more, but I got excited."

My mother looked at me then. "Where's yours, Les?"

"Here," I said and pointed to my two geese on the ground beside me.

My mother nodded in a nice way, and I think she liked everything then and wanted the day to turn out right and for all of us to be happy. "Six, then. You've got six in all."

"One's still out there," I said and motioned where the one goose was swimming in circles on the water.

"Okay," my mother said and put her hand over her eyes to look. "Where is it?"

Glen Baxter looked at me then with a strange smile, a smile that said he wished I had never mentioned anything about the other goose. And I wished I hadn't either. I looked up in the sky and could see the lines of geese by the thousands shining silver in the light, and I wished we could just leave and go home.

"That one's my mistake there," Glen Baxter said and grinned. "I shouldn't have shot that one, Aileen. I got too excited."

My mother looked out on the lake for a minute, then looked at Glen and back again. "Poor goose." She shook her head. "How will you get it, Glen?"

"I can't get that one now," Glen said.

My mother looked at him. "What do you mean?" she said.

"I'm going to leave that one," Glen said.

"Well, no. You can't leave one," my mother said. "You shot it. You have to get it. Isn't that a rule?"

"No," Glen said.

And my mother looked from Glen to me. "Wade out and get it, Glen," she said, in a sweet way, and my mother looked young

then for some reason, like a young girl, in her flimsy short-
sleeved waitress dress, and her skinny, bare legs in the wheatgrass.

"No." Glen Baxter looked down at his gun and shook his head.
And I didn't know why he wouldn't go, because it would've
been easy. The lake was shallow. And you could tell that anyone
could've walked out a long way before it got deep, and Glen had
on his boots.

My mother looked at the white goose, which was not more
than thirty yards from the shore, its head up, moving in slow
circles, its wings settled and relaxed so you could see the black
tips. "Wade out and get it, Glenny, won't you please?" she said.
"They're special things."

"You don't understand the world, Aileen," Glen said. "This
can happen. It doesn't matter."

"But that's so cruel, Glen," she said, and a sweet smile came
on her lips.

"Raise up your own arms, Leeny," Glen said. "I can't see any
angel's wings, can you Les?" He looked at me, but I looked away.

"Then you go on and get it, Les," my mother said. "You
weren't raised by crazy people." I started to go, but Glen Baxter
suddenly grabbed me by my shoulder and pulled me back
hard, so hard his fingers made bruises in my skin that I saw
later.

"Nobody's going," he said. "This is over with now."

And my mother gave Glen a cold look then. "You don't have
a heart, Glen," she said. "There's nothing to love in you. You're
just a son of a bitch, that's all."

And Glen Baxter nodded at my mother as if he understood
something that he had not understood before, but something
that he was willing to know. "Fine," he said, "that's fine." And
he took his big pistol out from against his belly, the big blue
revolver I had only seen part of before and that he said protected him, and he pointed it out at the goose on the water, his
arm straight away from him, and shot and missed. And then he
shot and missed again. The goose made its noise once. And then
he hit it dead, because there was no splash. And then he shot it
three times more until the gun was empty and the goose's head
was down and it was floating toward the middle of the lake

where it was empty and dark blue. "Now who has a heart?" Glen said. But my mother was not there when he turned around. She had already started back to the car and was almost lost from sight in the darkness. And Glen smiled at me then and his face had a wild look on it. "Okay, Les?" he said.

"Okay," I said.

"There're limits to everything, right?"

"I guess so," I said.

"Your mother's a beautiful woman, but she's not the only beautiful woman in Montana." I did not say anything. And Glen Baxter suddenly said, "Here," and he held the pistol out at me. "Don't you want this? Don't you want to shoot me? Nobody thinks they'll die. But I'm ready for it right now." And I did not know what to do then. Though it is true that what I wanted to do was to hit him, hit him as hard in the face as I could, and see him on the ground, bleeding and crying and pleading for me to stop. Only at that moment he looked scared to me, and I had never seen a grown man scared before — though I have seen one since — and I felt sorry for him, as though he were already a dead man. And I did not end up hitting him at all.

A light can go out in the heart. All of this went on years ago, but I still can feel now how sad and remote the world was to me. Glen Baxter, I think now, was not a bad man, only a man scared of something he'd never seen before — something soft in himself — his life going a way he didn't like. A woman with a son. Who could blame him there? I don't know what makes people do what they do or call themselves what they call themselves, only that you have to live someone's life to be the expert.

My mother had tried to see the good side of things, tried to be hopeful in the situation she was handed, tried to look out for us both, and it hadn't worked. It was a strange time in her life then and after that, a time when she had to adjust to being an adult just when she was on the thin edge of things. Too much awareness too early in life was her problem, I think.

And what I felt was only that I had somehow been pushed out into the world, into the real life then, the one I hadn't lived yet. In a year I was gone to hard-rock mining and no-paycheck jobs and not to college. And I have thought more than once about my mother's saying that I had not been raised by crazy people, and I don't know what that could mean or what difference it could make, unless it means that love is a reliable commodity, and even that is not always true, as I have found out.

Late on the night that all this took place I was in bed when I heard my mother say, "Come outside, Les. Come and hear this." And I went out onto the front porch barefoot and in my underwear, where it was warm like spring, and there was a spring mist in the air. I could see the lights of the Fairfield Coach in the distance on its way up to Great Falls.

And I could hear geese, white birds in the sky, flying. They made their high-pitched sound like angry yells, and though I couldn't see them high up, it seemed to me they were everywhere. And my mother looked up and said, "Hear them?" I could smell her hair wet from the shower. "They leave with the moon," she said. "It's still half wild out here."

And I said, "I hear them," and I felt a chill come over my bare chest, and the hair stood up on my arms the way it does before a storm. And for a while we listened.

"When I first married your father, you know, we lived on a street called Bluebird Canyon, in California. And I thought that was the prettiest street and the prettiest name. I suppose no one brings you up like your first love. You don't mind if I say that, do you?" She looked at me hopefully.

"No," I said.

"We have to keep civilization alive somehow." And she pulled her little housecoat together because there was a cold vein in the air, a part of the cold that would be on us the next day. "I don't feel part of things tonight, I guess."

"It's all right," I said.

"Do you know where I'd like to go?" she said.

"No," I said. And I suppose I knew she was angry then, angry with life, but did not want to show me that.

"To the Straits of Juan de Fuca. Wouldn't that be something? Would you like that?"

"I'd like it," I said. And my mother looked off for a minute, as if she could see the Straits of Juan de Fuca out against the line of mountains, see the lights of things alive and a whole new world.

"I know you liked him," she said after a moment. "You and I both suffer fools too well."

"I didn't like him too much," I said. "I didn't really care."

"He'll fall on his face, I'm sure of that," she said. And I didn't say anything because I didn't care about Glen Baxter anymore, and was happy not to talk about him. "Would you tell me something if I asked you? Would you tell me the truth?"

"Yes," I said.

And my mother did not look at me. "Just tell the truth," she said.

"All right," I said.

"Do you think I'm still very feminine? I'm thirty-two years old now. You don't know what that means. But do you think I am?"

And I stood at the edge of the porch, with the olive trees before me, looking straight up into the mist where I could not see geese but could still hear them flying, could almost feel the air move below their white wings. And I felt the way you feel when you are on a trestle all alone and the train is coming, and you know you have to decide. And I said, "Yes, I do." Because that was the truth. And I tried to think of something else then and did not hear what my mother said after that.

And how old was I then? Sixteen. Sixteen is young, but it can also be a grown man. I am forty-one years old now, and I think about that time without regret, though my mother and I never talked in that way again, and I have not heard her voice now in a long, long time.

TESS GALLAGHER

Bad Company

FROM PLOUGHSHARES

Mrs. Herbert drove into the cemetery, parked near the mausoleum, and got out with her flowers. The next day was Memorial Day, and the cemetery would be thronged with people. Entire families would arrive to bring flowers to the graves of their loved ones. Tiny American flags would decorate the graves of the veterans. But today the cemetery was still and deserted.

When she reached her husband's grave she saw that someone had been there before her. The little metal vase affixed to the headstone was crammed with daffodils and dandelions. Whoever had put them there hadn't known the difference between a flower and a weed. She put her flowers down on the flat gravestone and stared at the unsightly wad of flowers. Only a man could have thrown together such a bouquet, she thought.

She raised her hand to her brow and looked around. A short distance away she saw a girl stretched out next to a grave. She hadn't seen her at first because the girl had not been standing. The girl lay propped on one elbow so she could look down at the gravestone next to her. When Mrs. Herbert walked toward her, the girl did not lift her head or move. Then she saw the girl pluck a blade of grass and touch it to her lips before letting it fall. Mrs. Herbert's shadow fell across the girl, and the girl looked up.

"Did you happen to see anyone at that grave over yonder?" Mrs. Herbert asked.

The girl raised herself to a sitting position. She looked at the woman, but didn't say anything.

She's crazy, Mrs. Herbert thought, or else she can't talk. She regretted having spoken to the girl at all. Then the girl stood up and touched her hands together.

"There was a man. About an hour ago," the girl said. "He could of been to that grave."

"It's my husband," Mrs. Herbert said. "His grave. But I don't know who could have left those flowers." She noticed that the grave next to the girl had no flowers. She wondered at this, that anyone would come to a grave and then leave nothing behind. At this time of day the shadows of the evergreens at the near end of the graveyard crept gradually across the grass. It sent a chill through her shoulders. She drew her sweater together at the neck and folded her arms.

"He didn't stay long," the girl volunteered. And then she smiled.

Mrs. Herbert thought it was a nice thing after all to speak to this stranger and to be answered courteously in this sorrowful place.

"He was over at the mausoleum too," the girl said.

Mrs. Herbert thought hard who it might be. She only knew one person buried in the mausoleum. He had been dead ten years now and only one member of his family still survived. "It must have been Lloyd Medly," she said. "His brother, Homer, is over there in the mausoleum. His ashes, anyway. They grew up with my husband and me, those boys." She had spoken to Lloyd just last week on the telephone. He was in the habit of calling up every few weeks to see how she was. "Homer's on my mind a lot," he'd said to her when they last talked.

"I don't know anybody in the mausoleum," the girl said.

Mrs. Herbert looked down and saw a little white cross engraved over the name on the stone. There were some military designations she didn't understand and, below the name, the dates 1914–1967. "Nineteen-fourteen! That's the year I was born," she said, as if surprised that anyone born in that year had already passed on. For a moment it seemed as if she and the one lying there in the ground had briefly touched lives.

"I can barely remember him," the girl said. "But when I stay here awhile, things come back to me." She was a pretty girl with high Indian cheekbones. Mrs. Herbert noticed the way her hips went straight down from her waist. She had slow, black eyes, and appeared to be in her late twenties.

"I can't remember what Homer looked like," Mrs. Herbert said. "But he could yodel like nobody's business. Yodeling had just come in." She thought of Lloyd and how he and Arby, another brother, had been lucky to get out of California alive after they'd gone there to bring Homer's body back. Homer had been found dead in a fleabag hotel with Lloyd's phone number in his shirt pocket. "They'd as soon knock you in the head in them places as to look at you," Lloyd said afterwards.

"He was a street wino," she said to the girl. "But he was a beautiful yodeler. And he could play the guitar too."

"I think my dad used to whistle," the girl said. "I think I remember him whistling." She gazed toward the grove of trees, then across the street to the elementary school building. No one was coming in or going out of the building. It occurred to Mrs. Herbert that she had been to the cemetery hundreds of times and had never once seen any children coming or going from the school. But she knew they did, as surely as she knew that the people buried under the ground had once walked the earth, eaten meals, and answered to their names. She knew this as surely as she knew Homer Medly had been a beautiful yodeler.

"If I died tomorrow, I wonder what my little girls would remember," the girl said suddenly. Mrs. Herbert didn't know what to say to this so she didn't say anything. After a moment the girl said, "I'd like to start bringing my girls with me out here, but I hate to see kids run over the graves."

"I know what you mean," Mrs. Herbert said. But then she thought of her own father. Something he had said when he'd refused to be buried in the big county cemetery back home in Arkansas. "I want to be close enough to home that my grandkids can trample on my grave if they want to." But, as it turned out, everyone had moved away, and it hadn't mattered where he was buried.

"I always try to walk at the foot of the graves," the girl said. "But sometimes I forget." She put her hands into the hip pockets of her jeans and looked toward the mausoleum. "Those ones that are ashes, they don't have to worry," she said. She took her hands out of her pockets and sat down again on the grass next to the grave. "Nobody walks over them," she said. "I guess they just sit forever in those little cups."

Mrs. Herbert considered the idea of Homer's remains being contained in a little cup. She remembered that Lloyd had said he and his brother had wanted to bring Homer's body back, but there'd been too much red tape. And then there was the expense. So they'd had him cremated and, between them, they'd taken turns on the train holding the box with his ashes in it until they got home. Remembering this made her want to say a few words about Homer. She'd met Homer in her girlhood at nearly the same time she'd met her husband. For a moment, it came to her that Homer could have been her husband. But just as quickly she dismissed the thought. What had happened to Homer had made a deep, unsettling impression on her. She and Lloyd had talked about it once when they'd spoken in the supermarket. Lloyd had shaken his head and said, "Homer could of been something. He just fell in with the wrong company." And then he hadn't said anything else.

The girl brushed at something on the headstone. "My father was killed in an accident," she said. "We'd all been in swimming and then we kids went to the cabin to nap. My mother woke us up, crying. 'Your daddy's drowned,' she said. This drunk tried to swim the river and when my father tried to save him, the man pulled him down. 'Your daddy's drowned,' she kept saying. But you don't understand things when you're a kid," the girl said. "And you don't understand things later, either."

Mrs. Herbert was struck by this. She touched her teeth against her bottom lip, then ran her tongue over the lip. She didn't know what to say, so she said, "There's Homer that lived through the Second World War and then died in California a pure alcoholic." She shook her head. She didn't understand any of it.

The girl stretched out on the ground once more and made herself comfortable. She looked up and nodded once. Mrs. Herbert felt the girl slipping into a reverie, into a place she couldn't follow, and she wanted to say something to hold her back. But all she could think of was Homer Medly. She couldn't feature why she couldn't get Homer off her mind. She wanted to tell the girl everything that was important to know about Homer

Medly. How he had fallen into bad company in the person of Lester Yates, a boy who had molested a young girl and been sent to the penitentiary. How Beulah Looney had gone to the horse races in Santa Rosa, California, in 1935, and brought back word that Homer was married, and to a fine-looking woman! But the woman didn't live very long with Homer. He got drunk and hammered out the headlights of their car, then threatened to bite off her nose.

But she didn't tell the girl any of this. She couldn't. Besides, the girl looked to be half asleep. Mrs. Herbert looked down at the girl and it seemed the most natural thing in the world for the girl to be lying there alongside her father's grave. Then the girl rose on one elbow.

"I came out here the day of my divorce," the girl said. "And then I kept coming out here. One time I lay down and fell asleep," she said. "The caretaker came over and asked me was I all right. Sure, I said. I'm all right." The girl laughed softly and tossed her black hair over her shoulder. "Fact is, I don't know if I was all right. I been coming here trying to figure things out. If my dad was alive I'd ask him what was going to become of me and my girls. There's another man ready to step in and take up where my husband left off. But even if a man runs out on you it's no comfort just to pick up with the next one that comes around. I got to do better," the girl said. "I got to think of my girls, but I got to think of me too."

Mrs. Herbert felt she'd listened in on something important, and she wished she knew what to say to the girl for comfort. She and her husband hadn't been able to have children and, like so much of her life, she'd reconciled herself to it and never looked back. But now she could imagine having a daughter to talk with and to advise. Someone she could help in a difficult time. She felt she'd missed something precious and that she had nothing to offer the girl except to stand there and listen. Since her husband's death nearly a year ago it seemed that she seldom did more than exchange a few words with people. And here she was telling a stranger about Homer and listening to the girl tell her things back. Her memory of Homer seemed to insist on being told, and though she didn't understand why this should be, she didn't want this meeting to end until she'd said what she had to say.

The shadows from the stand of trees had darkened the portion of the cemetery that lay in front of the school building. The girl tilted her head toward the place her father was lying, and Mrs. Herbert thought she might be praying — or about to pray.

"Well, I've got peonies to put out," Mrs. Herbert said, and she moved back a few steps. But the girl did not acknowledge her leaving. Mrs. Herbert waited a minute, then turned and headed back across the graves. The ground felt softer than it had been when she'd approached the girl, and she couldn't help thinking that she had stepped on someone each time she put her foot down.

She felt relieved when she reached her husband's grave. She stood on the grave as if there at least she had a right to do as she pleased. The grave was like a green island in the midst of other green islands. Then she heard a car start up. She turned to look for the girl, but the girl was no longer there. The girl was gone. Just then Mrs. Herbert saw a little red car head out of the cemetery.

She took hold of her flowers and began to fit them into a vase next to the flowers she guessed must be from Lloyd. Once, a few weeks earlier, Lloyd had stopped at her house on the way to the cemetery and she'd given him some flowers to take to Homer and some for her husband. "They were roarers, those two," Lloyd had said as she'd made up the two bouquets. She thought of her husband again. He'd been a drinker like Homer and, except for having married her, he might have fallen in with bad company and ended the way Homer had.

She took her watering can and walked toward the spigot that stood near the mausoleum. She bent down and ran water into the can as she rested her eyes on the mausoleum. Bad company, she thought. And it occurred to her that her husband had been *her* bad company for all those years. And when he hadn't been bad company, he'd been no company at all. She listened to water run into the metal can and wondered what had saved her from being pulled down by the likes of such a man, even as Lester Yates had pulled Homer Medly down.

She let herself recall the time her husband had flown into a rage after a drinking bout and accused her of sleeping around, even though every night of their married life she'd slept nowhere but in the same bed with him. He'd taken her set of china cups out onto the sidewalk and smashed them with the whole neighborhood looking on. From then on they'd passed their evenings in silence. She would knit and he would look after the fire and smoke cigarettes. God knows it wasn't the way she'd wanted things. She'd thought she'd done the best she could. But the memory of those long, silent evenings struck at her heart now, and she wished she could go back to that time and speak to her husband. She knew there were old couples who lived differently, couples who took walks together or played checkers or cards in the evenings. And then it came to her, the thought that she had been bad company to him, had even denied him her company, going and coming from the house with barely a nod in his direction, putting his meals on the table out of duty alone, keeping house like a jailer. The idea startled and pained her, especially when she remembered how his illness had come on him until, in the last months, he was docile and then finally helpless near the end. What had she given him? What had she done for him? She could answer only that she had been there — like an implement, a shovel or a hoe. A lifetime of robbery! she thought. Then she understood that it was herself she had robbed as much as her husband. And there was no way now to get back their life together.

The water was running over the sides of the can, and she turned off the spigot. She picked up the watering can and stood next to the mausoleum and stared at it as if someone had suddenly thrown an obstacle in her pathway. She couldn't understand why anyone would want to be put into such a place when they died. The front was faced with rough stones and one wall was mostly glass so that visitors could peer inside. She had tried the door to this place once, but it was locked. She supposed the relatives had keys, or else they were let in by the caretaker. Homer was situated along the wall on the outside of the mausoleum. Thinking of Homer made her glad her husband hadn't ended up on the wall of the mausoleum as a pile of ashes. There was that to be thankful for.

When she reached his grave she poured water into the vase and then stared at the bronze nameplate where enough space had been left for her own name and dates.

She remembered the day she and her husband had quarreled

about where to buy their burial plots. Her husband had said he wasn't about to be buried anyplace that was likely to cave into the ocean. There were two cemeteries in their town — this one, just off the main highway near the elementary school, and the other, which was located at the edge of a bluff overlooking the ocean. He did not want to be near the ocean. He had said this several times. Then he had gone down and purchased two plots side by side across from the school and close to the mausoleum. She hadn't said much. Then he had shown her the papers with the location of the graves marked with little X's on a map of the cemetery. The more she thought about it though, the more she set her mind on buying her own plot in the cemetery overlooking the ocean. Then one day she arranged to go there, and she paid for a gravesite that very day.

She hadn't meant to tell her husband about her purchase, but one night they'd quarreled bitterly, and she'd flung the news at him. She had *two* gravesites, she said — one with him and one away from him — and she would do as she pleased when the time came. "Take your old bones and throw them in the ocean for all I care," he told her.

They'd left it like that. Right up until he died, her husband hadn't known where his wife was going to be buried. But what a thing to have done to him! To have denied him even that small comfort. She realized now that if anyone had told her about a woman who had done such a thing to a dying husband, she would have been shocked and ashamed for her. But this was the story of herself she was considering, and she was the one who'd sent her life's company lonely to the grave. This thought was so painful to her she felt her body go rigid — as if some force had struck her from the outside, and she had to brace herself to bear it.

She'd taken comfort in the idea of the second grave, even when she couldn't make up her mind where she would finally lie. She had prolonged her decision and she saw this clearly now for what it was: a way to deny this man with whom she had spent her life. Even when she came to the cemetery where her husband lay, she would still be thinking, as she was now, about the cemetery near the ocean — how when she went there she could gaze out at the little fishing boats on the water or listen to the gulls as they wheeled over the bluff. An oil tanker or a freighter might appear and slide serenely across the horizon. She loved how slowly the ships passed, and how she could follow them with her eyes until they were lost in the distance.

She gave the watering can a shake. There was water left in it, and she raised the can to her lips and drank deeply and thought again of the ocean. What she also loved about that view was the thought that those who walked in a cemetery, any cemetery, ought to be able to forget the dead for a moment and gaze out at something larger than themselves. Something mysterious. The ocean tantalized her even as she felt a kind of foreboding when she looked on it with her own death in mind. She could imagine children galloping over the graves, then coming to a stop at the sharp cliff edge to stare down at the waves far below. Her visits to the cemetery near the ocean gave her pleasure even after her grave there was no longer a secret. When her husband asked, "Have you been out there?" she knew what he meant. "I have," she said. And that was the extent of it. She thought she understood those who committed adultery and then returned home — unfaithful and divided. Yet she did nothing to change the situation. Then he had died, and some of the pleasure in her visits to the other grave seemed to have gone with him.

As Mrs. Herbert's life alone had settled into its own routine, weeks might go by until, with a start, she would realize she hadn't been to either cemetery. The fact of her two graves became a mystery to her. The shadows of the evergreens had reached where she was standing. She saw that the school building across the street was entirely in shadow now. She gathered up the containers she'd used to carry flowers to the grave and picked up her garden shears. On her way to the car she turned and looked at the flowers on her husband's grave. They seemed to accuse her of some neglect, some falsehood. She had decorated his grave, but there was no comfort in it for her. No comfort, she thought, and she knew she had simply been dutiful toward her husband in death as she had been in life. The thought quickened her step away from there. She reached her car and got in. For a moment she could not think where it was she was supposed to go next.

·

A month passed after her visit to the cemetery. Daisies and carnations were in bloom, but Mrs. Herbert made no visit to her husband's grave. It was early on a Sunday when she finally decided to go again. She expected the cemetery to be empty at that time of the morning, but no sooner had she arrived than a little red car drove into the narrow roadway through the cemetery and parked near the mausoleum. Then the driver got out. Mrs. Herbert was not surprised to see that it was the young woman she'd met before Decoration Day. She felt glad when the girl raised her hand in greeting as she passed on her way to her father's grave.

The girl stood by the grave with her head down, thinking. She had on a short red coat and a dress this time, as if she might be on her way to church. Mrs. Herbert approved of this — that the girl was dressed up and that she might go on to church. This caused another kind of respect to come into the visit. But what she felt most of all was that this was a wonderful coincidence. She had met the girl twice now in the cemetery and she wondered at this. Mrs. Herbert thought it must mean something, but she couldn't think what.

Mrs. Herbert took the dead flowers from the vases and emptied the acrid water. There was a stench, as if the water itself had a body that could decay and rot. She remembered a time in her girlhood when she and Homer and her husband had been driving to a dance in the next county. The car radiator had boiled over and they'd walked to a farm and asked for water. The farmer had given them some in a big glass jug. "It's fine for your car, but I wouldn't drink it," the man said. But the day was hot and after they'd filled the radiator each of them lifted the jug and took a drink. The water tasted like something had died in it. "Jesus save me from water like that!" Homer had said. "They invented whiskey to cover up water like that." Her husband agreed that the water tasted bad, but he took another drink anyway.

Mrs. Herbert straightened and glanced again toward the girl. She seemed deep in thought as she stood beside the grave. Mrs. Herbert saw that once again the girl had brought no flowers with her.

"Would you like some flowers for your grave?" Mrs. Herbert

called to her. The girl looked startled, as if the idea had never occurred to her. She waited a moment. Then she smiled and nodded. Mrs. Herbert busied herself choosing flowers from her own bunch to make a modest bouquet. Then she stepped carefully over the graves toward the girl. The girl took the flowers and pressed them to her face to smell them, as if these were the first flowers she'd held in a long time.

"I love carnations," she said. Then, before Mrs. Herbert could stop her, the girl began to dig a hole with her fingers at the top of her father's headstone.

"Wait! Just a minute," Mrs. Herbert said. "I'll find something." She walked to her car and found a jar in the trunk. She returned with this and the girl walked with her toward the mausoleum to draw water to fill the container. The water spigot was near the corner of the mausoleum where Homer's ashes lay, and she remembered having told the girl about his death.

"There's Homer," Mrs. Herbert said, and pointed to the wall of the mausoleum. There were four nameplates to each marble block and near each name a small fluted vase was attached to the stone. Most of the vases had faded plastic flowers in them, but Homer's vase was empty. The girl opened and closed her black eyes, then lifted her flowers and poured a little of the fresh water into the container fastened to Homer's stone. Then she took two carnations and fitted them into the vase. It was the right thing to do and Mrs. Herbert felt as if she'd done it herself.

As they walked back toward the graves Mrs. Herbert had the impulse to tell the girl about her gravesite near the ocean. But before she could say anything, the girl said, "I've got what I came for. I been coming here asking what I'm supposed to do with my life. Well, I'm not for sale. That's what he let me know. I'm free now and I'm going to stay free," the girl said. Mrs. Herbert heard the word "free" as if from a great distance. *Free,* she thought, but the word was meaningless to her. It came to her that in all her visits to her husband's grave she'd gotten nothing she needed. She'd just as well go and stand in her own backyard for all she got here. But she didn't let on to the girl she was feeling any of this, and when they set the container of carnations on the grave she said only, "That's better, isn't it?"

"Yes," the girl said. "Yes, it is." She seemed then to want to be alone, so Mrs. Herbert made her way back to her husband's grave. But after a few minutes she saw that instead of staying around to enjoy the flowers, the girl was leaving. She waved and Mrs. Herbert thought, *I'll never see her again.* Before she could bring herself to lift her hand to wave goodbye, the girl got into her car. Then the motor started, and she watched the car drive out of the cemetery.

A week later the widow drove to the cemetery again. She looked around as she got out of the car, half expecting to see the little red car drive up and the girl get out. But she knew this wouldn't happen. At her husband's grave she cleared away the dead flowers from her last visit.

She had brought no flowers and didn't quite know what to do with herself. She looked past the mausoleum and saw that a new field was being cleared to make room for additional graves at the far end of the cemetery. The sight brought a feeling of such desolation that she shuddered. She felt more alone than she had ever felt in her life. For the first time she realized she would continue on this way to the end. Her whole body took on the dull hopelessness of the feeling. She felt that if she had to speak she would have no voice. She was glad the girl wasn't there, that she would not have to speak to anyone in this place of regret and loneliness. Suddenly the caretaker came out of a shed in the trees, turned on a sprinkler and disappeared back into the shed. Then, once again, there was no one.

She waited a minute, and then lowered herself onto the grave. The water from the sprinkler whirled and looped over the graves, but it did not reach as far as her husband's grave. She looked around her, but saw no one. She leaned back on the grave and stretched out her legs. She put her head on the ground and closed her eyes. The sun was warm on her face and arms, and she began to feel drowsy.

As she lay there she thought she heard children running and laughing somewhere in the cemetery. But she couldn't separate this sound from the sound of the water, and she did not open her eyes to see if there really were children. The sprinkler made a *whit-whit* noise like a scythe going through a field of tall grass.

"I'm going to rest here a moment," she said out loud without opening her eyes. Then she said, "I've decided. You bought a place for me here, and that's what you wanted. And that's what I want too."

She opened her eyes then and with an awful certainty she knew that her husband had heard nothing of what she had said. And not in all of time would he hear her. She'd cut herself off from him as someone too good, someone too proud to do anything but injury to the likes of him. And this was her reward, that it would not matter to anyone on the face of the earth what she did. This, she thought, was eternity — to be left so utterly alone and to know that even her choice to be buried next to him would never reach her husband. Was she any better than the meanest wino who died in some fleabag hotel and was eventually reduced to ashes? No, she understood, no better. She had been no better than her husband all those years, and if she had saved him from a death like Homer's, it was only to die disowned at her own hearth. The enormity of this settled on her as she struggled to raise herself up.

A light mist from the sprinkler touched her face, and when she looked around her, she saw a vastness like that of the ocean. Headstones marked off the grass as far as she could see. She saw plainly a silent and fixed company set out there, a company she had not chosen.

She looked and saw the caretaker in the doorway of the shed. He drew on his cigarette as he stood watching her. She raised her hand and then brought it down to let him know she had seen him. He inclined his head and went on smoking.

AMY HEMPEL

Today Will Be a Quiet Day

FROM THE MISSOURI REVIEW

"I THINK IT's the other way around," the boy said. "I think if the quake hit now the *bridge* would collapse and the *ramps* would be left."

He looked at his sister with satisfaction.

"You are just trying to scare your sister," the father said. "You know that is not true."

"No, really," the boy insisted, "and I heard birds in the middle of the night. Isn't that a warning?"

The girl gave her brother a toxic look and ate a handful of Raisinets. The three of them were stalled in traffic on the Golden Gate Bridge.

That morning, before waking his children, the father had canceled their music lessons and decided to make a day of it. He wanted to know how they were, is all. Just — how were they. He thought his kids were as self-contained as one of those dogs you sometimes see carrying home its own leash. But you could read things wrong.

Could you ever.

The boy had a friend who jumped from a floor of Langley Porter. The friend had been there for two weeks, mostly playing Ping-Pong. All the friend said the day the boy visited and lost every game was never play Ping-Pong with a mental patient because it's all we do and we'll kill you. That night the friend had cut the red belt he wore in two and left the other half on his bed. That was this time last year when the boy was twelve years old.

You think you're safe, the father thought, but it's thinking you're invisible because you closed your eyes.

This day they were headed for Petaluma — the chicken, egg, and arm-wrestling capital of the nation — for lunch. The father had offered to take them to the men's arm-wrestling semifinals. But it was said that arm wrestling wasn't so interesting since the new safety precautions, that hardly anyone broke an arm or a wrist anymore. The best anyone could hope to see would be dislocation, so they said they would rather go to Pete's. Pete's was a gas station turned into a place to eat. The hamburgers there were named after cars, and the gas pumps in front still pumped gas.

"Can I have one?" the boy asked, meaning the Raisinets.

"No," his sister said.

"Can I have two?"

"Neither of you should be eating candy before lunch," the father said. He said it with the good sport of a father who enjoys his kids and gets a kick out of saying Dad things.

"You mean dinner," said the girl. "It will be dinner before we get to Pete's."

Only the northbound lanes were stopped. Southbound traffic flashed past at the normal speed.

"Check it out," the boy said from the back seat. "Did you see the bumper sticker on that Porsche? 'If you don't like the way I drive, stay off the sidewalk.' "

He spoke directly to his sister. "I've just solved my Christmas shopping."

"I got the highest score in my class in Driver's Ed," she said.

"I thought I would let your sister drive home today," the father said.

From the back seat came sirens, screams for help, and then a dirge.

The girl spoke to her father in a voice rich with complicity. "Don't people make you want to give up?"

"Don't the two of you know any jokes? I haven't laughed all day," the father said.

"Did I tell you the guillotine joke?" the girl said.

"He hasn't laughed all day, so you must've," her brother said.

The girl gave her brother a look you could iron clothes with. Then her gaze dropped down. "Oh-oh," she said, "Johnny's out of jail."

Her brother zipped his pants back up. He said, "Tell the joke."

"Two Frenchmen and a Belgian were about to be beheaded," the girl began. "The first Frenchman was led to the block and blindfolded. The executioner let the blade go. But it stopped a quarter inch above the Frenchman's neck. So he was allowed to go free, and ran off shouting, 'C'est un miracle! C'est un miracle!' "

"It's a miracle," the father said.

"Then the second Frenchman was led to the block, and same thing — the blade stopped just before cutting off his head. So *he* got to go free, and ran off shouting, 'C'est un miracle!'

"Finally the Belgian was led to the block. But before they could blindfold him, he looked up, pointed to the top of the guillotine, and cried, 'Voilà la difficulté!' "

She doubled over.

"Maybe *I* would be wetting *my* pants if I knew what that meant," the boy said.

"You can't explain after the punch line," the girl said, "and have it still be funny."

"There's the problem," said the father.

The waitress handed out menus to the party of three seated in the corner booth of what used to be the lube bay. She told them the specialty of the day was Moroccan chicken.

"That's what I want," the boy said. "Morerotten chicken."

But he changed his order to a Studeburger and fries after his father and sister had ordered.

"So," the father said, "who misses music lessons?"

"I'm serious about what I asked you last week," the girl said. "About switching to piano? My teacher says a real flutist only breathes with the stomach, and I can't."

"The real reason she wants to change," said the boy, "is her waist will get two inches bigger when she learns to stomach-breathe. That's what *else* her teacher said."

The boy buttered a piece of sourdough bread and flipped a chunk of cold butter onto his sister's sleeve.

"Jeezo-beezo," the girl said, "why don't they skip the knife and fork and just set his place with a slingshot!"

"Who will ever adopt you if you don't mind your manners?" the father said. "Maybe we could try a little quiet today."

"You sound like your tombstone," the girl said. "Remember what you wanted it to say?"

Her brother joined in with his mouth full: "Today will be a quiet day."

"Because it never is with us around," the boy said.

"You guys," said the father.

The waitress brought plates. The father passed sugar to the boy and salt to the girl without being asked. He watched the girl shake out salt onto the fries.

"If I had a sore throat, I would gargle with those," he said.

"Looks like she's trying to melt a driveway," the boy offered.

The father watched his children eat. They ate fast. They called it Hoovering. He finished while they sucked at straws in empty drinks.

"Funny," he said thoughtfully, "I'm not hungry anymore."

Every meal ended this way. It was his benediction, one of the Dad things they expected him to say.

"That reminds me," the girl said. "Did you feed Rocky before we left?"

"Uh-uh," her brother said. "I fed him yesterday."

"*I* fed him yesterday!" the girl said.

"Okay, we'll compromise," the boy said. "We won't feed the cat today."

"I'd say you are out of bounds on that one," the father said.

He meant you could not tease her about animals. Once, during dinner, that cat ran into the dining room shot from guns. He ran around the table at top speed, then spun out on the parquet floor into a leg of the table. He fell over onto his side and made short coughing sounds. "Isn't he smart?" the girl had crooned, kneeling beside him. "He knows he's hurt."

For years, her father had to say that the animals seen on shoulders of roads were napping.

"He never would have not fed Homer," she said to her father.

"Homer was a dog," the boy said. "If I forgot to feed him, he could just go into the hills and bite a deer."

"Or a Campfire Girl selling mints at the front door," their father reminded them.

"Homer," the girl sighed. "I hope he likes chasing sheep on that ranch in the mountains."

The boy looked at her, incredulous.

"You *believed* that? You actually *believed* that?"

In her head, a clumsy magician yanked the cloth and the dishes all crashed to the floor. She took air into her lungs until they filled, and then she filled her stomach, too.

"I thought she knew," the boy said.

The dog was five years ago.

"The girl's parents insisted," the father said. "It's the law in California."

"Then I hate California," she said. "I hate its guts."

The boy said he would wait for them in the car, and left the table.

"What would help?" the father asked.

"For Homer to be alive," she said.

"What would help?"

"Nothing."

"Help."

She pinched a trail of salt on her plate.

"A ride," she said. "I'll drive."

The girl started the car and screamed, "Goddammit."

With the power off, the boy had tuned in the Spanish station. Mariachis exploded on ignition.

"Dammit isn't God's last name," the boy said, quoting another bumper sticker.

"Don't people make you want to give up?" the father said.

"No talking," the girl said to the rearview mirror, and put the car in gear.

She drove for hours. Through groves of eucalyptus with their damp peeling bark, past acacia bushes with yellow flowers pulsing off their stems. She cut over to the coast route and the stony gray-green tones of Inverness.

"What you'd call scenic," the boy tried.

Otherwise they were quiet.

No one said anything else until the sky started to close, and then it was the boy again, asking shouldn't they be going home.

"No, no," the father said, and made a show of looking out the window, up at the sky and back at his watch. "No," he said, "keep driving — it's getting earlier."

But the sky spilled rain, and the girl headed south toward the bridge. She turned on the headlights and the dashboard lit up green. She read off the odometer on the way home: "Twenty-six thousand, three hundred eighty three and eight-tenths miles."

"Today?" the boy said.

The boy got to Rocky first. "Let's play the cat," he said, and carried the Siamese to the upright piano. He sat on the bench holding the cat in his lap and pressed its paws to the keys. Rocky played "Born Free." He tried to twist away.

"Come on, Rocky, ten more minutes and we'll break."

"Give him to me," the girl said.

She puckered up and gave the cat a five-lipper.

"Bring the Rock upstairs," the father called. "Bring sleeping bags, too."

Pretty soon three sleeping bags formed a triangle in the master bedroom. The father was the hypotenuse. The girl asked him to brush out her hair, which he did while the boy ate a tangerine, peeling it up close to his face, inhaling the mist. Then he held each segment to the light to find seeds. In his lap, cat paws fluttered like dreaming eyes.

"What are you thinking?" the father asked.

"Me?" the girl said. "Fifty-seven T-bird, white with red interior, convertible. I drive it to Texas and wear skirts with rickrack. I'm changing my name to Ruby," she said, "or else Easy."

The father considered her dream of a checkered future.

"Early ripe, early rot," he warned.

A wet wind slammed the window in its warped sash, and the boy jumped.

"I hate rain," he said. "I hate its guts."

The father got up and closed the window tighter against the storm. "It's a real frog-choker," he said.

In darkness, lying still, it was no less camp-like than if they had been under the stars, singing to a stone-ringed fire burned down to embers.

They had already said good-night some minutes earlier when the boy and girl heard their father's voice in the dark.

"Kids, I just remembered — I have some good news and some bad news. Which do you want first?"

It was his daughter who spoke. "Let's get it over with," she said. "Let's get the bad news over with."

The father smiled. They are all right, he decided. My kids are as right as this rain. He smiled at the exact spots he knew their heads were turned to his, and doubted he would ever feel — not better, but *more* than he did now.

"I lied," he said. "There is no bad news."

DAVID MICHAEL KAPLAN

Doe Season

FROM THE ATLANTIC

THEY WERE ALWAYS the same woods, she thought sleepily as they drove through the early morning darkness — deep and immense, covered with yesterday's snowfall, which had frozen overnight. They were the same woods that lay behind her house, *and they stretch all the way to here,* she thought, *for miles and miles, longer than I could walk in a day, or a week even, but they are still the same woods.* The thought made her feel good: it was like thinking of God; it was like thinking of the space between here and the moon; it was like thinking of all the foreign countries from her geography book where even now, Andy knew, people were going to bed, while they — she and her father and Charlie Spoon and Mac, Charlie's eleven-year-old son — were driving deeper into the Pennsylvania countryside, to go hunting.

They had risen long before dawn. Her mother, yawning and not trying to hide her sleepiness, cooked them eggs and French toast. Her father smoked a cigarette and flicked ashes into his saucer while Andy listened, wondering *Why doesn't he come?* and *Won't he ever come?* until at last a car pulled into the graveled drive and honked. "That will be Charlie Spoon," her father said; he always said "Charlie Spoon," even though his real name was Spreun, because Charlie was, in a sense, shaped like a spoon, with a large head and a narrow waist and chest.

Andy's mother kissed her and her father and said, "Well, have a good time" and "Be careful." Soon they were outside in the bitter dark, loading gear by the back-porch light, their breath steaming. The woods behind the house were then only a black streak against the wash of night.

Andy dozed in the car and woke to find that it was half light. Mac — also sleeping — had slid against her. She pushed him away and looked out the window. Her breath clouded the glass, and she was cold; the car's heater didn't work right. They were riding over gentle hills, the woods on both sides now — the same woods, she knew, because she had been watching the whole way, even while she slept. They had been in her dreams, and she had never lost sight of them.

Charlie Spoon was driving. "I don't understand why she's coming," he said to her father. "How old is she anyway — eight?"

"Nine," her father replied. "She's small for her age."

"So — nine. What's the difference? She'll just add to the noise and get tired besides."

"No, she won't," her father said. "She can walk me to death. And she'll bring good luck, you'll see. Animals — I don't know how she does it, but they come right up to her. We go walking in the woods, and we'll spot more raccoons and possums and such than I ever see when I'm alone."

Charlie grunted.

"Besides, she's not a bad little shot, even if she doesn't hunt yet. She shoots the .22 real good."

"Popgun," Charlie said, and snorted. "And target shooting ain't deer hunting."

"Well, she's not gonna be shooting anyway, Charlie," her father said. "Don't worry. She'll be no bother."

"I still don't know why she's coming," Charlie said.

"Because she wants to, and I want her to. Just like you and Mac. No difference."

Charlie turned onto a side road and after a mile or so slowed down. "That's it!" he cried. He stopped, backed up, and entered a narrow dirt road almost hidden by trees. Five hundred yards down, the road ran parallel to a fenced-in field. Charlie parked in a cleared area deeply rutted by frozen tractor tracks. The gate was locked. *In the spring,* Andy thought, *there will be cows here, and a dog that chases them,* but now the field was unmarked and bare.

"This is it," Charlie Spoon declared. "Me and Mac was up here just two weeks ago, scouting it out, and there's deer. Mac saw the tracks."

"That's right," Mac said.

"Well, we'll just see about that," her father said, putting on his gloves. He turned to Andy. "How you doing, honeybun?"

"Just fine," she said.

Andy shivered and stamped as they unloaded: first the rifles, which they unsheathed and checked, sliding the bolts, sighting through scopes, adjusting the slings; then the gear, their food and tents and sleeping bags and stove stored in four backpacks — three big ones for Charlie Spoon and her father and Mac, and a day pack for her.

"That's about your size," Mac said, to tease her.

She reddened and said, "Mac, I can carry a pack big as yours any day." He laughed and pressed his knee against the back of hers, so that her leg buckled. "Cut it out," she said. She wanted to make an iceball and throw it at him, but she knew that her father and Charlie were anxious to get going, and she didn't want to displease them.

Mac slid under the gate, and they handed the packs over to him. Then they slid under and began walking across the field toward the same woods that ran all the way back to her home, where even now her mother was probably rising again to wash their breakfast dishes and make herself a fresh pot of coffee. *She is there, and we are here:* the thought satisfied Andy. There was no place else she would rather be.

Mac came up beside her. "Over there's Canada," he said, nodding toward the woods.

"Huh!" she said. "Not likely."

"I don't mean *right* over there. I mean farther up north. You think I'm dumb?"

Dumb as your father, she thought.

"Look at that," Mac said, pointing to a piece of cow dung lying on a spot scraped bare of snow. "A frozen meadow muffin." He picked it up and sailed it at her. "Catch!"

"Mac!" she yelled. His laugh was as gawky as he was. She walked faster. He seemed different today somehow, bundled in his yellow-and-black-checkered coat, a rifle in hand, his silly floppy hat not quite covering his ears. They all seemed different as she watched them trudge through the snow — Mac and her father and Charlie Spoon — bigger, maybe, as if the cold landscape enlarged rather than diminished them, so that they, the only figures in that landscape, took on size and meaning just by being there. If they weren't there, everything would be quieter, and the woods would be the same as before. *But they are here,* Andy thought, looking behind her at the boot prints in the snow, *and I am too, and so it's all different.*

"We'll go down to the cut where we found those deer tracks," Charlie said as they entered the woods. "Maybe we'll get lucky and get a late one coming through."

The woods descended into a gully. The snow was softer and deeper here, so that often Andy sank to her knees. Charlie and Mac worked the top of the gully while she and her father walked along the base some thirty yards behind them. "If they miss the first shot, we'll get the second," her father said, and she nodded as if she had known this all the time. She listened to the crunch of their boots, their breathing, and the drumming of a distant woodpecker. And the crackling. In winter the woods crackled as if everything were straining, ready to snap like dried chicken bones.

We are hunting, Andy thought. The cold air burned her nostrils.

They stopped to make lunch by a rock outcropping that protected them from the wind. Her father heated the bean soup her mother had made for them, and they ate it with bread already stiff from the cold. He and Charlie took a few pulls from a flask of Jim Beam while she scoured the plates with snow and repacked them. Then they all had coffee with sugar and powdered milk, and her father poured her a cup too. "We won't tell your momma," he said, and Mac laughed. Andy held the cup the way her father did, not by the handle but around the rim. The coffee tasted smoky. She felt a little queasy, but she drank it all.

Charlie Spoon picked his teeth with a fingernail. "Now, you might've noticed one thing," he said.

"What's that?" her father asked.

"You might've noticed you don't hear no rifles. That's because there ain't no other hunters here. We've got the whole damn woods to ourselves. Now, I ask you — do I know how to find 'em?"

"We haven't seen deer yet, neither."

"Oh, we will," Charlie said, "but not for a while now." He leaned back against the rock. "Deer're sleeping, resting up for the evening feed."

"I seen a deer behind our house once, and it was afternoon," Andy said.

"Yeah, honey, but that was *before* deer season," Charlie said, grinning. "They know something now. They're smart that way."

"That's right," Mac said.

Andy looked at her father — had she said something stupid?

"Well, Charlie," he said, "if they know so much, how come so many get themselves shot?"

"Them's the ones that don't *believe* what they know," Charlie replied. The men laughed. Andy hesitated, and then laughed with them.

They moved on, as much to keep warm as to find a deer. The wind became even stronger. Blowing through the treetops, it sounded like the ocean, and once Andy thought she could smell salt air. But that was impossible; the ocean was *hundreds* of miles away, farther than Canada even. She and her parents had gone last summer to stay for a week at a motel on the New Jersey shore. That was the first time she'd seen the ocean, and it frightened her. It was huge and empty, yet always moving. Everything lay hidden. If you walked in it, you couldn't see how deep it was or what might be below; if you swam, something could pull you under and you'd never be seen again. Its musky, rank smell made her think of things dying. Her mother had floated beyond the breakers, calling to her to come in, but Andy wouldn't go farther than a few feet into the surf. Her mother swam and splashed with animal-like delight while her father, smiling shyly, held his white arms above the waist-deep water as if afraid to get them wet. Once a comber rolled over and sent them both tossing, and when her mother tried to stand up, the surf receding behind, Andy saw that her mother's swimsuit top had come off, so that her breasts swayed free, her nipples like two dark eyes. Embarrassed, Andy looked around: except for two women under a yellow umbrella farther up, the beach was empty. Her mother stood up unsteadily, regained her footing. Taking what seemed the longest time, she calmly refixed her top. Andy lay on the beach towel and closed her eyes. The sound of the surf made her head ache.

And now it was winter; the sky was already dimming, not just with the absence of light but with a mist that clung to the hunters' faces like cobwebs. They made camp early. Andy was chilled. When she stood still, she kept wiggling her toes to make sure they were there. Her father rubbed her arms and held her to him briefly, and that felt better. She unpacked the food while the others put up the tents.

"How about rounding us up some firewood, Mac?" Charlie asked.

"I'll do it," Andy said. Charlie looked at her thoughtfully and then handed her the canvas carrier.

There wasn't much wood on the ground, so it took her a while to get a good load. She was about a hundred yards from camp, near a cluster of high, lichen-covered boulders, when she saw through a crack in the rock a buck and two does walking gingerly, almost daintily, through the alder trees. She tried to hush her breathing as they passed not more than twenty yards away. There was nothing she could do. If she yelled, they'd be gone; by the time she got back to camp, they'd be gone. The buck stopped, nostrils quivering, tail up and alert. He looked directly at her. Still she didn't move, not one muscle. He was a beautiful buck, the color of late-turned maple leaves. Unafraid, he lowered his tail, and he and his does silently merged into the trees. Andy walked back to camp and dropped the firewood.

"I saw three deer," she said. "A buck and two does."

"Where?" Charlie Spoon cried, looking behind her as if they might have followed her into camp.

"In the woods yonder. They're gone now."

"Well, hell!" Charlie banged his coffee cup against his knee.

"Didn't I say she could find animals?" her father said, grinning.

"Too late to go after them," Charlie muttered. "It'll be dark in a quarter hour. Damn!"

"Damn," Mac echoed.

"They just walk right up to her," her father said.

"Well, leastwise this proves there's deer here." Charlie began snapping long branches into shorter ones. "You know, I think I'll stick with you," he told Andy, "since you're so good at finding deer and all. How'd that be?"

"Okay, I guess," Andy murmured. She hoped he was kidding; no way did she want to hunt with Charlie Spoon. Still, she was pleased he had said it.

Her father and Charlie took one tent, she and Mac the other. When they were in their sleeping bags, Mac said in the darkness, "I bet you really didn't see no deer, did you?"

She sighed. "I did, Mac. Why would I lie?"

"How big was the buck?"

"Four point. I counted."

Mac snorted.

"You just believe what you want, Mac," she said testily.

"Too bad it ain't buck season," he said. "Well, I got to go pee."

"So pee."

She heard him turn in his bag. "You ever see it?" he asked.

"It? What's 'it'?"

"It. A pecker."

"Sure," she lied.

"Whose? Your father's?"

She was uncomfortable. "No," she said.

"Well, whose then?"

"Oh I don't know! Leave me be, why don't you?"

"Didn't see a deer, didn't see a pecker," Mac said teasingly.

She didn't answer right away. Then she said, "My cousin Lewis. I saw his."

"Well, how old's he?"

"One and a half."

"Ha! A baby! A baby's is like a little worm. It ain't a real one at all."

If he says he'll show me his, she thought, *I'll kick him. I'll just get out of my bag and kick him.*

"I went hunting with my daddy and Versh and Danny Simmons last year in buck season," Mac said, "and we got ourselves one. And we hog-dressed the thing. You know what that is, don't you?"

"No," she said. She was confused. What was he talking about
now?

"That's when you cut him open and take out all his guts, so
the meat don't spoil. Makes him lighter to pack out, too."

She tried to imagine what the deer's guts might look like,
pulled from the gaping hole. "What do you do with them?" she
said. "The guts?"

"Oh, just leave 'em for the bears."

She ran her finger like a knife blade along her belly.

"When we left them on the ground," Mac said, "they smoked.
Like they were cooking."

"Huh," she said.

"They cut off the deer's pecker, too, you know."

Andy imagined Lewis's pecker and shuddered. "Mac, you're
disgusting."

He laughed. "Well, I gotta go pee." She heard him rustle out
of his bag. "Broo!" he cried, flapping his arms. "It's cold!"

He makes so much noise, she thought, *just noise and more noise.*

Her father woke them before first light. He warned them to talk
softly and said that they were going to the place where Andy
had seen the deer, to try to cut them off on their way back from
their night feeding. Andy couldn't shake off her sleep. Stuffing
her sleeping bag into its sack seemed to take an hour, and tying
her boots was the strangest thing she'd ever done. Charlie
Spoon made hot chocolate and oatmeal with raisins. Andy
closed her eyes and, between beats of her heart, listened to the
breathing of the forest. *When I open my eyes, it will be lighter,* she
decided. But when she did, it was still just as dark, except for
the swaths of their flashlights and the hissing blue flame of the
stove. *There has to be just one moment when it all changes from dark
to light,* Andy thought. She had missed it yesterday, in the car;
today she would watch more closely.

But when she remembered again, it was already first light and
they had moved to the rocks by the deer trail and had set up
shooting positions — Mac and Charlie Spoon on the up-trail
side, she and her father behind them, some six feet up on a
ledge. The day became brighter, the sun piercing the tall pines,
raking the hunters, yet providing little warmth. Andy now

smelled alder and pine and the slightly rotten odor of rock
lichen. She rubbed her hand over the stone and considered that
it must be very old, had probably been here before the giant
pines, *before anyone was in these woods at all.* A chipmunk sniffed
on a nearby branch. She aimed an imaginary rifle and pressed
the trigger. The chipmunk froze, then scurried away. Her legs
were cramping on the narrow ledge. Her father seemed to doze,
one hand in his parka, the other cupped lightly around the rifle.
She could smell his scent of old wool and leather. His cheeks
were speckled with gray-black whiskers, and he worked his jaws
slightly, as if chewing a small piece of gum.

Please let us get a deer, she prayed.

A branch snapped on the other side of the rock face. Her
father's hand stiffened on the rifle, startling her — *He hasn't
been sleeping at all,* she marveled — and then his jaw relaxed, as
did the lines around his eyes, and she heard Charlie Spoon call,
"Yo, don't shoot, it's us." He and Mac appeared from around
the rock. They stopped beneath the ledge. Charlie solemnly
crossed his arms.

"I don't believe we're gonna get any deer here," he said drily.

Andy's father lowered his rifle to Charlie and jumped down
from the ledge. Then he reached up for Andy. She dropped
into his arms and he set her gently on the ground.

Mac sidled up to her. "I knew you didn't see no deer," he
said.

"Just because they don't come when you want 'em to don't
mean she didn't see them," her father said.

Still, she felt bad. Her telling about the deer had caused them
to spend the morning there, cold and expectant, with nothing
to show for it.

They tramped through the woods for another two hours, not
caring much about noise. Mac found some deer tracks, and they
argued about how old they were. They split up for a while and
then rejoined at an old logging road that deer might use, and
followed it. The road crossed a stream, which had mostly frozen
over but in a few spots still caught leaves and twigs in an icy
swirl. They forded it by jumping from rock to rock. The road
narrowed after that, and the woods thickened.

They stopped for lunch, heating up Charlie's wife's corn
chowder. Andy's father cut squares of applesauce cake with his

hunting knife and handed them to her and Mac, who ate his almost daintily. Andy could faintly taste knife oil on the cake. She was tired. She stretched her leg; the muscle that had cramped on the rock still ached.

"Might as well relax," her father said, as if reading her thoughts. "We won't find deer till suppertime."

Charlie Spoon leaned back against his pack and folded his hands across his stomach. "Well, even if we don't get a deer," he said expansively, "it's still great to be out here, breathe some fresh air, clomp around a bit. Get away from the house and the old lady." He winked at Mac, who looked away.

"That's what the woods are all about, anyway," Charlie said. "It's where the women don't want to go." He bowed his head toward Andy. "With your exception, of course, little lady." He helped himself to another piece of applesauce cake.

"She ain't a woman," Mac said.

"Well, she damn well's gonna be," Charlie said. He grinned at her. "Or will you? You're half a boy anyway. You go by a boy's name. What's your real name? Andrea, ain't it?"

"That's right," she said. She hoped that if she didn't look at him, Charlie would stop.

"Well, which do you like? Andy or Andrea?"

"Don't matter," she mumbled. "Either."

"She's always been Andy to me," her father said.

Charlie Spoon was still grinning. "So what are you gonna be, Andrea? A boy or a girl?"

"I'm a girl," she said.

"But you want to go hunting and fishing and everything, huh?"

"She can do whatever she likes," her father said.

"Hell, you might as well have just had a boy and be done with it!" Charlie exclaimed.

"That's funny," her father said, and chuckled. "That's just what her momma tells me."

They were looking at her, and she wanted to get away from them all, even from her father, who chose to joke with them.

"I'm going to walk a bit," she said.

She heard them laughing as she walked down the logging trail. She flapped her arms; she whistled. *I don't care how much noise I make*, she thought. Two grouse flew from the underbrush,

startling her. A little farther down, the trail ended in a clearing
that enlarged into a frozen meadow; beyond it the woods began
again. A few moldering posts were all that was left of a fence
that had once enclosed the field. The low afternoon sunlight
reflected brightly off the snow, so that Andy's eyes hurt. She
squinted hard. A gust of wind blew across the field, stinging her
face. And then, as if it had been waiting for her, the doe
emerged from the trees opposite and stepped cautiously into
the field. Andy watched: it stopped and stood quietly for what
seemed a long time and then ambled across. It stopped again
about seventy yards away and began to browse in a patch of
sugar grass uncovered by the wind. Carefully, slowly, never taking her eyes from the doe, Andy walked backward, trying to
step into the boot prints she'd already made. When she was far
enough back into the woods, she turned and walked faster, her
heart racing. *Please let it stay,* she prayed.

"There's doe in the field yonder," she told them.

They got their rifles and hurried down the trail.

"No use," her father said. "We're making too much noise any
way you look at it."

"At least we got us the wind in our favor," Charlie Spoon said,
breathing heavily.

But the doe was still there, grazing.

"Good Lord," Charlie whispered. He looked at her father.
"Well, whose shot?"

"Andy spotted it," her father said in a low voice. "Let her
shoot it."

"What!" Charlie's eyes widened.

Andy couldn't believe what her father had just said. She'd
only shot tin cans and targets; she'd never even fired her father's .30-.30, and she'd never killed anything.

"I can't," she whispered.

"That's right, she can't," Charlie Spoon insisted. "She's not
old enough and she don't have a license even if she was!"

"Well, who's to tell?" her father said in a low voice. "Nobody's
going to know but us." He looked at her. "Do you want to shoot
it, punkin?"

Why doesn't it hear us? she wondered. *Why doesn't it run away?*

"I don't know," she said.

"Well, I'm sure as hell gonna shoot it," Charlie said. Her

father grasped Charlie's rifle barrel and held it. His voice was steady.

"Andy's a good shot. It's her deer. She found it, not you. You'd still be sitting on your ass back in camp." He turned to her again. "Now — do you want to shoot it, Andy? Yes or no."

He was looking at her; they were all looking at her. Suddenly she was angry at the deer, who refused to hear them, who wouldn't run away even when it could. "I'll shoot it," she said. Charlie turned away in disgust.

She lay on the ground and pressed the rifle stock against her shoulder bone. The snow was cold through her parka; she smelled oil and wax and damp earth. She pulled off one glove with her teeth. "It sights just like the .22," her father said gently. "Cartridge's already chambered." As she had done so many times before, she sighted down the scope; now the doe was in the reticle. She moved the barrel until the cross hairs lined up. Her father was breathing beside her.

"Aim where the chest and legs meet, or a little above, punkin," he was saying calmly. "That's the killing shot."

But now, seeing it in the scope, Andy was hesitant. Her finger weakened on the trigger. Still, she nodded at what her father said and sighted again, the cross hairs lining up in exactly the same spot — the doe had hardly moved, its brownish-gray body outlined starkly against the blue-backed snow. *It doesn't know,* Andy thought. *It just doesn't know.* And as she looked, deer and snow and faraway trees flattened within the circular frame to become like a picture on a calendar, not real, and she felt calm, as if she had been dreaming everything — the day, the deer, the hunt itself. And she, finger on trigger, was only a part of that dream.

"Shoot!" Charlie hissed.

Through the scope she saw the deer look up, ears high and straining.

Charlie groaned, and just as he did, and just at the moment when Andy knew — *knew* — the doe would bound away, as if she could feel its haunches tensing and gathering power, she pulled the trigger. Later she would think, *I felt the recoil, I smelled the smoke, but I don't remember pulling the trigger.* Through the scope the deer seemed to shrink into itself, and then slowly knelt, hind legs first, head raised as if to cry out. It trembled, still straining to keep its head high, as if that alone would save it; failing, it collapsed, shuddered, and lay still.

"Whoee!" Mac cried.

"One shot! One shot!" her father yelled, clapping her on the back. Charlie Spoon was shaking his head and smiling dumbly.

"I told you she was a great little shot!" her father said. "I told you!" Mac danced and clapped his hands. She was dazed, not quite understanding what had happened. And then they were crossing the field toward the fallen doe, she walking dreamlike, the men laughing and joking, released now from the tension of silence and anticipation. Suddenly Mac pointed and cried out, "Look at that!"

The doe was rising, legs unsteady. They stared at it, unable to comprehend, and in that moment the doe regained its feet and looked at them, as if it too were trying to understand. Her father whistled softly. Charlie Spoon unslung his rifle and raised it to his shoulder, but the doe was already bounding away. His hurried shot missed, and the deer disappeared into the woods.

"Damn, damn, damn," he moaned.

"I don't believe it," her father said. "That deer was dead."

"Dead, hell!" Charlie yelled. It was gutshot, that's all. Stunned and gutshot. Clean shot, my ass!"

What have I done? Andy thought.

Her father slung his rifle over his shoulder. "Well, let's go. It can't get too far."

"Hell, I've seen deer run ten miles gutshot," Charlie said. He waved his arms. "We may never find her!"

As they crossed the field, Mac came up to her and said in a low voice, "Gutshoot a deer, you'll go to hell."

"Shut up, Mac," she said, her voice cracking. It was a terrible thing she had done, she knew. She couldn't bear to think of the doe in pain and frightened. *Please let it die,* she prayed.

But though they searched all the last hour of daylight, so that they had to recross the field and go up the logging trail in a twilight made even deeper by thick, smoky clouds, they didn't find the doe. They lost its trail almost immediately in the dense stands of alderberry and larch.

"I am cold, and I am tired," Charlie Spoon declared. "And if you ask me, that deer's in another county already."

"No one's asking you, Charlie," her father said.

They had a supper of hard salami and ham, bread, and the rest of the applesauce cake. It seemed a bother to heat the coffee, so they had cold chocolate instead. Everyone turned in early.

"We'll find it in the morning, honeybun," her father said, as she went to her tent.

"I don't like to think of it suffering." She was almost in tears.

"It's dead already, punkin. Don't even think about it." He kissed her, his breath sour and his beard rough against her cheek.

Andy was sure she wouldn't get to sleep; the image of the doe falling, falling, then rising again, repeated itself whenever she closed her eyes. Then she heard an owl hoot and realized that it had awakened her, so she must have been asleep after all. She hoped the owl would hush, but instead it hooted louder. She wished her father or Charlie Spoon would wake up and do something about it, but no one moved in the other tent, and suddenly she was afraid that they had all decamped, wanting nothing more to do with her. She whispered, "Mac, Mac," to the sleeping bag where he should be, but no one answered. She tried to find the flashlight she always kept by her side, but couldn't, and she cried in panic, "Mac, are you there?" He mumbled something, and immediately she felt foolish and hoped he wouldn't reply.

When she awoke again, everything had changed. The owl was gone, the woods were still, and she sensed light, blue and pale, light where before there had been none. *The moon must have come out,* she thought. And it was warm, too, warmer than it should have been. She got out of her sleeping bag and took off her parka — it was that warm. Mac was asleep, wheezing like an old man. She unzipped the tent and stepped outside.

The woods were more beautiful than she had ever seen them. The moon made everything ice-rimmed glimmer with a crystallized, immanent light, while underneath that ice the branches of trees were as stark as skeletons. She heard a crunching in the snow, the one sound in all that silence, and there, walking down the logging trail into their camp, was the doe. Its body, like everything around her, was silvered with frost and moonlight. It walked past the tent where her father and Charlie Spoon were sleeping and stopped no more than six feet from her. Andy saw that she had shot it, yes, had shot it cleanly, just where she thought she had, the wound a jagged, bloody hole in the doe's chest.

A heart shot, she thought.

The doe stepped closer, so that Andy, if she wished, could have reached out and touched it. It looked at her as if expecting her to do this, and so she did, running her hand, slowly at first, along the rough, matted fur, then down to the edge of the wound, where she stopped. The doe stood still. Hesitantly, Andy felt the edge of the wound. The torn flesh was sticky and warm. The wound parted under her touch. And then, almost without her knowing it, her fingers were within, probing, yet still the doe didn't move. Andy pressed deeper, through flesh and muscle and sinew, until her whole hand and more was inside the wound and she had found the doe's heart, warm and beating. She cupped it gently in her hand. *Alive,* she marveled. *Alive.*

The heart quickened under her touch, becoming warmer and warmer until it was hot enough to burn. In pain, Andy tried to remove her hand, but the wound closed about it and held her fast. Her hand was burning. She cried out in agony, sure they would all hear and come help, but they didn't. And then her hand pulled free, followed by a steaming rush of blood, more blood than she ever could have imagined — it covered her hand and arm, and she saw to her horror that her hand was steaming. She moaned and fell to her knees and plunged her hand into the snow. The doe looked at her gently and then turned and walked back up the trail.

In the morning, when she woke, Andy could still smell the blood, but she felt no pain. She looked at her hand. Even though it appeared unscathed, it felt weak and withered. She couldn't move it freely and was afraid the others would notice. *I will hide it in my jacket pocket,* she decided, *so nobody can see.* She ate the oatmeal that her father cooked and stayed apart from them all. No one spoke to her, and that suited her. A light snow began to fall, It was the last day of their hunting trip. She wanted to be home.

Her father dumped the dregs of his coffee. "Well, let's go look for her," he said.

Again they crossed the field. Andy lagged behind. She averted her eyes from the spot where the doe had fallen, already filling up with snow. Mac and Charlie entered the woods first, followed by her father. Andy remained in the field and considered the smear of gray sky, the nearby flock of crows pecking at unyielding stubble. *I will stay here,* she thought, *and not move for a long while.* But now someone — Mac — was yelling. Her father appeared at the woods' edge and waved for her to come. She ran and pushed through a brake of alderberry and larch. The thick underbrush scratched her face. For a moment she felt lost and looked wildly about. Then, where the brush thinned, she saw them standing quietly in the falling snow. They were staring down at the dead doe. A film covered its upturned eye, and its body was lightly dusted with snow.

"I told you she wouldn't get too far," Andy's father said triumphantly. "We must've just missed her yesterday. Too blind to see."

"We're just damn lucky no animal got to her last night," Charlie muttered.

Her father lifted the doe's foreleg. The wound was blood-clotted, brown, and caked like frozen mud. "Clean shot," he said to Charlie. He grinned. "My little girl."

Then he pulled out his knife, the blade gray as the morning. Mac whispered to Andy, "Now watch this," while Charlie Spoon lifted the doe from behind by its forelegs so that its head rested between his knees, its underside exposed. Her father's knife sliced thickly from chest to belly to crotch, and Andy was running from them, back to the field and across, scattering the crows who cawed and circled angrily. And now they were all calling to her — Charlie Spoon and Mac and her father — crying *Andy, Andy* (but that wasn't her name, she would no longer be called that); yet louder than any of them was the wind blowing through the treetops, like the ocean where her mother floated in green water, also calling *Come in, come in,* while all around her roared the mocking of the terrible, now inevitable, sea.

DAVID LIPSKY

Three Thousand Dollars

FROM THE NEW YORKER

My mother doesn't know that I owe my father three thousand
dollars. What happened was this: My father sent me three thousand dollars to pay my college tuition. That was the deal he and
my mom had made. We'd apply for financial aid without him,
to get a lower tuition, and then he'd send me a check, and then
I'd put the check in my bank account and write one of my own
checks out to the school. This made sense not because my father
is rich but because he makes a lot more money than my mother
does — she's a teacher — and if we could get a better deal using
her income instead of his, there was no reason not to. Only,
when the money came, instead of giving it to the school, I spent
it. I don't even know what I spent it on — books and things,
movies. The school never called me in about it. They just kept
sending these bills to my mother, saying we were delinquent in
our payments. That's how my father found out. My mother kept
sending him the bills, he kept looking on them for the money
he'd sent me, and I kept telling him that the school's computer
was making an error and that I'd drop by the office one day
after class and clear it up.

So when I came home to New York for the summer my
mother was frantic, because the school had called her and she
couldn't understand how we could owe them so much money. I
explained to her, somehow, that what we owed them was a
different three thousand dollars — that during the winter the
school had cut our financial aid in half. My mother called my
father to ask him to send us the extra money, and he said that
he wanted to talk to me.

I waited till the next day so I could call him at his office. My stepmother's in finance, and she gets crazy whenever money comes up — her nightmare, I think, is of a river of money flowing from my father to me without veering through her — so I thought it would be better to talk to him when she wasn't around. My father has his own advertising agency in Chicago — Paul Weller Associates. I've seen him at his job when I've visited him out there, and he's pretty good. His company does all the ads for a big midwestern supermarket chain, and mostly what he does is supervise on these huge sets while camera crews stand around filming fruit. It's a really big deal. The fruit has to look just right. My father stands there in a coat and tie, and he and a bunch of other guys keep bending over and making sure that the fruit is O.K. — shiny-looking. There are all these other people standing around with water vapor and gloss. One word from my father and a thousand spray cans go off.

When he gets on the phone, I am almost too nervous to talk to him, though his voice is slow and far off, surrounded by static. I ask him to please send more money. He says he won't. I ask why, and he says because it would be the wrong thing to do. He doesn't say anything for a moment and then I tell him that I agree with him, that I think he is right not to send the money. He doesn't say anything to acknowledge this, and there is a long pause during which I feel the distance between us growing.

Just before he gets off the phone, he says, "What I'm really curious about, Richard, is what your mother thinks of all this," and this wakes me up, because he doesn't seem to realize that I haven't told her yet. I was afraid to. Before I came home, I thought of about twenty different ways of telling her, but once she was right there in front of me it just seemed unbearable. What I'm afraid of now is that my father will find that out, and then he will tell her himself. "I mean," he says, "if I were her, I probably couldn't bear having you in the house. What is she planning to do? Isn't the school calling you up? I can't imagine she has the money to pay them. Isn't she angry at you, Rich?"

I say, "She's pretty angry."

"I hope so," my father says. "I hope she's making you feel terrible. When I talked to her on the phone yesterday — and we only talked for a couple of seconds — she seemed mostly concerned with getting me to give you this money, but I hope that deep down she's really upset about this. Tell her it's no great tragedy if you don't go back to school in the fall. You can get a job in the city and I'll be happy to pay your tuition again next year. I'm sorry, but it just doesn't feel right for me to keep supporting you while you keep acting the way you've been acting, which to me seems morally deficient."

My mother is tall, with light hair and gray, watery eyes. She is a jogger. She has been jogging for six years, and as she's gotten older her body has gotten younger looking. Her face has gotten older, though. There are lines around her lips and in the corners of her eyes, as if she has taken one of those statues without arms or a head and put her own head on top of it. She teaches art at a grammar school a few blocks up from our house, and the the walls of our apartment are covered with her drawings. That's the way she teaches. She stands over these kids while she has them drawing a still life or a portrait or something, and if they're having trouble she sits down next to them to show them what to do, and usually she ends up liking her own work so much that she brings it home with her. We have all these candlesticks and clay flowerpots that she made during class. She used to teach up in Greenwich, Connecticut, which is where we lived before she and my dad got divorced, right before I started high school. Every summer, she and a bunch of other teachers rent a house together in Wellfleet; she will be leaving New York to go up there in six days, so I only have to keep her from finding out until then.

When I get off the phone, she is in the living room reading the newspaper. She gives me this ready-for-the-worst look and asks, "What did he say?"

I explain to her that I will not be going back to college in September. Instead, I will be staying in the apartment and working until I have paid the school the rest of the money.

My mother gets angry. She stands up and folds the paper together and stuffs it into the trash. "Not in this apartment," she says.

"Why not?" I ask. "It's big enough."

"A boy your age should be in college. Your friends are in college. Your father went to college. I'd better call him back." She walks to the phone, which sits on the windowsill.

"Why?" I ask quickly. "He said he wasn't going to do it."

"Well, of course, that's what he'd say to you. He knows you're afraid of him." She sees I'm going to protest this. "Who could blame you? Who wouldn't be afraid of a man who won't even support his own son's education?"

"He said he doesn't have the money."

"And you believe him?" she asks. "With two Volvos and a town house and cable TV? Let him sell one of his cars if he has to. Let him stop watching HBO. Where are his priorities?"

"I'm not his responsibility."

"Oh, no. You're just his son, that's all; I forgot. Why are you protecting him?"

I look up, and my mother's eyes widen a little — part of her question — and it feels as if she is seeing something in my face, so I realize I'd better get out of the room. "I'm not protecting him," I say. "It's just that you always want everything to be somebody's fault. It's the school's fault. It's nobody's fault. It's no great tragedy if I don't go back to school in the fall; you're the only person who thinks so. Why can't you just accept things, like everyone else?" I walk into my bedroom, shutting the door behind me. I lie on my bed and look up at the ceiling, where the summer bugs have already formed a sooty layer inside the bottom of my light fixture. My ears are hot.

Our apartment is small. There are only the two bedrooms, the living room, the bathroom, and the kitchen, and so if you want to be alone it's pretty impossible. My mother comes in after a few minutes. She has calmed down. She walks over to the air conditioner and turns it on, then waves her hand in front of the vents to make sure that cold air is coming out. I sit up and frown at her.

She sits down next to me and puts her arm around my shoulders. "I'm sorry you're so upset," she says. As she talks she rubs the back of my neck. "But I just think that there are a lot of things we can do before you have to go and look for a full-time job. There are relatives we can call. There are loans we can take out. There are a lot of avenues open to us."

"O.K., Mom."

"I know it must be pretty hard on you, having a father like this." She gives me time to speak, then says, "I mean, a man who won't even pay for his son's school."

"It's not that," I say. "It's not even that I'm that upset. It's just that I don't want us to be beholden to him anymore. I don't even like him very much."

My mom laughs. "What's to like?" she says.

I laugh with her. "It's just that he's so creepy."

"You don't have to tell me. I was married to him."

"Why did you marry him?" I ask.

"He was different when I met him."

"How different could he be?"

Mom laughs, shaking he head. Her eyes blank a little, remembering. She was twenty when she met my father — a year older than I am now. I imagine her in a green flannel skirt and blue knee socks. "I don't know," she says, looking past me. "Not very." We laugh together again. "I don't know. I wanted to get away from my parents, I guess."

"Who could blame you?" I say, but I can tell from a shift in her face that I have pushed too far. Her father died two years back.

"What do you mean?" she asks, turning back to me.

"I don't know," I say. "I mean, you were young."

She nods, as if this fact, remembering it, comes as something of a surprise to her. She blinks. "I was young," she says.

I get a job working at a B. Dalton bookstore. The manager has to fill out some forms, and when he asks me how long I will be working — for the whole year or just for the summer — I say, "Just for the summer," without thinking, and by the time I realize, he has already written it down and it doesn't seem worth the trouble of making him go back and change it. Still, I go through the rest of the day with the feeling that I've done something wrong. It's the store on Fifth Avenue, and it's not a bad place to work. I am sent to the main floor, to the middle register, where old women come in pairs and shuffle through the Romance section. I eat lunch in a little park a block from the store, where a mad-made waterfall keeps tumbling down and secretaries drink diet soda. There is a cool breeze, because of the water. It is the second week of the summer, and on returning from lunch I am told I will have Wednesday off, because it is the Fourth of July.

Riding the bus home, I begin thinking that maybe my mother called my father anyway. It's terrible. The bus keeps stopping and people keep piling in, and meanwhile I am imagining their conversation going on. If I could make the bus go faster, maybe I could get home in time to stop them. I try to make mental contact with the bus driver by concentrating. I think, Skip the next stop; but he, out of loyalty to the other passengers or simple psychic deafness, doesn't, and instead the bus keeps stopping and people keep getting off and on. Walking into our building, I get the feeling everyone knows. Even the people on the elevator scowl. Maybe if I had told my mother myself, I would have softened it somehow. What would upset her now is not only the money — although the money would be a big part of it — but also that I tried to put something over on her. I am almost afraid to open our door. "Hello," I call, stepping inside.

As it turns out, my mother isn't home. There is a note on the table. She has gone shopping. I look at the note for a while, to see if I can figure anything out from it. For example, it is a short note. Would she usually write a longer one? It isn't signed "Love" or anything — just "Mom," in the scratchy way she draws her pictures.

I hang my jacket in the closet and then turn on my mom's answering machine. There is one hang-up, and then a message from my father. It makes my whole body go cold. His voice sounds farther away than when we talked the last time. "Richard?" he says. His voice is slow. "This is your father. I just wanted to call to see how things were going. I had an interesting discussion with your mother this afternoon, and we can talk about it later, if you'd like to. Call back if you get a chance." Then there is the clatter of his phone being hung up, and then a little electronic squawk as the connection is broken, which the machine has recorded. I play it again, but there is no way of telling just what he and Mom talked about. I walk into the bathroom and splash cold water on my face and look in the mirror. Then I try reading my mom's note again, but all I can really make it say is that she has gone to the supermarket.

My mother comes home, carrying two big bags of groceries. She pushes the door open with her shoulder. "Can you give me a hand?" she says.

I stand up and take the bags from her and carry them into the kitchen. They are heavy even for me. I hold them close to my chest, where the edges brush against my nose, giving me their heavy, dusty smell. My mom stands in the dining area. She rests one hand on the table. She is wearing running shorts and a T-shirt that on the front says "Perrier" and on the back has the name and date of a race she ran. "Any messages?" she asks me.

I look at her, but I can't tell anything from her face, either. She looks angry, but that could be just because it was hot outside, or because there was too long a line at the supermarket. "I didn't look," I answer. "Don't you even say hello anymore?"

"Hello," she says. She picks up her note and holds it so I can see. "You could throw this away, you know," she says. "Or are you saving it for any particular reason?"

"No, you can throw it away."

"That's nice. How about you throw it away?"

"I'm unloading the groceries right now."

She puts the note back down on the table and then walks into the living room. I unload the rest of the groceries. There is a box of spaghetti, Tropicana orange juice, brown rice, pita bread, a few plain Dannon yogurts. I put everything away and then I fold up the bags and stuff them into the broom closet, where we save them for garbage.

In the living room I hear my mom turn on the machine. There is the hang-up and then my father's message begins again. "Richard?" he says. "This is your father." I walk into the living room. Mom is standing over the machine, one hand on the buttons. "Oh, God," she says, in a bored way when she hears his voice, and she shuts it off. Then she turns around and looks at me. I am standing near the wall. "Why do you have that funny look on your face, Richard?" she asks.

I shrug. "How was your day?" I say.

"Bad." She steps over her chair and sits down on the sofa. From the way she arranged herself, I can tell she is upset. She keeps her arms folded across her stomach, and there is something compressed and angry about her face. The way her lips are pressed together — and also something around her eyes. "You want to make me some tea?"

"What happened?" I ask.

"Nothing happened. I ran. I went shopping. I spoke to your father."

I pull a chair over from the table and sit down across from her. I count to five and then ask, "What did he say?"

She shakes her head and laughs through her nose. "Oh, God. He was awful, Richard. Just awful. Right when he got on the phone, he started asking if you'd found a job, and then when I asked him if he was planning to pay the rest of your tuition he laughed and said of course not. He said it was time for you to learn to take care of yourself. He said it was going to be good for you. I couldn't talk to him. Really, Richard, he was awful. I mean it. Just awful."

"I told you not to call him."

"Well, then, I was stupid, Richard."

"Are you going to call him again?"

"How do I know if I'm going to call him again? Not if he keeps acting that way on the phone to me. But I can't pay the school myself." Her lips go back to being tight, and she pulls her arms closer together, so that each hand curls under the opposite elbow.

It occurs to me that what's pressing down on her face is the money we owe the school. "Did the school call again?" I guess.

She nods. "Yesterday."

"Don't call him," I say.

"Thanks, Richard. You want to get me some tea?"

"How about 'please'?"

"How about throwing that note away? Or are you planning to leave it there till Christmas?"

The next day, I get the same feeling that she has called my father again. I go outside during lunch to phone her. It is very hot, and the undersides of my arms are soggy. I have to walk about two blocks down Fifth Avenue before I can find a free phone, and then when I dial our number there is no answer. I think I may have dialed the number wrong, because even if no one is home there should still be the machine, but when I try again there is still no answer. As I hang up, I catch my reflection in the shiny front of the phone for a second and I look awful, sweaty. The rest of the day is terrible. I can hardly work. I keep ringing up the paperbacks as Calendars and the children's books as Software. On the way home, I think that even if my father didn't tell her I will have to tell her myself. I'm afraid that if I don't something awful will happen, like we'll never speak to each other again or something. But when I get home she is sitting on the sofa, reading the newspaper with her feet up on a chair, and when I walk into the living room she smiles at me, and it just doesn't seem like the right time. I take off my tie and blazer and then pour myself a glass of milk and sit down next to her. She smells like Ben Gay — a strong, wintergreenish smell — which is what she rubs on her legs after running.

"How was your day?" she asks me. She has a mug of tea on the cushion next to her, and when I sit down she folds the newspaper and picks up the mug.

"Fine," I say. Then I ask, "Did you go somewhere? I tried calling around noon, but there was no answer."

"I drove up to Greenwich," she says.

"Why didn't you turn on the machine?"

"What are you, the police inspector? I didn't feel like it, that's why."

"But why'd you drive up to Greenwich?"

She laughs. "I feel like I should have one of those big lights on me." She brings her arms very close in to her sides and speaks very quickly, like a suspect: "I don't know. I don't know why I went up to Greenwich." She drinks from her cup, which she holds with both hands. Then she shakes her head and laughs.

We eat dinner. When we lived in Greenwich, she used to teach art in the summers, too. They had a summer day program, with a bunch of little kids running around — I was in it, too, when I was younger — and she used to take them out into the fields and have them draw trees and flowers. She hated it. While we were eating, I get the idea that maybe this is what she went up there for, to talk to someone about this job. Dinner is cool things: tuna fish and pita bread and iced coffee. My mother has a salad. We don't talk for a while. All we do is crunch.

"Why'd you go up to Greenwich?" I ask her again.

She looks up at me, a little angry. The rule, I know, is that we don't talk about anything once she has clearly finished talking about it. "I felt like it," she says. Then she forks some more salad into her mouth, and maybe thinks that her response is off key, because she says, "I had a great idea while I was up there, though."

"What?"

"I thought we could go up tomorrow. You know, for the Fourth of July. See the fireworks. I thought it'd be a lot of fun."

"It sounds great."

"Yes," she says, "I thought you'd like that."

I sleep late the next day, and when I wake up she has gone jogging. She has left me a note saying so, which I throw away. She comes back sweaty and happy, drinking a bottle of club soda, and I ask her why she isn't drinking tea, and we joke, and it all feels very nice, until I remember about Dad and the money and her job and then I feel awful again, because it seems as if all our talking and joking is going on in midair, without anything underneath it to hold it up. We eat lunch, and then my mom makes some sandwiches and we get into our car and drive up the thruway to Connecticut. It's fun seeing the place where you used to live. We drive by our old house, and it looks the same, though there are some toys in the back yard and some lawn furniture — chairs and a big wooden table — which we didn't own. I get this funny feeling while we are in the car that we could still be living inside, as a family; that my father could walk out on the lawn and wave to us, or that if we stayed long enough we might see ourselves going past a window or walking over to sit at that big table. When we get to the high school, cars are everywhere, loading and unloading, families carrying big plastic coolers filled with food. I ask my mother if it was always this popular. "Yes," she says. "You just don't remember." We have to drive up the street about two blocks to find a space. By the time we have taken our own cooler out of the trunk, two more cars have already parked in front of us.

The fireworks are always held at the same place. The people sit on the athletic field and the fireworks are set off from behind the baseball diamond about a hundred yards away. Thousands of people are sitting on blankets or walking around and talking to each other. It's like a scene from one of those movies where the dam bursts and everyone is evacuated to a municipal building, only instead of all their belongings the people here are carrying pillows and Cokes and Twinkies. We find a spot right in the middle of the field. Some kids are playing a game of tag. They keep running through the crowd, laughing, screaming, just barely missing the people on the ground, which of course is part of the fun. When one of the kids brushes against my mother's shoulder I can see that she wants to stop him, give him a talking to, but I ask her not to. I remember when I would have been playing, too.

There is a black platform in the center of the baseball field, and after about three-quarters of an hour a presentation begins. A fireman and a policeman and a man from the Chamber of Commerce walk back and forth to the microphone and give each other awards, for safety and diligence and community service. Then they step down and a group of boys and girls collect onstage, most of them blond, all of them in robes. The man from the Chamber of Commerce, wearing his silver community-service medal, introduces tham as the Royal Danish Boys and Girls Choir, "all the way from Holland." Then he leaves the stage, and though I imagine that the children will sing Danish folk songs, or maybe European anthems, what they sing is a medley of Broadway show tunes, in English, designed around the theme of a foreigner's impressions of America: "Oklahoma!" and "Getting to Know You" and "Gary, Indiana," though it is hard to make out the exact words through their accents.

By the time they have finished, the sky has turned dark blue, with the moon hanging just to one side. The policeman and the fireman return with the man from the Chamber of Commerce. "Good evening," he says. His voice echoes all over the field. "We'd like to welcome all of you to this year's celebration of the Greenwich, Connecticut, Fourth of July. In keeping with the spirit of this very special day, we'd like all of you to rise for the singing of our national anthem." My mother and I stand to sing, and there is something nice about being part of this wave of people, of voices. During the last line, there is a popping sound like a champagne bottle opening, and a yellow streak rises over the platform, nosing its way into the sky. The words "and the home, of the, brave" are lost in a chorus of "Oh"s. We sit down again, en masse. I hand my mother her sweater. I can barely see her, but her voice comes from where I know she should be: "Thank you." The fireworks go off over the outfield, sometimes one, sometimes two or three at a time. Each one leaves a little shadow of smoke that the next one, bursting, illuminates. Some bloom like flowers; others are simply midair explosions, flashes. A few burst and then shoot forward, like the effect in *Star Wars* when the ship goes into hyperspace. Some are designed to fool us: One pops open very high in the air, sending out a circle of streamers like the frame of an umbrella; the crowd begins to "Ooh." Then one of these streamers, falling, pops open itself, sending out another series, and the rest of the crowd goes "Ah." Finally, one of those pops right over our heads, giving off a final shower of color, and the crowd whistles and applauds. The display gets more and more elaborate, until, for the last few minutes, there are ten or twenty rockets in the air at once, bursting and unfolding simultaneously. Everyone starts cheering, and the noises keep booming over us, making us duck our heads. The air smells like sulfur.

In the car, I am close to sleep. My mother is driving, outside it is dark, and I feel safe. The roads are crowded at first, but farther away from the school the traffic gets thinner, until we are driving alone down mostly empty roads. We seem to drive for a long time before joining up with the highway, where we become again simply one car among many.

"I'm working this summer," my mother announces after a little while.

I know, but I ask "Where" anyway.

"Here," she says. "At the school. I got my old job back."

"Mom."

She stops me. "I thought about it, and I decided that it really was important for me to have you in school right now. It was my decision to make, and I made it."

I turn to look at her. Her face is lit up by the meters in the dashboard. It's a surprise to remember that she has a body to go with her voice. I look at her profile, at her cheek and at the skin underneath her chin beginning to sag. I remember how frightened she had been when we first moved to the city, how odd it had felt being in a house without my father's voice filling it, and how when we drove up to college for the first time last fall and she saw my name on top of my registration folder she walked out of the reception hall. I found her outside, on the main green, crying. "I can't believe we did it, we pulled it off," she said, meaning college.

"I just don't want to be a burden," I say now.

"You are," she says. "But it's O.K. I mean, I'm your mother, and you're supposed to be my burden." She turns to look at me in the dark. "I am your mother, aren't I?"

"As far as I know."

She laughs, and then we don't talk for a while. She turns on the air conditioner. I close my eyes and lean my head against the window. Every so often we hit a bump, which makes the window jiggle, which makes my teeth click together. "I'm sorry you have to work," I say.

"Look, you should be. Don't ask me to get rid of your guilt for you. If you feel guilty, that's fine. This was just important to me, that's all."

Her using the word "guilt" frightens me. I sit up and open my eyes. "What did Dad say to you on the phone?" I ask.

"Nothing. He said he wasn't going to pay for you. He said that he was doing the right thing. He said you understood. Do you?"

"No."

She nods, driving. "That's what I told your father. He said you should call him, if you want to. Do you?"

I laugh. "No."

She nods again. "I told him that, too."

She seems ready to stop talking, but I keep going. I want her to tell me that it's O.K., that she missed working outdoors, that she missed the little kids, missed Connecticut. "I just feel bad because now you can't go to Wellfleet for the summer."

My mother says, "Let's not talk."

We drive. Through the windshield everything looks purple and slick — the road and the taillights of the cars passing us and the slender, long-necked lights hanging over the highway. We seem sealed in, as if we are traveling under water.

My mother reaches over and turns off the air conditioner. "There is something I want to talk to you about, Richard," she says.

"What?" I ask.

She keeps her face turned toward the highway. "If anything like this ever happens again, I want you to tell me immediately. Don't make it so I have to find out myself. This whole thing wouldn't have happened if you had told me about it in the spring. We could have gotten loans and things. As it is, we're stuck."

I don't say anything.

"If you ever have anything to tell me," she says, "tell me when it happens, O.K.? We're very close. You can tell me anything you want to. O.K.?"

She looks over at me. I try to keep my face from showing anything, and when I can't do that I look away, at my feet under the dashboard. It is an offer. I can tell her or not. The funny thing is, I can feel that she doesn't really want me to. If she has guessed, she doesn't want me to confirm it. And though I am relieved, it seems to me that if I don't tell her now I never will, and this thing will always be between us, this failure, my father's voice embedded in static.

I look up. We are passing under the George Washington Bridge.

"O.K.," I say.

THOMAS McGUANE

Sportsmen

FROM PLAYBOY

WE KEPT THE PERCH in a stone pool in front of the living room window. An elm shaded the pool, and when the heavy drapes of the living room were drawn, so that my mother could see the sheet music on the piano, the window reflected the barred shapes of the fish in the pool.

We caught them from the rocks on the edge of the lake, rocks that were submerged when the wakes of passing freighters hit the shore. From a distance, the freighters pushed a big swell in front of them without themselves seeming to move on the great flatness of the lake. My friend that year was a boy named Jimmy Meade and he was learning to identify the vessel stacks of the freighters. We liked the Bob-Lo Line, Cleveland Cliffs, and Wyandotte Transportation with the red Indian tall on the sides of the stacks. We looked for whalebacks and tankers and the laden ore ships and listened to the moaning signals from the horns as they carried over the water. The wakes of those freighters moved slowly toward the land along the unmoving surface of water. The wakes were the biggest feature out there, bigger than Canada behind them, which lay low and thin like the horizon itself.

Jimmy Meade and I were thirteen then. He had moved up from lower Ohio the previous winter and I was fascinated by his almost-southern accent. His father had an old pickup truck in a town which drove mostly sedans, and they had a big loose-limbed hound that seemed to stand for a distant, unpopulated place.

Hoods were beginning to appear in the school, beginning to grow drastic haircuts, wear Flagg Flyer shoes, and sing Gene Vincent songs. They hung inside their cars from the wind vanes and stared at the girls I had grown up with, revealing an aspect of violence I had not known. They wolf-whistled. They laughed with their mouths wide open and their eyes glittering, and when they got into fights, they used their feet. They spent their weekends at the drags in Flat Rock. Jimmy and I loved the water, but when the hoods came near it, all they saw were the rubbers. We were downright afraid of the hoods, of how they acted, of the steel taps on their shoes, of the way they saw things, making us feel we would be crazy to ever cross them. We were sportsmen.

But then, we were lost in our plans. We wanted to refurbish a Civil War rifle Jimmy's father owned. We were going to make an ice boat, a duck blind, and a fishing shanty. We were going to dig up an Indian mound, sell the artifacts, and buy a racing hydroplane that would throw a rooster tail five times its own length. But above all, we wanted to be duck hunters.

That August we were diving off the pilings near the entrance to the Thoroughfare Canal. We were talking about salvaging boats from the Black Friday storm of 1916 when the Bob-Lo steamer passed. The wash came in and sucked the water down around the pilings. Jimmy dove from the tallest one, arcing down the length of the creosoted spar into the green, clear water. And then he didn't come up. Not to begin with. When he did, the first thing that surfaced was the curve of his back, white and Ohio-looking in its oval of lake water. It was a back that was never to widen with muscle or stoop with worry because Jimmy had just then broken his neck. I remember getting him out on the gravel shore. He was wide awake and his eyes poured tears. His body shuddered continuously and I recall his fingers fluttered on the stones with a kind of purpose. I had never heard sounds like that from his mouth in the thousands of hours we had talked. I learned from a neighbor that my screams brought help and, similarly, I can't imagine what I would sound like screaming. Perhaps no one can.

My father decided that month that I was a worthless boy who blamed his troubles on outside events. He had quite a long theory about all of this, and hanging around on the lake or in the flat woods hunting rabbits with our .22s substantiated that theory. I forget how.

He found me a job over in Burr Oak cleaning die-cast aluminum molds with acid and a wire brush. That was the first time I had been around the country people who work in small factories across the nation. Once you get the gist of their ways, you can get along anyplace you go, because they are everywhere and they are good people.

When I tried to call Jimmy Meade from Burr Oak, his father said that he was unable to speak on the telephone. He said Jimmy was out of the hospital and he would always be paralyzed. In his father's voice, with its almost-southern Ohio accent, I could feel myself being made to know that though I had not done this to Jimmy, I had been there, and that there was villainy, somehow, in my escape.

I really don't think I could have gotten out of the factory job without crossing my own father worse than I then dared. But it's true, I missed the early hospitalization of Jimmy and of course I had missed having that accident happen to me in the first place. I still couldn't picture Jimmy not being able to move anything, being kind of frozen where we left off.

I finished up in August and stayed in Sturgis for a couple of days, in a boardinghouse run by an old woman and her sixty-year-old spinster daughter. I was so comfortable with them that I found myself sitting in the front hall watching the street for prospective customers. I told them I was just a duck hunter. Like the factory people, they had once had a farm. After that, I went home to see Jimmy.

He lived in a small house on Macomb Street about a half mile from the hardware. There was a layout duck boat in the yard and quite a few cars parked around, hot rods mostly. What could have explained this attendance? Was it popularity? A strange feeling shot through me.

I went in the screen door at the side of the house, propped ajar with a brick. There were eight or ten people inside, boys and girls our own age. My first feeling, that I had come back from a factory job in another town with tales to tell, vanished and I was suddenly afraid of the people in the room, who were faster, tougher kids than Jimmy and I had known. There were open beer bottles on the table and the radio played hits.

Jimmy was in the corner where the light came through the screens from two directions. He was in a wheelchair and his arms and legs had been neatly folded within the sides of the contraption. He had a ducktail haircut and a girl held a beer to his lips, then replaced it with a Camel in a fake pearl-and-ebony cigarette holder. His weight had halved and there were copper-colored shadows under his eyes. He looked like a modernized station of the cross.

When he began to talk, his Ohio accent was gone. How did that happen? Insurance was going to buy him a flathead Ford. "I'm going to chop and channel it," he said, "kick the frame, french the headlights, bullnose the hood, and lead the trunk." He stopped and twisted his face to draw on the cigarette. "There's this hillbilly in Taylor Township who can roll and pleat the interior."

I didn't get the feeling he was particularly glad to see me. But what I did was just sit there and tough it out until the room got tense and people just began to pick up and go. That took no time at all: The boys crumpled beer cans in their fists conclusively. The girls smiled with their mouths open and snapped their eyes. Everyone knew something was fishy. They hadn't seen me around since the accident, and the question was: What was I doing there now?

"I seen a bunch of ducks moving," Jimmy said.

"I did too."

"Seen them from the house." Jimmy sucked on his cigarette. "Remember how old Minnow Milton used to shoot out of his boathouse when there was ducks?" Minnow Milton had lived in a floating house that had a trap attached to it from which he sold shiners for bait. The floating house was at the foot of Jimmy's road.

"I remember him."

"Well, Minnow's no longer with us. And the old boat is just setting there doing nothing."

The next morning before daybreak, Jimmy and I were in Minnow Milton's living room with the lake slapping underneath and the sash thrown up. There were still old photographs of the Milton family on the walls. Minnow was a bachelor and no one had come for them. I had my father's 12-gauge pump gun propped on the windowsill and I could see the blocks, the old

Mason decoys, all canvasbacks, that I had set out beneath the window, thirty of them bobbing, wooden beaks to the wind, like steamboats seen from a mile up. I really couldn't see Jimmy. I had wheeled him in terror down the gangplank and into the dark. I set the blocks in the dark, and when I lit his cigarette, he stared down the length of the holder, intently, so I couldn't tell what he was thinking. I said, "What fun is there if you can't shoot?"

"Shoot," he said.

"I'm gonna shoot. I was just asking."

"You ain't got no ducks anyways."

To my relief, that was true. But it didn't last. A cold wind came with daylight. A slight snow spit across the dark gray water, touching and scattering down into the whitecaps. I saw a flight of mallards rocket over and disappear behind us. Then they reappeared and did the same thing again right across the roof over our heads. When they came the third time, they set their wings and reached their feet through hundreds of feet of cold air toward the decoys. I killed two and let the wind blow them up against the floating house. Jimmy grinned from ear to ear.

I built a fire in Minnow Milton's old stove and cooked those ducks on a stick. I had to feed Jimmy off the point of my Barlow knife, but we ate two big ducks for breakfast and lunch at once. I stood the pump gun in the corner.

Tall columns of snow advanced toward us across the lake, and among them, right in among them, were ducks, some of everything, including the big canvasbacks that stirred us like old music. Buffleheads raced along the surface.

"Fork me some of that there duck meat," said Jimmy Meade in his Ohio voice.

We stare down from our house window as our decoys fill with ducks. The weather gets so bad the ducks swim among the decoys without caring. After half a day we don't know which is real and which is not. I wrap Jimmy's blanket up under his chin.

"I hope those ducks keep on coming," he says. And they do. We are in a vast raft of ducks. We don't leave until the earth has turned clean around and it is dark again.

CHRISTOPHER McILROY

All My Relations

FROM TRIQUARTERLY

WHEN JACK OLDENBURG first spoke to him, Milton Enos leaned over his paper plate, scooping beans into his mouth as if he didn't hear. Breaking through the murmur of *o'otham* conversation, the white man's speech was sharp and harsh. But Oldenburg stood over him, waiting.

Oldenburg had just lost his ranch hand, sick. If Milton reported to the Box-J sober in the morning, he could work for a couple of weeks until the cowboy returned or Oldenburg found a permanent hand.

"O.K.," Milton said, knowing he wouldn't go. Earlier in the day his wife and son had left for California, so he had several days' drinking to do. Following his meal at the convenience mart he would hitch to the Sundowner Lounge at the edge of the reservation.

After a sleepless night Milton saddled his horse for the ride to Oldenburg's, unable to bear his empty house. As Milton crossed the wide, dry bed of the Gila River, leaving the outskirts of Hashan, the house ceased to exist for him and he thought he would never go back. Milton's stomach jogged over the pommel with the horse's easy gait. Two hours from Hashan, Oldenburg's Box-J was the only ranch in an area either left desert or irrigated for cotton and sorghum. Its twenty square miles included hills, arroyos, and the eastern tip of a mountain range — gray-pink granite knobs split by ravines. The sun burned the tops of the mountains red.

Oldenburg stood beside his corral, tall and thin as one of its

mesquite logs. First, he said, sections of the barbed-wire fence
had broken down, which meant chopping and trimming new
posts.

Milton's first swings of the ax made him dizzy and sick. He
flailed wildly, waiting with horror for the bite of the ax into his
foot. But soon he gained control over his stroke. Though soft,
his big arms were strong. Sweat and alcohol poured out of him
until he stank.

In the afternoon Milton and Oldenburg rode the fence line.

"Hasn't been repaired in years," Oldenburg said. "My hand
Jenkins is old." Oldenburg himself was well over sixty, his crew
cut white and his face dried up like a dead man's. He had bright
eyes, though, and fine white teeth. Where the fence was flattened to the ground, Milton saw a swatch of red and white
cowhide snagged on the barbed wire. He'd lost a few head in
the mountains, Oldenburg said, and after the fence was secure
they'd round them up.

"One thing I'll tell you," Oldenburg said. "You can't drink
while you work for me. Alcohol is poison in a business."

Milton nodded. By reputation he knew Oldenburg had a tree
stump up his ass. Milton's wife C.C. had said she'd bring their
son Allen back when Milton stopped drinking. For good? he'd
asked. How would she know when was for good. For all anybody
knew tomorrow might be the first day of for good, or 25,500
days later he might get drunk again. For a moment Milton
remembered playing Monopoly with C.C. and Allen several
weekends before. As usual, Milton and Allen were winning.
Pretending not to be furious, C.C. smiled her big, sweet grin.
Milton and the boy imitated her, stretching their mouths, until
she couldn't help laughing. Milton clicked them off like a TV
set and saw only mesquite, and rocky sand, sky, and the line of
fence. After his two weeks, Milton thought, he'd throw a drunk
like World War Ten.

At the end of the day Milton accepted Oldenburg's offer: $75
a week plus room and board, weekend off. Oldenburg winced
apologetically proposing the wage; the ranch didn't make
money, he explained.

They ate at a metal table in the dining room. Milton, whose
pleasure in food went beyond filling his stomach, appreciated

Oldenburg's meat loaf — diced with onion, the center conceal-
ing three hard-boiled eggs. Milton couldn't identify the season-
ings except for chili. "What's in this?" he asked.

"Sage, chili, cumin and Worcestershire sauce."

"*Heyyy.*"

Inside his two-room adobe, Milton was so tired he couldn't
feel his body, and lying down felt the same as standing up. He
slept without dreaming until Oldenburg rattled the door at daybreak.

Milton dug holes and planted posts. By noon his sweat had
lost its salt and tasted like pure spring water. Then he didn't
sweat at all. Chilled and shaking at the end of the day, his body
felt as if he'd been thrown by a horse. The pain gave him a
secret exultation which he hoarded from Oldenburg, saying
nothing. Yet he felt he was offering the man part of the ache
as a secret gift. Slyly, he thumped his cup on the table and
screeched his chair back with exaggerated vigor. Milton was
afraid of liking Oldenburg too much. He liked people easily,
even those who were not *o'otham* — especially those, perhaps,
because he wanted them to prove he needn't hate them.

Milton worked ten-, eleven-hour days. The soreness left his
muscles, though he was as tired the fourth evening as he had
been the first. Thursday night Oldenburg baked a chicken.

"You're steady," Oldenburg said. "I've seen you Pimas work
hard before. What's your regular job?"

"I've worked for the government." Milton had ridden rodeo,
sold wild horses he captured in the mountains, broken horses.
Most often there was welfare. Recently he had completed two
CETA training programs, one as a hospital orderly and the
other baking cakes. But the reservation hospital wasn't hiring,
and the town of Hashan had no bakeries. For centuries, Milton
had heard, when the Gila flowed, the *o'otham* had been farmers.
Settlements and overgrazing upstream had choked off the river
only a few generations past. Sometimes Milton tried to envision
green plots of squash, beans, and ripening grains, watered by
earthen ditches, spreading from the banks. He imagined his
back flexing easily in the heat as he bent to the rows, foliage
swishing his legs, finally the villagers diving into the cool river,
splashing delightedly.

"I don't think Jenkins is coming out of the hospital," Olden-burg said. "This job is yours if you want it." Milton was stunned. He had never held a permanent position.

In just a week of hard work, good eating, and no drinking, Milton had lost weight. Waking Friday morning, he pounded his belly with his hand; it answered him like a drum. He danced in front of the bathroom mirror, swiveling his hips, urging him-self against the sink as if it were a partner. At lunch he told Oldenburg he would spend the weekend with friends in Ha-shan.

When he tossed the post-hole digger into the shed, Milton felt light and strong, as if instead of sinking fence posts he'd spent the afternoon in a deep, satisfying nap. On the way to the guest house, his bowels turned over and a sharp pain set into his head. He saw the battered station wagon rolling down the drive, C.C. at the wheel, Allen's tight face in the window.

Milton threw his work clothes against the wall. After a sting-ing shower, he changed and mounted his horse for the ride to Vigiliano Lopez's.

Five hours later, the Sundowner was closing. Instead of his customary beer, Milton had been drinking highball glasses of straight vodka. He felt paler and paler, like water, until he was water. His image peeled off him like a wet decal and he was only water in the shape of a man. He flowed onto the bar, hooking his water elbows onto the wooden ridge for support. Then he was lifted from the stool, tilted backward, floating on the pickup bed like vapor.

Milton woke feeling the *pong, pong* of a baskeball bouncing outside. The vibration traveled along the dirt floor of Lopez's living room, up the couch Milton lay on. The sun was dazz-ling. Looking out the window, Milton saw six-foot-five, three-hundred-pound Bosque dribbling the ball with both hands, knocking the other players aside. As he jammed the ball into the low hoop, it hit the back of the rim, bouncing high over the makeshift plywood backboard. A boy and two dogs chased it.

Seeing beer cans in the dirt, Milton went outside. He took his shirt off and sat against the house with a warm Bud. The lean young boys fired in jump shots, or when they missed, their fathers and older brothers pushed and wrestled for the rebound. Lopez grabbed a loose ball and ran with it, whirling for a turnaround fadeaway that traveled three feet. He laughed, and said to Milton, "When we took you home you started fighting us. Bosque had to pick you up and squeeze you, and when he did, everything came out like toothpaste."

"Try our new puke-flavored toothpaste," someone said, laughing.

"Looks like pizza."

"So we brought you here."

Milton said nothing. He watched the arms and broad backs collide. The young boys on the sidelines practiced lassoing the players' feet, the dogs, the ball. When he finished a beer, Milton started another. Later in the afternoon he sent boys to his house for the rest of his clothes and important belongings.

When the game broke up, some of the men joined the women in the shade of a mesquite. Saddling a half-broke wild colt, the boys took turns careening across the field. Lopez drove a truckload to the rodeo arena, where a bronc rider from Bapchule was practicing. Compact and muscular, with silver spurs and collar tabs, he rode out the horse's bucks, smoothing the animal to a canter. Two of Milton's drunk friends tried and were thrown immediately. For a third, the horse didn't buck but instead circled the arena at a dead run, dodging the lassos and open gates. From the announcer's booth Lopez called an imaginary race as horse and rider passed the grandstand again and again — "coming down the backstretch now, whoops, there he goes for another lap, this horse is not a quitter, ladies and gentlemen."

"Go ahead, Milton," Lopez said. "You used to ride."

Milton shook his head. Allen, thirteen, recently had graduated from steers to bulls. In both classes he had finished first or second in every start, earning as much money in the past months as his father and mother combined. Would there be rodeo in California? Milton wondered. In school, too, Allen was a prodigy, learning high school geometry in eighth grade. If he studied hard, the school counselor said, he could finish high school in three years and win a college scholarship. Milton didn't know where the boy's talent came from.

Tears filled Milton's eyes.

"Aaaah," Bosque said. His big hand gripped Milton's arm. They walked back to Lopez's house and split a couple of sixes under the mesquite until the men returned. Audrey Lopez and the other wives prepared chili and chimuth dough while the men played horseshoes and drank in the dusk.

By the end of dinner everyone was drunk. Milton, face sweating, was explaining to Audrey Lopez, "Just a few weeks ago, Allen wins some kind of puzzle contest for the whole state, O.K.? And he's on TV. And C.C. and I have got our faces up to the screen so we can hear every word he's saying. And we can't believe it. He's talking on TV, and his hair's sticking up on the side, just like it always does.

"I see them so real. When C.C. plays volleyball she's like a rubber ball, she's so little and round. She *dives* for those spikes, and her hair goes flying back."

Lopez slid his leg along Audrey's shoulder. "Good song," he said. "Let's dance." The radio was playing Top Forty.

"Wait. I'm listening to this man."

"Milton talks you into tomorrow afternoon. Come on." Lopez pulled her shoulder.

Audrey shrugged him off and laid her hand on Milton's arm. "His wife and son are gone."

"Dried-up old bitch," Lopez said. "C.C.'s too old for you, man, she's way older than he is. You lost nothing."

Grabbing a barbecue fork, ramming Lopez against the wall, Milton chopped the fork into Lopez's shoulder. A woman screamed, Milton heard his own grunts as the glistening tines rose and stabbed. Lopez ducked and his knife came up. Milton deflected the lunge with his fork, the knife blade springing down its long shank. Milton shouted as the knife thudded into the wall. His little finger had bounded into the air and lay on the floor, looking like a brown pebble.

Bosque drove both men to the hospital. The doctor cauterized, stitched, and bandaged the wound, and gave Milton a tetanus shot. If Milton had brought the severed finger — the top two joints — the doctor said, he might have sewn it on. The men refused to stay overnight. When they returned to the party, couples were dancing the choti and bolero to a Mexican radio station. Gulps of vodka deadened the pain in Milton's finger.

He and Lopez kept opposite corners of the living room until dawn, when Lopez pushed Audrey into Milton's arms and said, "Get some dancing, man."

Sunday Milton slept under the mesquite until evening, when he rode to the Box-J.

"That's your mistake, Milton," Oldenburg said. "Everyone's entitled to one mistake. Next time you drink you're gone. You believe me?"

Milton did. He felt like weeping. The next day he roamed the fence line, his chest and neck clotted with the frustration of being unable to work. The horse's jouncing spurted blood through the white bandage on his finger. Finally he rode out a back gate and into the midst of the granite mountains. Past a sparkling dome broken by a slump of shattered rock, Milton trotted into a narrow cut choked with mesquite. As a boy, he would hunt wild horses for days in these ravines, alone, with only a canvas food bag tied to the saddle. He remembered sleeping on the ground without a blanket, beneath a lone sycamore that had survived years of drought. Waking as dawn lit the mountain crests, he would force through the brush, gnawing a medallion of jerked beef. Most often when he startled a horse, the animal would clatter into a side gully, boxing itself in. Then roping was easy. Once when Milton flushed a stringy gray mustang, the horse charged him instead; Milton had no time to uncoil his rope before the gray was past. Milton wheeled, pursuing at a full gallop out the canyon and onto the *bajada*. Twig-matted tail streaming behind, the mustang was outrunning him, and Milton had one chance with the rope. He dropped the loop around the gray's neck, jarring the animal to its haunches. It was so long ago. Today, Milton reflected, the headlong chase would have pinned him and the horse to Oldenburg's barbed-wire fence.

The sycamore held its place, older and larger. Though encountering no horses, Milton returned three stray cattle to Oldenburg's ranch. For a month, while the slightest jolt could rupture the wound, he hunted down mavericks in the miles of ravine, painted the ranch buildings, and repaired the roofs, one-handed. Even as the finger healed, the missing segment unbalanced his grip. Swinging the pick or ax, shoveling, he would clench his right hand so tightly the entire arm would tremble. By the second month a new hand had evolved, with the musculature of the other fingers, the palm, and the wrist more pronounced. The pinky stub acted as a stabilizer against pickshaft or rope. Milton had rebuilt the fence and combed the granite mountains, rounding up another two dozen head. Oldenburg's herd had increased to 120.

In late August Milton rode beyond the granite range to the Ka kai Mountains, a low, twisted ridge of volcanic rock that he had avoided because he once saw the Devil there. Needing to piss, he had stumbled away from a beer party and followed a trail rising between the boulders. Watching the ground for snakes, Milton had almost collided with a man standing in the path. The stranger was a very big, ugly Indian, but Milton knew it was the Devil because his eyes were black, not human, and he spoke in a booming voice that rolled echoes off the cliffs. Milton shuddered uncontrollably and shriveled to the size of a spider. Afterwards he found he had fallen and cut himself. Cholla segments were embedded in his leg. The Devil had said only: "Beware of Satan within you."

The meeting enhanced Milton's prestige, and Allen was impressed, though not C.C. "You see?" she said. "What did I always tell you?"

In daylight the mountains looked like no more than a pile of cinders. Milton chose an arroyo that cut through the scorched black rubble into red slabs, canyon walls which rose over Milton's head, then above the mesquite. Chasing a calf until it disappeared in a side draw, Milton left the animal for later. The canyon twisted deeper into the mountains, the red cliffs now three hundred feet high. The polished rock glowed. Milton was twelve years old, and his brothers were fighting.

"You took my car," Steven said.

"So what," Lee said. Milton's favorite brother, he was slim and handsome, with small ears and thick, glossy hair that fell almost into his eyes. Weekends he took Milton into Phoenix to play pool and pinball, sometimes to the shopping mall for Cokes. He always had girls, even Mexicans and whites.

"I told you if you took my car I was going to kill you." Steven always said crazy things. At breakfast, if Milton didn't pass him the milk right away — "How'd you like this knife in your eye?" About their mother — "Bitch wouldn't give me a dime. I'm going to shit on her bed." He wore a white rag around his head and hung out with gangs. Now they would call him a cholo.

"So what," Lee said. "Kill me." Cocking his leg, he wiped the dusty boot heel carefully against the couch. Milton was sitting on the couch.

Steven ran down the hall and came back with a .22. He pointed it at Lee's head, there was a shocking noise, a red spot appeared in Lee's forehead, and he collapsed on the rug.

"Oh my GOD," Steven said. Fingers clawed against his temples, he rushed out the door. Milton snatched the gun and chased him, firing on the run. Steven, bigger and faster, outdistanced him in the desert. Milton didn't come home for three days. Steven wasn't prosecuted and he moved to Denver. If he returned, Milton would kill him, even twenty years later.

Milton's horse ambled down the white sand, the dry bed curving around a red outcropping. Trapped by the canyon walls, the late summer air was hot and close. The weight of Milton's family fell on his back like a landslide — his father, driving home drunk from Casa Grande, slewing across the divider, head-on into another pickup. The four children had flown like crickets from the back, landing unhurt in the dirt bank. The driver of the other truck died, and Milton's mother lost the shape of her face.

Milton felt himself turning to water. He circled his horse, routed the calf from the slit in the wall, and drove it miles to the ranch. At dinner he told Oldenburg he needed a trip to town.

"You'll lose your job," Oldenburg said.

Milton ate with his water fingers, spilling food and the orange juice that Oldenburg always served. "The lives of *o'otham* is a soap opera," he cried, trying to dispel his shame by insulting himself. "I love my boy, O.K.? But it's him who has to hold me when I go for C.C. He doesn't hold me with his strength. He holds me because I see him, and I stop. Sometimes I don't stop."

Oldenburg served Milton cake for dessert and told him to take the next day off, if he wanted.

The following morning Milton lay on his bed, sweating. In his mind were no thoughts or images save the swirls of chill, unpleasant water that washed over him. He could transform the water, making it a cold lake that pumped his heart loudly and shrank his genitals, or a clear stream immersing him in swift currents and veins of sunlight, but he could not change the water into thoughts. The green carpeting and blue-striped drapes in his room sickened him. He could have finished a pint of vodka before he knew he was drinking.

He could not imagine losing his work.

Abruptly Milton rose. In the corral he fitted a rope bridle over the horse's head. As he rode past Oldenburg, the man looked up from a bench of tack he was fussing with, then quickly lowered his head.

"I'm going to the mountains," Milton said.

He let the horse carry him into the charred crust of the canyon. The scarlet walls rose high and sheer, closing off the black peaks beyond. Tethering the horse to a mesquite, Milton sat in the sand. The cliffs seemed almost to meet above him. Heat gathered over his head and forced down on him. A lizard skittered by his ear, up the wall. A tortoise lumbered across the wash. The water rippling through Milton became a shimmering on the far wall, scenes of his life. Milton racing after Steven, aiming at the zigzagging blue shirt, the crack of the gun, a palo verde trunk catching the rifle barrel and spinning Milton to his knees. His father's empty boots beside the couch, where he slept. His mother in baggy gray slacks, growing fatter. C.C.'s head snapping back from Milton's open palm. The pictures flickered over the cliff. Milton sat while shadow climbed the rock, and a cool breeze funneled through the canyon, and night fell. Scooping a hole in the sand, Milton lay face to the stone while the canyon rustled and sighed. The wind rushed around a stone spur, scattering sand grains on his face. Several times in the night footsteps passed so near that the ground yielded beneath Milton's head. Huddled, shivering, he thought his heart had stopped and fell asleep from terror. He dreamed of the cliffs, an unbroken glassy red.

Early in the morning, Milton woke and stretched, refreshed by the cool air. The only prints beside him were his own. That evening he wrote to C.C. in care of her California aunt, telling her he'd quit drinking.

When C.C. didn't respond, Milton wrote again, asking at least for word of Allen, who would have entered high school. C.C. replied, "When I got here the doctor said I had a broken nose. Allen says he has no father."

Milton knew he must hide to avoid drinking. When he asked Oldenburg's permission to spend a day in the granite mountains, Oldenburg said he would go, too. They camped against a rock turret. The light in the sky faded and the fire leaped up. In the weeks since the former hand Jenkins's death, Oldenburg had become, if possible, more silent. Milton, meanwhile, admitted he had been a "chatterbox," recalling high school field trips to Phoenix fifteen years before, and rodeos in Tucson, Prescott, Sells, and White River. Oldenburg, fingertips joined at his chin, occasionally nodded or smiled. Tonight Milton squatted, arms around his knees, staring into the fire. About to share his most insistent emotions with Oldenburg, Milton felt a giddy excitement, as if he were showing himself naked to a woman for the first time. Intimacy with a white man evoked stepping off the school bus in Phoenix, where buildings like great stone crystals, blanketed in dreamy smog, spilled thousands of white people into the street.

Milton told Oldenburg what C.C. had said.

"Your drinking has scarred them like acid. It will be time before they heal," Oldenburg said.

"There shouldn't be *o'otham* families," Milton exclaimed. "We should stop having children."

Oldenburg shook his head. After a while he said, "Milton, I hope you're not bitter because I won't let you drink. Drawing the line helps you. It's not easy living right. I've tried all my life and gained nothing — I lost both my sons in war and my wife divorced me to marry a piece of human trash. And still, in my own poor way, I try to live right." Oldenburg relaxed his shoulders and settled on his haunches.

Milton laid another mesquite limb across the fire. As the black of the sky intensified, the stars appeared as a glinting powder. Milton sipped two cups of coffee against the chill. Oldenburg, firelight sparkling off his silver tooth, wool cap pulled low over his stretched face, looked like an old grandmother. Laughing, Milton told him so. Oldenburg laughed too, rocking on his heels.

Soon after Oldenburg went to bed, Milton's mood changed. He hated the embers of the fire, the wind sweeping the rock knoll, the whirring of bats. He hated each stone and twig littering the campsite. His own fingers, spread across his knees, were like dumb, sleeping snakes. Poisonous things. He was glad one of them had been chopped off. Unrolling his blanket, he lay on his back, fists clenched. He dug his hands and heels into the ground as if staked to it. After lying stiffly, eyes open, for an hour, he got up, slung his coiled rope over his shoulder, and walked down the hillside.

Brush and cactus were lit by a rising moon. Reaching a sheer drop, Milton jammed boot toes into rock fissures, seized tufts of saltbush, to let himself down. In the stream bed he walked quickly until he joined the main river course. After a few miles' meandering through arroyos and over ridges, he arrived at the big sycamore and went to sleep.

Waking before dawn. Milton padded along the wash, hugging the granite. The cold morning silence was audible, a high, pure ringing. Milton heard the horse's snort before he saw it tearing clumps of grass from the gully bank, head tossing, lips drawn back over its yellow teeth. Rope at his hip, Milton stalked from boulder to boulder. When he stepped forward, whirling the lariat once, the horse reared, but quieted instantly as the noose tightened around its neck. Milton tugged the rope; the animal neighed and skipped backward, but followed.

During the next two days, Milton and Oldenburg captured three more spindly, wiry horses. Oldenburg would flush the mustangs toward Milton, who missed only once with the lasso. The stallions Milton kept in separate pens and later sold as rodeo broncs. Within a couple of weeks he had broken the mares.

Milton consumed himself in chores. Though the Box-J was a small ranch, labor was unremitting. In the fall, summer calves were rounded up and "worked" — branded with the Box-J, castrated, and dehorned. The previous winter's calves, now some

400–500 pounds each, were held in side pens for weighing and loading onto the packer's shipping trucks. The pens were so dilapidated that Milton tore them down and built new ones. Winter, Milton drove daily pickup loads of sorghum hay, a supplement for the withered winter grasses, to drop spots at the water holes. Oldenburg hired extra help for spring roundup, working the new winter calves. Summer, Milton roved on horseback, troubleshooting. The fence line would need repair. Oldenburg taught Milton to recognize cancer eye, which could destroy a cow's market value. A low water tank meant Oldenburg must overhaul the windmill. Throughout the year Milton inspected the herd, groomed the horses, maintained the buildings, kept tools and equipment in working order.

Certain moments, standing high in the stirrups, surveying the herd and the land which stretched from horizon to horizon as if mirroring the sky, Milton could believe all belonged to him.

Every two weeks, when Oldenburg drove into Casa Grande for supplies, Milton deposited half his wages — his first savings account — and mailed the rest to C.C. These checks were like money thrown blindly over the shoulder. So thoroughly had Milton driven his family from his mind that he couldn't summon them back, even if he wished to. When, just before sleep, spent from the day's work, he glimpsed C.C. and Allen, the faces seemed unreal. They were like people he had met and loved profoundly one night at a party, then forgotten.

The night of the first November frost, soon after the wild-horse roundup, Oldenburg had asked Milton if he played cards. Milton didn't.

"Too bad," Oldenburg said. "It gets dull evenings. Jenkins and I played gin rummy. We'd go to five thousand, take us a couple of weeks, and then start again."

"We could cook," Milton said.

On Sunday he and Oldenburg baked cakes. Milton missed the pressurized frosting cans with which he'd squirted flowers and desert scenes at the CETA bakery, but Oldenburg's cherry-chocolate layer cake was so good he ate a third of it. Oldenburg complimented him on his angel food.

Oldenburg bought a paperback *Joy of Cooking* in Casa Grande. Though he and Milton had been satisfied with their main dishes, they tried Carbonnade Flamande, Chicken Paprika, Quick Spaghetti Meat Pie. Milton liked New England Boiled Dinner. Mostly they made desserts. After experimenting with mousses and custard, they settled on cakes — banana, golden, seed, sponge, four-egg, Lady Baltimore, the Rombauer Special. Stacks of foil-wrapped cakes accumulated in the freezer. The men contributed cakes to charitable bake sales. Milton found that after his nightly slab of cake sleep came more easily and gently.

The men were serious in the kitchen. Standing side by side in white aprons tacked together from sheets, Milton whisking egg whites, Oldenburg drizzling chocolate over pound cake, they would say little. Milton might ask the whereabouts of a spice; Oldenburg's refusal to label the jars irritated him. Then they sat by the warm stove, feet propped on crates, and steamed themselves in the moist smells.

As they relaxed on a Sunday afternoon, eating fresh, hot cake, Oldenburg startled Milton by wondering aloud if his own wife were still alive. She had left him in 1963, and they'd had no contact since their second son was killed in 1969, more than ten years before.

"She wanted a Nevada divorce," Oldenburg said, "but I served papers on her first, and I got custody of the boys. I prevented a great injustice." He had sold his business in Colorado and bought the ranch. "The boys hated it," he said. "They couldn't wait to join the Army."

In Hashan, Milton said, she and her lover would have been killed.

Oldenburg shook his head impatiently. "He's deserted her, certainly. He was a basketball coach, and much younger than she was."

A Pima phrase — he knew little Pima — occurred to Milton. *Ne ha: jun* — all my relations. "Here is the opposite," Milton said. "We should call this the No Relations Ranch."

Oldenburg sputtered with laughter. "Yes! And we'd need a new brand. Little round faces with big X's over them."

"You'd better be careful. People would start calling it the Tick-tack-toe Ranch."

"Or a manual, you know, a sex manual, for fornication. The X's doing it to the O's."

Lightheaded from the rich, heavily frosted cake, they sprayed crumbs from their mouths, laughing.

At the Pinal County Fair in May, Oldenburg entered a walnut pie and goaded Milton into baking his specialty, a jelly roll. It received honorable mention, while Oldenburg won second prize.

Milton wrote C.C., "I'm better than a restaurant."

C.C. didn't answer. When Valley Bank opened a Hashan branch in June, Milton transferred his account and began meeting his friends for the first time in a year. They needled him, "Milton, you sleeping with that old man?" His second Friday in town, Milton was writing out a deposit slip when he heard Bosque say, "Milton Oldenburg."

"Yes, Daddy just gave him his allowance," said Helene Mashad, the teller.

Bosque punched him on the shoulder and put out his hand. Milton shook it, self-conscious about his missing finger.

Bosque was cashing his unemployment check. The factory where he'd manufactured plastic tote bags for the past six months had closed. "Doesn't matter," Bosque said, "I'm living good." Before leaving, he said to come on by.

"You know what Oldenburg's doing, don't you?" Helene said, smoothing the wrinkles from Milton's check. She still wore her long, lavender Phoenix nails and a frothy perm. After years in Phoenix, she'd relocated at the new branch, closer to her home in Black Butte. "Oldenburg wants to marry you. Then he'll get some kind of government project money for his Indian wife. Or he'll adopt you. Same deal."

"It's not me who's the wife or child, I run that place." Nervous speaking to a woman again, Milton rambled, boasting of his authority over hired crews, what Oldenburg called his "quick mind and fast hands" cutting calves or constructing a corner brace, his skill with new tools. Even his baking. "He has to be the wife," Milton said. "He's a better cook." Milton leaned his hip against the counter. "Older woman. He's so old he turned white. And he lost his shape." Milton's hands made breasts. "Nothing left."

They both laughed. Elated by the success of his joke, Milton asked her to dinner. Helene said yes, pick her up at six.

Milton was uneasy in Hashan. The dusty buildings — adobes, sandwich houses of mud and board, slump-block tract homes — seemed part of the unreal life that included his family. To kill time, he rode to the trading post in Black Butte, a few miles in the direction of Oldenburg's ranch, and read magazines. When he arrived at the bank, Helene slapped her forehead: she hadn't known he was on horseback. Phew, she said, she didn't want to go out with a horse. Milton should follow her home and take a bath first.

They never left her house. She was eager for him, and Milton realized that as a man he'd been dead for a year. They made love until early morning. Milton lay propped against the headboard, his arm encircling her, her cheek resting on his chest. She briskly stroked his hand.

"Your poor finger," she said. "I hear Lopez has little circles in his shoulder like where worms have gone into a tomato."

"It was bad," Milton said, closing his hand.

"I can't stand the men in this town, the drunken pigs," Helene said. "I don't know why I came back."

Helene wasn't what Milton wanted, but he liked her well enough to visit once or twice a month. Because she lived outside Hashan, few people knew of the affair. They would eat dinner and see a movie in Casa Grande or Phoenix, and go to bed. Sometimes they simply watched TV in bed, or drove Helene's Toyota through the desert, for miles without seeing another light.

When Milton returned from his second weekend with Helene, Oldenburg was peevish. "You drink with that woman?" he said. "You going to send her picture to your wife?" Emergencies arose that kept Milton on the ranch weekends. After selling two wild colts to a stable, Milton took Helene to Phoenix overnight. Oldenburg berated him, "The cows don't calve on Saturday and Sunday? They don't get sick? A shed doesn't blow down on Sunday?" Still the men baked together. At the beginning of the school year they entered a fund-raising bake-off sponsored by the PTO. Oldenburg won first with a Boston cream pie, and Milton's apple ring took second.

Helene transferred to Casa Grande, and Milton brought his account with her, relieved to avoid Hashan. Conversations with his friends were strained and dead. He worked; they didn't. They drank; he didn't. They had families. Milton nodded when he saw them but no longer stopped to talk.

Fridays after Helene punched out, they might browse in the Casa Grande shopping center. Milton was drawn to the camera displays, neat lumps of technology embedded in towers of colorful film boxes. The Lerners Shop manikins fascinated him — bony stick figures like the bleached branches of felled cottonwood, a beautiful still arrangement. "Imagine Pimas in those," Helene said, pointing to the squares and triangles of glittering cloth. She puffed out her cheeks and spread her arms. Milton squeezed her small buttocks. Helene's legs were the slimmest of any *o'otham* woman he'd known.

During the second week of October, when Milton and a hired crew had set up shipping pens and begun culling the calves, a rare fall downpour, tail end of a Gulf hurricane, struck. For six hours thunder exploded and snarls of lightning webbed the sky. The deluge turned the ground to slop, sprang leaks in the roof, and washed out the floodgates at the edge of the granite mountains. Cattle stampeded through the openings; one died, entangled in the barbed wire. When the skies cleared, Oldenburg estimated that a quarter of the cash animals, some three hundred dollars apiece, had escaped. The shipping trucks were due in two days.

The next morning, a new hired man brought further news: over the weekend, a fight had broken out at the Sundowner. The fat end of a pool cue had caught Audrey Lopez across the throat, crushing her windpipe. Her funeral was to be at two in the afternoon.

Milton stood helplessly before Oldenburg. In the aftermath of the storm, the sky was piercingly blue, and a bracing wind stung his cheeks. Oldenburg's collar fluttered.

"You have to go," Oldenburg said. "There's no question."

"You'll lose too much money," Milton said stubbornly. "The cattle are in the mountains and I knew every little canyon where they run."

"There's no question," Oldenburg repeated. "The right way is always plain, though we do our best to obscure it."

The service took place in a small, white, Spanish-style church. At the cemetery the mourners stood bareheaded, the sun glinting off their hair. The cemetery was on a knoll, and in the broad afternoon light the surrounding plains, spotted by occasional cloud shadows, seemed immensely distant, like valleys at the foot of a solitary butte. Milton imagined the people at the tip of a rock spire miles in the clouds. The overcast dimmed them, and shreds of cumulus drifted past their backs and bowed heads.

Afterwards the men adjourned to the Lopez house, where Vigiliano Lopez rushed about the living room, flinging chairs aside to clear a center space. A ring of some twenty men sat on chairs or against the wall. Bosque arrived carrying three cold cases and two quarts of Crown Russe. More bottles appeared. Lopez started one Crown Russe in each direction and stalked back and forth from the kitchen, delivering beer and slapping bags of potato chips at the men's feet.

At his turn, Milton passed the bottle along.

"Drink, you goddamn Milton Oldenburg," Lopez said.

Milton said, "I'll lose my job."

"So?" Lopez shrugged distractedly. "I haven't had a job in a year. I don't need a job." Lopez had been the only Pima miner at the nearby Loma Linda pit until Anaconda shut it down. He pushed his hair repeatedly off his forehead, as if trying to remember something, then turned up the radio.

Milton sat erect in the chair, hands planted on his knees. He gobbled the potato chips. No one avoided him, nor he anyone else, yet talk was impossible. Grief surged through the party like a wave. Milton felt it in over-loud conversation, silences, the restlessness — no one able to stay in one place for long. Laughter came in fits. Over the radio, the wailing tremolos of the Mexican ballads were oppressive and nerve-racking. The power of feeling in the room moved Milton and frightened him, but he was outside it.

Joining the others would be as simple as claiming the vodka bottle on its next round, Milton knew. But he remembered standing tall in the stirrups, as if he could see over the edge of the yellow horizon, the end of Oldenburg's land, and he kept his hands spread on his knees. At the thought of vodka's sickly tastelessness, bile rose in his throat. Pretending to drink, tipping the bottle and plugging it with his tongue, would be foolish and shameful. Out of friendship and respect for Lopez, he could not leave. Their wounding each other, Milton realized, had bound him more closely to Lopez.

As night fell the men became drunker and louder. Bosque went out for more liquor. When he returned, he danced with the oil-drum cookstove, blackening his hands and shirt.

"Hey, not with my wife," Lopez said, grabbing the drum and humping it against the wall. "Need somebody to do you right, baby," he said. The drum clanged to the floor. The men cheered. Lopez, knees bent and hands outstretched as if waiting for something to drop into them, lurched to the middle of the room. A smile was glazed over his face. He saw Milton.

"Drink with me, you son of a bitch," he shouted.

Milton motioned for the Crown Russe, a third full. "Half for you, half for me," he said. Marking a spot on the label with his finger, Milton took two long swallows and held out the bottle for Lopez. Lopez drank and flipped the empty bottle over his shoulder. Side by side, arms around each other, Milton and Lopez danced the *cumbia*. Lopez's weight sagged until Milton practically carried him. The man's trailing feet hooked an extension cord, sending a lamp and the radio crashing to the floor. Lopez collapsed.

Milton ran outside and retched. Immediately he was refreshed and lucid. The stars burned like drill-points of light. Patting the horse into an easy walk, Milton sat back in the saddle, reins loose in his lap, and gave himself to the brilliant stillness. As his eyes adjusted to the night, he could distinguish the black silhouettes of mountains against the lesser dark of the sky. Faint stars emerged over the ranges, bringing the peaks closer. The mountains were calm and friendly, even the jagged line of the Ka kai.

That night Milton dreamed that a chocolate-colored flood swept through Hashan. The *o'otham* bobbed on the foam; from the shore others drove backward into the torrent, arms raised symmetrically by their heads. Receding, the flood left bodies swollen in the mud — Milton's brother Lee, their mother, belly down, rising in a mound. Milton, long hair fixed in the mud, stared upward. His hands were so full of fingers they had become agaves, clusters of fleshy, spiny leaves. Peering down at him, C.C. and Allen were black against the sun, arms crooked as if for flight. Milton was glad they had escaped.

Milton woke serene and energetic, the dream forgotten. Over breakfast Oldenburg studied him intently — clear gray eyes, a slight frown — but said nothing. The penned calves were weighed and loaded onto the shipping trucks. Many remained free, and the year would be a loss.

Milton wrote C.C. of Audrey Lopez's death. "I had a big drink to keep Lopez company," he added, "but I threw it up. It was the first booze in more than a year. I don't like it anymore."

Lying beside Milton the following weekend, Helene said, "Poor finger. I'll give you another one." She laid her pinky against the stub so a new finger seemed to grow. Her lavender nail looked like the fancy gem of a ring. She lifted, lowered the finger. "And Lopez with the purple spots on his shoulder like the eyes of a potato," she said. She shifted, and her small, hard nipple brushed Milton's side. "It's a wonder you two didn't fight."

"Shut up," Milton said. "His wife is dead."

"I know. It's terrible." She had worried for him, Helene said, knowing he would be at the funeral with Lopez. He should have brought her.

"I didn't want you there," Milton said. "You don't have the right feelings." He left before dawn and hadn't returned to Helene when C.C. replied.

"I was shocked to hear about Audrey," C.C. wrote. "I feel sad about it every day. Hashan is such a bad place. But it isn't any better here. At Allen's school there are gangs and not just Mexicans but black and white too."

She wrote again: "I miss you. I've been thinking about coming back. Allen says he won't but he'll come with me in the end. The money has helped. Thank you."

Milton threw up his arms and danced on the corral dirt, still moist and reddened from fluke autumn rains. Shouting, he danced on one leg and the other, dipping from side to side as if soaring, his head whirling. Oldenburg's nagging — where will they live? — worried him little. Over dinner Oldenburg suggested, "They'll live in your old place, and you can visit them on weekends. We'll have to move our baking to the middle of the week."

Milton knew he must be with the *o'otham*. Announcing a ride into the mountains, he saddled up and galloped toward Ha-shan. Because he couldn't see the faces of his family his joy felt weirdly rootless. The past year he had killed them inside. The sudden aches for Allen, the sensation of carrying C.C.'s weight in his arms from the adobe to the ranch house, were like the twinges of heat, cold and pain from his missing finger. As if straining after their elusive faces, Milton rode faster. His straw hat, blown back and held by its cord, flapped at his ear. The horse's neck was soaked with sweat.

Bosque's fat wife said he wasn't home. Milton made a plan for the Sundowner: after one draft for sociability, he would play the shuffleboard game. Tying up at a light pole, Milton hesi-tated in the lounge doorway. The familiarity of the raw wood beams crisscrossing the bare Sheetrock walls frightened him. But Bosque, sliding his rear off a barstool, called, "Milton Ol-denburg."

"C.C.'s hauling her little tail home," Milton announced. "And the boy."

"All *riiight*." Bosque pumped his hand up and down. Milton's embarrassment at his missing finger disappeared in the vast-ness of Bosque's grip. Friends he hadn't spoken to in months surrounded him. "When's she coming? They going to live on the ranch? Oldenburg will have a whole Indian family now." Warmed by their celebration of his good luck, Milton ordered pitchers. His glass of draft was deep gold and sweeter than he had remembered, though flat. Others treated him in return. Someone told a story of Bosque building a scrap wood raft to sail the shallow lake left by the rains. Halfway across, the raft had broken apart and sunk. "Bosque was all mud up to his eyes," the storyteller said. "He looked like a bull rolling in cow flop." Everyone laughed.

Fuzzy after a half-dozen beers. Milton felt his heart pound, and his blood. He saw them then — C.C., wings of hair, white teeth, dimpled round cheeks. Allen's straight bangs and small, unsmiling mouth. Their eyes were black with ripples of light, reflections on a pool. Milton was drawn into that pool, lost. Terror washed over him like a cold liquid, and he ordered a vodka.

"I'm a drunk," he told the neighbor on his right.

"Could be. Let's check that out, Milton," the man said.

"I never worked."

"No way," the man said, shaking his head.

"I didn't make a living for them."

"Not even a little bitty bit," the man agreed.

"Not even this much," Milton said, holding his thumb and forefinger almost closed, momentarily diverted by the game. "I hurt them."

Holding up his hands, the man yelled, "Not me."

"I tortured them. They don't belong to me. I don't have a family," Milton mumbled. Quickly he drank three double vodkas. The jukebox streamed colors, and he floated on its garbled music.

Shoving against the men's room door, Milton splashed into the urinal, wavering against the stall. He groped for the Sundowner's rear exit. The cold bit through his jacket. Milton pitched against a stack of bricks.

Waking in the dark, Milton jumped to his feet. C.C. was coming, and his job was in danger. He was foreman of a white man's ranch. Allen and C.C. would be amazed at his spread. With a bigger bank account than three-quarters of Hashan, Milton could support them for a year on savings alone. The night before was an ugly blur. But his tongue was bitter, his head thudded, he had the shakes. Cursing, Milton mounted and kicked the horse into a canter. To deceive Oldenburg he must work like a crazy man and sweat out his hangover. The fits of nausea made him moan with frustration. He kicked the horse and struck his own head.

Milton arrived an hour after sunup. Shooing the horse into the corral with a smack to the rump, he stood foggily at the gate, unable to remember his chore from the previous day. A ladder leaning against the barn reminded him: patching. He lugged a roll of asphalt roofing up the ladder. Scrambling over the steep pitch didn't frighten him, even when he slipped and tore his hands. He smeared tar, pressed the material into place, drove the nails. Every stroke was true, two per nail. Milton had laid half a new roof when Oldenburg called him.

"Come down." Oldenburg was pointing to the corral. The gate was still ajar. Milton's horse, head drooping, dozed against the wall, but the other three were gone.

Milton stood before him, wobbly from exertion, blood draining from his head.

"You lied," Oldenburg said. "You abandoned your job. The week is *my* time. You've been drunk. I'm going to have to let you go, Milton."

Milton couldn't speak.

"You understand, don't you?" Oldenburg said more rapidly. His eyes flicked down, back to Milton. "Do you see what happens?" His arms extended toward the empty corral.

"So I lose a day running them down."

Smiling slightly, Oldenburg shook his head. "You miss the point. It would be wrong for me to break my word. You'd have no cause to believe me again and our agreement would be meaningless."

"Once a year I get drunk," Milton burst out. "We'll put a name on it, November Something Milton's Holiday."

Oldenburg smiled again. "Once a month . . . once a week . . . I'm sorry. I'll give you two weeks' pay but you can leave any time." He turned.

"I've worked hard for you!" Milton's throat felt as if it were closing up.

Oldenburg stopped, brow furrowed. "It's sad," he said. "You've managed the Box-J better than I could. I'm going to miss our baking." He paused. "But we have to go on, Milton, don't you see? My family leaves me, Jenkins leaves me, you leave me. But *I* go on." He walked away.

Two long steps, a knee in the back, arms around the neck, and he could break the man in half — Milton's arms dropped. He had lost his urge for violence. Long after Oldenburg had disappeared into the open green range where the horses were, Milton stood by the corral. Then, arms over his head as if escaping a cloudburst, he ran into the adobe, packed his belongings in a sheet, and that afternoon rode the exhausted horse back to his old home.

To C.C. Milton wrote, "I don't have my job anymore but there's plenty of money in the bank." Weeks later she replied, "Milton, I know what's going on. I can't come home to this." But she would continue to write him, she said. Milton saw no one. Pacing the house, he talked to the portraits over the TV — Allen's eighth-grade class picture, a computer-drawn black-dot composition of C.C. from the O'otham Tash carnival. He disturbed nothing, not even the year-and-a-half-old pile of dishes in the sink.

For several weeks he laid fence for a Highway Maintenance heavy equipment yard. Working with a new type of fence, chain link topped with barbed wire, cheered him. The foreman was lax, married to one of Milton's cousins, so when Milton requested the leftover spools of barbed wire, he said, "Sure. It's paid for."

Milton dug holes around his house and cut posts from the warped, gnarled mesquite growing in the vacant land. As he worked, the blue sky poured through chinks in the posts, reminding Milton pleasantly of the timeless first days repairing the line at Oldenburg's range. When he had finished stringing the wire, Milton's house was enclosed in a neat box — two thorned strands, glinting silver. Sunlight jumped off the metal in zigzag bolts. In Hashan, where fences were unknown and the beige ground was broken only by houses, catcus, and drab shrubs, the effect was as startling as if Milton had wrapped his home in Christmas lights.

Milton sat on the back doorstep, drinking beer. Discouraged by the fence, no one visited at first. But dogs still ran through the yard, as did children, who preferred scaling the fence to slithering under it. Their legs waggled precariously on the stiffly swaying wire; then they hopped down, dashed to the opposite side, and climbed out, awkward as spiders. Milton's fence became a community joke, which made him popular. Instead of walking through the gap behind the house, friends would crawl between the strands or try to vault them. Or they would lean on the posts, passing a beer back and forth while they chatted.

Keeping her promise, C.C. wrote that Allen had shot up tall. Even running track he wore his Walkman, she said. But he smoked, and she had to yell at him. Last term he'd made nearly all A's.

Milton grew extremely fat, seldom leaving the house except to shop or work the odd jobs his new skills brought him. Through spring and summer he drowsed on the doorstep. In November, almost a year after he'd left Oldenburg's, he fell asleep on the concrete slab and spent the night without jacket or blanket. The next day he was very sick, and Bosque and Lopez drove him to the hospital. The doctor said he had pneumonia.

Milton's first day in ICU, Bosque and Lopez shot craps with him during visiting hours. But as Milton's lungs continued to fill with fluids, his heart, invaded by fatty tissues from his years of drinking, weakened. Four days after entering the hospital, he suffered a heart attack.

In the coronary ward, restricted to ten-minute visits, Milton dreamed, feeling as if the fluids had leaked into his skull and his brain was sodden. In one dream the agaves again sprouted from his wrists, their stalks reaching into the sky. Milton gave the name *ne ha: jun* — all my relations — to his agave hands.

The next morning C.C. and Allen appeared in the doorway. Huge, billowing, formless as smoke, they approached the bed in a peculiar rolling motion. Milton was afraid. From the dreams he realized his deepest love was drawn from a great lake far beneath him, and that lake was death. But understanding, he lost his fear. He held out his arms to them.

ALICE MUNRO

Monsieur les Deux Chapeaux

FROM GRAND STREET

"Is THAT your brother out there?" Davidson said. "What's he up to?"

Colin went over to the window to see what Ross was up to. Not much. Ross was using the long-handled clippers to clip the grass along the sidewalk to the front door of the school. He was working at a normal rate and seemed to be paying attention to what he was doing.

"What's he up to?" Davidson said.

Ross was wearing two hats. One was the green and white peaked cap he had got last summer at the feed store, and the other one, on top, was the old floppy hat of pinkish straw that their mother wore in the garden.

"Search me," said Colin.

Davidson was going to think that was smart-arse.

"You mean why has he got the two hats on? I don't know. I honestly don't know. Maybe he forgot."

This was in the front office, during school hours on Friday afternoon, the secretaries bent over their desks but keeping their ears open. Colin had a gym class going on at the moment — he had just come into the office to find out what had happened about a boy who had begged off sick half an hour before — and he hadn't expected to find Davidson prowling around here. He hadn't come prepared to provide explanations about Ross.

"Is he a forgetful kind of person?" the principal said.

"No more than average."

"Maybe it's supposed to be funny."

Colin was silent.

"I've got a sense of humor myself but you can't start being funny around kids. You know the way they are. They'll see enough to laugh at anyway, without giving them extra. They'll make any little thing an excuse for distraction and then you know what you've got."

"You want me to go out and talk to him?" Colin said.

"Leave it for now. There's probably a couple of classrooms already have their eye on him and that'd just get them more interested. Mr. Box can speak to him if somebody has to. Actually Mr. Box was mentioning him."

Coonie Box was the school janitor, who had hired Ross for the spring cleanup on the grounds.

"Oh? What?" said Colin.

"He says your brother keeps his own hours a bit."

"Does he do the work all right?"

"He didn't say he didn't." Davidson gave Colin one of his tight-lipped, dismissive, much-imitated smiles. "Just that he's inclined to be independent."

Colin and Ross looked rather alike, being tall, as their father had been, and fair-skinned and fair-haired, like their mother. Colin was athletic, with a shy, severe expression. Ross, though younger, was soft around the middle, and had a looser look. And he had an expression which seemed both leering and innocent.

Ross was not retarded. He had kept up with his age group in school. His mother said he was a genius of the mechanical kind. Nobody else would go that far.

"So? Is Ross getting used to getting up in the morning? Has he got an alarm?" Colin said to his mother.

"They're lucky to have him," Sylvia said.

Colin hadn't known whether he'd find her home. She worked shifts as a nurse's aide at the hospital, and when she wasn't working she was often out. She had a lot of friends and commitments.

"And you're lucky I'm in," she said. "I'm on the early shift this week and next but usually I go over to Eddy's after work and do a big of housecleaning for him."

Eddy was Sylvia's boyfriend, a dapper seventy-year-old, twice a widower, with no children and plenty of money, a retired garage owner and car dealer who could certainly have afforded to hire somebody to clean his house. What did Sylvia know about housecleaning, anyway? All last summer she had kept the winter plastic tacked up over her front windows, to save the trouble of putting it up again. Colin's wife, Glenna, said that gave her the same feeling as bleary glasses — she couldn't stand it. And the house — the same insul-brick-covered cottage Sylvia and Ross and Colin had always lived in — was so full of furniture and junk some rooms had turned into passageways. Most surfaces were piled high with magazines, newspapers, plastic and paper bags, catalogues, circulars, and fliers for sales that had come and gone, in some cases for businesses that had folded and products that had disappeared from the market. In any ashtray or ornamental dish you might find a button or two, keys, cut-out coupons promising ten cents off, an earring, a cold capsule still in its plastic wrap, a vitamin pill turning to powder, a mascara brush, a broken clothespin. And Sylvia's cupboards were full of all kinds of cleaning fluids and polishes — not the regular kind bought in stores, but products supposedly of unique and dazzling effectiveness, signed for at parties. She was kept broke paying for all the things she had signed for at parties — cosmetics, pots and pans, baking utensils, plastic bowls. She loved giving and going to those parties, also bridal showers and baby showers, and good-bye showers for her co-workers leaving the hospital. Here in these deeply cluttered rooms she had dispensed, on her own, a great deal of careless, hopeful hospitality.

She poured water from the kettle onto the powdered coffee in their cups, which she had rinsed lightly at the sink.

"Was it boiling?" said Colin.

"Near enough."

She shook some pink-and-white marshmallow cookies out of their plastic package.

"I told Eddy I needed the afternoon off. He's getting to think he owns me."

"Can't have that," said Colin.

About her boyfriends, he usually took a lightly critical tone.

Sylvia was a short woman with a large head — made larger by her fluffy, graying hair — and broad hips and shoulders. One of her boyfriends used to tell her she looked like a baby elephant, and she took that — at first — as an endearment. Colin thought there was something clumsy and appealing about her figure and her wide-open face with its pink, soft skin, clear blue eyes under almost nonexistent eyebrows, her eager all-purpose smile. Something maddening as well.

The subject of Ross was one of the few things that could make her face tighten up. That, and the demands and peculiarities of boyfriends, once they were on the wane.

Was Eddy on the verge of waning?

Sylvia said, "I've been telling him he's just too darn possessive." Then she told Colin a joke that was going round at the hospital, about a black man and a white man at the urinal.

"If you're working the early shift," said Colin, "how do you know what time Ross gets up?"

"Somebody complaining about Ross, is that it?"

"Well. They're just saying he likes to keep his own hours."

"They'll find out. If they have any mechanical thing or electrical thing that goes wrong, they'll be glad they got Ross. Ross has just as many brains as you do but they have gone in a different direction."

"I won't argue that," said Colin. "But his job is on the grounds."

Glenna said that the reason Sylvia proclaimed Ross to be a genius — aside from the fact that he really was clever about engines — was that he had the other side of a genius. He was absent-minded and not very clean. He called attention to himself. He was weird, and that was the way a genius was supposed to be. But taken by itself, said Glenna, that wasn't enough proof.

Then she always said, "I like Ross, though. You can't help liking him. I like him *and* your mother. I like her too." Colin believed she did like Ross. He wasn't so sure she liked his mother.

"I only go over to your place when I'm invited, Colin," was what his mother said. "It's your home but it's Glenna's home too. Nevertheless I'm glad Ross feels so welcome."

"I went in the office today," Colin said, "and there was Davidson looking out the window." He hadn't known whether or not he was going to tell his mother about the hats. As usual, he wanted to get her a little upset about Ross, but not too upset. The sight of Ross working away there, with the electric clippers, all alone on the school grounds, a floppy pink straw hat perched on his seed-corn cap, had seemed to Colin something new, newly disturbing. He had seen Ross in odd get-ups before — once in the supermarket wearing Sylvia's blond wig. That seemed more calculated than today's appearance, more definitely a joke with an audience in mind. Today, too, he could be thinking about all the kids behind the windows. And teachers and typists and Davidson and anybody driving by. But not them particularly. Something about Ross today suggested the audience had grown and faded — it included the whole town, the whole world, and Ross was almost indifferent to it. A sign, Colin thought. He didn't know what of — just a sign that Ross was further along the way that Ross was going.

Sylvia didn't seem concerned with that part of it. She was upset, but for another reason.

"My hat. He's bound to lose it. I'll give him 'Hail Columbia.' I'll give him proper *hell*. It may not look like much, but I really value that hat."

The first words Ross every spoke directly to Glenna were, "Do you know the only thing that's the matter with you?"

"What?" said Glenna, looking alarmed. She was a tall, frail girl with dark curly hair, white skin, very light blue eyes, and a habit of holding on to her bottom lip with her teeth, which gave her a wistful, worried air. She was the sort of girl who often wears pale blue (she had a fuzzy sweater on of that color) and a delicate chain around her neck with a cross or heart on it, or a name. (Glenna wore her name, because people had trouble spelling it.)

"The only thing the matter with you," said Ross, chewing and nodding, "is that I didn't find you first!"

A relief. They all laughed. This was during Glenna's first dinner at Sylvia's house. Sylvia and Colin and Glenna were eating take-out Chinese food — Sylvia had set a pile of plates and forks and even paper napkins beside the cardboard cartons — and Ross was eating a pizza, which Sylvia had ordered especially for him because he didn't like Chinese food.

Glenna suggested that Ross might like to come to the drive-in with them that night, and he did. The three of them sat on top of Colin's car, with Glenna in the middle, drinking beer.

It became a family joke. What would have happened if Glenna had met Ross first?

Colin wouldn't have had a chance.

Finally Colin had to ask her, "What if you *had* met him first? Would you have gone out with him?"

"Ross is sweet," Glenna said.

"But would you have gone out with him?"

She looked embarrassed, which was really all the answer Colin needed.

"Ross isn't the type you go out with."

Sylvia said, "Ross, some day you are going to find a wonderful girl."

But Ross seemed to have given up looking. He stopped calling up girls and crowing like a rooster into the phone, he no longer drove slowly along the street, trailing them, sounding the horn as if in Morse code. One Saturday night at Colin and Glenna's house, he said he had given up on women, it was so hard to find a decent one, and anyway he had never gotten over Wilma Barry.

"Wilma Barry, who was that?" said Glenna. "Were you in love, Ross? When?"

"Grade nine."

"Wilma Barry! Was she pretty? Did she know how you felt about her?"

"Yeah. Yeah. Yeah, I guess."

Colin said, "Jesus, the whole school knew!"

"Where is she now, Ross?" said Glenna.

"Gone. Married."

"Did she like you too?"

"Couldn't stand me," said Ross complacently.

Colin was remembering the persecution of Wilma Barry: how Ross would go into empty classrooms and write her name on the blackboard in little dots of colored chalk, or little hearts;

how he went to watch the girls' basketball games, in which she played, and carried on like a madman every time she got near the ball or the basket. She dropped out of the team. She took to hiding in the girls' washroom and sending out scouts to tell her if the coast was clear. Ross knew this and hid in broom closets, so he could pop out and mournfully whistle at her. She dropped out of school altogether and married at seventeen. Ross was too much for her.

"What a shame," said Glenna sympathetically.

"I did love that Wilma," Ross said, and shook his head. "Colin, tell Glenna about me and the piece of pie!"

So Colin told that story, a favorite with everybody who had gone to high school around their time. Colin and Ross always brought their lunch to school because their mother worked and the cafeteria was too expensive. They always had bologna and ketchup sandwiches and store pie. One day they were all being kept in at noon for some reason, grades nine and ten together, so Ross and Colin were in the same room. Ross had his lunch in his desk, and right in the middle of whatever lecture they were getting, he took out a big piece of apple pie and started to eat it. What in the devil do you think you're doing? the teacher yelled, and Ross without a moment's hesitation thrust the pie under his bum and sat on it, bringing his sticky hands together in a clap of innocence.

"I didn't do it to be funny!" Ross told Glenna. "I just couldn't think what to do with that pie but stick it underneath me!"

"I can just see you!" said Glenna, laughing. "Oh, Ross, I can just see you! Like some character on television!"

"Didn't we ever tell you that before?" said Ross. "How come we never?"

"I kind of think we did," said Colin.

Glenna said, "You did, but it's funny to hear it again."

"All right, Colin, tell her about the time you shot me dead!"

"You told me that too, and I don't want to ever have to hear it again," said Glenna.

"Why not?" said Ross, disappointed.

"Because it's horrible."

Colin knew that when he got home from Sylvia's Ross would be there ahead of him, working on the car. He was right. It was nearly the end of May now, and Ross had started his car wrecking and combo building in Colin's yard as soon as the snow was gone. There wasn't enough room for this activity at Sylvia's.

Plenty of room for it here. Colin and Glenna had bought a run-down cottage set far back from the street in the remains of an orchard. They were fixing it up. They used to live over the Laundromat, and when Glenna had to quit work — she was a teacher, too, a Primary Specialist — because of being pregnant with Lynnette, she took on the job of managing the Laundromat so they could live rent free and save money. They talked then about moving — right away, to someplace remote and adventurous-sounding like Labrador or Mooseknee or Yellowknife. They talked about going to Europe and teaching the children of Canadian servicemen. Meanwhile this house came up for sale, and it happened to be a house Glenna had always looked at and wondered about when she took Lynnette for a walk in the carriage or stroller. She had grown up in air force bases all over the country, and she loved to look at old houses.

Now, Glenna said, with all the work there was to do on this place, it looked as if they knew where they'd be and what they'd be doing forevermore.

Ross had two cars to wreck and one to build. The Chevy was a 1958 model that had been in an accident. The windshield was smashed, and the radiator and fan shoved back on the engine. The wiring was burned. Ross hadn't been able to tell how the engine ran until he got the fan and the radiator and the banged-up sheet metal out of the way. Then he hot-wired it and filled the block with water. It ran. Ross said he knew it would. That was what he had bought the car for, the body being so damaged it was no use to him. The body he was using belonged to a 1971 Camaro. The top coat of paint had fallen off in sheets when he used the stripper, but now he was having to work with the hose and scouring pads on what was underneath. He was going to have to take out the dents in the roof with a body hammer and cut out the rusted sections of the floorboards to put in an aluminum panel. That and a lot more. It looked as if the job might take all summer.

Right now Ross was working on the wheels with Glenna helping him. Glenna was polishing the trim rings and center caps, which had been taken off, while Ross scoured the wheels themselves and went over them with a wire brush. Lynnette was in her playpen by the front door.

Colin sniffed the air for stripper. Ross didn't use a respirator; he said you didn't need to in the fresh air. Colin knew he should trust Glenna not to expose herself and Lynnette to that. But he sniffed, and it was all right; they hadn't been using any. To cover up, he said, "Smells like spring."

"You don't need to tell me," said Glenna, who was subject to hay fever. "I can feel the clouds of pollen just getting ready to move in."

"Did you get your shots?" said Colin.

"Not today."

"That was dumb."

"I know," said Glenna polishing like mad. "I was going to walk over to the hospital, then I got fooling around with these and I got sort of hypnotized."

Lynette walked cautiously around the sides of her playpen, holding on, then lifted her arms and said, "Up, Dad." Colin was delighted with the firm, businesslike way she said "Dad" — not "Da" as other babies did.

"What I've decided I'm going to do," said Ross. "I'm going to put on a rust remover that's a conditioner and then a conversion coating and then a primer. But I got to get every last bit of the old filler out because the stripper could've got into it and it'd look like a mess through the new paint. I'm going to use acrylic lacquer. What do you think?"

"What color?" said Colin. He was talking to two rear ends, both in jeans. Glenna's jeans were cut-offs, baring her long, powdery-white legs. No sign of either hat on Ross, now. He sobered up remarkably whenever he got near his car.

"I was thinking yellow. Then I thought red always looks good on a Camaro."

"We'll get the paint chart and hold it up in front of Lynnette and let her choose," said Glenna. "Okay, Ross? Whatever she points to? Will we do that?"

"Okay," said Ross.

"She'll point to red. She loves red."

"Take it easy," said Colin to Lynnette as he went past her into the house. She started to complain, not too seriously. He got three bottles of beer out of the refrigerator. During the winter they had worked inside the house, pulling off wallpaper and tearing up linoleum, and they had got the place now to a stage in which all the innards were showing. There were bats of pink insulating material held in place under sheets of plastic. Piles of lumber to be used in the new partitions sat around drying. You walked on springy wide boards in the kitchen. Ross had shown up regularly to help but he had not offered since he started on the car.

Glenna had said, "I think he started thinking about the car when he realized he wasn't going to live with us in the house."

Colin said, "Ross always fooled around with cars."

But Ross had never cared so much before about what a car looked like. He had cared about the getaway speed and top speed and whatever menacing or ridiculous-sounding noise he could get out of it. He had had two accidents. Once he rolled his car into a ditch and walked away without a scratch. Another time he had taken a short cut, as he said, through a vacant lot in town and run into a heap of junk that included an old bathtub. When Colin came home from college on the weekend there was Ross with purple bruises along the side of his face, a cut over one ear, and his ribs taped.

"I had a collision with a bathtub."

Was he drunk, or high?

"I don't think so," said Ross.

This time he seemed to have something else in mind than gunning the engine and fishtailing down the street, leaving a trail of burn marks on the pavement. He wanted a real car, what the magazines he read called a "street car." Could that be to get girls? Or just to show himself off in, driving in a respectable style with an occasional flash of speed or powerful growl when he took off at the lights? Maybe this time he could even do without a trick horn.

"This is one car isn't going to be run up and down the main street like a maniac or hittin' a hundred on the gravel," he said.

"That's right, Ross," said Glenna. "Time you graduated."

"Beer," said Colin, and put it down where Ross could reach.

"Ross?" said Glenna ("Thank you," she said to Colin). "Ross, you're going to have to rip the carpet off the doors. You are. It looks okay but really it stinks. I can smell it. Over here."

Colin sat on the step with Lynnette on one knee, knowing he wasn't going to bring up the matter of being on time, let alone of hats. He wasn't going to remind Ross that this was the first job he'd had in over a year. He was too tired and now he felt too peaceful. Some of this peacefulness was Glenna's doing. Glenna didn't ally herself with anybody who was completely weird or with any futile undertaking. And there she was, looking at her face in the caps, sniffing the carpet panels, taking Ross and his car seriously — so seriously that when Colin first got out of the car and saw her squatted down, polishing, he had felt like asking if this was the way things were going to go all summer, with her so involved with Ross's car she wouldn't have time to work on the house. He'd be kicking himself now if he'd said that. What would he do if she didn't like Ross, if she hadn't like him from the start and agreed to have him around? When Ross said what the one thing wrong was, at their first meeting, and Glenna smiled, not politely or condescendingly but with true surprise and pleasure, Colin had felt more than relief. He had felt as if from now on Ross could stop being a secret weight on him; he would have someone to share Ross with. He had never counted Sylvia.

The other thought that had crossed Colin's mind was dirty in every sense of the word. Ross never would. He was a prude. Ross glowered and stuck his big lip out and looked as if he half felt like crying when there was a sexy scene at the movies.

On Saturday morning there was a large package of chicken pieces thawing on the counter, reminding Colin that Glenna had asked Sylvia and Eddy and her friend — their friend — Nancy to come over for supper.

Glenna had gone to the hospital, walking, with Lynnette in the stroller, to get her hay fever shots. Ross was already working. He had come into the house and put a tape on, leaving the door open so that he could hear it. *Chariots of Fire.* That was Glenna's. Ross usually listened to country and western.

Colin was just home from the Builder's Supply, where they

didn't have his ceiling panels in yet in spite of promises. He went out to look at the grass he had planted last Saturday, a patch of lawn to the side of the house, fenced off with string. He gave it some water, then watched Ross sanding the wheels. Before long and without quite intending to, he was sanding as well. It was hypnotizing, as Glenna had said, you just kept on at it. After they were sufficiently sanded down, the wheels had to be painted with primer (the tires protected from that with masking tape and paper), and when the primer was dry, they had to be scuffed off with a copper pad and cleaned again with a wax and grease remover. Ross had all this planned out.

They worked all morning and then all afternoon. Glenna made hamburgers for lunch. When Colin told her he couldn't do the kitchen ceiling because the panels hadn't come, she said he couldn't have worked on the kitchen anyway because she had to make a dessert.

Ross went uptown and bought a touch-up gun and some metallic charcoal paint, as well as Armor-All for the tires. This was a good idea — the touch-up gun made it a lot easier to get into the recesses of the wheels.

Nancy arrived about the middle of the afternoon, driving her dinky little Chevette and wearing a strange new outfit — rather long, loose shorts and a top that was like a bag with holes cut for the head and arms, the whole thing dirt-colored and held at the waist with a long raggedy purple sash. Nancy had been brought in that year to teach French from kindergarten to grade eight, that being the new requirement. She was a rangy, pale, flat-chested girl with frizzy corn-yellow hair and an intelligent, mournful face. Colin found her likable and disturbing. She came around like an ordinary old friend, bringing her own beer and her own music. She chattered to Lynnette, and had a made-up name for her — Winnie-Winnie. But whose old friend was she? Before last September none of them had ever set eyes on her. She was in her early thirties, had lived with three different men and did not think she would ever marry. The first time she met Sylvia and Eddy she had told them all about the three men and about the drugs she had taken. Sylvia egged her on, of course. Eddy didn't know what she was talking about, and

when she mentioned acid, he may have thought she was referring to battery acid. She told you how she felt every time you
saw her. Not that she had a headache or a cold or swollen glands
or sore feet, but whether she was depressed or elated or whatever. And she had an odd way of talking about this town. She
talked about it as if it were a substance, a lump, as if the people
in it were all glued together, and as if the lump had — for her
— peculiar and usually discouraging characteristics.

"I saw you yesterday, Ross," said Nancy. She sat on the step,
having opened a beer and put on Joan Armatrading, "Show
Some Emotion." She got up and lifted Lynnette out of the playpen. "I saw you at the school. You were beautiful."

Colin said, "There's stuff lying all around here she could put
in her mouth. Little nuts and stuff. You have to watch her."

"I'll watch her," said Nancy. "Winnie-Winnie." She was tickling Lynnette with the fringe of her sash.

"Monsieur les Deux Chapeaux," she said. "I had grade three
all looking out the window and admiring you. That's what we
decided to call you. Monsieur les Deux Chapeaux. Monsieur of
the Two Hats."

"We do know some French. Strange as it may seem," said
Colin.

"I don't," said Ross. "I don't know what she's talking about."

"Oh, Ross," said Nancy, tickling Lynnette. "Aren't you my
little honey bear, my little Winnie-Winnie? Ross, you were beautiful. What an inspiration on a dull dragged-out old Friday
afternoon."

Nancy had a way of making Ross turn sullen. To her face,
behind her back, he often said that she was crazy.

"You're crazy, Nancy. You never saw me. You're seeing
things. You got double vision."

"Sure," said Nancy. "Absolutely, Monsieur les Deux Chapeaux. So what are you doing? Tell me. You taking up car
wrecking?"

"We're painting these wheels at the moment," said Colin. Ross
wouldn't say anything.

"I once took a course," said Nancy. "I took a course in elementary mechanics so I would know what was going on with my
car and I wouldn't have to go into the garage squeaking like a

little woman." She squeaked like a little woman, "Oh, there's this funny noise and tell me what's under the hood, please? Good heavens, it's an engine! Well, so I wouldn't do that I took this course and I got so interested I took another course and I was actually thinking about becoming a mechanic. I was going to get down in the grease pit. But really I'm too conventional. I couldn't face the hassle. I'd rather teach French."

She put Lynnette on her hip and walked over to look at the engine.

"Ross? You going to steam-clean this?"

"Yeah," said Ross. "I'll have to see about renting one."

"Also I lived with a guy who was involved with cars and you know what he did? When he had to rent a steamer he used to ask around to see if anybody else wanted it done, and then he'd charge them ten dollars. So he made money on the rent."

"Yeah," Ross said.

"Just suggesting. You'll need a different radiator brace, won't you? V-eights mount the radiator behind the brace."

After that Ross came out of his sulk — he saw he might as well — and started showing her things.

"Come on, Colin," Nancy said, "Glenna says we need more whipping cream. We can go in my car. You hold Lynnette."

"I haven't got a shirt on," said Colin.

"Lynnette doesn't care. I'll go into the store. Come on. Glenna wants it now."

In the car she said, "I wanted to talk to you."

"I figured that."

"It's about Ross. About what he's doing."

"You mean him going around in those hats? What? What did Davidson say?"

"I don't mean anything about that. I mean that car."

Colin was relieved. "What about the car?"

"That engine. Colin, that engine is too big. He can't put that engine in that body."

Her voice was dramatically deep and calm.

"Ross knows quite a bit about cars," Colin said.

"I believe you. I never said Ross was dumb. He does know.

But that engine, if he puts it in, I'm afraid it will simply break the drive shaft, not immediately but sooner or later. And sooner rather than later. Kids do that a lot. They put in a big powerful engine for the pickup and speed they want, and one day, you know, really, it can take the whole car over. It literally flips it over. Breaks the shaft. The thing is, with kids, something else often goes wrong first or they wreck it up. So he could have done this before and got away with it. Thought he was getting away with it. I'm not just doing the big expert, Colin. I swear to God I'm not."

"Okay," said Colin. "You're not."

"You know I'm not? Colin?"

"I know you're not."

"I just could not bring myself to say anything to Ross. He is so steamed up about it. That's what they say here, isn't it? Steamed up? I couldn't come out with a major criticism like that. Anyway he might not believe me."

"I don't know if he'd believe me," said Colin. "Look. You are dead sure?"

"Don't say dead!" Nancy begged him, in that phony-sounding voice he had to believe was sincere. "I am absolutely and undeniably sure, and if I wasn't I would not have opened my big mouth."

"He knows he's putting in a bigger engine. He knows that. He must figure it's all right."

"He figures wrong. Colin, I love Ross. I don't want to upset his project."

"You better not let Sylvia hear you say that."

"Say what? She doesn't want him killed, either."

"That you love Ross."

"I love you all, Colin," said Nancy, pulling into the Mac's Milk lot. "I really do."

"This is what I did, I'll tell you," said Sylvia, speaking mostly to Nancy, after a fourth glass of rosé. "I gave myself a twenty-fifth wedding anniversary party. What do you think of that?"

"Marvelous!" said Nancy. Sylvia had just told her the joke about the black man and white man at the urinal and Colin could see that it had given her some difficulty.

"I mean, without a husband. I mean, he wasn't still living with me, I wasn't still living with him. He was still living. In Peterborough. He isn't still living now. But I said, I have been married twenty-five years, and I still am married. So don't I deserve to have a party?"

Nancy said, "Certainly."

They were sitting at the picnic table out in the backyard, just a few steps from the kitchen door, under the blossoming black-cherry tree. Glenna had spread a white cloth and used her wedding china.

"This will be a patio by next year," Glenna said.

"See," said Sylvia, "if you had've used plastic, you could scoop all this up now and put it in the garbage."

Eddy lit her cigarette. He himself had not stopped smoking throughout the meal.

Nancy picked a soggy strawberry out of the ruined crown of meringue. "It's lovely here now," she said.

"At least no bugs yet," said Glenna.

Sylvia said, "True. Strawberries would have been a lot cheaper by next week but you couldn't've ate out here because of the bugs."

That seemed funny to Nancy. She started laughing, and Eddy joined in. For some unstated reason — with him it would have to be unstated — he admired Nancy and all she did. Sylvia, bewildered but good-humored, with her face as pink as a tissue-paper rose starting to look pretty crumpled round the edges, said, "I don't see what's funny. What did I say?"

"Go on," said Ross.

"Go on what?"

"Go on and tell about the anniversary party."

"Oh, Ross," said Glenna. She got up and turned on the lights in the colored plastic lanterns that were strung along the wall of the house. "I should have made Colin get up and put some in the cherry tree," she said.

"Well. Colin was thirteen at the time and Ross was twelve," Sylvia said. "Oh, everybody knows this backwards and forwards except you, Nancy. So, twenty-five years married and my oldest kid is thirteen? You could say that was the problem. Such a long time without kids, we were just counting on never having any.

First counting on having them and then being disappointed and then getting used to it, and being used to it so long, over ten years married, and I'm pregnant! That was Colin. And not even twelve months later, eleven months and three days later, another one! That was Ross!"

"Whoopee!" said Ross.

"The poor man, I guess he got scared from then on I would just be dropping babies every time he turned around, so he took off."

"He was transferred," Colin said. "He worked for the railway and when they took off the passenger train through here they transferred him to Peterborough."

He had not many memories of his father. Once, walking down the street, his father had offered him a stick of gum. There was a kindly, official air about this gesture — his father was wearing his uniform at the time — rather than a paternal intimacy. Colin had the impression that Sylvia couldn't manage sons and a husband somehow — that she had mislaid her marriage without exactly meaning to.

"He didn't just work for the railway," said Sylvia. "He was a conductor on it. After he first was transferred he used to come back sometimes on the bus but he hated traveling on the bus and he couldn't drive a car. He just gradually quit visiting and he died just before he would've retired. So maybe he would've come back then, who knows?"

(It was Glenna's idea, relayed to Colin, that all this easygoing talk about throwing her own anniversary party was just Sylvia's bluff — that she had asked or told her husband to come, and he hadn't.)

"Well, never mind him, it was a party," Sylvia said. "I asked a lot of people. I would've asked Eddy but I didn't know him then so well as I do now. I thought he was too high class." She jabbed Eddy's arm with her elbow. Everybody knew it was his second wife who had been too high class. "It was August, the weather was good, we were able to be outside, like we are here. I had trestle tables set up and I had a washtub full of potato salad. I had spareribs and fried chicken and desserts and pies and an anniversary cake I got iced by the bakery. And two fruit punches, one with and one without. The one with got a lot more with as the evening wore on and people kept pouring in vodka and brandy and whatever they had and I didn't know it!"

Ross said, "Everybody thought Colin got into the punch!"

"Well, he didn't," said Sylvia. "That was a lie."

Earlier, Colin and Nancy had cleared the table together and when they were alone in the kitchen Nancy said, "Did you say anything to Ross?"

"Not yet."

"You will, though? Colin? It's serious."

Glenna coming in with a platter of chicken bones heard that, though she didn't say anything.

Colin said, "Nancy thinks Ross is making a mistake with his car."

"A fatal mistake," said Nancy. Colin went back outside, leaving her talking in a lowered, urgent voice to Glenna.

"And we had music," Sylvia said. "We were dancing on the sidewalk, round the front, as well as partying at the back. We had records playing in my front room and the windows open. The night constable came down and he was dancing along with us! It was just after they put the pink streetlights up on that street, so I said, look at the lights they put up for my party! Where are you going?" she said to Colin, who had stood up.

"I want to show Eddy something."

Eddy stood up, looking pleased, and padded around the table. He was wearing brown-and-yellow checked pants, not too bold a check, a yellow sports shirt and dark-red neckerchief. "Doesn't he look nice?" said Sylvia, not for the first time. "Eddy, you're such a dresser! Colin just don't want to hear me tell the rest."

"The rest is the best," Ross said. "Coming up!"

"I want to show Eddy something and ask him something," Colin said. "In private."

"This part of it is like something you would read in the newspaper," said Sylvia.

Glenna said, "It's horrible."

"He's going to show Eddy his precious grass," said Sylvia. "Plus, he really does want to get away from me telling it. Why?

Wasn't his fault. Well, partly. But it's the kind of thing has happened over and over again with others only the outcome has been worse. Tragic."

"It sure could've been tragic," Ross said, laughing.

Colin, guiding Eddy around to the front of the house, could hear Ross laughing. He got Eddy past the string fence and the new grass. In the front yard there was some light from the streetlight, not really enough. He turned on the light by the front door.

"Now. How good can you see Ross's car?" Colin said.

Eddy said. "I seen it all before."

"Wait."

Colin's car was parked so that the lights would shine where he wanted them to, and he had the keys in his pocket. He got in and started the motor and turned on the lights.

"There," he said. "Take a look at the engine now while I got the lights on."

Eddy said, "Okay," and walked over into the car light and stood contemplating the engine.

"Now look at the body."

"Yeah," said Eddy, doing a quarter-turn but not stooping to look. In those clothes, he wouldn't want to get too close to anything.

Colin turned off the lights and the motor and got out of the car. In the dark he heard Ross laughing again.

"Somebody was saying to me that the engine was too big to be put in there," Colin said. "This person said it would break the universal and the drive shaft would go and the car would somersault. Now, I don't know enough about cars. Is that true?"

He wasn't going to say that the person was Nancy, not because Nancy was a woman but because Eddy was apt to regard anything Nancy said or did with such mesmerized delight that you would never be able to get an opinion out of him. It was not easy to get opinions out of him in any case.

"It's a big engine," Eddy said. "It's a V-eight three-fifty. It's a Chevy engine."

Colin didn't say he knew this already.

"Is it too big?" he said. "Is it a danger?"

"It is a bit big."

"Have you seen them put this kind of engine in this kind of body before?"

"Oh, yeah. I seen them do everything."

"Would it cause an accident, like this person said?"

"Hard to say."

After most people say that, they go on and tell you what it is that is hard to say. Not Eddy.

"Would it be sure to break the universal?"

"Oh, not sure," said Eddy agreeably. "I wouldn't say that."

"It might?"

"Well."

"Should I say anything to Ross?"

Eddy chuckled nervously. "Sylvia don't take it too well when you say anything to Ross."

Colin had not been into the spiked punch. He and Ross and the half-dozen other boys did not go that close to the heart of the party. They ignored the party, staying on the fringes of it, drinking only out of cans — cans of Coca-Cola and orange that somebody had brought and left beside the back steps. They ate potato chips that were provided, but did not bother with the food set out on tables that required plates or forks. They did not pay attention to what the adults were doing. A few years ago they would have been hanging around watching everything, with the idea, mostly, of making fun of and distrupting it. Now they would not give that world — the world of adults, at the party or anywhere else — credit for existing.

Things that belonged to adults were another story. Those were still interesting, and in the cars parked along the back lane they found plenty. Tools, shovels, last winter's chains, boots, some traps. Torn raincoats, a blanket, magazines with dirty pictures. A gun.

The gun was lying along the back seat of an unlocked car. It was a hunting rifle. There was no question that they would have to lift it out, look at it and comment on it in a knowledgeable way, aim it at imaginary birds.

Some said to be careful.

"It isn't loaded."

"How do you know?"

Colin never heard how that boy knew. He was thinking how Ross must not get his hands on this gun or, loaded or not, it would explode. To prevent such a thing happening Colin grabbed it himself, and what happened then he absolutely did not know, or remember, ever. He didn't remember pointing the gun. He couldn't have pointed it. He didn't remember pulling the trigger because that was what he couldn't have done. He couldn't have pulled the trigger. He couldn't remember the sound of a shot but only the knowledge that something had happened — the knowledge you have when a loud noise wakes you out of sleep and just for a moment seems too distant and inevitable to need your attention.

Screams and yells broke on his ears at this same time. One of the screams came from Ross (which should have told Colin something — do people shot dead usually scream?). Colin didn't see Ross fall. What he did see — and always remembered — was Ross lying on the ground, on his back, with his arms flung out, a dark stain spilled out from the top of his head.

(That could not actually have been there — was there a puddle?)

Not despising the world or help of adults anymore, one or two boys raced down the lane to Sylvia's house, yelling, "Ross is shot! Colin shot him! Ross! He's shot! Colin shot him! Ross! Colin! Ross!"

By the time they made the people sitting around the table in the backyard understand this — some had heard the shot but thought of firecrackers — and by the time the first men, running down the lane, came to the scene of the tragedy, Ross was sitting up, stretching his arms, with a sly, abashed look on his face. The boys who hadn't run to get help had seen him stir, and thought he must be alive but wounded. He wasn't wounded at all. The bullet hadn't come near him. It had hit the shed a little way down the lane, a shed where an old man sharpened skates in the wintertime. Nobody was hurt.

Ross claimed he had been knocked out, or knocked over, by the sound of the shot. But everybody, knowing Ross, believed or suspected that he had put on an act on purpose, on the spur of the moment. The gun was lying in the grass by the side of the lane, where Colin had thrown it. None of the boys had picked it up, nobody wanted to touch it or be associated with it. Though it was clear to them, now, that everything must come out — how they took it from the car when they had no business to, how they were all to blame.

But Colin chiefly. Colin was to blame. And he had run.

That was the cry, after the first commotion about Ross.

"What happened? Ross, are you all right? Are you hit? Where is the gun? Are you really all right? Where did you get the gun? Why did you act like you were shot? Are you sure you're not shot? Who shot the gun? *Who?* Colin!"

"Where is Colin?"

Nobody even remembered the direction he had gone in. Nobody remembered seeing him go. They called, but there was no answer. They looked along the lane to see if he might be hiding. The constable got into the police car, and other people got into their cars, and they drove up and down the streets, even drove a few miles out onto the highway, to see if they could catch him running away. No sign of him. Sylvia went into the house and looked in the closets and under the beds. People were wandering around, bumping into each other, shining flashlights into bushes, calling for Colin.

Then Ross said he knew the place to look.

"Down at the Tiplady Bridge."

This was an iron bridge of the old-fashioned kind, spanning the Tiplady River. It had been left in place though a new, concrete bridge had been built upriver, so that the widened highway now bypassed that bit of town. The road leading down to the old bridge was closed off to cars and the bridge itself declared unsafe, but people swam or fished off it, and at night cars bumped around the ROAD CLOSED sign to park. The pavement there was broken up, and the streetlight had burned out and not been replaced. There were rumors and jokes about this light, implying that members of the council were among those who parked, and preferred darkness.

The bridge was only a couple of blocks from Sylvia's house. Boys ran ahead, not led but followed by Ross, who took a thoughtful pace. Sylvia stuck close to him and told him to get a move on. She was wearing high heels and a teal-blue sheath dress, too tight across the hips, which hampered her.

"You better be right," she said, confused now as to which son she was most angry at. She hadn't had time to recover from Ross's not being shot when she had to wonder if she would ever see Colin again. Some party guests were drunk or tactless enough to wonder out loud if he could have jumped into the Tiplady River.

The constable stuck his head out of the car and told them to remove the roadblock. Then he drove through, and shone his headlights on the bridge.

The top of the bridge did not show up very well in this light, but they could see somebody sitting there.

"Colin!"

Colin had climbed up and settled on the iron girders. He was there.

"Colin! I can't believe you did that!" Sylvia yelled up at him. "Come on down off that bridge!"

Colin didn't move. He seemed dazed. He was in fact so blinded by the lights of the police car that he couldn't have climbed down if he had wanted to.

Now the constable ordered him, and others ordered him. He wouldn't budge. In the midst of the orders and reproaches it struck Sylvia that of course he didn't know that Ross wasn't dead.

"Colin, your brother isn't shot!" she called to him. "Colin! Your brother is alive here beside me! Ross is alive!"

Colin didn't answer but she thought she saw his head move, as if he was peering down.

"Get those stupid lights off him," she said to the constable, who was a sort of boyfriend. "Turn the lights on Ross if you want to turn them on something."

"Why don't we stand Ross out in the lights?" the constable said. "Then we can turn them off and let the boy climb down."

"Okay, Colin," the constable called out. "We're going to show you Ross standing down here, he isn't hurt or anything!"

Sylvia pushed Ross into the light.

"Open your mouth for crying out loud," she said. "Tell your brother you're alive."

Colin was helping Glenna clean up. He thought about what his mother had said, about plastic dishes and tablecloths that you could just scoop up and throw in the garbage. There was not a chance in a million that Glenna would ever do that. His mother understood nothing about Glenna, nothing at all.

Now Glenna was exhausted, having created a dinner party more elaborate than necessary, which nobody but herself could appreciate.

No, that was wrong. He appreciated, even if he didn't understand the necessity. Every step she took him away from his mother's confusion he appreciated.

"I don't know what to say to Ross," he said.

"What about?" said Glenna.

She was so tired, he thought, that she had forgotten what Nancy told her.

He found himself thinking of the night before their wedding. Glenna had five bridesmaids, chosen for their size and coloring rather than particular friendship, and she had made all their dresses to a design of her own. She made her wedding dress as well, and all the gloves and headdresses. The gloves had sixteen little self-covered buttons each. She finished them at nine-thirty the night before the wedding. Then she went upstairs, looking very white. Colin, who was staying in the house, went up to see how she was and found her weeping, still holding some scraps of colored cloth. He couldn't get her to stop, and called her mother, who said, "That's just the way she is, Colin. She overdoes things."

Glenna sobbed and said, among other things, that she saw no use in being alive. The next day she was calm and pretty, showing no ravages, drinking in praise and wishes for her happiness.

This dinner wasn't likely to have worn her out as much as the bridesmaids' outfits, but she had reached the stage where she had a forbidding look, a harsh pallor, as if there were a lot of things that she might call in question.

"He is not going to want to go hunting for another engine," Colin said. "How can he afford one? He owes Sylvia for that one. Anyway he wants a big engine. He wants the power."

Glenna said, "Does it make that much difference?"

"It makes a difference. In the pickup and the power, sure. An engine like that makes a difference."

Then he saw that she might not have meant that. She might not have meant, Does the engine make a difference?

She might have meant, If it's not this, it'll be something else.

(She sat on the grass; she polished the caps; she sniffed at the door panels. She said, Let Lynette choose the color.)

She might have meant, Why don't we just let it go?

Colin shook the garbage down in the plastic bag and tied it at the neck.

"I don't want you and Lynnette riding around with him, if there's anything like that."

"Colin, I wouldn't," said Glenna in a gentle, amazed voice. "Do you think I ever would ride with him in that car or let Lynette ride with him? I never would."

He took the garbage out and she began to sweep the floor. When he came back she said, "I just thought of something. I thought, soon I'll be sweeping the black and white tiles and I won't even be able to picture what these old boards look like. We won't be able to remember. We should take some pictures so we can remember what we've done."

Then she said, "I think Nancy sort of dramatizes sometimes. I mean it about me and Lynnette. But I think she overdramatizes."

Glenna had surprised him, in fact, with the way she could picture things. The house, each of its rooms, in its finished state. She had placed the furniture they hadn't yet bought; she had chosen the colors in accordance with a northern or southern exposure, morning or evening light. Glenna could hold in her mind an orderly succession of rooms, an arrangement that was ordained, harmonious, and, by her, completely understood.

A problem wouldn't just thrust itself on Glenna and throw her into doubts and agonies. Solutions were waiting, like a succession of rooms. There was a way she would see, of dealing with things, without talking or thinking about them. And all her daily patience and sweetness wouldn't alter that way, or touch it.

At first with the lights and the hollering, his only idea was that they had come to blame him. That didn't interest him. He knew

what he had done. He hadn't run away and cut down here and
climbed the bridge in the dark so that they couldn't punish
him. He was not afraid; he wasn't shivering with the shock. He
sat on the narrow girders and felt how cold the iron was,
even on a summer night, and he himself was cold but still
calm, with all the jumble of his life, and other people's lives in
this town, rolled back, just like a photograph split and rolled
back, so it shows what was underneath all along. Nothing.
Ross lying on the ground with a pool around his head.
Ross silenced, himself a murderer. Still, nothing. He wasn't
glad or sorry. Such feelings were too puny and personal, they
did not apply. Later on he found out that most people, and
apparently his mother, believed he had climbed up there
because he was in a frenzy of remorse and was contemplating
throwing himself into the Tiplady River. That never occurred to him. In a way, he had forgotten the river was
there. He had forgotten that a bridge was a structure over a
river and that his mother was a person who could order him
to do things.

No, he hadn't forgotten those things, so much as grasped how
silly they were. How silly it was that he should have a name and
it should be Colin, and that people should be shouting it. It was
silly, in a way, even to think that he had shot Ross, though he
knew he had. What was silly was to think in these chunks of
words. Colin. Shot. Ross. To see it as an action, something sharp
and separate, an event, a *difference*.

He wasn't thinking of throwing himself into the river or of
anything else he might do next, or of how his life would progress from this moment. Such progress seemed not only unnec-
essary but impossible. His life had split open, and nothing had
to be figured out anymore.

They were telling him Ross wasn't dead.

He isn't dead, Colin.

You never shot him.

It was a hoax.

It was Ross playing a joke.

Ross's joke.

You never shot anybody, Colin. Gun went off but nobody was
hurt.

See, Colin. Here he is.

Here's Ross. He ain't dead.

"I ain't dead, Colin!"

"Did you hear that? Did you hear what he said? He said he ain't dead!"

So now you can come on down.

Now you can come down.

Colin. Come on down.

That was when everything started to go back to being itself again. He saw Ross unwounded, unmistakably himself, lit up by car lights. Ross risen up, looking cheerful and slightly apprehensive but not really apologetic. Ross, who seemed to caper even when he was standing still, and to laugh loud even when he was working hard at keeping his mouth shut.

The same.

Colin felt dizzy and sick with the force of things coming back to life, the chaos and emotion. It was as painful as fiery blood pushing into frozen parts of your body. Doing as he was told, he started to climb down. Some people clapped and cheered. He had to concentrate to keep from slipping. He was weak and cramped from sitting up there. He had to keep himself from thinking, too suddenly, about what had just missed happening.

And he ended up with the idea that to watch out for something like that happening — to Ross and to himself — was going to be his job in life from then on.

JESSICA NEELY

Skin Angels

FROM NEW ENGLAND REVIEW AND BREAD LOAF QUARTERLY

IN THE BEGINNING of the summer my mother memorized the role of Lady Macbeth four mornings a week and worked the late shift in Geriatrics. She had always wanted to act in a play, a real play, and in the months after my father left home, when it was clear to us that he'd left for good, she would take me to the old converted church, the Bread and Circuses theater. The company players had painted the limestone walls and the windows of the church gray so that no sunlight would interfere with the stage floods. In real life, these people were all students and teachers and housewives. But in the muggy mornings of that summer they would park their cars and walk through the back door of the theater to put on make-up and costumes, to curl their hair and put on large gaudy earrings that only the right shade of blue could make beautiful. Sy was the manager of Bread and Circuses. He told my mother that she could play Lady Macbeth because she had crazy eyes and red hair. So my mother and I went to the theater four mornings each week. She stood just off stage while three witches hunched over a bucket of dry ice and practiced incantations. I sat in the front pew and watched. I was eight years old then.

Before dawn, when my mother came home from work at the hospital, she would double-lock the door. I could smell the cold air and cigarette smoke on her uniform as she lifted me out of bed, carried me into her room. I stood on the bed to take the bobby pins out of her hair. Then I undid the zipper. My mother unclipped her nurse's badge that said "Andrea" in script and

laid it on the dresser. When she was nude, she'd stand in front
of the mirror with outstretched arms and stare at herself. I'd
jump on the bed behind her. I'd bounce high until I could see
myself in the mirror above her head. Sometimes she'd laugh so
hard she'd have to bend over and hold her stomach. We'd get
into bed and pull the covers over our heads to make a tent.

"There's nobody in the world except you and me," my mother
would whisper. "No cars, no families, no people, no old people."

"We're in a cave."

"That's right." she'd curl up around my back and pull me
close against her warm stomach and breasts.

My sister Serina, who is nine years older than I, had a job dancing at the Brass Monkey. Her boyfriend Ponce usually drove
her home around eight. I would hear her key first in one lock,
then the other; hear my sister whisper, "Goodbye. Okay, all
right. Goodbye," and hold back a giggle, as if she were home
late from a date and didn't want to be caught. I'd open my eyes
to the windows in my mother's room where the broad sunlight
framed Venetian blinds. Serina came into the room and shook
me by the shoulders. The fringe on her leotard tickled my face.

"Get ready for school," she said. Then she walked around the
bed to our mother, bent down and yelled, "Andy, get up or
you'll be late for play practice!"

In the bathroom I turned on the shower, but I could still hear
them fighting. My mother screamed, "Does he pay you? How
much does that nigger pay you?"

Sy told my mother that she didn't know much about being an
actress. She would need to spend afternoons with him going
over lines and gestures. He taught her the way actresses dress:
purple suede miniskirts, black cigarette holders, berets. On the
last day of third grade, when I came home, my mother and Sy
were in the kitchen smoking pot in their underwear.

"We're going to be beatniks, Carlie," my mother said. "What
do you think of that?"

"I don't know."

Sy wore green bikini underpants. He had curly brown hair
frosted grey at the temples and a chest and beard furry as a
bear's. His fat stomach hung over the edge of his underpants

and a little tear split the elastic near his thigh. I turned away
and looked at my mother's painted toe nails.

"Hey, Carlie, would you like Daddy Sy to get you a new wardrobe?"

"Daddy Sy!" My mother slapped the table. "That's rich.
Daddy, Sy in my ear and I'm yours forever."

Sy fell out of his chair, laughing. My mother laughed too.
One hand over her mouth, the other hitting her thigh, she
looked at me, coaxing. And Sy rolled around on the floor until
he bumped into the refrigerator.

I put my report card on the table.

Sy bought me fringed go-go boots like the ones Serina wore to
work. He bought me tights in every color, earrings, and he also
bought me Conchita, a wooden doll with a black tiara and a red
taffeta skirt. Almost every Saturday my mother and Sy took me
to the lake. We had a checkered tablecloth that we spread on
the deserted part of the beach where Sy's family once had a
house. At first we all got sunburns. My mother made me wear a
T-shirt so mine wasn't bad, but we had to make Sy a cold bath
with tea bags in it.

Sy would lie on my mother's bed and pay me quarters to peel
the thin strips of skin off his back. When I'd get a long one he'd
say, "Hold it up in front of the window and let the breeze catch
it." I'd pinch the top between my fingers and watch it flutter.
"Those are skin angels," he said. I'd flick the skin angels out
through the window and watch them float away. Sy told me they
went straight to heaven.

Some nights while my mother worked, Serina and Ponce stayed
home with me. Serina worked on her painting, a mosaic called
Blasted Jesus. She hated water colors and oils were too expensive,
so she used to hold crayons over a lit candle and pat the wax
drips onto the canvas. Serina used black for Jesus' face, brown
for his eyes, white for his teeth. Ponce would stretch out on the
sofa while Serina worked. He was a tall, skinny man who wore
tight bell bottoms and turtlenecks and he had an afro that
looked perfectly sculpted, like a globe. Serina spent hours on
that afro.

One night Ponce said he wanted to take Serina to Greenwich

Village to meet gallery owners. "With your legs and my capital . . ."

Serina said her legs would have nothing to do with it, but Ponce leaned back and laughed. "Lady Cakes, you don't know the score yet, do you?"

"I know what nice legs will get you," Serina said and she pointed over her shoulder to my mother's bedroom.

Ponce laughed. "What about you, Carlie? Do you want to run away to Greenwich Village with us?" he asked. "It's only about five hours south. You could go visit your mommy every second Sunday."

I looked across the room to my mother's doorway. It was open and dark. "Only if you buy me a ten-speed," I said.

"Sweetheart, I'll buy you a Cutlass Supreme. Won't I, Serina?"

"Sure you will."

"We'll sell Serina's mosaics and buy three Supremes in pastel colors. We'll drive down Houston parade-style. You don't want to live with your bird of a mother anymore, do you?"

"She's not a bird," I said. "My mother says your face is dirty."

Ponce arched his back and yawned. "It's her mind that's dirty, honey. Your mommy is a loon."

"Shut up." Serina laughed.

My mother would tell me that she and I were the oddballs in the family, the only ones with red hair. No one was ever allowed to cut my hair except her — a quarter inch off the ends every six months. She put the clippings in a pink shellacked jewelry box and when that was full, she'd put the hair into a paper bag in the closet. When she dies, my mother said, I was to make her a pillow out of the clippings. She said that's what God does. He hires swans to fill up pillows with their softest underdown and kick them off the clouds to all of the funeral parlors. But she wanted her pillow to be special, she said; she wanted it filled with my thin red hair.

We sat at the kitchen table. My mother had put an apron over her uniform to keep it clean and her hair was pinned up in a bun. But she had on too much make-up for work. She looked as if she were on her way to perform on the set of a hospital play.

She was telling me that Serina loved Ponce only because she was afraid of him.

"This is something I want you to remember," she said. "A chain is only as strong as its weakest link. Do you know what that means?"

I shook my head.

"I'm trying to teach you about self-respect, Carlie. You don't want to love out of fear. You have to be strong enough to dare everything." She lit a cigarette. "That's the only way we know how to love, you and me, right?"

I said I didn't know and my mother frowned. She watched me move my fork back and forth across my plate. "Answer the question. Do you know what I'm saying?"

"That you aren't afraid."

My mother blew her smoke out in a stream. "Absolutely not. I'm not afraid of Sy and I was not afraid of your father. I loved him completely, until there was nothing left to love him with, but I was never afraid of him. Never. I'm telling you, Carlie, Ponce will leave Serina the way your father left me. He'll leave just like that, in the middle of the night. He won't say anything. He won't slam anything."

She put her hand against her forehead and shut her eyes. The cigarette stuck out between her fingers and the smoke lifted to flat layers above her hair. "He didn't even take his clothes. I kept them in drawers for so long. I thought he might get cold."

I wanted my doll, Conchita. I wanted to hold her, but I had left her in the bedroom. Slowly I pushed my chair away from the table and stood as quietly as I could. My mother sat still. The only motion around her was the thin twist of smoke in the air.

The next afternoon Sy came over to practice a scene from *Macbeth*. I knocked on my mother's bedroom door because I heard Sy yelling and wanted to know what was going on.

Sy opened the door. "I told you, Carlie, when this door's closed it means no admittance." he said.

My mother snapped her fingers and pointed to the far corner of the room. "Over there. Be quiet."

Sy had put a red light in the sunlamp. He had it pointed up

toward the bed where my mother stood with a blanket wrapped around her. A fan on the dresser blew my mother's hair back from her face in tangled strands.

"Okay, I want your voice to build, baby." He walked to my mother and pushed her chin slightly to the right. "You've read the letter and you're enraged. Do you hear? You're begging for evil."

Sy smudged my mother's lipstick across the top of her mouth. "Yeah," he whispered, "evil. Take it from 'Make thick.' " He squatted down by the sunlamp.

My mother lifted her arms so that the blanket slid back. " 'Make thick my blood,' " she said. " 'Stop up the access and passage to remorse, that no compunctuous visitings of nature shake my fell purpose nor —' "

"Stop!" Sy grabbed my mother. "Slow down. Compunctuous. Compunctuous. Roll your lips around the sound, lick the word. You're Satan's mistress. Okay. Start at 'Stop up the access.' "

" 'Stop up the access and passage to remorse, that no compunctuous visitings of nature shake my fell purpose nor keep peace between the effect and it!' " My mother ran her hands up along her sides. " 'Come to my woman's breasts and take my milk for gall, you murthering ministers, wherever —' "

"Cut!" Sy turned the fan off. "Andy, you're making an ass of yourself. If you're not going to take this seriously . . ."

My mother went into the kitchen. Conchita and I followed. She poured herself a glass of water then splashed some on her face.

Sy stood in the kitchen doorway. "Look at that," he said. "You're slumped over like some kind of beggar. Hold that glass in front of you. Drink it as if it's the nectar of the gods."

"Knock it off," my mother said.

Sy crossed his arms and stared at my mother and me. "Andy, the only possible way you'll be successful is by listening to me. You've got to be onstage every single minute; breathe and live the tragedy."

"Get out of here."

"Louder."

"Get out of here!"

"Marvelous."

My mother threw the glass on the floor. "Out!"

"Good night, all." Sy bowed slightly and walked out.

Opening night for *Macbeth* was only three weeks away and Sy decided to have a party for the cast. My mother bought four dozen lilies for the party. We went to Sy's condo and taped the lilies to the walls, put them in bud vases, cut the tops off and let them float in coffee cups.

I was supposed to sleep in Sy's bed with Conchita, but that night I was too afraid to sleep. I got out of bed and went to the end of the hallway where I could watch. There were no lights on in the house, only lit candles. Most of the cast members were outside on the pool patio smoking cigarettes and joints. Some wore Batman capes. Others had on dwarf boots, Peter Pan hats. Sy had bought plastic champagne goblets with removable bottoms. A woman in a feathered dress was throwing the plastic bottoms around like tiny Frisbees. Sy came in from the patio. Conchita and I crouched in a shadow. He stood beside a thin man who kept peeling lilies off the wall and eating them.

"Banquo, that's no way to treat a lily," Sy said.

"Hey, Sy, how about this?" He offered Sy the top of a lily. " 'If you can look into the seeds of time and say which grain will grow and which will not, speak then to me.' "

Sy held the skinny man's wrist and looked at the flower. " 'Your children shall be kings.' "

"Beautiful." The man bit off a petal and chewed it up.

I held Conchita and went back to the bedroom. As we fell asleep, I could hear people dancing and jumping on the floor.

Later I awoke because I heard my mother scream. No one was in the living room so I ran out to the patio. I saw Sy and two other men standing naked beside the pool; they were holding my mother above the water, swinging her back and forth. Sy yelled, "One, two, three!" and they threw my mother into the air. Her back arched as she came down.

Under the water I could see her long body sink and her hair fan out like blood against the pool lights. The men dove in, one at a time, and headed for my mother. They took turns swimming between her legs, quick as eels.

I screamed for Sy to let my mother up. She needed air. They

had to let her up for air. I ran with Conchita into the kitchen to
dial the Brass Monkey where Serina worked.

"I need to talk to my sister, Serina," I said.

"She's busy. She can't come to the phone," the Monkey said.

"It's an emergency. Please," I said, "let me talk to her."

"Who?"

"Serina!" I yelled. "Tell her someone's killing her mother!"

The Monkey screeched into the phone and hung up.

I ran with Conchita out the front door. I was too afraid to
look for my mother and I didn't want Sy or the other men to
find me. I crouched down beside the house in some trees and
bushes. It was raining a little so I made Conchita a lean-to out
of leaves and sticks. I put rocks around her bed to make
a bumper. There were no sounds from the pool. I could
hear only the rain on the leaves around me. I tucked my
knees in close to my chest and pulled my nightgown down over
them.

After a long while, music began blaring from the house. I
heard Sy's voice, then my mother laughing. Her laugh was high
and scary. I put my face down on my knees, held my hands over
my ears. I didn't want to hear that music, hear Sy's words or the
way my mother was laughing. I sat there on the ground until
the rain soaked through my nightgown and I began to shiver.
And I did not go back inside until the music had stopped and
all of the lights in the house were off.

When I opened the door to Sy's room, I could see the bodies
of my mother and Sy wrapped up in the blankets. My mother's
dress and shoes were on the floor. I took off my wet nightgown
and put on my mother's dress. "Mom?" I whispered, but not
loud enough to wake her. I walked to the side of the bed and
lifted the blanket. Sy's body was curled around my mother's
back, his hand flat across her breasts. I bent over and whispered
to her again.

A night wind blew the rain in through the screened window.
It fell in a mist across my face and neck. I knew it was hours
before sunrise, so I pulled the blanket over my mother again
and sat down on the end of the bed. I was then I remembered
that I had left Conchita outside.

The next morning Sy made breakfast. I sat at the table and watched. He cracked six eggs into a large ceramic bowl.

"I'll bet you love scrambled eggs," he said.

I didn't answer. I watched him cut a square of butter and drop it into the frying pan.

"I'll bet they're your absolute favorite food," he said, but he didn't turn toward me for an answer and again I was quiet.

When my mother came into the kitchen she was still in her bathrobe. Her eye make-up was smeared and her hair was in snarls. She hadn't bothered to brush it.

"Andy, *you'll* eat some of these eggs," Sy said.

"I'm not hungry." My mother looked at me and then she looked down. "Sy, I feel ill." She sat down at the table.

Sy walked to my mother and gently raised her chin. "A star's got to keep her strength up," he said. He took a film container out of his pants pocket, opened it and sprinkled some dope onto a rolling paper. "This will give you an appetite. Because you're a star, Andy. You know that? You're beautiful."

My mother smiled up at him like a child.

"You're my baby, Andy, my little baby." He licked the side of the joint and lit the end.

"Tell me about opening night," my mother said.

Sy inhaled the dope and held the smoke in his mouth. He looked at my mother and tucked a strand of hair behind her ear. With his face up close, he blew the smoke out and said, "Opening night." The words rushed around her cheeks. "Yes, you're standing alone on the stage. You've got the floods on you, and the backdrop is lit up red and purple. There's silence for one, maybe two minutes."

Sy smoked the joint again. "The audience is transfixed. They can't take their eyes off you, Andy, your long red hair flowing around your shoulders. They're amazed. You're a star."

My mother leaned back and laughed softly.

"Then you stretch out your hands. There's a knife in them. The lights reflect off the blade. You don't say a word. You start moving, undulating, waving the knife like you're cutting a big S in the air. And then the lights go down. You're a silhouette against the backdrop. Here." Sy handed her the joint. "Take a hit."

My mother took a drag and started to laugh.

"That's better," Sy said. "I love it when you laugh. Laugh."

My mother began to laugh. She leaned back and laughed straight at the ceiling. Sy started laughing too. Sometimes he giggled and took puffs off the joint. Sometimes he laughed out loud; but my mother just laughed at the ceiling, until it was one long sound, like a yell, which she only broke to catch her breath.

Ponce told Serina that if she didn't go to Greenwich Village he'd burn her with a hot comb. He put the metal teeth on the electric burner until it heated up and the grease smoked a little.

"You're going, Serina, right?" He picked up the wooden handle and waved the teeth at her.

I grabbed my sister's arm, tried to pull her away. But Serina wouldn't move.

Ponce held the hot comb in front of Serina's face. "You pack your bags and be ready by dawn, darling. Got it?"

Serina smiled with the side of her mouth. "Sit down," she said.

Ponce winked at me, but I wouldn't smile back. He sat at the kitchen table and Serina divided his hair into sections. She rubbed grease on his scalp and straightened his hair from the roots upward.

"I just want to make sure when we leave I don't owe nobody nothing," he said.

"You don't," Serina said. She pulled his hair up tall and smooth.

That was the night Serina and Ponce left. I woke up around five. The sun sifted in from the bottom of my mother's blinds, fell in spots on the rug. I moved the flat of my palm along the mattress, but my mother was not home yet and there was no one there. I went down the hall to the lit door of Serina's room. Ponce had gone somewhere.

"Carlie, I'm sorry. I've got to get out of here." She had a big suitcase and she was stuffing it with her dresses, sweaters and blue jeans.

"Why?"

"You don't realize, but Mom is driving me crazy. I'll be happy in New York. Ponce will get a job and I'll try to sell my paintings. Look, you can have this. You'll grow into it."

"I don't *want* your sweater," I said. "Serina, don't leave."

Serina took a belt from one of her dresses and folded it in quarters.

"You don't have to be afraid of him."

Serina stared at me. Then she began to fold her clothes again. "Carlie, I'm in love with Ponce. Mom doesn't choose to see that. You don't have to . . . change yourself for a man and you don't have to be a martyr." Serina looked behind me at the door.

My mother was leaning against the wall in her coat. She had her nurse cap in her hand and she was smoking.

"What do you think you're doing?"

"I'm leaving." Serina put the suitcase on the floor and sat down on it to close the latches.

"Mom, tell her not to go."

"I'll do no such thing." My mother raised her chin and spoke in a loud voice as if she were on stage. "Go, Serina, you make no pretense of living here anyway."

Serina pulled her coat out of the closet. "I'll leave a number with the Brass Monkey," she said to me and kissed the top of my head.

My mother walked toward Serina. "You don't give a damn about *me*, do you? Do you? For the first time in my life I'm doing something that's important to me. I'm acting in a play. I've always wanted to act and you know it. But you can't stay home a few afternoons to take care of Carlie." She pointed toward the door. "*You* have to go galavanting all over East Jesus with that man."

"Just cut the theatrics, mother."

"Where did you get that? That's your father's suitcase. Put it back in my closet. Now!"

"Mother, move." Serina picked up the suitcase.

"No, Serina, wait a minute. Let's talk for a second," she pleaded. "Okay? Okay?" She stubbed out her cigarette. "There, we'll just talk about this."

Serina put down the suitcase. She looked at me and said, "The only thing I regret is how screwed up Carlie's going to be while you play around with Sy and his sick friends."

My mother stared at her for a second and then she slapped Serina across the face.

Serina stared back at her.

"Oh God, honey, I'm sorry. Serina sweetheart, I didn't mean to do that. I love you so much, honey. Wait a second, wait, don't take that suitcase."

Serina pushed my mother away from the door. Then she left.

My mother sat on the floor and hugged her knees. She kept rocking back and forth, calling my sister's name.

Later that day we packed up Serina's room. We put all of her remaining clothes and shoes in shopping bags. My mother stripped Serina's bed and threw the sheets in the trash. Then she took the curtains off the windows and vacuumed the carpet.

My mother asked me to stay in bed with her. She had drawn her shades and unplugged the phone. "Brush my hair," she asked, so I sat on her back, made hairdos with rubber bands and barrettes. I continued to brush my mother's long hair for hours, it seemed, while she slept. Once in a while she would wake up and roll over.

"You love me, don't you Carlie?" she'd ask.

I'd hug her.

"Say it."

"I love you," I'd say and brush the hair back from her face. I lay down on my mother's back and held my cheek against her forehead. I thought about Serina, then I thought of Conchita lying, face down, in the woods behind Sy's house. The rain would twist her wooden body and wash the paint from her lips. It would smooth her arms and fingers flat until they were level and whole with the ground. I felt a loneliness so wide, a loss that would only continue, constant as my mother's breathing and lulled merely by the need for sleep.

KENT NELSON

Invisible Life

FROM THE VIRGINIA QUARTERLY REVIEW

I had over-prepared the event, that much was ominous.
— Ezra Pound, *Villanelle: The Psychological Hour*

MY MOTHER had little to add. She sat with her coffee after dinner and stared toward the plate-glass window that faced the
front yard. The porch light was on outside, and I could see
the dead spring grass and the stark branches alive with buds in
the warm and misted night air. At the same time, my mother's
reflection shimmered in the dark window: shadowy, confused
color mixed with details of the yard beyond. From her expression I could not tell whether she was gauging herself in the glass
or merely thinking. She had been in fine health all her life, and
she looked it. Her complexion was still smooth and her eyes
clear. Her long hair had grayed, but was streaked with rich
brown. Yet at that moment I thought she looked tired, as
though the news Allison had given her had made her suddenly
and irrevocably old.

Allison had gone upstairs to feed Livingston and to put Tricia
to bed, and my mother had fallen into some dark memory, as
she did sometimes when she came to visit and was reminded of
my father. Finally she turned away from the window. "Is it
really such a disaster?" she asked.

"Well, it's not divorce, if that's what you mean."

"I should think you'd be proud."

"There's nothing to be proud of yet," I said. "Anyway, if she
wants graduate school, she could go to Penn in the city."

"But just the idea of history!" my mother said. She paused. "Perhaps she won't be admitted, is that what you mean? I suppose age is something they consider."

We were caught by loud, rapid footsteps upstairs. Hillary had slammed the bathroom door, and Allison yelled at her. The house seemed still for a moment, as it had often been lately, just a pause, barely noticeable, like a sigh between one word and another. Then Tricia appeared, modeling the new nightgown my mother had brought her.

"What was that about?" I asked.

"Hillary talked back," Tricia said. "She said she was not going to any party with Freeny Lewis."

"What's Livy doing?"

"Nothing, as usual."

"Did you sing him a song?"

"Mom wants me to go to bed."

Tricia whirled around so that the nightgown flowed away from her thin legs. At seven she was already gangly, thin as a rail, and sensitive. She read too much, if that was possible, and was so quiet we had been afraid that when Livingston was born she would disappear altogether.

I drew her toward me and hugged her. "You tell your mother I said you could sing him one song."

"Okay." She whirled away again. "Do you like it, Nanoo?"

"On you it shines," my mother said.

"Do I have to go to bed?"

"Yes," I said.

"Can I read?"

"Kiss your old Nanoo," I said. "One song. No reading."

Tricia climbed the stairs, pausing upon each step as though to catch our secrets.

"Tell your mother we're talking about her," I called up.

We waited a little longer until Tricia had padded down the hall. A breeze blew across the yard, stirring branches and telephone wires, but the room was still. "It's not as though we were starting out in life," I said.

My mother looked back toward the window. "You said she hasn't told any of her friends?"

"No, but she wanted to tell you."

"Why would she do that?"

I had no answer. Allison and my mother had never been particularly close, and while Allison was always cordial, I had felt in her a certain critical attitude about the way my parents lived their lives. Allison had always been reluctant to visit them in Bryn Mawr, even when my father was alive.

"Perhaps to enlist your sympathy," I said finally.

"But you don't object to school."

"It's partly the timing," I said casually. "The children . . ."

"Children adapt."

"You know what I mean."

I stood up and went to the window. A dog passed through the edge of the light near the street, his legs clicking and his head down upon some scent. "The kitchen was just remodeled four months ago because Allison thought we needed more space. And we got a station wagon last year, trading in Dad's good Buick. I agreed to those things — now and then we have to accommodate others."

I turned when I caught movement in the glass. Allison was leaning against the jamb in the doorway.

"Go on," she said easily, without malice. She looked at me in a straightforward way. "Say what you think."

"It just isn't the time to be liberated."

"Not the time for her or for you?" my mother asked.

Allison smiled briefly. She was not a beautiful woman — her mouth was too large and her skin sagged along her jaw and her curly hair was forever matted in sweat or flying out of some loose pin — but at that moment, as she moved into the center of the room, she looked so composed, so certain, that I felt a chill run across my shoulders.

"But I'm not trying to be liberated," she said, turning to my mother. "I'm trying to live my life."

The whole muddle had begun two weeks after Livingston was born, when Allison had announced that she was applying to graduate schools at Stanford and Harvard. That had been in November, and I had dismissed the idea out of hand. Given Allison's history, it was unlikely she truly wanted to study again after a fourteen-year hiatus, and even less likely that she would leave a small infant. The doctor, of course, had warned both of us about postpartum depression. A woman's body restructured itself after pregnancy and new hormones created havoc with the emotions. The additional burden of fatigue could overwhelm the unsuspecting. I assumed Allison's inspiration was in large measure a fantasy of escape.

If anything, she seemed happier and more dutiful than ever. She carried on about Livy to friends, nursed him cautiously (though more privately), and spoke to me of her guilt at feeling so much love for her son. The only difference, really, between her reactions to Hillary's and Tricia's births and to Livy's was that with Livy she seemed more intense.

In December she took the Graduate Record Examinations. She had been bright in college — Phi Beta Kappa at Mt. Holyoke, in fact — though she admitted her grades had been predicated more upon her acute memory than upon curiosity or ambition. She had said then, when we met, that she detested the deadlines and confining minutiae of college life so much that she could not even consider going on to an advanced degree. And in the twelve years of our marriage, I had never heard her voice a desire for a career.

"Just how do you propose to implement this dream?" I asked her one evening after the exams. I had prepared myself with a couple of Scotches.

"I will go to Palo Alto or Cambridge, and you will stay here."

"The logistics, I mean."

"We have enough money, don't we?"

"We are a family," I said rather harshly. "Perhaps not a glamorous family, maybe too serious on the whole, but steadfast and bright. Hillary vacillates between enthusiasm and silence, but she has not given us too much trouble. And Tricia has been mercilessly indulgent with Livy. She sings to him by the hour."

"Hillary and Tricia are in school," Allison said. "You may have to arrange Tricia's afternoons for recreation, but Hillary is old enough to and would rather fend for herself. You can either stay home with Livingston or hire someone to come in."

"Just like that?"

"I will think of you all the time."

"No emotion, though. You will go off, no muss or fuss, and never look back."

Allison turned away as though she did not want to think of it.

"You don't think Livy needs you?" I asked impatiently. "You don't think Tricia will miss you terribly?"

She turned around and her cheeks were wet with tears.

"We just can't get along without you," I said more softly.

"Certainly you can," she whispered. "What would you do if I died?"

Hypothetical questions have always irritated the hell out of me. I didn't know what I would do if she were to die, but she was not about to. I would not know what to do if my law practice suddenly evaporated, or if Allison were miraculously beautiful, or if Hillary were taking cocaine. I only know what I do at the moment, in response to a real event or a real threat. And I began to consider Allison's scheme a threat.

My mother was no help. She seemed to side with Allison, not outwardly but in subtle ways, as though she were the apologist for Allison's plan. "She has not confided in me," my mother said over the telephone one day. "I'm certain she has not told me anything she has not told you."

"But I know she's called you."

"Yes, that's different."

"Does she feel guilty? Do you sense that?"

"She wants me to know she still cares about you and the family."

"What else?"

"Nothing."

"What do you think? You must have some feel for it."

My mother paused on the line.

"What has changed her?" I went on. "I can't think of anything except Livy's birth that might have been traumatic, and why would she react to that? She loves him. I mean, why after all these years does she want to go away to graduate school?"

"There's the obvious," my mother said slowly, "that for her it's now or not at all."

"But she's never wanted a job or a career."

"Then she wants something else," my mother said quietly.

One Saturday in April, at Allison's urging, we drove to Bryn Mawr to wish my mother a happy birthday, her sixty-third.

Hillary complained that she had promised friends she would jog with them, and when that excuse failed, that she had homework.

"Bring your homework with you," I said. "Your cousin Rob will be there to help you."

"That creep?" Hillary said. "That's another reason not to go."

"Can I play in the gazebo?" Tricia asked.

"You can ask Nanoo."

"Why don't you invite her here?" Hillary asked.

"Because your mother wants to go there."

"I thought Mom didn't like to go to Nanoo's."

"Apparently she's changed her mind."

"And Aunt Tillie always talks about Grandpa. It's dull and Mom hates it."

"It's not dull," Tricia said. "There's the gazebo and the woods."

"It's dull," Hillary said.

Allison came downstairs with Livy in one arm and a large package in the other. "Can you get the port-a-crib?" she asked.

"What's that?" I asked, pointing to the package.

"A present."

"What present? I already got the bracelet you picked out for her."

"This is another one," Allison said blithely, and she breezed out the door.

The day was warm and sunny, and after lunch I took Tricia into the woods behind the house to explore with her the places I remembered from my own childhood. A dark stream ran through the woodland, and leaves were yellow-green against the fast-moving clouds and blue sky. I pointed out, as my father had to me, the warblers darting among the oaks and maples. The stream swirled lazily over rocks and sodden logs, and for a while we sat upon a boulder and watched the water flow.

"Did you know there are tiny creatures in that water?" I asked. "Animals that you can't see?"

Tricia lowered her face toward the pool beneath us. "Are there?"

My father had demonstrated the existence of the invisible teeming life by taking a sample of creek water and showing me slides under a microscope. I remembered the elaborate bulbous forms of protozoa and the bizarre wriggling cilia that waved in the droplets of water.

"How do you suppose we could tell whether such creatures were there?" I asked.

Tricia continued to stare into the water. "By the fish," she said.

"The fish?"

"I can see fish, and the fish have to eat something smaller than they are, and those things must eat something smaller . . ."

I nodded and laughed at what seemed so logical, and at myself for thinking I should believe only what I could see with my own eyes.

The birthday party went well enough. My divorced sister, Tillie the Hun, came over for dessert with her children, Rob and Virginia, and when my mother was ready to open her presents, we had to drag Hillary and Rob from the porch.

"What's in the big box?" my mother asked the smaller children. "Should I open it first or last?"

"Last," Tricia said. She liked surprises.

I expected Tillie to begin her neurotic melancholy spiel about our father's absence, but she sat stoically with Allison on the sofa. My mother liked the housecoat Tillie gave her, and both Virginia and Tricia had made ceramic dishes in school. When she opened the bracelet, my mother uttered the appropriate words of joy and thanks.

Then she settled back in her flower-print chair amidst the explosion of colorful blue and white wrapping paper. The children crowded around the last big present, which Allison had kept hidden from me.

To heighten the children's eagerness, my mother spoke in an exaggerated whisper as she slowly pulled the ribbon. "Now what do you suppose this could be? It's such a big package! What do you imagine is in it?"

"A stuffed animal," Virginia giggled. "No, you wouldn't get *that!*"

"What does Nanoo need?" Tricia asked.

I turned, feeling an uncomfortable sensation, and Allison was staring at me with a studied air, as though measuring me. Her

eyes were relaxed, her mouth slack in a half-expectant smile. I
noticed for the first time that she had recently cut her hair, and
though it was still unkempt, it no longer covered a childhood
scar at her temple.

Inside the large box was a smaller one, also wrapped, and
inside that, yet another. The children clapped and pressed
closer.

Inside the third box was an envelope, and my mother raised
her eyes at the children and held it up with two fingers.

"An envelope?" Tricia asked.

"It's a ticket to Greece," Hillary guessed.

My mother slipped open the flap and before drawing out its
contents, she paused and looked at Allison. In that simple moment there was a sigh in the room, as though my mother and
Allison shared some silent pleasure. I knew too well, then, what
was in the envelope, and I turned away.

The drive home to Haddonfield over the Schuylkill Express-
way and the Walt Whitman Bridge was tedious, nerve-wrench-
ing. Livingston cried half the way, and Allison sat in the back
seat and fed him. I did not want to argue in front of the children, but when Tricia had lain down in the far back, and
Livy was asleep in the infant seat, I could restrain myself no
longer.

"At least tell me why you would tell her before you told me."

"I told you both at the same time."

"But why not give me advance warning?"

"I knew she would be glad for me."

"And I'm made to look ridiculous!"

"To whom? Tillie?" Allison smiled at the thought.

"I'm glad for you, too."

"Tom, I didn't mean to hurt you, but you aren't exactly sympathetic."

"Not exactly," I said. "I wish *I* could go back to school."

"Then go ahead."

I ran down a list of the responsibilities we had acquired together, in case they had escaped Allison's notice.

"You're driving forty," she said.

"I have to earn a living," I said. I looked in the rearview and
saw the cars piling up behind me on the bridge.

"You're doing what you have to do," she said, "and I'm doing
what I have to."

Allison's acceptances to Stanford and Harvard made the situation quite different. The issue was no longer theoretical. For
Allison, it was no longer whether she would be able to go, but
where she would go.

I still resisted with as many rational arguments as I could
make, but even my skills as a lawyer were no match for her
determination. She weighed the merits of the two history departments, the climates, distances from home. She preferred
palm trees to the harsh winter of Boston, and the strengths of
the departments were close; but the determining factor was that
Harvard was closer. I felt mildly appeased.

That summer we drove to Boston to scout a place for her to
live. I had called ahead for a real estate agent to show us apart-
ments — a place with large windows and bright walls was what
Allison would like, and it should be close enough to walk to the
Square.

"Who is going to live here?" Allison asked, standing in the
middle of a sunny room overlooking the Charles.

"You are."

"I don't want it."

The real estate agent showed the children around while we
talked it over.

"It's convenient. It's modern. There is good fire protection
and adequate security. Think about . . ."

"I'm thinking about my mental health."

She refused to make a decision and then the next weekend
went back to Cambridge alone. When she returned home, she
said she had found a place.

"How did you manage with the children?" she asked.

"What's the place like?"

"Did Livingston take his bottle? Did he wake up at night?"

"Yes and yes."

"Were you able to get to work on Friday?"

"The children aren't in school," I said. "It wasn't too bad."

"You didn't call your mother for help?"

"You told me not to."

"Good. Well, the apartment is small. You won't approve, but I like it well enough."

She hurried up the stairs to see Livy.

The next week Allison went through the usual ritual of buying clothes for the girls for school. Hillary had grown three inches in one year, and none of her jeans and blouses fit. Tricia wanted to be a newly polished silver star.

"What about you, Mom?" Hillary asked before they left. "Do you get clothes?"

"She doesn't grow," Tricia said. "That must be awful."

"But I can keep longer the things I have," Allison said cheerfully.

"Aren't you worried at all?" Hillary asked.

"Yes, I'm worried."

"You can always come home if you don't like it," Tricia said.

"I'm worried it's the right thing," Allison said. She smiled and then added, "But I will need your help."

"We'll be good," Tricia promised.

"Not that so much. I know you'll be all right." Again she stopped, and her voice quieted. "But I want you to be new. Be new every single day."

We had a party for friends — the Saxes and the Gerards and the Hamiltons — and then the summer was over. The children started school, and we had an anxious two weeks before Allison actually went off to Cambridge.

I was cynical, suspicious, even jealous. I had perhaps been too supportive, too willing to let her try her experiment. Perhaps she had only meant to test me, to see whether I would comply or resist. Yes, I was sympathetic to her wanting to do something more than volunteer work and child care. But she had chosen that herself. And I could not just shrug my shoulders the way Phil Sax had when his wife had started a dress shop and had an affair with a seller from New York. Nor could I be so analytical as Harry Gerard. "Economically you might be better off," he said. "And perhaps psychologically, too, in the long run."

I was not convinced. Allison had some other motive, I was

certain, some demon as invisible as the protozoa in that dark stream behind my mother's house. But what could I do to learn what it was?

We drove two cars to Cambridge — the BMW, which I had jammed full of clothes and boxes, and the station wagon packed with furniture. Allison thought it better to leave the older children with the Gerards next door, and we brought Livingston.

The apartment was exactly what I feared. It was a one-bedroom place in an old converted clapboard house on one of the back streets of North Cambridge. We climbed to the second floor, turned on the timed light, and climbed to the third. The place was not even clean. The previous tenant had departed hurriedly, leaving newspapers and bottles in the pantry and grease in the oven. The landlord had not fixed the light in the ancient refrigerator, and the windows above the kitchen sink were streaked with city grime. The whole place smelled of wax and acrid smoke.

We unloaded the furniture, and Allison went off in the station wagon to buy a bed. I carried in the boxes from the BMW, cleaned up as best I could, and began to assemble the metal bookcase we had brought. I was sitting on the floor, swearing at screws and angle joints, when suddenly I turned and Allison was there. Sweat glinted from her forehead, and she looked terribly sad. I don't know how long she had stood there before I noticed her.

"I got the bed," she said.

"Are you all right?"

"I will be."

"I'll bring up the bed when I finish this."

She paused in the doorway and looked around the room, as if grasping the full measure of her choice. Finally she said, "Can I have the key to the BMW? I'll go get some Chinese food."

"I thought we'd go out. Sort of a celebration."

"There's too much to do," she answered slowly, "if you're going to go back. I'd rather you did."

I nodded and threw her the keys.

She took nearly an hour. I finished setting up the bookcase and went downstairs to get the bed. I opened the hatch of the station wagon, and I knew why she had looked so sad, why she was taking a long time to get the food: she had bought a single bed.

In the first two years of our marriage, and before that, we had slept in a single bed, sometimes illicitly in dorm rooms, sometimes at friends' places, and even after we had bought the house in Haddonfield, while I was getting my law practice started. We had pressed together in the narrow space, holding each other in sleep, while the night unraveled beyond our walls.

Later our lives changed: we moved along in our world, with our children, new furnishings, new friends. Sometimes, long after we had acquired a big brass double bed, we had occasion to sleep upon a sofa or, skiing in Vermont, in a friend's small guest room with a single bed. We laughed, wondering how we had got through *years* in a small bed when now, twisted and cramped, we could not endure even one night.

Allison came back with the Chinese food, and I said nothing about the bed. The bookcase was against the wall beside her desk, and the bed was pushed into the corner near the lone window. We ate the Chinese food sitting on the floor, without speaking much, and later I drove home in the station wagon.

Hillary was either kind or mutinous, but overall she was helpful. Tricia had a toothache one morning, and I rushed her to the dentist. And Livingston's nurse walked out after a fight with her boyfriend, so I stayed home from work one day, then prevailed upon Angie Hamilton to babysit until I found someone else to come in.

We survived. Livy cried at night, and I got up to comfort him, heat his bottle, and pat him back to sleep. With Allison gone, Hillary became slightly more responsible, certainly more independent, and Tricia more silent. Sometimes there were moments when the four of us sat around the table in uneasy truce, and I felt near tears and proud for having put in a day's work and got dinner on the table.

Yet I missed Allison terribly. At first I called her often to complain about the small details I did not know and about the dilemmas that constantly recurred. Where were the winter sweaters? What was I supposed to do about the new drapes she had ordered? Did Tricia need shots? I told her how Livingston

was faring, about Hillary's 98 in algebra, what Tricia was reading.

"It takes some time to adjust," Allison said.

"I don't want to adjust."

There was a moment's pause, and I felt we had nothing more
to say. I was bitter; she was far away.

"Allison, listen to me . . ."

"No, I can't now. I love you, and I have to go."

The next time I called, two days later, her telephone had been
disconnected.

The telephone company could give me no satisfactory answers, and the police refused to look for someone who was not
officially missing. The history department kept no records of
who attended classes and who did not.

I began to think perverse thoughts. Perhaps it had been Allison's intention all along to deceive me. She wanted adventure,
to test herself with other men, and graduate school was a believ-
able ruse. Why else had she given only vague reasons for her
decision? And she knew, once her flight was under way, she
could still choose whether to soar higher or to come home again.

Yet I did not believe those things about her. Allison was not
the kind of woman for whom such excitement was alluring. She
would have been more tempted by a brazen fling than by a
drawn-out subterfuge, and I could more easily have imagined
her desire to see Europe or the Far East than her desire to be
with another man.

I wrestled with the issue of her privacy — whether, for the
good of all of us, I had a right to know her intentions. I wanted
to know the future of the family, whether I would have to begin
the subtle explanations to Tricia and to Hillary.

By the weekend I resolved to confront her: I would drive up
unannounced and would not leave until I had answers.

"I want to see where Mom lives," Tricia said when I told her
I was going.

"You can't, honey. There's no room to stay."

"Why are you taking Livingston?"

"Because I have to. I think your mother would want me to
because he's changing so fast."

"Are you getting divorced?"

"Not that I know of."

I drove all afternoon, stopping once to change Livy and again to buy more milk at a Howard Johnson's. I prepared a self-righteous speech: "All the sacrifices, the willingness to give free rein . . . I'm sorry I was not the man you wanted . . ." It sounded maudlin, impossible. "What do you think, Livy?" I asked.

I took a wrong turn at the traffic circle on Route 2 and ended up on Memorial Drive. Darkness was settling in, and with the sun behind me, the river looked icy, bleak against the far bank and the burgeoning skyline of Boston in the distance. I weaved through Harvard Square and west again on Massachusetts Avenue. When I found her house, not far from Porter Square, Allison was not there. The BMW was parked out front, collecting soot and leaves, but her window was dark. I rang the bell anyway, but no one answered.

The door downstairs was open, so I took Livingston in and waited at the landing outside her door. I was not by nature a prying person, but in these circumstances when Allison herself was so secretive, I felt justified in trying to get into the apartment. When I couldn't jimmy the lock, I snooped under her door. There was a note there, just a corner visible.

Then the light went off, and Livy cried until I could find the switch.

A person with no telephone received notes. I tried to scrape the piece of paper from beneath the door, but my fingers were too thick and the penknife I had too short. "Wait here," I said to Livy. "I'll get something from the car."

I raced down the stairs. In the car I searched through the jumble that had accumulated in the cargo space and found the cross-beam of an old kite.

Livingston screamed when the light went out again.

I tore the shreds of the kite away and was about to sprint back to the house when a woman turned the corner and came ahead. She was about Allison's height, but her hair was very short and she was quite thin. I hid the stick along my body.

"Tom?"

I stopped and turned back. "Is that you?"

"What are you doing here?"

"I came to see you. Hurry, Livy is crying."

I went in and turned on the light from below, and the wailing stopped. Allison took the stairs by twos. She snatched Livy from his seat and held him close, tight enough to smother him.

"I would have called," I said vaguely.

"Is anything wrong?"

Suddenly I felt crazy, stupid, as though, having believed a burglar was rummaging through the house, I had found only the family cat. "Nothing is wrong."

"Can you find the keys in my purse?" she asked. "What were you doing with that stick?"

I threw down the cross-beam of the kite and found the keys.

The notes — two of them — lay on the floor, and I picked them up and examined the handwriting. One was a woman's, the other a man's. Allison pushed past me, still hugging Livy.

"Did you bring diapers?" she asked, laying him on the bed.

I put the two notes on the table and went into the hallway to get the diapers. The apartment was bleak: nothing on the walls, the bed unmade, books and papers scattered across the desk and piled on the floor. In the small kitchen, a few dishes were stacked carelessly in the sink.

After she had changed Livy, Allison opened the notes. One was from a woman inviting her to a breakfast conference; the other, she said, was from a man who had found some sources of Russian history she had wanted.

That night, sleeping on the edge of the narrow bed, I understood less than ever.

By Thanksgiving little had changed. Allison came home for the holiday, and we went to my mother's house for dinner. Tillie had a thousand questions about how Allison was faring, how much she had to study, where she did her laundry. It was curious that Tillie seemed so interested until I realized how much Tillie and I were alike. Anything in the world outside seemed to her a subject of wonder.

"What do you *do* with history?" Tillie asked.

"You make it," Allison answered, perhaps too blithely.

"I mean are there careers?"

"Teaching, government, politics. If you want, there are lots of fields which might use the discipline of study."

The children had gone out to play in the yard, and we sat at the table littered with empty glasses and plates and used napkins.

"Boston is a lovely city," my mother said. "Don't you ever get a free moment?"

Allison nodded. "I've been to the museum several times, and once to the symphony. But I'm afraid I've spent most of my time reading."

"The work must be quite hard," my mother said.

"Novels," Allison went on. "I've never had such luxury."

I thought of her apartment, the unmade bed, and the dirty dishes.

"What novels?"

"Particularly Russian novels. The slant of fiction upon history has fascinated me. Chekhov; of course, Dostoevsky, Kuprin . . ."

"Dostoevsky is so gloomy," Tillie said.

"But haunting," Allison said wistfully. "And I admire Tolstoy."

We went on to other topics, and as often happened when Tillie was there, the conversation drifted toward my father.

"He would have lived ten more years," Tillie said, "if he had kept working."

"He had cancer of the colon," I said calmly, stating the facts as we all knew them. "His life would not have been pleasant."

"But he wouldn't have *had* cancer."

I tried to soothe Tillie, who had begun to cry. Allison excused herself and went to the kitchen with some plates. I heard dishes clattering, and my mother got up to help.

Tillie had dwelled upon our father's death. He had died two years after retiring from a lifelong career in the trust department of the City Bank of Philadelphia, and she saw no reason for him to die when he was on the brink of enjoying his life for the first time. I explained to her again that no logical connection existed between his retirement and his contracting cancer.

"We don't plan those things," I said, getting up to look out the window.

"But it's so unfair!"

I watched the children running in their good clothes across the lawn, the woods beyond, and their joy in the face of Tillie's

tiresome sorrow made me feel as though I were detached, suspended forever in the role of the one who comforted and provided. I was about to deliver my speech about fairness when a
taxi pulled up outside the front door.

Allison came out from the kitchen. "I'm sorry," she said politely and without rancor. "I have to leave."

"Allison . . ."

"I have work to do," she said. "Your mother understands.
Will you bring the children?"

She smiled at Tillie and went to the door, pausing a moment
to look at me closely before she went out.

I considered taking a leave of absence from the firm. Allison
needed help, and I thought the family's moving to Cambridge
might be the answer. The children would have lived through
the trauma, *adjusted,* as Allison might have said. We could have
closed up the house or rented it. But for three years, maybe
four? We were such a part of the town. The children had their
friends. We knew the Saxes and the Gerards, the streets, the
names of the shopkeepers. Allison and I had fought to save the
sycamores along Kings' Highway, and the children's summer
camp existed only because Harry Gerard and I canvassed the
neighborhood for the cause.

Besides, I have never understood how people just pulled up
stakes. How did they leave their homes and homelands and
strike out into the void? They were not like the Portuguese or
Columbus, or searchers of riches like Cortez, or dreamers of
glory. They were people who had too little, who clung to a tiny
speck of hope. They were cursed by their pasts and were willing
to give up friends, family, and familiar surroundings, even their
countries, for some tenuous vision of survival.

No, I would not move. And so I waited.

Allison called the children every week from a pay telephone,
and it made me anxious to think of her upon some sidewalk or
street corner, gazing into the reflection of herself in the glass
cell. I could hear the traffic beyond her, the horns of cars,
voices.

Once I asked her, "Is someone waiting for you?"

"No."

"I can only do this if you tell the truth."

"No one is waiting," she said. "You can believe what you wish."

I did not know what to believe.

Christmas, I hoped, would be better. Allison insisted we go to my mother's again, this time for two days.

"Are you sure you want us?" I asked my mother on the telephone.

"Of course. Allison wrote me a letter saying she's looking forward to it."

"I hope she apologized," I said.

"She explained."

"I wish she would explain to me."

My mother hesitated. "But mostly she wrote about her studies and how much she likes what she is doing."

I nodded, though I knew my mother could not see me. "If only we all did."

The day we drove to my mother's, December twentieth, was gray and cold. Low clouds moved slowly across the Delaware River, and as we headed for Bryn Mawr, I sensed a new mood in Allison.

"At least Tillie won't be there," I said, as though my sister's presence had somehow been the catalyst for Allison's behavior.

Allison looked at me, that subtle glance, but I kept my eyes on the road.

"It wasn't Tillie," she said.

"You know how she gets."

"I'm used to Tillie's problems."

Tricia put her head over the back of the seat and rested her chin upon my shoulder. "Is it going to snow?" she asked.

"It's supposed to."

"What happens to the little things in the creek when it freezes?"

"I don't know."

"Do they hibernate?"

"What do fish do?" I asked.

"Do you know, Mom?" Tricia asked.

Allison shook her head. "No, what?"

At my mother's we got settled in the various rooms. Livy was crawling and pulling himself up beside tables and chairs, so we cleared the low places of vases and glass figurines. Hillary disappeared into the attic, her place of refuge, while Tricia went into the backyard to look into the barren woodland.

I started a fire in the grate, and Allison made hot buttered rum. We had a couple of these, and I joked about Allison's running away at Thanksgiving. "She won't do it again."

"I can't promise," she said, smiling.

"There is no need to promise anything," my mother said.

"Tillie should learn," I went on. "I thought perhaps her . . ."

"It was Tolstoy," Allison said.

"Tolstoy?" Even my mother seemed surprised.

"I had been reading him — we were talking about it casually — reading the way he lived, what he wrote. Dostoevsky, too. What energy they had! Tolstoy never stopped questioning for his whole life. Did you know that when he was eighty-eight he tried to leave his wife?"

Neither my mother nor I could answer.

"He may have been terrible in some ways, but imagine living every day, wondering whether you had done the right thing, whether you ought to strike out for some new place, whether you still loved your wife . . ." Allison paused and drew a deep breath.

We were silent a moment, watching Livy pull himself up beside Allison on the sofa. She picked him up and set him on her lap.

Then Tricia came in from the veranda and shouted, "It's snowing! Look!"

Gray flakes swirled across the dark woodland and onto bare yellow lawn. Hillary, having apparently noticed, too, rushed down the stairs.

"Will you come?" Tricia asked me.

"I'll watch."

I got up and stood by the window. Hillary and Tricia ran across the lawn, trying to catch snowflakes in their mouths.

I turned back toward the room. The fire had ebbed, and the room seemed dark compared to the gray light outside.

My mother got up to put another piece of oak on the fire.

"Do you still remember what you felt when he died?" Allison asked.

My mother moved away from the fireplace and stood for a moment, visibly caught by the question. She seemed to know Allison spoke to her.

"It's strange that I have forgotten him," she said. "He determined so much of my life, but . . . I don't mean that cruelly." Her voice trailed away.

"Do you miss him?" Allison went on.

The question shocked me — so tactless and direct — and yet, voiced as it was in the silence, with the low fire and the gray snowlight beyond the room, it did not seem so much an intrusion as a reaching out.

Livingston was still, and even the children outside had tired and ceased their joyful yelling. My mother hesitated.

"I think of his carrying his *case,* as he called it, to the car, getting into the car, and driving to the station. I know that ritual is not uncommon — Tom probably does it, too — but I wondered sometimes what he thought as he went through these motions, whether he ever thought of *me,* whether he thought different things from day to day. He came home, kissed me, and never talked of his work, which took most of his conscious time. Did he care about it? Was there any satisfaction? Sometimes he would speak of the people he worked with or about some incident which happened on the train. But in a way he was like a man who never spoke about his dreams because he never dreamed."

My mother's soft tone ebbed, and I wanted to argue with her, but I could not bring myself to disagree. Words came to my lips and dissipated like the wisps of children's breaths in the cold air outside.

"No, I don't miss him," my mother went on. "I know that sounds ungrateful after all he did for me for so many years. I don't know what I mean exactly. I don't mean it as it sounds . . ." She looked at Allison. "I knew everything about him, but at the same time, nothing. He always did what he thought he should do. He was that kind of man."

That night I got up with Tricia when she cried out in the darkness of the strange house. I held her and smoothed her hair. Hillary stirred in the next bed but did not wake. When Tricia slept again, I went in to look in on Livy, who had thrown off his blankets. I tucked him in and gazed at him. Even in sleep he did not look peaceful.

For a long time I stood at the window of my old room, looking toward the woods. As a child I used to imagine people roaming those woods at night, eyes sharp as owls', intent upon some vague and nameless evil. Those men had nothing better to do than to creep through the darkness, and more than once I was certain I had seen a shadow lurking at the edge of the lawn. I would rush to my father's room, just short of screaming, and he would take me by the hand and lead me into the backyard.

"Now what do you think you see?" he asked, shining the flashlight into the woods.

"Men who can find me in the dark."

"And do you see them now?"

"No."

"Then we shall all be able to sleep."

But the trees seemed closer now, as I stood and listened to Livy's even breathing. The rough, curved horizon was dark against the dim gray sky. Snow fell invisibly through the air, filling the woods, covering the lawn with gray.

In the morning I dressed warmly and put on my boots in the vestibule before anyone else was up.

"Where are you going?" Tricia asked, surprising me, barefooted, on the kitchen steps.

"For a walk."

"Can I come?"

"You may come after breakfast. Will you tell your mother where I've gone?"

"Why can't I come now?"

"There will be tracks in the snow you can follow."

The snow had stopped and low clouds hung along the flanks of the hills. I plodded straight across the white lawn and, near the gazebo, crossed the tracks of two deer. Beyond that, at the edge of the yard where the tall dead grass replaced the manicured lawn, I found the wing prints of quail.

A slight breeze stirred snow from the trees, and it trickled down through the branches onto my face. My footsteps crackled leaves beneath the snow, and once out of sight of the house, I paused and listened. Far away a truck's engine whined, spinning wheels, and when that stopped, the whole world was silent, and the gray trees and spiny limbs and the whiteness filled me. My father had often taken me here, even in winter, pointing out small details — woodpeckers' holes or the tracks of mice. The stream swirled lazily over rocks and sodden logs, and I sat upon a snowy boulder and watched the water flow. Not much had changed, except the trails had grown over and the water in the stream was low. I sat for a long time, watching the slow current curl among the rocks, wondering what did happen to the invisible creatures in the water, waiting for Tricia to come to me.

GRACE PALEY

Telling

FROM MOTHER JONES

I was standing in the park under that tree. They call it the
Hanging Elm. Once upon a time it made a big improvement on
all kinds of hooligans. Nowadays if once in a while . . . No? No.
So this woman comes up to me, a woman minus a smile. I said
to my grandson, Uh-oh Emanuel. Here comes a lady, she was
once a beautiful customer of mine in the pharmacy I showed
you.

Emanuel says, Grandpa, who?

She looks OK now, but not so hot. Well, what can you do,
time takes a terrible toll off the ladies.

This is her idea of a hello: Iz, what are you doing with that
black child? Then she says, Who is he? Why are you holding on
to him like that? She gives me a look like God in judgment. You
could see it in famous paintings. Then she says, Why are you
yelling at that poor kid?

What yelling? A history lesson about the park. This is a tree
in guide books. How are you by the way, Miss . . . Miss? I was
embarrassed. I forgot her name absolutely.

Well who is he? You got him pretty scared.

Me? Don't be ridiculous. It's my grandson. Say hello, Emanuel, don't put on an act.

Emanuel shoves his hand in my pocket to be a little more
glued to me. Are you going to open your mouth sonny, yes or
no?

She says, Your grandson? Really Iz, your grandson? What do
you mean, your grandson? Emanuel closes his eyes tight. Did

you ever notice children get all mixed up. They don't want to
hear about something, they squinch up their eyes. Many children do this.

Now listen Emanuel I want you to tell this lady who is the
smartest boy in kindergarten.

Not a word.

Goddamnit open your eyes. It's something new with him. Tell
her who is the smartest boy. He was just five, he can already
read a whole book by himself.

He stands still. He's thinking. I know his little cute mind.
Then he jumps up and down yelling Me, Me, Me. He makes a
little dance. His grandma calls it his smartness dance. My other
ones (three children grown up for some time already) were also
very smart, but they don't hold a candle to this character. Soon
as I get a chance, I'm gonna bring him to the city to Hunter for
gifted children, he should get a test.

But this Miss . . . Miss . . . she's not finished with us yet. She's
worried. Whose kid is he? You adopt him?

Adopt? At my age? It's Cissy's kid. You know my Cissy? I see
she knows something. Why not, I had a public business. No
surprise.

Of course I remember Cissy. She says this, her face is a little
more ironed out.

So, my Cissy if you remember she was a nervous girl.

I'll *bet* she was.

Is that a nice way to answer? Cissy *was* nervous . . . The ner-
vousness to be truthful ran in Mrs. Z's family. Ran? Galloped
. . . tarum tarum tarum.

When we were young I used to go over there to visit and
while me and her brother and uncles played pinochle, in the
kitchen three aunts would sit drinking tea. Everything was Oi!
Oi! Oi! What for? Nothing to oi about. They got husbands . . .
perfectly fine gentlemen. One in business, two of them real
professionals. They just got in the habit somehow. So I said to
Mrs. Z, One oi out of you and it's divorce.

I remember your wife very well, this lady says. *Very* well. She
puts on the same face like before; her mouth gets small. Your
wife *is* a beautiful woman.

So . . . would I marry a mutt?

But she was right. My Nettie when she was young, she was very fair, like some Polish Jews you see once in a while. Like for instance maybe some big blond peasant made a pogrom on her great-grandma.

So I answered her, Oh yes, very nice looking; even now she's not so bad, but a little bit on the grouchy side.

OK. She makes a big sigh like I'm a hopeless case. What did happen to Cissy?

Emanuel go over there and play with those kids. No? No.

Well, I'll tell you, it's the genes. The genes are the most important. Environment is OK. But the genes . . . that's where the whole story is written down. I think the school had something to do with it also. Cissy's more an artist like your husband. Am I thinking of the right guy? When she was a kid you should of seen her. She's a nice-looking girl now, even when she has an attack. But then she was something. The family used to go to the mountains in the summer. We went dancing, her and me. What a dancer. People were surprised. Sometimes we danced until 2 A.M.

I don't think that was good, she says. I wouldn't dance with my son all night . . .

Naturally, you're a mother. But "good." Who knows what's good. Maybe a doctor. I could have been a doctor by the way. Her brother-in-law in business would of backed me. But then what? You don't have the time. People call you day and night. I cured more people in a day than a doctor in a week. Many an M.D. called me. Said, Zagrowsky, does it work . . . that Parke-Davis medication they put out last month or it's a fake? I got immediate experience and I'm not too stuck up to tell.

Oh Iz you are, she said. She says this like she means it but it makes her sad. How do I know this? Years in a store. You observe. You watch. The customer is always right, but plenty of times you know he's wrong and also a goddamn fool.

All of a sudden I put her in a certain place. Then I said to myself, Why are you standing here with this woman? I looked her straight in the face and I said, Faith? Right? Listen to me. Now you listen, because I got a question. Is it true, no matter what time you called, even if I was closing up, I came to your house with the penicillin or the tetracycline later? You lived on

the fourth floor walk-up. Your friend what's her name Susan
with the three girls next door? I can see it very clear. Your face
is all smeared up with crying, your kid got a hundred five de-
grees, maybe more, burning up, you didn't want to leave him in
the crib screaming, you're standing in the hall, it's dark. You
were living alone, am I right? So young. Also your husband he
comes to my mind, very jumpy fellow, in and out, walking
around all night. He drank? I betcha. Irish? Imagine, you didn't
get along so you got a divorce. Very simple. You kids knew how
to live.

She doesn't even answer me. She says . . . you want to know
what she says? She says Oh shit! Then she says, Of course I
remember. God, Richie was sick! Thanks, she says. Thanks, God
almighty thanks.

I was already thinking something else: the mind makes its
own business. When she first came up to me. I couldn't remember. I knew her well but where? Then out of no place, a word,
her bossy face maybe, exceptionally round, which is not usual,
her dark apartment, the four flights, the other girls — all once
lively, young . . . you could see them walking around on a sunny
day, dragging a couple kids, a carriage, a bike, beautiful girls,
but tired from all day, mostly divorced, going home alone. Boyfriends? Who knows how that type lives? I had a big apprecia-
tion for them. Sometimes, five o'clock I stood in the door to see
them. They were mostly the ways models *should* be. I mean not
skinny; round, like they were made of little cushions and bigger
cushions, depending where you looked, young mothers. I hollered a few words to them, they hollered back. Especially I remember her friend Ruthy — she had two little girls with long
black braids, down to here. I told her, In a couple of years Ruthy
you'll have some beauties on your hands. You better keep an
eye on them. In those days the women always answered you in
a nice way, not afraid to smile. Like this: They said, You really
think so? Thanks Iz.

But this is all used-to-be and in that place there is not only
good but bad and the main fact in regard to *this* particular lady:
I did her good but to me she didn't always do so much good.

So we stood around a little. Emanuel says, Grandpa let's go to
the swings. Go yourself — it's not so far, there's kids, I see them.

No, he says and stuffs his hand in my pocket again. So don't go. Ach what a day, I said. Buds and everything. She says, That's a catalpa tree over there. No kidding! I said. What do you call that one, doesn't have a single leaf. Locust, she says. Two locusts, I say.

Then I take a deep breath: OK. You still listening? Let me ask you, If I did you so much good including I saved your baby's life, how come you did that? You know what I'm talking about. A perfectly nice day. I look out the window of the pharmacy and I see four customers that I seen at least two in their bathrobes crying to me in the middle of the night Help Help! They're out there with signs. "Zagrowsky Is a Racist." "Years after Rosa Parks Zagrowsky Refuses to Serve Blacks."

It's like an etching right *here*. I point out to her my heart. I know exactly where it is.

She's naturally very uncomfortable when I tell her. Listen, she says, We were right.

I grab on to Emanuel. You?

Yes, we wrote a letter first, did you answer it? We said Zagrowsky come to your senses. Ruthy wrote it. We said we would like to talk to you. We tested you. At least four times, you kept Mrs. Green and Josie our friend Josie who was kind of Spanish black . . . she lived on the first floor in our house . . . you kept them waiting a long time till everyone ahead of them was taken care of. Then you were very rude, I mean nasty, you can be extremely nasty Iz. And then Josie left the store, she called you some pretty bad names. You remember Iz?

No I happen not to remember. There was plenty of yelling in the store. People *really* suffering; come in yelling for codeine or what to do their mother was dying. That's what I remember not some crazy Spanish lady hollering.

But listen, she says, like all this is not in front of my eyes, like the past is only a piece of paper in the yard — you didn't finish with Cissy.

Finish? *You* almost finished my business and don't think that Cissy didn't hold it up to me. Later when she was so sick.

Then I thought, Why should I talk to this woman? I see myself: how I was standing that day how many years ago? Like an idiot behind the counter waiting for customers. Everybody is peeking in past the picket line. It's the kind of neighborhood, if they see a picket line half don't come in. The cops say they have a right. To destroy a person's business. I was disgusted but I went into the street. After all I knew the ladies. I tried to explain, Faith, Ruthy, Mrs. Kratt — a stranger comes into a store naturally you have to serve the old customers first. Anyone would do the same. Also they sent in black people, brown people, all colors and to tell the truth I didn't like the idea my pharmacy should get the reputation of being a cut-rate place for them. They move into a neighborhood, goodbye property values. I did what everyone did. Not to insult people too much, but to discourage them a little. They shouldn't feel so welcome, they could just move in because it's a nice area.

All right. A person looks at my Emanuel and says, Hey! He's not altogether from the white race, what's going on? I'll tell you what: Life is going on. You have no opinion. I have an opinion. Life don't have an opinion.

I moved away from this Faith lady. I didn't like to be near her. I sat down on the bench. I'm no spring chicken. Cock-a-doodle-do, I only holler once in a while. I'm tired. I'm mostly the one in charge of our Emanuel. Mrs. Z stays home, her legs swell up. It's a shame.

In the subway once she couldn't get off at the right stop. The door opens, she can't get up. She tried (she's a little overweight). She says to a big guy with a notebook, a big colored fellow, Please help me get up. He says to her, You kept me down three hundred years, you can stay down another ten minutes. I asked her, Nettie didn't you tell him we're raising a little boy brown like a coffee bean. But he's right, says Nettie, we done that. We kept them down.

We? We? My two sisters and my father were being fried up for Hitler's supper in 1944 and you say We? Nettie sits down. Please bring me some tea. Yes Iz, I say *We.*

I can't even put up the water I'm so mad. You know, my Mrs., you are crazy like your three aunts, crazy like our Cissy. Your whole family put in the genes to make it for sure that she wouldn't have a chance. Nettie looks at me. She says Ai Ai. She doesn't say oi anymore. She got herself assimilated into ai . . . That's how come she also says "we" done it. Don't think this will

make you an American, I said to her, that you included yourself
in with Robert E. Lee. Naturally it was a joke, only what is there
to laugh?

I'm tired right now. This Faith could even see I'm a little
shaky. What should she do she's thinking. But she decides the
discussion ain't over so she sits down sideways. The bench is
damp. It's only April.

What about Cissy? Is she all right?

It ain't your business how she is.

OK. She starts to go.

Wait wait! Since I seen you in your nightgown a couple of
times when you were a handsome young lady . . . She really gets
up this time. I think she must be a woman's libber, they don't
like remarks about nightgowns. Bathrobes, she didn't mind. Let
her go! The hell with her . . . But she comes back. She says,
Once and for all, cut it out Iz. I really *want* to know. Is Cissy all
right?

You want. She's fine. She lives with me and Nettie. She's in
charge of the plants. It's an all-day job.

But why should I leave her off the hook. Oh boy Faith, I got
to say it, what you people put on me! And you want to know
how Cissy is. *You!* Why? Sure. You remember you finished with
the picket lines after a week or two. I don't know why. Tired?
Summer maybe, you got to go away make trouble at the beach.
But I'm stuck there. Did I have air conditioning yet? All of a
sudden I see Cissy outside. She has a sign also. She must of got
the idea from you women. A big sandwich board, she walks up
and down.

If someone talks to her, she presses her mouth together.

I don't remember that, Faith says.

Of course you were already on Long Island or Cape Cod or
someplace — the Jersey shore.

No, she says, I was not. I was not. (I see this is a big insult to
her that she should go away for the summer.)

Then I thought, Calm down Zagrowsky. Because for a fact I
didn't want her to leave, because, since I already began to tell I
have to tell the whole story. I'm not a person who keeps things
in. Tell! That opens up the congestion a little — the lungs are
for breathing, not secrets. My wife never tells, she coughs,

coughs. All night. Wakes up. Ai Iz open the window there's no air. You poor woman, if you want to breathe, you got to tell.

So I said to this Faith, I'll tell you how Cissy is but you got to hear the whole story how we suffered. I thought OK. Who cares! Let her get on the phone later with the other girls. They should know what they started.

How we took our own Cissy from here to there to the biggest doctor I had good contacts from the pharmacy. Dr. Francis O'Connell the heavy Irishman over the hospital sat with me and Mrs. Z for two hours, a busy man. He explained that it was one of the most great mysteries. They were ignoramuses, the most brilliant doctors were dummies in this field. But still in my place, I heard of this cure and that one. So we got her massaged fifty times from head to toe, whatever someone suggested. We stuffed her with vitamins and minerals — there was a real doctor in charge of this idea.

If she would take the vitamins — sometimes she shut her mouth. To her mother she said dirty words. We weren't used to it. Meanwhile in front of my place every morning she walks up and down. She could of got minimum wage she was so regular. Her afternoon job is to follow my wife from corner to corner to tell what my wife done wrong to her when she was a kid. Then after a couple months, all of a sudden she starts to sing. She has a beautiful voice. She took lessons from a well-known person. On Christmas week, in front of the pharmacy she sings half the *Messiah* by Handel. You know it? So that's nice, you think. Oh! that's beautiful. But where were you you didn't notice that she don't have on a coat. You didn't see she walks up and down, her socks are falling off? Her face and hands are like she's the super in the cellar. She sings! She sings! Two songs she sings the most: One is about the Gentiles will see the light and the other is Look! a virgin will conceive a son. My wife says, Sure, naturally, she wishes she was a married woman just like anyone. Baloney. She could of. She had plenty of dates. Plenty. She sings, the idiots applaud, some skunk yells, Go Cissy go. What? Go where? Some days she just hollers.

Hollers what?

Oh, I forgot about you. Hollers anything. Hollers racist! Hollers he sells poison chemicals! Hollers he's a terrible dancer, he got three left legs! Which isn't true, just to insult me publicly, plain silly. The people laugh, what'd she say? Some didn't hear so well; hollers you go to whores. Also not true. She met me once with a woman actually a distant relative from Israel. Not that I'm an angel. But everything is in her head. It's a garbage pail.

One day her mother says to her, Cissile comb your hair for godsakes darling. For this remark, she gives her mother a sock in the face. I come home I see a woman not at all young with two black eyes and a bloody nose. The doctor said, Before it's better with your girl it's got to be worse. That much he knew. He sent us to a beautiful place a hospital right at the city line, I'm not sure if it's Westchester or the Bronx, but thank god you could use the subway. That's how I found out what I was saving up my money for. I thought for retiring in Florida to walk around under the palm trees in the middle of the week. Wrong. It was for my beautiful Cissy she should have a nice home with other crazy people.

So little by little, she calms down. We can visit her. She shows us the candy store, we give her a couple of dollars; soon our life is this way. Three times a week my wife goes, gets on the subway with delicious food (no sugar, they're against sugar); she brings something nice, a blouse or a kerchief — a present, you understand, to show love; and once a week I go, but she don't want to look at me. So close we were, like sweethearts — you can imagine how I feel. Well you have children so you know little children little troubles, big children big troubles. It's a saying in Yiddish. Maybe the Chinese said it too.

Oh Iz. How could it happen? Like that. All of a sudden. No signs?

What's with this Faith? Her eyes are full of tears. Sensitive I suppose. I see what she's thinking. Her kids are teen-agers. So far they look OK but what will happen? People think of themselves. Human nature. At least she doesn't tell me it's my wife's fault or mine. I did something terrible! I loved my child. I know what's on people's minds. I know psychology *very* well. Since this happened to us, I read up on the whole business.

Oh Iz.

She puts her hand on my knee. I looked at her. Maybe she's

just a nut. Maybe she thinks I'm plain old (I almost am). Well I
said it before. Thank god for the head. Inside the head is the
only place you go to be young when the usual place gets used
up. For some reason she gives me a kiss on the cheek. A peculiar
person. Right?

Faith I still can't figure it out why you girls were so rotten to
me.

But we were right.

Then this lady Queen of Right makes a small lecture. She
don't remember my Cissy walking up and down screaming bad
language but she remembers: After Mrs. Kendrick's big fat
snotty maid walked out with Kendrick's diabetes order, I made
a face and said Ho! Ho! The great lady! That's terrible? She
says whenever I saw a couple walk past on the block, a black and
white couple, I said Ugh — disgusting! It shouldn't be allowed!
She heard this remark from me a few times. So? It's a matter of
taste. Then she tells me about this Josie, probably Puerto Rican,
once more — the one I didn't serve in time. Then she says,
Really, Iz, what about Emanuel.

Don't you look at Emanuel, I said. Don't you dare. He has
nothing to do with it.

She rolls her eyes around in her head like they were marbles.
She got more to say. She also doesn't like how I talk to women.
She says I called Mrs. Z a grizzly bear a few times. It's my wife,
no? That I was winking and blinking at the girls, a few pinches.
A lie . . . Maybe I patted, but I never pinched. Besides I know
for a fact a couple of them loved it. She says No, none of them
liked it. Not one. They only put up with it because it wasn't time
yet in history to holler. (An American-born girl has some nerve
to mention history.)

But, she says, Iz forget all that. I'm sorry you have so much
trouble now. She's really sorry. In a second she changes her
mind. She's not so sorry. I could see her face change. It's her
mouth. With some people the eyes. She takes her hand back.
This woman is like a book, only the pages are turning top speed.
You have to be a fast reader.

Emanuel climbs up on my lap. He pats my face. Don't be sad
Grandpa, he says. He can't stand if he sees a tear on a person's
face. Even a stranger. If his mama gets a black look, he's smart,
he doesn't go to her anymore. He comes to my wife. Grandma

he says, my poor mama is very sad. My wife jumps and runs in. Worried. Scared. Did Cissy take her pills? What's going on? Once he went to Cissy and said, Mama why are you crying? So this is her answer to a little boy: She stands up straight and starts to bang her head on the wall. Hard. My mama! he screams. Lucky I was home. Since then he goes straight to his grandma for his little troubles. What will happen? We're not so young. My oldest son is doing very well, he used his brains — only he lives in a very exclusive neighborhood in Rockland County. Our other boy — well he's in his own life, he's from that generation. He went away.

She looks at me this Faith. She can't say a word. She sits there. She opens her mouth almost. I know what she wants to know: How did Emanuel come into the story? When?

Then she says to me exactly those words. Well, where does Emanuel fit in?

He fits, he fits. Like a golden present from Nasser.

Nasser?

OK. Egypt, not Nasser — he's from Isaac's other son, get it? A close relation. I was sitting one day thinking why? why? The answer: to remind us. That's the purpose of most things.

It was Abraham, she interrupts me. He had two sons Isaac and Ishmael. God promised him he would be the father of generations. He was. But you know, she says, he wasn't such a good father to those two little boys. Not so unusual, she has to add on.

You see that's what they make of the Bible, those women; because they got it in for men. Of *course* I meant Abraham. Abraham. Did I say Isaac? Once in a while I got to admit it, she says something true. You remember one son he sent out of the house altogether, the other he was ready to chop up if he only heard a noise in his head saying Go! Chop!

But the question is where did Emanuel fit. I didn't mind telling. I wanted to tell, I explained that already . . .

So it begins. One day my wife goes to the administration of Cissy's hospital and she says. What kind of a place you're running here? I have just looked at my daughter. A blind person could almost see it. My daughter is pregnant. What goes on here at night? Who's the supervisor? Where is she this minute?

Pregnant? they say like they never heard of it. And they run around and the regular doctor comes and says, Yes, pregnant. Sure. You got more news? my wife says. And then: meetings with the weekly psychiatrist, the day-by-day psychologist, the nerve doctor, the social worker, the supervising nurse, the nurse's aide. My wife says, She knows, Cissy knows. She's not an idiot, only mixed up and depressed. She *knows* she has a child in her womb inside of her like a normal woman. She likes it, my wife said. She even said to her, Mama I'm having a baby and she gave my wife a kiss. The first kiss in a couple of years. How do you like that?

Meanwhile they investigated thoroughly. It turns out the man is a colored fellow. One of the gardeners. But he left a couple months ago for the Coast. I could imagine what happened. Cissy always loved flowers. When she was a little girl she was planting seeds every minute and sitting all day in front of the flower pot to see the little flower cracking up the seed. So she must of watched him and watched him. He dug up the earth. He put in the seeds. She watched.

The office apologized. Apologized? An accident. The supervisor was on vacation that week. I could sue them for a million dollars. Don't think I didn't talk to a lawyer. That time, then, when I heard, I called a detective agency to find him. My plan was to kill him. I would tear him limb from limb. What to do next. They called them all in again. The psychiatrist, the psychologist, they only left out the nurse's aide.

They only hope she could live a half-normal life — not in the institution: She must have this baby, she could carry it full term. No, I said, I can't stand it. I refuse. Out of my Cissy, who looked like a piece of gold, would come a black child. Then the psychologist says, Don't be so bigoted. What nerve! Little by little my wife figured out a good idea. OK, we'll put it out for adoption. Cissy doesn't even have to see it in person.

You are laboring under a misapprehension, says the boss of the place. They talk like that. What he meant, he meant we got to take that child home with us and if we really loved Cissy . . . Then he gave us a big lecture on this baby; it's Cissy's connection to life, also it happens she was crazy about this gardener, this son of a bitch, a black man with a green thumb.

You see I can crack a little joke because look at this pleasure. I got a little best friend here. Where I go, he goes, even when I go down to the Italian side of the park to play a little boccie with the old goats over there. They invite me if they see me in the supermarket, Hey Iz! Tony's sick. You come on and play, OK? My wife says, Take Emanuel, he should see how men play games. I take him, those old guys they also seen plenty in their day. They think I'm some kind of a do-gooder. Also a lot of those people are ignorant. They think the Jews are a little bit colored anyways, so they don't look at him too long. He goes to the swings and they make believe they never even seen him.

I didn't mean to get off the subject. What is the subject? The subject is how we took the baby. My wife, Mrs. Z, Nettie, she plain forced me. She said, We got to take this child on us. I will move out of here into the project with Cissy and be on welfare Iz, you better make up your mind. Her brother a top social worker he encouraged her, I think he's a communist also, the way he talks the last twenty, thirty years . . . He says:

You'll live Iz. It's a baby after all. It's got your blood in it. Unless of course you want Cissy to rot away in that place till you're so poor they don't keep her anymore. Then they'll stuff her into Bellevue or Central Islip or something. First she's a zombie, then she's a vegetable. That's what you want Iz?

After this converation I get sick. I can't go to work. Meanwhile every night Nettie cries. She don't get dressed in the morning. She walks around with a broom. Doesn't sweep up. Starts to sweep bursts into tears. Puts a pot of soup on the stove runs into the bedroom lies down. Soon I think I'll have to put her away too.

I give in.

My listener says to me, Right Iz, you did the right thing. What else could you do?

I feel like smacking her. I'm not a violent person just very excitable, but who asked her. Right Iz. She sits there looking at me, nodding her head from rightness. Emanuel is finally in the playground. I see him swinging and swinging. He could swing for two hours. He likes that. He's a regular swinger.

Well, the bad part of the story is over. Now the good part.

Naming the baby. What should we name him? A perfect stranger. Little brown baby. An intermediate color. Very cute if I have to admit.

In the maternity ward, you know where the mothers lie with the new babies, Nettie is saying, Cissy Cissile darling my sweetest heart (this is how my wife talked to her, like she was made of gold — or eggshells) my darling, what should we name this little child?

Cissy is nursing. On her white flesh is this little black curly head. Cissy says right away: Emanuel, Immediately. When I hear this, I say, Ridiculous. Ridiculous, such a long Jewish name on a little baby. I got old uncles with such names. Then they all get called Manny. Uncle Manny. Again she says — Emanuel . . .

David is nice, I suggest in a pleasant voice. It's your grandpa's he should rest in peace. Michael is nice too, my wife says. Joshua is beautiful. Many children have these beautiful names nowadays. They're nice modern names. People like to say them.

No, she says. Emanuel. Then she starts her screaming. Emanuel Emanuel. We almost had to give her extra pills. But we were careful on account of the milk. The milk could get affected.

OK, everyone hollered, OK. Calm yourself Cissy. OK. Emanuel. Bring the birth certificate. Write it down. Put it down. Let her see it.

Emanuel . . . In a few days, the rabbi came. He raised up his eyebrows a couple times. Not that he didn't know beforehand. Then he did his job, which is to make the bris. In other words, a circumcision. This is done so the child will be a man in Israel. That's the expression they use. He isn't the first colored child. They tell me long ago we were mostly dark. And now I think of it, I wouldn't mind going over there to Israel. They say there are plenty black Jews. It's not unusual over there at all. They ought to put out more publicity on it. Because I have to think where he should live. Maybe it won't be so good for him here. Because my son, his fancy ideas . . . ach forget it.

What about the building, your neighborhood, I mean where you live now? Are there other black people in the community?

Oh yeah, but they're very snobbish. Don't ask what they got to be so snobbish.

Because, she says, he should have friends his own color, he shouldn't have the burden of being the only one in school.

Listen, it's New York, it's not Oshkosh, Wisconsin. But she gets going, you can't stop her.

After all, she says, he should eventually have his own people. It's their life he'll have to share. I know it's a problem to you Iz, I know, but that's the way it is. A friend of mine with the same situation moved to a more integrated neighborhood.

Is that a fact? I say, Where's that?

Oh there are . . .

I start to tell her, Wait a minute we live thirty-five years in this apartment. But I can't talk. I sit very quietly for a while, I think and think. I say to myself, Be like a Hindu Iz, calm like a cucumber. But it's too much. Listen Miss, Miss Faith, do me a favor. Don't teach me.

I'm not teaching you Iz, It's just . . .

Don't answer me every time I say something. Talking talking. It's true. What for? To whom? Why? Nettie's right. It's our business. She's telling me Emanuel's life.

You don't know nothing about it, I yell at her. Go make a picket line. Don't teach me.

She gets up and looks at me kind of scared. Take it easy Iz.

Emanuel is coming. He hears me. He got his little worried face. She sticks out a hand to pat him, his grandpa is hollering so loud.

But I can't put up with it. Hands off, I yell, It ain't your kid. Don't lay a hand on him. And I grab his shoulder and push him through the park past the playground and the big famous arch. She runs after me a minute. Then she sees a couple friends. Now she has what to talk about. Three, four women. They make a little bunch, they talk. They turn around, they look. One waves hiya Iz.

This park is full of noise. Everybody got something to say to the next guy. Playing this music, standing on their heads, juggling. Someone even brought a piano can you believe it, some job.

I sold the store four years ago. I couldn't put in the work no more. But I wanted to show Emanuel my pharmacy, what a beautiful place it was, how it sent three children to college, saved a couple lives — imagine: one store!

I tried to be quiet for the boy. You want ice cream Emanuel. Here's a dollar sonny. Buy yourself a Good Humor. The man's over there. Don't forget to ask for the change. I bend down to give him a kiss. I don't like that he heard me yell at a woman and my hand is still shaking. He hugs me tight. Grandpa don't go away, stay right here . . . He runs a few steps, he looks back to make sure I didn't move an inch.

I got my eye on him too. He waves a chocolate Popsicle. It's a little darker than him. Out of that crazy mob a young fellow comes up to me. He has a baby strapped on his back. That's the style now. He asks like it's an ordinary friendly question, he points to Emanuel . . . Gosh what a cute kid. Whose is he? I don't answer. He says it again, Really some cute kid.

I just look in his face. What does he want? I should tell him the story of my life? I don't need to tell. I already told and told. So I said very loud no one else should bother me. How come it's your business mister? Who do you think he is? By the way, whose kid you got on your back? It don't look like you.

He says, Hey there buddy, be cool be cool. I didn't mean anything. (You met anyone lately who meant something when he opened his mouth?) While I'm hollering at him, he starts to back away. The women are gabbing in a little clutch by the statue. It's a considerable distance, lucky they got radar . . . They turn around sharp like birds and fly over to the man. They talk very soft. Why are you bothering this old man? He got enough trouble. Why don't you leave him alone?

The fellow says, I wasn't bothering him. I just asked him something.

Well, he thinks you're bothering him, Faith says.

Then her friend a woman maybe forty, very angry starts to holler. How come you don't take care of your own kid are you deaf? she's crying. Naturally the third woman makes a remark, doesn't want to be left out. She taps him on his jacket. I seen you around here before buster, you better watch out.

Then this Faith comes back to me, with a big smile. She says, Honestly, some people are a pain aren't they Iz? We sure let him have it, didn't we? And she gives me one of her kisses. Say Hello to Cissy OK? She puts her arms around her pals. They say a few words back and forth, like cranking up a motor. Then they bust out laughing. They wave goodbye to Emanuel. Laughing. Laughing. So long Iz . . . see you . . .

So I say, What is going on Emanuel? Could you explain to me what just happened? Did you notice anywhere a joke?

This is the first time he doesn't answer me. He's writing his name on the sidewalk Emanuel Emanuel in big capital letters.

And the women walk away. Talking. Talking. Stories.

MONA SIMPSON

Lawns

FROM THE IOWA REVIEW

I STEAL. I've stolen books and money and even letters. Letters
are great. I can't tell you the feeling walking down the street
with twenty dollars in my purse, stolen earrings in my pocket. I
don't get caught. That's the amazing thing. You're out on the
sidewalk, other people all around, shopping, walking, and
you've got it. You're out of the store, you've done this thing
you're not supposed to do, but no one stops you. At first it's a
rush. Like you're even for everything you didn't get before. But
then you're left alone, no one even notices you. Nothing
changes.

I work in the mailroom of my dormitory, Saturday mornings.
I sort mail, put the letters in these long narrow cubbyholes. The
insides of mailboxes. It's cool there when I stick in my arm.

I've stolen cash — these crisp, crackling, brand-new twenty-
dollar bills the fathers and grandmothers send, sealed up in
sheets of wax paper. Once I got a fifty. I've stolen presents, too.
I got a sweater and a football. I didn't want the football, but
after the package was messed up on the mail table, I had no
choice, I had to take the whole thing in my day pack and throw
it out on the other side of campus. I found a covered garbage
can. It was miles away. Brand new football.

Mostly, what I take are cookies. No evidence. They're edible.
I can spot the coffee cans of chocolate chip. You can smell it
right through the wrapping. A cool smell, like the inside of a
pantry. Sometimes I eat straight through the can during my
shift.

Tampering with the United States mail is a federal crime, I know. Listen, let me tell you, I know. I got a summons in my mailbox to go to the Employment Office next Wednesday. Sure I'm scared.

The university cops want to talk to me. Great. They think, "suspect" is the word they use, that one of us is throwing out mail instead of sorting it. Wonder who? Us is the others, I'm not the only sorter. I just work Saturdays, mail comes, you know, six days a week in this country. They'll never guess it's me.

They say this in the letter, they think it's out of *laziness*. Wanting to hurry up and get done, not spend the time. But I don't hurry. I'm really patient on Saturday mornings. I leave my dorm early, while Lauren's still asleep, I open the mailroom — it's this heavy door and I have my own key. When I get there, two bags are already on the table, sagging, waiting for me. Two old ladies. One's packages, one's mail. There's a small key opens the bank of doors, the little boxes from the inside. Through the glass part of every mail slot, I can see. The Astroturf field across the street over the parking lot, it's this light green. I watch the sky go from black to gray to blue while I'm there. Some days just stay foggy. Those are the best. I bring a cup of coffee in with me from the vending machine — don't want to wake Lauren up — and I get there at like seven-thirty or eight o'clock. I don't mind it then, my whole dorm's asleep. When I walk out it's as quiet as a football game day. It's eleven or twelve when you know everyone's up and walking that it gets bad being down there. That's why I start early. But I don't rush.

Once you open a letter, you can't just put it in a mailbox. The person's gonna say something. So I stash them in my pack and throw them out. Just people I know. Susan Brown I open, Annie Larsen, Larry Helprin. All the popular kids from my high school. These are kids who drove places together, took vacations, they all ski, they went to the prom in one big group. At morning nutrition — nutrition, it's your break at ten o'clock for donuts and stuff. California state law, you have to have it.

They used to meet outside on the far end of the math patio, all in one group. Some of them smoked. I've seen them look at

each other, concerned at ten in the morning. One touched the
inside of another's wrist, like grown-ups in trouble.

And now I know. Everything I thought those three years,
worst years of my life, turns out to be true. The ones here get
letters. Keri's at Santa Cruz, Lilly's in San Diego, Kevin's at
Harvard, and Beth's at Stanford. And like from families, their
letters talk about problems. They're each other's main lives. You
always knew, looking at them in high school, they weren't just
kids who had fun. They cared. They cared about things.

They're all worried about Lilly now. Larry and Annie are
flying down to talk her into staying at school.

I saw Glenn the day I came to Berkeley. I was all unpacked and
I was standing there leaning into the window of my father's car,
saying, "Smile, Dad, jeez, at least try, would you?" He was crying
because he was leaving. I'm thinking oh, my god, some of these
other kids carrying in their trunks and backpacks are gonna see
him, and then finally, he drives away and I was sad. That was
the moment I was waiting for, him gone and me alone and there
it was and I was sad. I took a walk through campus and I'd been
walking for almost an hour and then I see Glenn, coming down
on a little hill by the infirmary, riding one of those lawn mowers
you sit on, with grass flying out of the side and he's smiling. Not
at me but just smiling. Clouds and sky behind his hair, half of
Tamalpais gone in fog. He was wearing this bright orange vest
and I thought, fall's coming.

I saw him that night again in our dorm cafeteria. This's the
first time I've been in love. I worry. I'm a bad person, but
Glenn's the perfect guy, I mean for me at least, and he thinks
he loves me and I've got to keep him from finding out about
me. I'll die before I'll tell him. Glenn, OK, Glenn. He looks like
Mick Jagger, but sweet, ten times sweeter. He looks like he's
about ten years old. His father's a doctor over at UC Med.
Gynecological surgeon.

First time we got together, a whole bunch of us were in
Glenn's room drinking beer, Glenn and his roommate collect
beer cans, they have them stacked up, we're watching TV and
finally everybody else leaves. There's nothing on but those gray
lines and Glenn turns over on his bed and asks me if I'd rub his
back.

I couldn't believe this was happening to me. In high school, I was always ending up with the wrong guys, never the one I wanted. But I wanted it to be Glenn and I knew it was going to happen, I knew I didn't have to do anything. I just had to stay there. It would happen. I was sitting on his rear end, rubbing his back, going under his shirt with my hands.

All of a sudden, I was worried about my breath and what I smelled like. When I turned fourteen or fifteen, my father told me once that I didn't smell good. I slugged him when he said that and didn't talk to him for days, not that I cared about what I smelled like with my father. He was happy, though, kind of, that he could hurt me. That was the last time, though, I'll tell you.

Glenn's face was down in the pillow. I tried to sniff myself but I couldn't tell anything. And it went all right anyway.

I don't open Glenn's letters but I touch them. I hold them and smell them — none of his mail has any smell.

He doesn't get many letters. His parents live across the Bay in Marin County, they don't write. He gets letters from his grandmother in Michigan, plain, even handwriting on regular envelopes, a sticker with her return address printed on it, Rural Route #3, Guns Street, see, I got it memorized.

And he gets letters from Diane, Di, they call her. High school girlfriend. Has a pushy mother, wants her to be a scientist, but she already got a C in Chem 1A. I got an A+, not to brag. He never slept with her, though, she wouldn't, she's still a virgin down in San Diego. With Lilly. Maybe they even know each other.

Glenn and Di were popular kids in their high school. Redwood High. Now I'm one because of Glenn, popular. Because I'm his girlfriend, I know that's why. Not 'cause of me. I just know, OK, I'm not going to start fooling myself now. Please.

Her letters I hold up to the light, they've got fluorescent lights in there. She's supposed to be blond, you know, and pretty. Quiet. The soft type. And the envelopes. She writes on these sheer cream-colored envelopes and they get transparent and I can see her writing underneath, but not enough to read what it says, it's like those hockey lines painted under layers of ice.

I run my tongue along the place where his grandmother

sealed the letter. A sharp, sweet gummy taste. Once I cut my tongue. That's what keeps me going to the bottom of the bag, I'm always wondering if there'll be a letter for Glenn. He doesn't get one every week. It's like a treasure. Cracker Jack prize. But I'd never open Glenn's mail. I kiss all four corners where his fingers will touch, opening it, before I put it in his box.

I brought home cookies for Lauren and me. Just a present. We'll eat 'em or Glenn'll eat 'em. I'll throw them out for all I care. They're chocolate chip with pecans. This was one good mother. A lucky can. I brought us coffee, too. I *bought* it.

Yeah, OK, so I'm in trouble. Wednesday, at ten-thirty, I got this notice I was supposed to appear. I had a class, Chem 1C, pre-med staple. Your critical thing. I never missed it before. I told Glenn I had a doctor's appointment.

OK, so I skip it anyway and I walk into this room and there's these two other guys, all work in the mailroom doing what I do, sorting. And we all sit there on chairs on this green carpet. I was staring at everybody's shoes. And there's a cop. University cop, I don't know what's the difference. He had this sagging, pear-shaped body. Like what my dad would have if he were fat, but he's not, he's thin. He walks slowly on the carpeting, his fingers hooked in his belt loops. I was watching his hips.

Anyway, he's accusing us all and he's trying to get one of us to admit we did it. No way.

"I hope one of you will come to me and tell the truth. Not a one of you knows anything about this? Come on, now."

I shake my head no and stare down at the three pairs of shoes. He says they're not going to do anything to the person who did it, right, wanna make a bet, they say they just want to know, but they'll take it back as soon as you tell them.

I don't care why I don't believe him. I know one thing for sure and that's they're not going to do anything to me as long as I say no, I didn't do it. That's what I said, no, I didn't do it, I don't know a thing about it. I just can't imagine where those missing packages could have gone, how letters got into garbage cans. Awful. I just don't know.

The cop had a map with X's on it every place they found mail. The garbage cans. He said there was a group of students trying

to get an investigation. People's girlfriends sent cookies that
never got here. Letters are missing. Money. These students put
up Xeroxed posters on bulletin boards showing a garbage can
stuffed with letters.

Why should I tell them, so they can throw me in jail? And
kick me out of school? Four-point-oh average and I'm going to
let them kick me out of school? They're sitting there telling us
it's a felony. A federal crime. No way, I'm gonna go to medical
school.

This tall, skinny guy with a blond mustache, Wallabees, looks
kind of like a rabbit, he defended us. He's another sorter, works
Monday/Wednesdays.

"We all do our jobs," he says. "None of us would do that."
The rabbity guy looks at me and the other girl for support. So
we're going to stick together. The other girl, a dark blonde
chewing her lip, nodded. I loved that rabbity guy that second. I
nodded too.

The cop looked down. Wide hips in the coffee-with-milk-
colored pants. He sighed. I looked up at the rabbity guy. They
let us all go.

I'm just going to keep saying no, not me, didn't do it and I
just won't do it again. That's all. Won't do it anymore. So, this is
Glenn's last chance for homemade cookies. I'm sure as hell not
going to bake any.

I signed the form, said I didn't do it, I'm OK now. I'm
safe. It turned out OK after all, it always does. I always think
something terrible's going to happen and it doesn't. I'm
lucky.

I'm afraid of cops. I was walking, just a little while ago, today,
down Telegraph with Glenn, and these two policemen, not the
one I'd met, other policemen, were coming in our direction. I
started sweating a lot. I was sure until they passed us, I was sure
it was all over, they were there for me. I always think that. But
at the same time, I know it's just my imagination. I mean, I'm a
four-point-oh student, I'm a nice girl just walking down the
street with my boyfriend.

We were on our way to get Happy Burgers. When we turned
the corner, about a block past the cops, I looked at Glenn and I
was flooded with this feeling. It was raining a little and we were

by People's Park. The trees were blowing and I was looking at all those little gardens coming up, held together with stakes and white string.

I wanted to say something to Glenn, give him something. I wanted to tell him something about me.

"I'm bad in bed," that's what I said, I just blurted it out like that. He just kind of looked at me, he was nervous, he just giggled. He didn't know what to say, I guess, but he sort of slung his arm around me and I was so grateful and then we went in. He paid for my Happy Burger, I usually don't let him pay for me, but I did and it was the best goddamn hamburger I've ever eaten.

I want to tell him things.

I lie all the time, always have, but I keep track of each lie I've ever told Glenn and I'm always thinking of the things I can't tell him.

Glenn was a screwed up kid, kind of. He used to go in his backyard, his parents were inside the house I guess, and he'd find this big stick and start twirling around with it. He'd dance, he called it dancing, until if you came up and clapped in front of him, he wouldn't see you. He'd spin around with that stick until he fell down dead on the grass, unconscious, he said he did it to see the sky break up in pieces and spin. He did it sometimes with a tire swing, too. He told me when he was spinning like that, it felt like he was just hearing the earth spinning, that it really went that fast all the time but we just don't feel it. When he was twelve years old his parents took him in the city to a clinic to see a psychologist. And then he stopped. See, maybe I should go to a psychologist. I'd get better, too. He told me about that in bed one night. The ground feels so good when you fall, he said to me. I loved him for that.

"Does anything feel that good now?" I said.

"Sex sometimes. Maybe dancing."

Know what else he told me that night? He said, right before we went to sleep, he wasn't looking at me, he said he'd been thinking what would happen if I died, he said he thought how he'd be at my funeral, all my family and my friends from high school and my little brother would all be around at the front and he'd be at the edge in the cemetery, nobody'd even know who he was.

I was in that crack, breathing the air between the bed and the wall. Cold and dusty. Yeah, we're having sex. I don't know. It's good. Sweet. He says he loves me. I have to remind myself. I talk to myself in my head while we're doing it. I have to say, it's OK, this is just Glenn, this is who I want it to be and it's just like rubbing next to someone. It's just like pushing two hands together, so there's no air in between.

I cry sometimes with Glenn, I'm so grateful.

My mother called and woke me up this morning. Ms. I'm-going-to-be-perfect. Ms. Anything-wrong-is-your-own-fault. Ms. If-anything-bad-happens-you're-a-fool.

She says if she has time, she *might* come up and see my dorm room in the next few weeks. Help me organize my wardrobe, she says. She didn't bring me up here, my dad did. I wanted Danny to come along. I love Danny.

But my mother has *no* pity. She thinks she's got the answers. She's the one who's a lawyer, she's the one who went back to law school and stayed up late nights studying while she still made our lunch boxes. With gourmet cheese. She's proud of it, she tells you. She loves my dad, I guess. She thinks we're like this great family and she sits there at the dinner table bragging about us, to us. She Xeroxed my grade card first quarter with my Chemistry A+ so she's got it in her office and she's got the copy up on the refrigerator at home. She's sitting there telling all her friends that and I'm thinking, you don't know it, but I'm not one of you.

These people across the street from us. Little girl, Sarah, eight years old. Maybe seven. Her dad, he worked for the army, some kind of researcher, he decides he wants to get a sex-change operation. And he goes and does it, over at Stanford. My mom goes out, takes the dog for a walk, right. The mother *confides* in her. Says the things she regrets most is she wants to have more children. The little girl, Sarah, eight years old, looks up at my mom and says, "Daddy's going to be an aunt."

Now that's sad, I think that's really sad. My mom thinks it's a good dinner table story, proving how much better we are than them. Yeah, I remember exactly what she said that night. "That's all Sarah's mother's got to worry about now is that she wants another child. Meanwhile, Daddy's becoming an aunt."

She should know about me.

So my dad comes to visit for the weekend. Glenn's dad came to speak at UC one night, he took Glenn out to dinner to a nice place, Glenn was glad to see him. Yeah, well. My dad. Comes to the dorm. Skulks around. This guy's a *businessman,* in a three-piece suit, and he acts inferior to the eighteen-year-old freshmen coming in the lobby. My dad. Makes me sick right now thinking of him standing there in the lobby and everybody seeing him. He was probably looking at the kids and looking jealous. Just standing there. Why? Don't ask me why, he's the one that's forty-two years old.

So he's standing there, nervous, probably sucking his hand, that's what he does when he's nervous, I'm always telling him not to. Finally, somebody takes him to my room. I'm not there, Lauren's gone, and he waits for I don't know how long.

When I come in he's standing with his back to the door, looking out the window. I see him and right away I know it's him and I have this urge to tiptoe away and he'll never see me.

My pink sweater, a nice sweater, a sweater I wore a lot in high school, was over my chair, hanging on the back of it, and my father's got one hand on the sweater shoulder and he's like rubbing the other hand down an empty arm. He looks up at me, already scared and grateful when I walk into the room. I feel like smashing him with a baseball bat. Why can't he just stand up straight?

I drop my books on the bed and stand there while he hugs me.

"Hi, Daddy, what are you doing here?"

"I wanted to see you." He sits in my chair now, his legs crossed and big, too big for this room, and he's still fingering the arm of my pink sweater. "I missed you so I got away for the weekend," he says. "I have a room up here at the Claremont Hotel."

So he's here for the weekend. He's just sitting in my dorm room and I have to figure out what to do with him. He's not going to do anything. He'd just sit there. And Lauren's coming back soon so I've got to get him out. It's Friday afternoon and the weekend's shot. OK, so I'll go with him. I'll go with him and get it over with.

But I'm not going to miss my date with Glenn Saturday night. No way. I'd die before I'd cancel that. It's bad enough missing dinner in the cafeteria tonight. Friday's eggplant, my favorite, and Friday nights are usually easy, music on the stereos all down the hall. We usually work, but work slow and talk and then we all meet in Glenn's room around ten.

"Come, sit on my lap, honey." My dad like pulls me down and starts bouncing me. *Bouncing me.* I stand up. "OK, we can go somewhere tonight and tomorrow morning, but I have to be back for tomorrow night. I've got plans with people. And I've got to study, too."

"You can bring your books back to the hotel," he says. "I'm supposed to be at a convention in San Francisco, but I wanted to see you. I have work, too, we can call room service and both just work."

"I still have to be back by four tomorrow."

"All right."

"OK, just a minute." And he sat there in my chair while I called Glenn and told him I wouldn't be there for dinner. I pulled the phone out into the hall, it only stretches so far, and whispered. "Yeah, my father's here," I said, "he's got a conference in San Francisco. He just came by."

Glenn lowered his voice, sweet, and said, "Sounds fun."

My dad sat there, hunched over in my chair, while I changed my shirt and put on deodorant. I put a nightgown in my shoulder pack and my toothbrush and I took my chem book and we left. I knew I wouldn't be back for a whole day. I was trying to calm myself, thinking, well, it's only one day, that's nothing in my life. The halls were empty, it was five o'clock, five-ten, everyone was down at dinner.

We walk outside and the cafeteria lights are on and I see everyone moving around with their trays. Then my dad picks up my hand.

I yank it out. "Dad," I say, really mean.

"Honey, I'm your father." His voice trails off. "Other girls hold their fathers' hands." It was dark enough for the lights to be on in the cafeteria, but it wasn't really dark out yet. The sky was blue. On the tennis courts on top of the garage, two Chinese guys were playing. I heard that *thonk-pong* and it sounded so carefree and I just wanted to be them. I'd have even given up Glenn, Glenn-that-I-love-more-than-anything, at that second, I would have given everything up just to be someone else, someone new. I got into the car and slammed the door shut and turned up the heat.

"Should we just go to the hotel and do our work? We can get a nice dinner in the room."

"I'd rather go out," I said, looking down at my hands. He went where I told him. I said the name of the restaurant and gave directions. Chez Panisse and we ordered the most expensive stuff. Appetizers and two desserts just for me. A hundred and twenty bucks for the two of us.

OK, this hotel room.

So, my dad's got the Bridal Suite. He claimed that was all they had. Fat chance. Two-hundred-eighty room hotel and all they've got left is this deal with the canopy bed, no way. It's in the tower, you can almost see it from the dorm. Makes me sick. From the bathroom, there's this window, shaped like an arch, and it looks over all of Berkeley. You can see the bridge lights. As soon as we got there, I locked myself in the bathroom, I was so mad about that canopy bed. I took a long bath and washed my hair. They had little soaps wrapped up there, shampoo, may as well use them, he's paying for it. It's this deep old bathtub and wind was coming in from outside and I felt like that window was just open, no glass, just a hole cut out in the stone.

I was thinking of when I was little and what they taught us in catechism. I thought a soul was inside your chest, this long horizontal triangle with rounded edges, made out of some kind of white fog, some kind of gas or vapor. I could be pregnant. I soaped myself all up and rinsed off with cold water. I'm lucky I never got pregnant, really lucky.

Other kids my age, Lauren, everybody, I know things they don't know. I know more for my age. Too much. Like I'm not a virgin. Lots of people are, you'd be surprised. I know about a lot of things being wrong and unfair, all kinds of stuff. It's like seeing a UFO, if I ever saw something like that, I'd never tell, I'd wish I'd never seen it.

My dad knocks on the door.

"What do you want?"

"Let me just come in and talk to you while you're in there."

"I'm done, I'll be right out. Just a minute." I took a long time toweling. No hurry, believe me. So I got into bed with my night-gown on and wet already from my hair. I turned away. Breathed against the wall. "Night."

My father hooks my hair over my ear and touches my shoulder. "Tired?"

I shrug.

"You really have to go back tomorrow? We could go to Marin or to the beach. Anything."

I hugged my knees up under my nightgown. "You should go to your conference, Dad."

I wake up in the middle of the night, I feel something's going on, and sure enough, my dad's down there, he's got my night-gown worked up like a frill around my neck and my legs hooked over his shoulders.

"Dad, stop it."

"I just wanted to make you feel good," he says, and looks up at me. "What's wrong? Don't you love me anymore?"

I never really told anybody. It's not exactly the kind of thing you can bring up over lunch. "So, I'm sleeping with my father. Oh, and let's split a dessert." Right.

I don't know, other people think my dad's handsome. They say he is. My mother thinks so, you should see her traipsing around the balcony when she gets in her romantic moods, which, on her professional lawyer schedule, are about once a year, thank god. It's pathetic. He thinks she's repulsive, though. I don't know that, that's what I think. But he loves me, that's for sure.

So next day, Saturday — that rabbity guy, Paul's his name, he did my shift for me — we go downtown and I got him to buy me this suit. Three hundred dollars from Saks. Oh, and I got shoes. So I stayed later with him because of the clothes, and I was a little happy because I thought at least now I'd have some-

thing good to wear with Glenn. My dad and I got brownie
sundaes at Sweet Dreams and I got home by five. He was crying
when he dropped me off.

"Don't cry, Dad. Please," I said. Jesus, how can you not hate
someone who's always begging from you.

Lauren had Poly Styrene on the stereo and a candle lit in our
room. I was never so glad to be home.

"Hey," Lauren said. She was on her bed with her legs
propped up on the wall. She'd just shaved. She was rubbing in
cream.

I flopped down on my bed. "Ohhhh," I said, grabbing the
sides of the mattress.

"Hey, can you keep a secret about what I did today?" Lauren
said. "I went to that therapist, up at Cowell."

"You have the greatest legs," I said, quiet. "Why don't you
ever wear skirts?"

She stopped what she was doing and stood up. "You think
they're good? I don't like the way they look, except in jeans."
She looked down at them. "They're crooked, see?" She shook
her head. "I don't want to think about it."

Then she went to her dresser and started rolling a joint.
"Want some?"

"A little."

She lit up, lay back on her bed and held her arm out for me
to come take the joint.

"So, she was this really great woman. Warm, kind of chubby.
She knew instantly what kind of man Brent was." Lauren
snapped her fingers. "Like that." Brent was the pool man Lauren had an affair with, home in LA.

I'm back in the room maybe an hour, putting on mascara, my
jeans are on the bed, pressed, and the phone rings and it's my
dad and I say, "Listen, just leave me alone."

"You don't care about me anymore."

"I just saw you. I have nothing to say. We just saw each other."

"What are you doing tonight?"

"Going out."

"Who are you seeing?"

"Glenn."

He sighs. "So you really like him, huh?"

"Yeah, I do and you should be glad. You should be glad I have a boyfriend." I pull the cord out into the hall and sit down on the floor there. There's this long pause.

"We're not going to end up together, are we?"

I felt like all the air's knocked out of me. I looked out the window and everything looked dead and still. The parked cars. The trees with pink toilet paper strung between the branches. The church all closed up across the street.

"No, we won't, Daddy."

He was crying. "I know, I know."

I hung up the phone and went back and sat in the hall. I'm scared, too. I don't know what'll happen.

I don't know. It's been going on I guess as long as I can remember. I mean, not the sex, but my father. When I was a little kid, tiny little kid, my dad came in before bed and said his prayers with me. He kneeled down by my bed and I was on my back. *Prayers.* He'd lift up my pajama top and put his hands on my breast. Little fried eggs, he said. One time with his tongue. Then one night, he pulled down the elastic of my pajama pants. He did it for an hour and then I came. Don't believe anything they ever tell you about kids not coming. That first time was the biggest I ever had and I didn't even know what it was then. It just kept going and going as if he were breaking me through layers and layers of glass and I felt like I'd slipped and let go and I didn't have myself anymore, he had me, and once I'd slipped like that I'd never be the same again.

We had this sprinkler on our back lawn, Danny and me used to run through it in summer and my dad'd be outside, working on the grass or the hedge or something and he'd squirt us with the hose. I used to wear a bathing suit bottom, no top — we were this modern family, our parents walked around the house naked after showers and then Danny and I ended up both being these modest kids, can't stand anyone to see us even in our underwear, I always dress facing the closet, Lauren teases me. We'd run through the sprinkler and my dad would come up and pat my bottom and the way he'd put his hand on my thigh, I felt like Danny could tell it was different than the way he touched him, I was like something he owned.

First time when I was nine, I remember, Dad and me were in
the shower together. My mom might have even been in the
house, they did that kind of stuff, it was supposed to be OK.
Anyway, we're in the shower and I remember this look my dad
had. Like he was daring me, knowing he knew more than I did.
We're both under the shower. The water pasted his hair down
on his head and he looked younger and weird. "Touch it. Don't
be afraid of it," he says. And he grabs my thighs on the outside
and pulls me close to him, pulling on my fat.

He waited till I was twelve to really do it. I don't know if you
can call it rape, I was a good sport. The creepy thing is I know
how it felt for him, I could see it on his face when he did it.
He thought he was getting away with something. We were supposed to go hiking but right away that morning when we got
into the car, he knew he was going to do it. He couldn't wait to
get going. I said I didn't feel good, I had a cold, I wanted to
stay home, but he made me go anyway and we hiked two miles
and he set up the tent. He told me to take my clothes off and I
undressed just like that, standing there in the woods. He's the
one who was nervous and got us into the tent. I looked old for
twelve, small but old. And right there on the ground, he spread
my legs open and pulled my feet up and fucked me. I bled. I
couldn't even breathe the tent was so small. He could have done
anything. He could have killed me, he had me alone on this
mountain.

I think about that sometimes when I'm alone with Glenn in
my bed. It's so easy to hurt people. They just lie there and let
you have them. I could reach out and choke Glenn to death,
he'd be so shocked, he wouldn't stop me. You can just take what
you want.

My dad thought he was getting away with something but he
didn't. He was the one who fell in love, not me. And after that
day, when we were back in the car, I was the one giving orders.
From then on, I got what I wanted. He spent about twice as
much money on me as on Danny and everyone knew it, Danny
and my mom, too. How do you think I got good clothes and a
good bike and a good stereo? My dad's not rich, you know. And
I'm the one who got to go away to college even though it killed
him. Says it's the saddest thing that ever happened in his life,

me going away and leaving him. But when I was a little kid that day, he wasn't in love with me, not like he is now.

Only thing I'm sad about isn't either of my parents, it's Danny. Leaving Danny alone there with them. He used to send Danny out of the house. My mom'd be at work on a Saturday afternoon or something or even in the morning and my dad would kick my little brother out of his own house. Go out and play, Danny. Why doncha catch some rays. And Danny just went and got his glove and baseball from the closet and he'd go and throw it against the house, against the outside wall, in the driveway. I'd be in my room, I'd be like dead, I'd be wood, telling myself this doesn't count, no one has to know, I'll say I'm still a virgin, it's not really happening to me, I'm dead, I'm blank, I'm just letting time stop and pass, and then I'd hear the sock of the ball in the mitt and the slam of the screen door and I knew it was true, it was really happening.

Glenn's the one I want to tell. I can't ever tell Glenn.

I called my mom. Pay phone, collect, hour-long call. I don't know, I got real mad last night and I just told her. I thought when I came here, it'd just go away. But it's not going away. It makes me weird with Glenn. In the morning, with Glenn, when it's time to get up, I can't get up. I cry.

I knew it'd be bad. Poor Danny. Well, my mom says she might leave our dad. She cried for an hour, no jokes, on the phone.

How could he *do* this to me, she kept yelping. To her. Everything's always to her.

But then she called an hour later, she'd talked to a psychiatrist already, she's kicked Dad out, and she arrives, just arrives here at Berkeley. But she was good. She says she's on my side, she'll help me, I don't know, I felt OK. She stayed in a hotel and she wanted to know if I wanted to stay there with her but I said no, I'd see her more in a week or something, I just wanted to go back to my dorm. She found this group. She says, just in San Jose, there's hundreds of families like ours, yeah, great, that's what I said. But there's groups. She's going to a group of other thick-o mothers like her, these wives who didn't catch on. She wanted me to go to a group of girls, yeah, molested girls, that's what they call them, but I said no, I have friends here already, she can do what she wants.

I talked to my dad, too, that's the sad thing, he feels like he's lost me and he wants to die and I don't know, he doesn't know what he's doing. He called in the middle of the night.

"Just tell me one thing, honey. Please tell me the truth. When did you stop?"

"Dad."

"Because I remember once you said I was the only person who ever understood you."

"I was ten years old."

"OK, OK. I'm sorry."

He didn't want to get off the phone. "You know, I love you, honey. I always will."

"Yeah, well."

My mom's got him lined up for a psychiatrist, too, she says he's lucky she's not sending him to jail. I *am* a lawyer, she keeps saying, as if we could forget. She'd pay for me to go to a shrink now, too, but I said no, forget it.

It's over. Glenn and I are, over. I feel like my dad's lost me everything. I sort of want to die now. I'm telling you I feel terrible. I told Glenn and that's it, it's over. I can't believe it either. Lauren says she's going to hit him.

I told him and we're not seeing each other anymore. Nope. He said he wanted to just think about everything for a few days. He said it had nothing to do with my father but he'd been feeling a little too settled lately. He said we don't have fun anymore, it's always so serious. That was Monday. So every meal after that, I sat with Lauren in the cafeteria and he's there on the other side, messing around with the guys. He sure didn't look like he was in any kind of agony. Wednesday, I saw Glenn over by the window in this food fight, slipping off his chair and I couldn't stand it, I got up and left and went to our room.

But I went and said I wanted to talk to Glenn that night, I didn't even have any dinner, and he said he wanted to be friends. He looked at me funny and I haven't heard from him. It's, I don't know, seven days, eight.

I know there are other guys. I live in a dorm full of them, or half full of them. Half girls. But I keep thinking of Glenn 'cause of happiness, that's what makes me want to hang on to him.

There was this one morning when we woke up in his room, it was light out already, white light all over the room. We were sticky and warm, the sheet was all tangled. His roommate, this little blond boy, was still sleeping. I watched his eyes open and he smiled and then he went down the hall to take a shower. Glenn was hugging me and it was nothing unusual, nothing special. We didn't screw. We were just there. We kissed, but slow, the way it is when your mouth is still bad from sleep.

I was happy that morning. I didn't have to do anything. We got dressed, went to breakfast, I don't know. Took a walk. He had to go to work at a certain time and I had that sleepy feeling from waking up with the sun on my head and he said he didn't want to say goodbye to me. There was that pang. One of those looks like as if at that second, we both felt the same way.

I shrugged. I could afford to be casual then. We didn't say goodbye. I walked with him to the shed by the Eucalyptus Grove. That's where they keep all the gardening tools, the rakes, the hoes, the mowers, big bags of grass seed slumped against the wall. It smelled like hay in there. Glenn changed into his uniform and we went to the North Side, up in front of the chancellor's manor, that thick perfect grass. And Glenn gave me a ride on the lawn mower, on the handlebars. It was bouncing over these little bumps in the lawn and I was hanging on to the handlebars, laughing. I couldn't see Glenn but I knew he was there behind me. I looked around at the buildings and the lawns, there's a fountain there, and one dog was drinking from it.

See, I can't help but remember things like that. Even now, I'd rather find some way, even though he's not asking for it, to forgive Glenn. I'd rather have it work out with him, because I want more days like that. I wish I could have a whole life like that. But I guess nobody does, not just me.

I saw him in the mailroom yesterday, we're both just standing there, each opening our little boxes, getting our mail — neither of us had any — I was hurt but I wanted to reach out and touch his face. He has this hard chin, it's pointy and all bone. Lauren says she wants to hit him.

I mean, I think of him spinning around in his backyard and that's why I love him and he should understand. I go over it all and think I should have just looked at him and said I can't believe you're doing this to me. Right there in the mailroom. Now when I think that, I think maybe if I'd said that, in those words, maybe it would be different.

But then I think of my father — he feels like there was a time when we had fun, when we were happy together. I mean, I can remember being in my little bed with Dad and maybe cracking jokes, maybe laughing, but he probably never heard Danny's baseball in his mitt the way I did or I don't know. I remember late in the afternoon, wearing my dad's navy-blue sweatshirt with a hood and riding bikes with him and Danny down to the diamond.

But that's over. I don't know if I'm sorry it happened. I mean I am, but it happened, that's all. It's just one of the things that happened to me in my life. But I would never go back, never. And what hurts so much is that maybe that's what Glenn is thinking about me.

I told Lauren last night. I had to. She kept asking me what happened with Glenn. She was so good, you couldn't believe it, she was great. We were talking late and this morning we drove down to go to House of Pancakes for breakfast, get something good instead of watery eggs for a change. And on the way, Lauren's driving, she just skids to a stop on this street, in front of this elementary school. "Come on," she says. It's early, but there's already people inside the windows.

We hooked our fingers in the metal fence. You know, one of those aluminum fences around a playground. There were pigeons standing on the painted game circles. Then a bell rang and all these kids came out, yelling, spilling into groups. This was a poor school, mostly black kids, Mexican kids, all in bright colors. There's a Nabisco factory nearby and the whole air smelled like blueberry muffins.

The girls were jump-roping and the boys were shoving and running and hanging on to the monkey bars. Lauren pinched her fingers on the back of my neck and pushed my head against the fence.

"Eight years old. Look at them. They're eight years old. One of their fathers is sleeping with one of those girls. Look at her. Do you blame her? Can you blame her? Because if you can forgive her you can forgive yourself."

"I'll kill him," I said.

"And I'll kill Glenn," Lauren says.

So we went and got pancakes. And drank coffee until it was time for class.

I saw Glenn yesterday. It was so weird after all this time. I just had lunch with Lauren. We picked up tickets for Talking Heads and I wanted to get back to the lab before class and I'm walking along and Glenn was working, you know, on the lawn in front of the Mobi Building. He was still gorgeous. I was just going to walk, but he yelled over at me.

"Hey, Jenny."

"Hi, Glenn."

He congratulated me, he heard about the NSF thing. We stood there. He has another girlfriend now. I don't know, when I looked at him and stood there by the lawn mower, it's chugging away, I felt the same as I always used to, that I loved him and all that, but he might just be one of those things you can't have. Like I should have been for my father and look at him now. Oh, I think he's better, they're all better, but I'm gone, he'll never have me again.

I'm glad they're there and I'm here, but it's strange, I feel more alone now. Glenn looked down at the little pile of grass by the lawn mower and said, "Well, kid, take care of yourself," and I said, "You too, 'bye," and started walking.

So, you know what's bad, though, I started taking stuff again. Little stuff from the mailroom. No packages and not people I know anymore.

But I take one letter a Saturday, I make it just one and someone I don't know. And I keep 'em and burn 'em with a match in the bathroom sink and wash the ashes down the drain. I wait until the end of the shift. I always expect it to be something exciting. The two so far were just everyday letters, just mundane, so that's all that's new, I-had-a-pork-chop-for-dinner letters.

But something happened today, I was in the middle, three-quarters way down the bag, still looking, I hadn't picked my letter for the day, I'm being really stern, I really mean just one, no more, and there's this little white envelope addressed to me. I sit there, trembling with it in my hand. It's the first one I've gotten all year. It was my name and address, typed out, and I just stared at it. There's no address. I got so nervous, I thought maybe it was from Glenn, of course, I wanted it to be from Glenn so bad, but then I knew it couldn't be, he's got that new girlfriend now, so I threw it in the garbage can right there, one of those with the swinging metal door, and then I finished my shift. My hands were sweating, I smudged the writing on one of the envelopes.

So all the letters are in boxes, I clean off the table, fold the bags up neat and close the door, ready to go. And then I thought, I don't have to keep looking at the garbage can, I'm allowed to take it back, that's my letter. And I fished it out, the thing practically lopped my arm off. And I had it and I held it a few minutes, wondering who it was from. Then I put it in my mailbox so I can go like everybody else and get mail.

JOY WILLIAMS

Health

FROM TENDRIL

PAMMY IS IN AN unpleasant Texas city, the city where she was
born, in the month of her twelfth birthday. It is cold and cloudy.
Soon it will rain. The rain will wash the film of ash off the car
she is traveling in, volcanic ash that has drifted across the Gulf
of Mexico, all the way from the Yucatán. Pammy is a stocky,
gray-eyed blonde, a daughter, traveling in her father's car,
being taken to her tanning lesson.

This is her father's joke. She is being taken to a tanning ses-
sion, twenty-five minutes long. She had requested this for her
birthday, ten tanning sessons in a health spa. She had also asked
for and received new wheels for her skates. They are purple
Rannallis. She had dyed her stoppers to match although the
match was not perfect. The stoppers were a duller, cruder purple. Pammy wants to be a speed skater but she worries that she
doesn't have the personality for it. "You've gotta have gravel in
your gut to be in speed," her coach said. Pammy has mastered
the duck walk but still doesn't have a good, smooth crossover,
and sometimes she fears that she never will.

Pammy and her father, Morris, are following a truck that is
carrying a jumble of televison sets. There is a twenty-four-inch
console facing them on the open tailgate, restrained by rope,
with a bullet hole in the exact center of the screen.

Morris drinks coffee from a plastic-lidded cup that fits into a
bracket mounted just beneath the car's radio. Pammy has a
friend, Wanda, whose stepfather has the same kind of plastic
cup in his car, but he drinks bourbon and water from his.

Wanda had been adopted when she was two months old. Pammy is relieved that neither her father nor Marge, her mother, drinks. Sometimes they have wine. On her birthday, even Pammy had wine with dinner. Marge and Morris seldom quarrel and she is grateful for this. This morning, however, she had seen them quarrel. Once again, her mother had borrowed her father's hairbrush and left long, brown hairs in it. Her father had taken the brush and cleaned it with a comb over the clean kitchen sink. Her father had left a nest of brown hair in the white sink.

In the car, the radio is playing a song called "Tainted Love," a song Morris likes to refer to as "Rancid Love." The radio plays constantly when Pammy and her father drive anywhere. Morris is a good driver. He is fast and doesn't bear grudges. He enjoys driving still, after years and years of it. Pammy looks forward to learning how to drive now, but after a few years, who knows? She can't imagine it being that enjoyable after a while. Her father is skillful here, on the freeways and streets, and on the terrifying, wide two-lane highways and narrow mountain roads in Mexico, and even on the rutted, soiled beaches of the Gulf Coast. One weekend, earlier that spring, Morris had rented a Jeep in Corpus Christi and he and Pammy and Marge had driven the length of Padre Island. They sped across the sand, the only people for miles and miles. There was plastic everywhere.

"You will see a lot of plastic," the man who rented them the Jeep said, "but it is plastic from all over the world."

Morris had given Pammy a lesson in driving the Jeep. He taught her how to shift smoothly, how to synchronize acceleration with the depression and release of the clutch. "There's a way to do things right," Morris told her and when he said this she was filled with a sort of fear. They were just words, she knew, words that anybody could use, but behind words were always things, sometimes things you could never tell anyone, certainly no one you loved, frightening things that weren't even true.

"I'm sick of being behind this truck," Morris says. The screen of the injured television looks like dirty water. Morris pulls to the curb beside an Oriental market. Pammy stares into the mar-

ket, where shoppers wait in line at a cash register. Many of the
women wear scarves on their heads. Pammy is deeply disturbed
by Orientals who kill penguins to make gloves and murder
whales to make nail polish. In school, in social studies class, she
is reading eyewitness accounts of the aftermath of the atomic
bombing of Hiroshima. She reads about young girls running
from their melting city, their hair burnt off, their burnt skin in
loose folds, crying, "Stupid Americans." Morris sips his coffee,
then turns the car back onto the street, a street now free from
fatally wounded television sets.

Pammy gazes at the backs of her hands, which are tan but,
she feels, not tan enough. They are a dusky peach color. This
will be her fifth tanning lesson. In the health spa, there are ten
colored photographs on the wall showing a woman in a bikini,
a pale woman being transformed into a tanned woman. In the
last photograph she has plucked the bikini slightly away from
her hip bone to expose a sliver of white skin and she is smiling
down at the sliver.

Pammy tans well. Without a tan, her face seems grainy and
uneven, for she has freckles and rather large pores. Tanning
draws her together, completes her. She has had all kinds of tans
— golden tans, pool tans, even a Florida tan, which seemed
yellow back in Texas. She had brought all her friends the same
present from Florida — small plywood crates filled with tiny
oranges that were actually chewing gum. The finest tan Pammy
has ever had, however, was in Mexico six months ago. She had
gone there with her parents for two weeks, and she had gotten
a truly remarkable tan and she had gotten tuberculosis. This
has caused some tension between Morris and Marge, as it had
been Morris's idea to swim at the spas in the mountains rather
than in the pools at the more established hotels. It was believed
that Pammy had become infected at one particular public spa
just outside the small, dusty town where they had gone to buy
tiles, tiles of a dusky orange with blue rays flowing from the
center, tiles that are now in the kitchen of their home, where
each morning Pammy drinks her juice and takes three hundred
milligrams of isoniazid.

"Here we are," Morris says. The health spa is in a small,
concrete block building with white columns, salvaged from the

wrecking of a mansion, adorning the front. There are gift shops, palmists, and all-night restaurants along the street, as well as an exterminating company that has a huge fiber glass bug with X's for eyes on the roof. This was not the company that had tented Wanda's house for termites. That had been another company. When Pammy was in Mexico getting tuberculosis, Wanda and her parents had gone to San Antonio for a week while their house was being tented. When they returned, they'd found a dead robber in the living room, the things he was stealing piled neatly nearby. He had died from inhaling the deadly gas used by the exterminators.

"Mommy will pick you up," Morris says. "She has a class this afternoon so she might be a little late. Just stay inside until she comes."

Morris kisses her on the cheek. He treats her like a child. He treats Marge like a mother, her mother.

Marge is thirty-five but she is still a student. She takes courses in art history and film at one of the city's universities, the same university where Morris teaches petroleum science. Years ago when Marge had first been a student, before she had met Morris and Pammy had been born, she had been in Spain in a museum studying a Goya and a piece of the painting had fallen at her feet. She had quickly placed it in her pocket and now has it on her bureau in a small glass box. It is a wedge of greenish-violet paint, as large as a thumbnail. It is from one of Goya's nudes.

Pammy gets out of the car and goes into the health spa. There is no equipment here except for the tanning beds, twelve tanning beds in eight small rooms. Pammy has never had to share a room with anyone. If asked to, she would probably say no, hoping that she would not hurt the other person's feelings. The receptionist is an old, vigorous woman behind a scratched metal desk, wearing a black jumpsuit and feather earrings. Behind her are shelves of powders and pills in squat brown bottles with names like Dynamic Stamina Builder and Dynamic Super Stress-End and Liver Concentrate Energizer.

The receptionist's name is Aurora. Pammy thinks that the name is magnificent and is surprised that it belongs to such an old woman. Aurora leads her to one of the rooms at the rear of the building. The room has a mirror, a sink, a small stool, a white rotating fan, and the bed, a long, bronze, coffin-like apparatus with a lid. Pammy is always startled when she sees the bed with its frosted ultraviolet tubes, its black vinyl headrest. In the next room someone coughs. Pammy imagines people lying in all the rooms, wrapped in white light, lying quietly as though they were being rested for a long, long journey. Aurora takes a spray bottle of disinfectant and a scrap of toweling from the counter above the sink and cleans the surface of the bed. She twists the timer and the light leaps out, like an animal in a dream, like a murderer in a movie.

"There you are, honey," Aurora says. She pats Pammy on the shoulder and leaves.

Pammy pushes off her sandals and undresses quickly. She leaves her clothes in a heap, her sweatshirt on top of the pile. Her sweatshirt is white with a transfer of a skater on the back. The skater is a man wearing a helmet and knee pads, side surfing goofy-footed. She lies down and with her left hand pulls the lid to within a foot of the bed's cool surface. She can see the closed door and the heap of clothing and her feet. Pammy considers her feet to be her ugliest feature. They are skinny and the toes are too far apart. She and Wanda had painted their toes the same color, but Wanda's feet were pretty and hers were not. Pammy thought her feet looked like they belonged to a dead person and there wasn't anything she could do about them. She closes her eyes.

Wanda, who read a lot, told Pammy that tuberculosis was a very romantic disease, the disease of artists and poets and "highly sensitive individuals."

"Oh yeah," her stepfather had said. "Tuberculosis has mucho cachet."

Wanda's stepfather speaks loudly and his eyes glitter. He is always joking, Pammy thinks. Pammy feels that Wanda's parents are pleasant but she is always a little uncomfortable around them. They had a puppy for a while, a purebred Doberman, which they gave to the SPCA after they disovered it had a slightly overshot jaw. Wanda's stepfather always called the puppy a sissy. "You sissy," he'd say to the puppy. "Hanging around with girls all the time." He was referring to his wife and to Wanda and Pammy. "Oh, you sissy, you sissy," he'd say to the puppy.

There was also the circumstance of Wanda's adoption. There

had been another baby adopted, but it was learned that the baby's background had been misrepresented. Or perhaps it had been a boring baby. In any case the baby had been returned and they got Wanda.

Pammy doesn't think Wanda's parents are very steadfast. She is surprised that they don't make Wanda nervous, for Wanda is certainly not perfect. She's a shoplifter and gets C's in Computer Language.

The tanning bed is warm but not uncomfortably so. Pammy lies with her arms straight by her sides, palms down. She hears voices in the hall and footsteps. When she first began coming to the health spa, she was afraid that someone would open the door to the room she was in by mistake. She imagined exactly what it would be like. She would see the door open abruptly out of the corner of her eye, then someone would say, "Sorry," and the door would close again. But this had not happened. The voices pass by.

Pammy thinks of Snow White lying in her glass coffin. The Queen had deceived her how many times? Three? She had been in disguise, but still. And then Snow White had choked on an apple. In the restaurants she sometimes goes to with her parents there are posters on the walls that show a person choking and another person trying to save him. The posters take away Pammy's appetite.

Snow White lay in a glass coffin, not naked of course but in a gown, watched over by the dwarfs. But surely they not not been real dwarfs. That had just been a word that had been given to them.

When Pammy had told Morris that tuberculosis was a romantic disease, he had said, "There's nothing romantic about it. Besides, you don't have it."

It seems to be a fact that she both has and doesn't have tuberculosis. Pammy had been given the tuberculin skin test along with her classmates when she began school in the fall and within forty-eight hours had a large swelling on her arm.

"Now that you've come in contact with it, you don't have to worry about getting it," the pediatrician had said in his office, smiling.

"You mean the infection constitutes immunity," Marge said.

"Not exactly," the pediatrician said, shaking his head, still smiling.

Her lungs are clear. She is not ill but has an illness. The germs are in her body, but in a resting state, still alive but rendered powerless, successfully overcome by her healthy body's strong defenses. Outwardly she is the same, but within a great drama had taken place and Pammy feels herself in possession of a bright, secret, and unspeakable knowledge.

She knows other things too, things that would break her parents' hearts, common, ugly, easy things. She knows a girl in school who stole her mother's green stamps and bought a personal massager with the books. She knows another girl whose brother likes to wear her clothes. She knows a boy who threw a can of motor oil at his father and knocked him unconscious.

Pammy stretches. Her head tingles. Her body is about a foot and a half off the floor and appears almost gray in the glare from the tubes. She has heard of pills one could take to acquire a tan. One just took two pills a day and after twenty days one had a wonderful tan, which could be maintained just by taking two pills a day thereafter. You ordered them from Canada. It was some kind of food-coloring substance. How gross, Pammy thinks. When she had been little she had bought a quarter of an acre of land in Canada by mail for fifty cents. That had been two years ago.

Pammy hears voices from the room next to hers, coming through the thin wall. A woman talking rapidly says, "Pete went up to Detroit two days ago to visit his brother who's dying up there in the hospital. Cancer. The brother's always been a nasty type, I mean very unpleasant. Younger than Pete and always mean. Tried to commit suicide twice. Then he learns he has cancer and decides he doesn't want to die. Carries on and on. Is miserable to everyone. Puts the whole family through hell, but nothing can be done about it, he's dying of cancer. So Pete goes up to see him his last days in the hospital and you know what happens? Pete's wallet gets stolen. Right out of a dying man's room. Five hundred dollars in cash and all our credit cards. That was yesterday. What a day."

Another woman says, "If it's not one thing, it's something else."

Pammy coughs. She doesn't want to hear other people's voices. It is as though they are throwing away junk the way some people use words, as though one word were as good as another.

"Things happen so abruptly anymore," the woman says. "You know what I mean?"

Pammy does not listen and she does not open her eyes for if she did she would see this odd, bright room with her clothes in a heap and herself lying motionless and naked. She does not open her eyes because she prefers imagining that she is a magician's accomplice, levitating on a stage in a coil of pure energy. If one thought purely enough, one could create one's own truth. That's how people accomplished astral travel, walked over burning coals, cured warts. There was a girl in Pammy's class at school, Bonnie Black, a small, owlish-looking girl who was a Christian Scientist. She raised rabbits and showed them at fairs, and was always wearing the ribbons they had won at school, pinned to her blouse. She had warts all over her hands, but one day Pammy noticed that the warts were gone and Bonnie Black had told her that the warts disappeared after she had clearly realized that in her true being as God's reflection, she couldn't have warts.

It seemed that people were better off when they could concentrate on something, hold something in their mind for a long time and really believe it. Pammy had once seen a radical skater putting on a show at the opening of a shopping mall. He leapt over cars and jumped up the sides of buildings. He did flips and spins. A disc jockey who was set up for the day in the parking lot interviewed him. "I'm really impressed with your performance," the disc jockey said, "and I'm impressed that you never fall. Why don't you fall?" The skater was a thin boy in baggy cut-off jeans. "I don't fall," the boy said, looking hard at the microphone, "because I've got a deep respect for the concrete surface and because when I make a miscalculation, instead of falling, I turn it into a new trick."

Pammy thinks it is wonderful that the boy was able to say something that would keep him from thinking he might fall.

The door to the room opened. Pammy had heard the turning of the knob. At first she lies without opening her eyes, willing the sound of the door shutting, but she hears nothing, only the ticking of the bed's timer. She swings her head quickly to the side and looks at the door. There is a man standing there, staring at her. She presses her right hand into a fist, and lays it between her legs. She puts her left arm across her breasts.

"What?" she says to the figure, frightened. In an instant she is almost panting with fear. She feels the repetition of something painful and known, but she has not known this, not ever. The figure says nothing and pulls the door shut. With a flurry of rapid ticking, the timer stops. The harsh lights of the bed go out.

Pammy pushes the lid back and hurriedly gets up. She dresses hastily and smoothes her hair with her fingers. She looks at herself in the mirror, her lips parted. Her teeth are white behind her pale lips. She stares at herself. She can be looked at and not discovered. She can speak and not be known. She opens the door and enters the hall. There is no one there. The hall is so narrow that by spreading her arms she can touch the walls with her fingertips. In the reception area by Aurora's desk, there are three people, a stoop-shouldered young woman and two men. The woman was signing up for a month of unlimited tanning, which meant that after the basic monthly fee she only had to pay a dollar a visit. She takes her checkbook out of a soiled handbag, which is made out of some silvery material, and writes a check. The men look comfortable lounging in the chairs, their legs stretched out. They know one another, Pammy guesses, but they do not know the woman. One of them has dark, spikey hair like a wet animal's. The other wears a tight red T-shirt. Neither is the man she had seen in the doorway.

"What time do you want to come back tomorrow, honey?" Aurora asks Pammy. "You certainly are coming along nicely. Isn't she coming along nicely?"

"I'd like to come back the same time tomorrow," Pammy says. She raises her hand to her mouth and coughs slightly.

"Not the same time, honey. Can't give you the same time. How about an hour later?"

"All right," Pammy says. The stoop-shouldered woman sits down in a chair. There are no more chairs in the room. Pammy opens the door to the street and steps outside. It has rained and the street is dark and shining. The air smells fresh and feels thick. She stands in it, a little stunned, looking. Her father will teach her how to drive, and she will drive around. Her mother will continue to take classes at the university. Whenever she meets someone new, she will mention the Goya. "I have a small Goya," she will say, and laugh.

Pammy walks slowly down the street. She smells barbecued meat and the rain lingering in the streets. By a store called Imagine, there's a clump of bamboo with some beer cans glittering in its ragged, grassy center. Imagine sells neon palm trees and silk clouds and stars. It sells greeting cards and chocolate in shapes children aren't allowed to see and it sells children's stickers and shoelaces. Pammy looks in the window at a huge satin pillow in the shape of a heart with a heavy zipper running down the center of it. Pammy turns and walks back to the building that houses the tanning beds. Her mother pulls up in the car. "Pammy!" she calls. She is leaning toward the window on the passenger side, which she has rolled down. She unlocks the car's door. Pammy gets in and the door locks again.

Pammy wishes she could tell her mother something, but what can she say? She never wants to see that figure looking at her again, so coldly staring and silent, but she knows she will, for already its features are becoming more indistinct, more general. It could be anything. She coughs, but it is not the cough of a sick person because Pammy is a healthy girl. It is the kind of cough a person might make if they were at a party and there was no one there but strangers.

Marge, driving, says, "You look very nice. That's a very pretty tan, but what will happen when you stop going there? It won't last. You'll lose it right away, won't you?"

She will. And she will grow older, but the world will remain as young as she was once, infinite in its possibilities and uncaring.

TOBIAS WOLFF

The Rich Brother

FROM VANITY FAIR

THERE WERE two brothers, Pete and Donald.

Pete, the older brother, was in real estate. He and his wife had a Century 21 franchise in Santa Cruz. Pete worked hard and made a lot of money, but not any more than he thought he deserved. He had two daughters, a sailboat, a house from which he could see a thin slice of the ocean, and friends doing well enough in their own lives not to wish bad luck on him. Donald, the younger brother, was still single. He lived alone, painted houses when he found the work, and got deeper in debt to Pete when he didn't.

No one would have taken them for brothers. Where Pete was stout and hearty and at home in the world, Donald was bony, grave, and obsessed with the fate of his soul. Over the years Donald had worn the images of two different Perfect Masters around his neck. Out of devotion to the second of these he entered an ashram in Berkeley, where he nearly died of undiagnosed hepatitis. By the time Pete finished paying the medical bills Donald had become a Christian. He drifted from church to church, then joined a pentecostal community that met somewhere in the Mission District to sing in tongues and swap prophecies.

Pete couldn't make sense of it. Their parents were both dead, but while they were alive neither of them had found it necessary to believe in anything. They managed to be decent people without making fools of themselves, and Pete had the same ambition. He thought that the whole thing was an excuse for Donald to take himself seriously.

The trouble was that Donald couldn't content himself with worrying about his own soul. He had to worry about everyone else's, and especially Pete's. He handed down his judgments in ways that he seemed to consider subtle: through significant silence, innuendo, looks of mild despair that said, *Brother, what have you come to?* What Pete had come to, as far as he could tell, was prosperity. That was the real issue between them. Pete prospered and Donald did not prosper.

At the age of forty Pete took up sky diving. He made his first jump with two friends who'd started only a few months earlier and were already doing stunts. They were both coked to the gills when they jumped but Pete wanted to do it straight, at least the first time, and he was glad that he did. He would never have used the word "mystical," but that was how Pete felt about the experience. Later he made the mistake of trying to describe it to Donald, who kept asking how much it cost and then acted appalled when Pete told him.

"At least I'm trying something new," Pete said. "At least I'm breaking the pattern."

Not long after that conversation Donald also broke the pattern, by going to live on a farm outside of Paso Robles. The farm was owned by several members of Donald's community, who had bought it and moved there with the idea of forming a family of faith. That was how Donald explained it in the first letter he sent. Every week Pete heard how happy Donald was, how "in the Lord." He told Pete that he was praying for him, he and the rest of Pete's brothers and sisters on the farm.

"I only have one brother," Pete wanted to answer, "and that's enough." But he kept this thought to himself.

In November the letters stopped. Pete didn't worry about this at first, but when he called Donald at Thanksgiving Donald was grim. He tried to sound upbeat but he didn't try hard enough to make it convincing. "Now listen," Pete said, "you don't have to stay in that place if you don't want to."

"I'll be all right," Donald answered.

"That's not the point. Being all right is not the point. If you don't like what's going on up there, then get out."

"I'm all right," Donald said again, more firmly. "I'm doing fine."

But he called Pete a week later and said that he was quitting the farm. When Pete asked him where he intended to go, Donald admitted that he had no plan. His car had been repossessed just before he left the city, and he was flat broke.

"I guess you'll have to stay with us," Pete said.

Donald put up a show of resistance. Then he gave in. "Just until I get my feet on the ground," he said.

"Right," Pete said. "Check out your options." He told Donald he'd send him money for a bus ticket, but as they were about to hang up Pete changed his mind. He knew that Donald would try hitchhiking to save the fare. Pete didn't want him out on the road all alone where some head case could pick him up, where anything could happen to him.

"Better yet," he said. "I'll come and get you."

"You don't have to do that. I didn't expect you to do that," Donald said. He added, "It's a pretty long drive."

"Just tell me how to get there."

But Donald wouldn't give him directions. He said that the farm was too depressing, that Pete wouldn't like it. Instead, he insisted on meeting Pete at a service station called Jonathan's Mechanical Emporium.

"You must be kidding," Pete said.

"It's close to the highway," Donald said. "I didn't name it."

"That's one for the collection," Pete said.

The day before he left to bring Donald home, Pete received a letter from a man who described himself as "head of household" at the farm where Donald had been living. From this letter Pete learned that Donald had not quit the farm, but had been asked to leave. The letter was written on the back of a mimeographed survey form asking people to record their response to a ceremony of some kind. The last question said:

What did you feel during the liturgy?
  a) *Being*
  b) *Becoming*
  c) *Being and Becoming*

d) *None of the Above*
e) *All of the Above*

Pete tried to forget the letter. But of course he couldn't. Each time he thought of it he felt crowded and breathless, a feeling that came over him again when he drove into the service station and saw Donald sitting against a wall with his head on his knees. It was late afternoon. A paper cup tumbled slowly past Donald's feet, pushed by the damp wind.

Pete honked and Donald raised his head. He smiled at Pete, then stood and stretched. His arms were long and thin and white. He wore a red bandanna across his forehead, a T-shirt with a couple of words on the front. Pete couldn't read them because the letters were inverted.

"Grow up," Pete yelled. "Get a Mercedes."

Donald came up to the window. He bent down and said, "Thanks for coming. You must be totally whipped."

"I'll make it." Pete pointed at Donald's T-shirt. "What's that supposed to say?"

Donald looked down at his shirt front. "Try God. I guess I put it on backwards. Pete, could I borrow a couple of dollars? I owe these people for coffee and sandwiches."

Pete took five twenties from his wallet and held them out the window.

Donald stepped back as if horrified. "I don't need that much."

"I can't keep track of all these nickels and dimes," Pete said. "Just pay me back when your ship comes in." He waved the bills impatiently. "Go on — take it."

"Only for now." Donald took the money and went into the service station office. He came out carrying two orange sodas, one of which he gave to Pete as he got into the car. "My treat," he said.

"No bags?"

"Wow, thanks for reminding me," Donald said. He balanced his drink on the dashboard, but the slight rocking of the car as he got out tipped it onto the passenger's seat, where half its contents foamed over before Pete could snatch it up again. Donald looked on while Pete held the bottle out the window, soda running down his fingers.

"Wipe it up," Pete told him. "Quick!"

"With what?"

Pete stared at Donald. "That shirt. Use the shirt."

Donald pulled a long face but did as he was told, his pale skin puckering against the wind.

"Great, just great," Pete said. "We haven't even left the gas station yet."

Afterwards, on the highway, Donald said, "This is a new car, isn't it?"

"Yes. This is a new car."

"Is that why you're so upset about the seat?"

"Forget it, okay? Let's just forget about it."

"I said I was sorry."

Pete said, "I just wish you'd be more careful. These seats are made of leather. That stain won't come out, not to mention the smell. I don't see why I can't have leather seats that smell like leather instead of orange pop."

"What was wrong with the other car?"

Pete glanced over at Donald. Donald had raised the hood of the blue sweatshirt he'd put on. The peaked hood above his gaunt, watchful face gave him the look of an inquisitor.

"There wasn't anything wrong with it," Pete said. "I just happened to like this one better."

Donald nodded.

There was a long silence between them as Pete drove on and the day darkened toward evening. On either side of the road lay stubble-covered fields. A line of low hills ran along the horizon, topped here and there with trees black against the gray sky. In the approaching line of cars a driver turned on his headlights. Pete did the same.

"So what happened?" he asked. "Farm life not your bag?"

Donald took some time to answer, and at last he said, simply, "It was my fault."

"What was your fault?"

"The whole thing. Don't play dumb, Pete. I know they wrote to you." Donald looked at Pete, then stared out the windshield again.

"I'm not playing dumb."

Donald shrugged.

"All I really know is they asked you to leave," Pete went on. "I don't know any of the particulars."

"I blew it," Donald said. "Believe me, you don't want to hear the gory details."

"Sure I do," Pete said. He added, "Everybody likes the gory details."

"You mean everybody likes to hear how someone else messed up."

"Right," Pete said. "That's the way it is here on Spaceship Earth."

Donald bent one knee onto the front seat and leaned against the door so that he was facing Pete instead of the windshield. Pete was aware of Donald's scrutiny. He waited. Night was coming on in a rush now, filling the hollows of the land. Donald's long cheeks and deep-set eyes were dark with shadow. His brow was white. "Do you ever dream about me?" Donald asked.

"Do I ever dream about you? What kind of a question is that? Of course I don't dream about you," Pete said, untruthfully.

"What do you dream about?"

"Sex and money. Mostly money. A nightmare is when I dream I don't have any."

"You're just making that up," Donald said.

Pete smiled.

"Sometimes I wake up at night," Donald went on, "and I can tell you're dreaming about me."

"We were talking about the farm," Pete said. "Let's finish that conversation and then we can talk about our various out-of-body experiences and the interesting things we did during previous incarnations."

For a moment Donald looked like a grinning skull; then he turned serious again. "There's not that much to tell," he said. "I just didn't do anything right."

"That's a little vague," Pete said.

"Well, like the groceries. Whenever it was my turn to get the groceries I'd blow it somehow. I'd bring the groceries home and half of them would be missing, or I'd have all the wrong things, the wrong kind of flour or the wrong kind of chocolate or whatever. One time I gave them away. It's not funny, Pete."

Pete said, "Who did you give the groceries to?"

"Just some people I picked up on the way home. Some field-
workers. They had about eight kids with them and they didn't
even speak English — just nodded their heads. Still, I shouldn't
have given away the groceries. Not all of them, anyway. I really
learned my lesson about that. You have to be practical. You
have to be fair to yourself." Donald leaned forward, and Pete
could sense his excitement. "There's nothing actually wrong
with being in business," he said. "As long as you're fair to other
people you can still be fair to yourself. I'm thinking of going
into business, Pete."

"We'll talk about it," Pete said. "So, that's the story? There
isn't any more to it than that?"

"What did they tell you?" Donald asked.

"Nothing."

"They must have told you something."

Pete shook his head.

"They didn't tell you about the fire?" When Pete shook his
head again Donald regarded him for a time, then said, "I don't
know. It was stupid. I just completely lost it." He folded his
arms across his chest and slumped back into the corner. "Everybody had to take turns cooking dinner. I usually did tuna casser-
ole or spaghetti with garlic bread. But this one night I thought
I'd so something different, something really interesting." Donald looked sharply at Pete. "It's all a big laugh to you, isn't it?"

"I'm sorry," Pete said.

"You don't know when to quit. You just keep hitting away."

"Tell me about the fire, Donald."

Donald kept watching him. "You have this compulsion to
make me look foolish."

"Come off it, Donald. Don't make a big thing out of this."

"I know why you do it. It's because you don't have any purpose in life. You're afraid to relate to people who do, so you
make fun of them."

"Relate," Pete said softly.

"You're basically a very frightened individual," Donald said.
"Very threatened. You've always been like that. Do you remember when you used to try to kill me?"

"I don't have any compulsion to make you look foolish, Donald — You do it yourself. You're doing it right now."

"You can't tell me you don't remember," Donald said. "It was after my operation. You remember that."

"Sort of." Pete shrugged. "Not really."

"Oh yes." Donald said. "Do you want to see the scar?"

"I remember you had an operation. I don't remember the specifics, that's all. And I sure as hell don't remember trying to kill you."

"Oh yes," Donald repeated, maddeningly. "You bet your life you did. All the time. The thing was, I couldn't have anything happen to me where they sewed me up because then my intestines would come apart again and poison me. That was a big issue, Pete. Mom was always in a state about me climbing trees and so on. And you used to hit me there every chance you got."

"Mom was in a state every time you burped," Pete said. "I don't know. Maybe I bumped into you accidentally once or twice. I never did it deliberately."

"Every chance you got," Donald said. "Like when the folks went out at night and left you to baby-sit. I'd hear them say good night, and then I'd hear the car start up, and when they were gone I'd lie there and listen. After a while I would hear you coming down the hall, and I would close my eyes and pretend to be asleep. There were nights when you would stand outside the door, just stand there, and then go away again. But most nights you'd open the door and I would hear you in the room with me, breathing. You'd come over and sit next to me on the bed — you remember, Pete, you have to — you'd sit next to me on the bed and pull the sheets back. If I was on my stomach you'd roll me over. Then you would lift up my pajama shirt and start hitting me on my stitches. You'd hit me as hard as you could, over and over. And I would just keep lying there with my eyes closed. I was afraid that you'd get mad if you knew I was awake. Is that strange or what? I was afraid that you'd get mad if you found out that I knew you were trying to kill me." Donald laughed. "Come on, you can't tell me you don't remember that."

"It might have happened once or twice. Kids do those things. I can't get all excited about something I maybe did twenty-five years ago."

"No maybe about it. You did it."

Pete said. "You're wearing me out with this stuff. We've got a long drive ahead of us and if you don't back off pretty soon we aren't going to make it. You aren't, anyway."

Donald turned away.

"I'm doing my best," Pete said. The self-pity in his own voice made the words sound like a lie. But they weren't a lie! He was doing his best.

The car topped a rise. In the distance Pete saw a cluster of lights that blinked out when he started downhill. There was no moon. The sky was low and black.

"Come to think of it," Pete said, "I did have a dream about you the other night." Then he added, impatiently, as if Donald were badgering him. "A couple of other nights too. I'm getting hungry," he said.

"The same dream?"

"Different dreams. I only remember one of them well. There was something wrong with me, and you were helping out. Taking care of me. Just the two of us. I don't know where everyone else was supposed to be."

Pete left it that. He didn't tell Donald that in this dream he was blind.

"I wonder if that was when I woke up," Donald said. He added, "I'm sorry I got into that thing about my scar. I keep trying to forget it but I guess I never will. Not really. It was pretty strange, having someone around all the time who wanted to get rid of me."

"Kid stuff," Pete said. "Ancient history."

They ate dinner at a Denny's on the other side of King City. As Pete was paying the check he heard a man behind him say, "Excuse me, but I wonder if I might ask which way you're going?" and Donald answer, "Santa Cruz."

"Perfect," the man said.

Pete could see him in the fish-eye mirror above the cash register: a red blazer with some kind of crest on the pocket, little black mustache, glossy black hair combed down on his forehead like a Roman emperor's. A rug, Pete thought. Definitely a rug.

Pete got his change and turned. "Why is that perfect?" he asked.

The man looked at Pete. He had a soft ruddy face that was doing its best to express pleasant surprise, as if this new wrinkle were all he could have wished for, but the eyes behind the aviator glasses showed signs of regret. His lips were moist and shiny. "I take it you're together," he said.

"You got it," Pete told him.

"All the better, then," the man went on. "It so happens I'm going to Santa Cruz myself. Had a spot of car trouble down the road. The old Caddy let me down."

"What kind of trouble?" Pete asked.

"Engine trouble," the man said. "I'm afraid it's a bit urgent. My daughter is sick. Urgently sick. I've got a telegram here." He patted the breast pocket of his blazer.

Pete grinned. Amazing, he thought, the old sick daughter ploy, but before he could say anything Donald got into the act again. "No problem," Donald said. "We've got tons of room."

"Not that much room," Pete said.

Donald nodded. "I'll put my things in the trunk."

"The trunks's full," Pete told him.

"It so happens I'm traveling light," the man said. "This leg of the trip anyway. In fact I don't have any luggage at this particular time."

Pete said, "Left it in the old Caddy, did you?"

"Exactly," the man said.

"No problem," Donald repeated. He walked outside and the man went with him. Together they strolled across the parking lot, Pete following at a distance. When they reached Pete's car Donald raised his face to the sky, and the man did the same. They stood there looking up. "Dark night," Donald said.

"Stygian," the man said.

Pete still had it in mind to brush him off, but he didn't do that. Instead he unlocked the door for him. He wanted to see what would happen. It was an adventure, but not a dangerous adventure. The man might steal Pete's ashtrays but he wouldn't kill him. If Pete got killed on the road it would be by some spiritual person in a sweatsuit, someone with his eyes on the far horizon and a wet Try God T-shirt in his duffel bag.

As soon as they left the parking lot the man lit a cigar. He blew a cloud of smoke over Pete's shoulder and sighed with pleasure. "Put it out," Pete told him.

"Of course," the man said. Pete looked into the rear-view mirror and saw the man take another long puff before dropping the cigar out the window. "Forgive me," he said. "I should have asked. Name's Webster, by the way."

Donald turned and looked back at him. "First name or last?"

The man hesitated. "Last," he said finally.

"I know a Webster," Donald said. "Mick Webster."

"There are many of us," Webster said.

"Big fellow, wooden leg," Pete said.

Donald gave Pete a look.

Webster shook his head. "Doesn't ring a bell. Still, I wouldn't deny the connection. Might be one of the cousinry."

"What's your daughter got?" Pete asked.

"That isn't clear," Webster answered. "It appears to be a female complaint of some nature. Then again it may be tropical." He was quiet for a moment, and then added: "If indeed it *is* tropical, I will have to assume some of the blame myself. It was my own vaulting ambition that first led us to the tropics and kept us in the tropics all those many years, exposed to every evil. Truly I have much to answer for. I left my wife there."

Donald said quietly, "You mean she died?"

"I buried her with these hands. The earth will be repaid, gold for gold."

"Which tropics?" Pete asked.

"The tropics of Peru."

"What part of Peru are they in?"

"The lowlands," Webster said.

Pete nodded. "What's it like down there?"

"Another world," Webster said. His tone was sepulchral. "A world better imagined than described."

"Far out," Pete said.

The three men rode in silence for a time. A line of trucks went past in the other direction, trailers festooned with running lights, engines roaring.

"Yes," Webster said at last, "I have much to answer for."

Pete smiled at Donald, but Donald had turned in his seat again and was gazing at Webster. "I'm sorry about your wife," Donald said.

"What did she die of?" Pete asked.

"A wasting illness," Webster said. "The doctors have no name for it, but I do." He leaned forward and said, fiercely, *"Greed."* Then he slumped back against his seat. "My greed, not hers. She wanted no part of it."

Pete bit his lip. Webster was a find and Pete didn't want to scare him off by hooting at him. In a voice low and innocent of knowingness, he asked, "What took you there?"

"It's difficult for me to talk about."

"Try," Pete told him.

"A cigar would make it easier."

Donald turned to Pete and said, "It's okay with me."

"All right," Pete said. "Go ahead. Just keep the window rolled down."

"Much obliged." A match flared. There were eager sucking sounds.

"Let's hear it," Pete said.

"I am by training an engineer," Webster began. "My work has exposed me to all but one of the continents, to desert and alp and forest, to every terrain and season of the earth. Some years ago I was hired by the Peruvian government to search for tungsten in the tropics. My wife and daughter accompanied me. We were the only white people for a thousand miles in any direction, and we had no choice but to live as the Indians lived — to share their food and drink and even their culture."

Pete said, "You knew the lingo, did you?"

"We picked it up." The ember of the cigar bobbed up and down. "We were used to learning as necessity decreed. At any rate, it became evident after a couple of years that there was no tungsten to be found. My wife had fallen ill and was pleading to be taken home. But I was deaf to her pleas, because by then I was on the trail of another metal — a metal far more valuable than tungsten."

"Let me guess," Pete said, "Gold?"

Donald looked at Pete, then back at Webster.

"Gold," Webster said. "A vein of gold greater than the Mother Lode itself. After I found the first traces of it nothing could tear me away from my search — not the sickness of my wife nor anything else. I was determined to uncover the vein, and so I did — but not before I laid my wife to rest. As I say, the earth will be repaid."

Webster was quiet. Then he said, "But life must go on. In the years since my wife's death I have been making the arrangements necessary to open the mine. I could have done it immediately, of course, enriching myself beyond measure, but I knew what that would mean — the exploitation of our beloved Indians, the brutal destruction of their environment. I felt I had too much to atone for already." Webster paused, and when he spoke again his voice was dull and rushed, as if he had used up all the interest he had in his own words. "Instead I drew up a program for returning the bulk of the wealth to the Indians themselves. A kind of trust fund. The interest alone will allow them to secure their ancient lands and rights in perpetuity. At the same time, our investors will be rewarded a thousandfold. Two-thousandfold. Everyone will prosper together."

"That's great," Donald said. "That's the way it ought to be."

Pete said, "I'm willing to bet that you just happen to have a few shares left. Am I right?"

Webster made no reply.

"Well?" Pete knew that Webster was on to him now, but he didn't care. The story had bored him. He'd expected something different, something original, and Webster had let him down. He hadn't even tried. Pete felt sour and stale. His eyes burned from cigar smoke and the high beams of road-hogging truckers. "Douse the stogie," he said to Webster. "I told you to keep the window down."

"Got a little nippy back there."

Donald said, "Hey, Pete. Lighten up."

"Douse it!"

Webster sighed. He got rid of the cigar.

"I'm a wreck," Pete said to Donald. "You want to drive for a while?"

Donald nodded.

Pete pulled over and they changed places.

Webster kept his counsel in the back seat. Donald hummed while he drove, until Pete told him to stop. Then everything was quiet.

Donald was humming again when Pete woke up. Pete stared sullenly at the road, at the white lines sliding past the car. After a few moments of this he turned and said, "How long have I been out?"

Donald glanced at him. "Twenty, twenty-five minutes."

Pete looked behind him and saw that Webster was gone. "Where's our friend?"

"You just missed him. He got out in Soledad. He told me to say thanks and goodbye."

"Soledad? What about his sick daughter? How did he explain her away?" Pete leaned over the seat. Both ashtrays were still in place. Floor mats. Door handles.

"He has a brother living there. He's going to borrow a car from him and drive the rest of the way in the morning."

"I'll bet his brother's living there," Pete said. "Doing fifty concurrent life sentences. His brother and his sister and his mom and his dad."

"I kind of liked him," Donald said.

"I'm sure you did," Pete said wearily.

"He was interesting. He'd been places."

"His cigars had been places, I'll give you that."

"Come on, Pete."

"Come on yourself. What a phony."

"You don't know that."

"Sure I do."

"How? How do you know?"

Pete stretched. "Brother, there are some things you're just born knowing. What's the gas situation?"

"We're a little low."

"Then why didn't you get some more?"

"I wish you wouldn't snap at me like that," Donald said.

"Then why don't you use your head? What if we run out?"

"We'll make it," Donald said. "I'm pretty sure we've got enough to make it. You didn't have to be so rude to him," Donald added.

Pete took a deep breath. "I don't feel like running out of gas tonight, okay?"

Donald pulled in at the next station they came to and filled the tank while Pete went to the men's room. When Pete came back, Donald was sitting in the passenger's seat. The attendant came up to the driver's window as Pete got in behind the wheel. He bent down and said, "Twenty-two fifty-five."

"You heard the man," Pete said to Donald.

Donald looked straight ahead. He didn't move.

"Cough up," Pete said. "This trip's on you."

Donald said, softly, "I can't."

"Sure you can. Break out that wad."

Donald glanced up at the attendant, then at Pete. "Please," he said. "Pete, I don't have it anymore."

Pete took this in. He nodded, and paid the attendnat.

Donald began to speak when they left the station but Pete cut him off. He said, "I don't want to hear from you right now. You just keep quiet or I swear to God I won't be responsible."

They left the fields and entered a tunnel of tall trees. The trees went on and on. "Let me get this straight," Pete said at last. "You don't have the money I gave you."

"You treated him like a bug or something," Donald said.

"You don't have the money," Pete said again.

Donald shook his head.

"Since I bought dinner, and since we didn't stop anywhere in between, I assume you gave it to Webster. Is that right? Is that what you did with it?"

"Yes."

Pete looked at Donald. His face was dark under the hood but he still managed to convey a sense of remove, as if none of this had anything to do with him.

"Why?" Pete asked. "Why did you give it to him?" When Donald didn't answer, Pete said, "A hundred dollars. Gone. Just like that. I *worked* for that money, Donald."

"I know, I know," Donald said.

"You don't know! How could you? You get money by holding out your hand."

"I work too," Donald said.

"You work too. Don't kid yourself, brother."

Donald leaned toward Pete, about to say something, but Pete cut him off again.

"You're not the only one on the payroll, Donald. I don't think you understand that. I have a family."

"Pete, I'll pay you back."

"Like hell you will. A hundred dollars!" Pete hit the steering wheel with the palm of his hand. "Just because you think I hurt some goofball's feelings. Jesus, Donald."

"That's not the reason," Donald said. "And I didn't just *give* him the money."

"What do you call it, then? What do you call what you did?"

"I *invested* it. I wanted a share, Pete." When Pete looked over at him Donald nodded and said again, "I wanted a share."

Pete said, "I take it you're referring to the gold mine in Peru."

"Yes," Donald said.

"You believe that such a gold mine exists?"

Donald looked at Pete, and Pete could see him just beginning to catch on. "You'll believe anything," Pete said. "Won't you? You really will believe anything at all."

"I'm sorry," Donald said, and turned away.

Pete drove on between the trees and considered the truth of what he had just said — that Donald would believe anything at all. And it came to him that it would be just like this unfair life for Donald to come out ahead in the end, by believing in some outrageous promise that would turn out to be true and that he, Pete, would reject out of hand because he was too wised up to listen to anybody's pitch anymore except for laughs. What a joke. What a joke if there really was a blessing to be had, and the blessing didn't come to the one who deserved it, the one who did all the work, but to the other.

And as if this had already happened Pete felt a shadow move upon him, darkening his thoughts. After a time he said, "I can see where all this is going, Donald."

"I'll pay you back," Donald said.

"No," Pete said. "You won't pay me back. You can't. You don't know how. All you've ever done is take. All your life."

Donald shook his head.

"I see exactly where this is going," Pete went on. "You can't work, you can't take care of yourself, you believe anything anyone tells you. I'm stuck with you, aren't I?" He looked over at Donald. "I've got you on my hands for good."

Donald pressed his fingers against the dashboard as if to brace himself. "I'll get out," he said.

Pete kept driving.

"Let me out," Donald said. "I mean it, Pete."

"Do you?"

Donald hesitated. "Yes," he said.

"Be sure," Pete told him. "This is it. This is for keeps."

"I mean it."

"All right. You made the choice." Pete braked the car sharply and swung it to the shoulder of the road. He turned off the engine and got out. Trees loomed on both sides, shutting out the sky. The air was cold and musty. Pete took Donald's duffel bag from the back seat and set it down behind the car. He stood there, facing Donald in the red glow of the taillights. "It's better this way," Pete said.

Donald just looked at him.

"Better for you," Pete said.

Donald hugged himself. He was shaking. "You don't have to say all that," he told Pete. "I don't blame you."

"Blame me? What the hell are you talking about? Blame me for what?"

"For anything," Donald said.

"I want to know what you mean by blame me."

"Nothing. Nothing, Pete. You'd better get going. God bless you."

"That's it," Pete said. He dropped to one knee, searching the packed dirt with his hands. He didn't know what he was looking for; his hands would know when they found it.

Donald touched Pete's shoulder. "You'd better go," he said.

Somewhere in the trees Pete heard a branch snap. He stood up. He looked at Donald, then went back to the car and drove away. He drove fast, hunched over the wheel, conscious of the way he was hunched and the shallowness of his breathing, refusing to look at the mirror above his head until there was nothing behind him but darkness.

Then he said, "A hundred dollars," as if there were someone to hear.

The trees gave way to fields. Metal fences ran beside the road, plastered with windblown scraps of paper. Tule fog hung above the ditches, spilling into the road, dimming the ghostly halogen lights that burned in the yards of the farms Pete passed. The fog left beads of water rolling up the windshield.

Pete rummaged among his cassettes. He found Pachelbel's Canon and pushed it into the tape deck. When the violins began to play he leaned back and assumed an attentive expression as if he were really listening to them. He smiled to himself like a man at liberty to enjoy music, a man who has finished his work and settled his debts, done all things meet and due.

And in this way, smiling, nodding to the music, he went another mile or so and pretended that he was not already slowing down, that he was not going to turn back, that he would be able to drive on like this, alone, and have the right answer when his wife stood before him in the doorway of his home and asked, Where is he? Where is your brother?

Biographical Notes

DONALD BARTHELME was born in Philadelphia and raised in Houston. His stories have appeared in a wide range of journals and magazines including *New American Review, Paris Review, Esquire,* and *The New Yorker.* He is the author of many books of fiction for adults and of a National Book Award–winning children's book, *The Slightly Irregular Fire Engine* (1972). Mr. Barthelme's newest novel, *Paradise,* is due out soon from Putnam.

CHARLES BAXTER lives in Ann Arbor and teaches at Wayne State University. His stories have appeared in *The Best American Short Stories 1982* and the *Pushcart Prize* anthologies. Viking Penguin has published two collections of his stories — *Harmony of the World* and *Through the Safety Net.*

ANN BEATTIE, who lives in Charlottesville, Virginia, has published many books of fiction, both novels and short story collections. Her latest collection, *Where You'll Find Me,* is due out this fall from Linden Press. She will serve as Guest Editor of *The Best American Short Stories 1987.*

JAMES LEE BURKE is the author of several novels and a collection of stories entitled *The Convict.* His forthcoming novels are *The Lost Get-Back Boogie* (LSU Press) and *The Neon Rain* (Henry Holt and Company). He lives with his children and his wife, Pearl, in Wichita, Kansas, where he teaches fiction writing in the M.F.A. program at Wichita State University.

ETHAN CANIN's first collection of short stories, which received a Houghton Mifflin Literary Fellowship, will be published in 1987. His work has appeared in *The Atlantic* and *Ploughshares,* among other magazines, and also in *The Best American Short Stories 1985.* He is a third-year medical student in Boston.

FRANK CONROY, author of the highly regarded autobiographical novel *Stop-Time,* teaches writing at Brandeis University and is director of the Literary Program of the National Endowment of the Arts. A longer version of "Gossip" is included in his recently published collection, *Midair* (Dutton).

RICHARD FORD is the author of the novel *The Sportswriter.* His new collection of short stories will be published by Atlantic Monthly Press in 1987.

TESS GALLAGHER's first collection of short stories, *The Lover of Horses,* will be published by Harper & Row this fall, and a book of her essays, *A Concert of Tenses,* will also be published this fall in the University of Michigan's Poets on Poetry series. Her story "The Leper" will appear in *Editor's Choice III* from Bantam. She lives most of the year in a house overlooking the Strait of Juan de Fuca.

AMY HEMPEL is the author of *Reasons to Live,* a collection of stories. She is a contributing editor of *Vanity Fair* and lives in New York City.

DAVID MICHAEL KAPLAN's fiction has appeared in *The Atlantic, The Ohio Review, The Mississippi Review,* and *The New Mexico Humanities Review,* and has been chosen for the 1985 PEN Syndicated Fiction Project. A first collection of stories, entitled *Comfort,* will be published by Viking in early 1987. He has received writing fellowships from the Fine Arts Work Center in Provincetown, Yaddo, and the Millay Colony for the Arts. He lives in Iowa City, Iowa, where he is working on a novel.

DAVID LIPSKY, a senior at Brown University in Providence, Rhode Island, was born in 1965 and grew up in New York City. His work has appeared in *The New Yorker.*

THOMAS McGUANE is the author of six novels and a forthcoming collection of stories, *To Skin a Cat* (Dutton/Seymour Lawrence). Mr. McGuane was educated at Michigan State University and the Yale School of Drama. He lives with his family in Livingston, Montana.

CHRISTOPHER McILROY has published short stories in *Sonora Review, Fiction, Story Quarterly, TriQuarterly,* and *The Missouri Review,* among others. He lives in Tucson, Arizona, with his wife, baby daughter, step-daughter, and raccoon, and is at work on a novel.

ALICE MUNRO was born in Wingham, Ontario, and attended the University of Western Ontario. She has published several books of fiction, two of which have received the Governor General's Award in Canada. Her newest collection of short stories, *The Progress of Love*, will be published this fall by Knopf. Ms. Munro lives in Clinton, Ontario.

JESSICA NEELY grew up in Rochester, New York. She attended Vassar College and Stanford University, and now lives in San Francisco. Her stories have appeared in *Tendril* and *New England Review and Bread Loaf Quarterly*, and she is at work on a collection of them.

KENT NELSON has lived in Colorado, Texas, South Carolina, and Georgia, and has had many part-time jobs, including city judge, tennis pro, and visiting professor. He has published nearly fifty stories in reviews such as *Southern, Missouri, Sewanee,* and *Virginia Quarterly,* and is the author of a novel, *Cold Wind River* (1981), and a story collection (1978). He lives in New Hampshire, where he is working on a novel.

GRACE PALEY, who was born in New York City in 1922, is the author of three volumes of stories: *The Little Disturbances of Man* (Doubleday, 1959; reprinted in the Penguin Fiction Series, 1985); *Enormous Changes at the Last Minute* (Farrar, Straus and Giroux, 1974); and *Later the Same Day* (Farrar, Straus and Giroux, 1985). Her book of poems, *Leaning Forward,* was also published in 1985, by Granite Press. Ms. Paley lives in New York City.

MONA SIMPSON's stories have appeared in *Ploughshares, The Iowa Review, North American Review,* and *The Paris Review,* and in the anthologies *Twenty under Thirty* and *Pushcart Prize.* Knopf will publish her first novel in January 1987.

JOY WILLIAMS lives in Florida. She is the author of two novels, *State of Grace* and *The Changeling,* and a collection of stories, *Taking Care.* A new collection of her short fiction will be published in 1987 by Vintage in its Contemporaries series.

TOBIAS WOLFF received the 1985 PEN/Faulkner Award for Fiction for his short novel, *The Barracks Thief.* "The Rich Brother" belongs to his most recent collection of stories, *Back in the World,* published last fall by Houghton Mifflin and by Bantam in the fall of 1986. He teaches at Syracuse University.

100 Other Distinguished Short Stories of the Year 1985

SELECTED BY SHANNON RAVENEL

DOLAN, J. D.
Grace. *Mississippi Review,* Spring.
DRISKELL, LEON V.
Martha Jean. *Prairie Schooner,* Fall.
DUBUS, ANDRE
Rose. *Ploughshares,* Vol. 11, Nos. 2 & 3.

ERDRICH, LOUISE
The Little Book. *Formations,* Spring.

FELDSHER, CONNIE HULL
Anniversary. *The Threepenny Review,* Summer.
FIDLER, SU
Night Bloom. *Carolina Quarterly,* Winter.
FREEMAN, CASTLE, JR.
Before He Went Out West. *The Massachusetts Review,* Summer/ Autumn.

GALLANT, MAVIS
From Cloud to Cloud. *The New Yorker,* July 8.
GERBER, MERRILL JOAN
At the Fence. *The Sewanee Review,* Winter.
GILDNER, GARY
Boats Coming Ashore. *The North American Review,* March.
Numbers. *Northwest Review,* Vol. 23, No. 1.
GILES, MOLLY
Talking to Strangers. *Five Fingers Review,* No. 2.
GLOVER, DOUGLAS
Heartsick. *The Iowa Review,* Vol. 14, No. 3.
GREENBERG, BARBARA, and GEORGE CHAMBERS
Monday. *Chicago Review,* Vol. 34, No. 4.
GURLEY, GEORGE H., JR.
Downturn. *Kansas Quarterly,* Vol. 17, Nos. 1 & 2.

HARABIN, VIRGINIA
Saturday, Sunday. *The Paris Review,* No. 97.
HARRIS, ELIZABETH
The World Record Holder. *Southwest Review,* Summer.
HOOD, MARY
Something Good for Ginnie. *The Georgia Review,* Fall.
HUDDLE, DAVID
Apache. *Denver Quarterly, Spring.*
Summer of the Magic Show. *Grand Street,* Summer.
HUMPHRIES, JENNY STONE
The Make-Believe Ballroom. *The North American Review,* June.

JACOBSEN, JOSEPHINE
Adios, Mr. Moxley. *Prairie Schooner,* Spring.
JANOWITZ, TAMA
Spells. *The New Yorker,* November 25.
JOHNSON, LESLIE
New Mexico. *Piedmont Literary Review,* Spring/Summer.
JOHNSON, WILLIS
The Girl Who Would Be Russian. *The Southern Review,* Winter.

KENNEY, SUSAN
In Case You Don't Come Back. *Hudson Review,* Summer.
KINSELLA, W. P.
Real Indians. *Waves,* Vol. 13, No. 4.
KORNBLATT, JOYCE R.
Offerings. *The Georgia Review,* Spring.

LEITMAN, D.
An Affair, I Guess. *Tendril,* No. 19– 20.

MATTISON, ALICE
They All Went Up to Amsterdam. *The New Yorker,* July 29.
MINOT, SUSAN
Allowance. *The New Yorker,* April 29.

SWENDSEN, LINDA
Flights. *Western Humanities Review,*
    Autumn.

TALLENT, ELIZABETH
Black Holes. *The New Yorker,* July.
TAYLOR, ROBERT, JR.
Fiddle and Bow. *Southwest Review,*
    Winter.
TURNER, RONALD F.
Luzon. *The Yale Review,* Summer.

UPDIKE, JOHN
The Wallet. *Yankee,* September.

WALKER, ALICE
Kindred Spirits. *Esquire,* August.
WARREN, ROSALIND
Penguin Flight. *Fiction Network,* Fall.
WASS, MARGARET P.
Seasons. *Story Quarterly,* No. 19.

WHISNANT, LUKE
Across from the Motoheads. *Grand
    Street,* Autumn.
WHITTEMORE, REED
The Death of Apples. *New Letters,*
    Spring.
WIEBE, DALLAS
Going to the Mountain. *Epoch,* Vol.
    14, No. 2.
WILLIAMS, JOY
Lu-Lu. *Grand Street,* Spring.
WOLFF, TOBIAS
Leviathan. *TriQuarterly,* Winter.
Soldier's Joy. *Esquire,* October.

YATES, DWIGHT
The Possum Is Not a Dream.
    Northwest Review, Vol. 23,
    No. 2.
YOURGRAY, BARRY
Sand. *The Paris Review,* No. 95.

Editorial Addresses of American and Canadian Magazines Publishing Short Stories

When available, the annual subscription rate, the average number of stories published per year, and the name of the editor follow the addresses.

Agni Review
P.O. Box 660
Amherst, MA 01004
$8, 10, Sharon Dunn

A.I.D. Review
American Institute of Discussion
P.O. Box 103
Oklahoma City, OK 73101
Ron Robinson

Amazing
Dragon Publishing
P.O. Box 110
Lake Geneva, WI 53147
George Scithers

Amelia
329 East Street
Bakersfield, CA 93304
$6, 10, Frederick A. Raborg, Jr.

Analog Science Fiction/Science Fact
380 Lexington Avenue
New York, NY 10017
$19.50, 70, Stanley Schmidt

Antaeus
18 West 30th Street
New York, NY 10001
$20, 15, Daniel Halpern

Antietam Review
33 West Washington Street
Hagerstown, MD 21740
$3, 10, Ellyn Bache

Antioch Review
P.O. Box 148
Yellow Springs, OH 45387
$18, 20, Robert S. Fogarty

Apalachee Quarterly
P.O. Box 20106
Tallahassee, FL 32304
$12, 10, Allen Woodman, Barbara Hanby, Monica Faeth

Arizona Quarterly
University of Arizona
Tucson, AZ 85721
$5, 12, Albert F. Gegenheimer

Ascent
English Department
University of Illinois
Urbana, IL 61801
$3, 20, Daniel Curley

Atlantic
8 Arlington Street
Boston, MA 02116
$9.75, 25, C. Michael Curtis

Aura Literary/Arts Review
P.O. Box University Center
University of Alabama
Birmingham, AL 35294
$6, 10, rotating editorship

Bennington Review
Bennington College
Bennington, VT 05201
$4, 10, Nicholas Delbanco

Black Ice
6022 Sunnyview Road NE
Salem, OR 97305
20, Dale Shank

Black Warrior Review
P.O. Box 2936
University, AL 35486
$5, 12, Gabby Hyman

Boston Review
991 Massachusetts Avenue
Cambridge, MA 02138
$9, 6, Nicholas Bromell, Gail Caldwell

Brown Journal of the Arts
Box 1852
Brown University
Providence, RI 02912
rotating editorship

California Quarterly
100 Sproul Hall
University of California
Davis, CA 95616
$10, 4, Nixa Schell

Canadian Fiction
Box 946
Station F
Toronto, Ontario
M4Y 2N9 Canada
$30, 16, Geoffrey Hancock

Capilano Review
Capilano College
2055 Purcell Way
North Vancouver
British Columbia
Canada
$9, 10, Dorothy Jantzen

Carolina Quarterly
Greenlaw Hall 066A
University of North Carolina
Chapel Hill, NC 27514
$10, 20, rotating editorship

Chariton Review
Division of Language & Literature
Northeast Missouri State University
Kirksville, MO 63501
$4, 10, Jim Barnes

Chattahoochee Review
DeKalb Community College
2101 Womack Road
Dunwoody, GA 30338
$12.50, 25, Lamar York

Chelsea
P.O. Box 5880
Grand Central Station
New York, NY 10163
$9, 6, Sonia Raiziss

Chicago Review
5801 South Kenwood
University of Chicago
Chicago, IL 60637
$10, 20, Steve Heminger, Steve Schroer

Choteau Review
Box 10016
Kansas City, MO 64111
David Perkins

Christopher Street
249 West Broadway
New York, NY 10013
$24, 12, Charles Ortleb

Cimarron Review
208 Life Sciences East
Oklahoma State University
Stillwater, OK 74078
$10, 15, Neil John Hatchett

Clockwatch Review
Driftwood Publications
737 Penbrook Way
Hartland, WI 53029
$6, 5, James Plath

Colorado State Review
360 Eddy Building
Colorado State University
Fort Collins, CO 80523
$15, 10, Wayne Ude

Columbia Magazine of Poetry and
    Prose
404 Dodge Hall
Columbia University
New York, NY 10027
$4.50, rotating editorship

Commentary
165 East 56th Street
New York, NY 10022
$33, 5, Marion Magid

Confrontation
English Department
C. W. Post College of Long Island
    University
Greenvale, NY 11548
$8, 25, Martin Tucker

Conjunctions
33 West 9th Street
New York, NY 10011
$16, 5, Brandford Morrow

Crazyhorse
Department of English
University of Arkansas
Little Rock, AR 72204
$8, 10, David Jauss

Crescent Review
P.O. Box 15065
Winston-Salem, NC 27103
$7.50, 24, Bob Shar

Crosscurrents
2200 Glastonbury Road
Westlake Village, CA 91361
$15, 50, Linda Brown Michelson

Crucible
Atlantic Christian College
Wilson, NC 27893
Agnes H. McDonald

CutBank
Department of English
University of Montana
Missoula, MT 59801
$6.50, 10, Craig Holden

Denver Quarterly
University of Denver
Denver, CO 80208
$12, 10, David Milofsky

Descant
P.O. Box 314
Station P
Toronto, Ontario
M5S 2S5 Canada
$18, 20, Karen Mulhallen

Epoch
251 Goldwin Smith Hall
Cornell University
Ithaca, NY 14853
$8, 15, C. S. Giscombe

Esquire
2 Park Avenue
New York, NY 10016
$17.94, 15, Rust Hills

event
c/o Douglas College
P.O. Box 2503
New Westminster
British Columbia
V3L 5B2 Canada
$8, 10, Leona Gem

Fantasy & Science Fiction
Box 56
Cornwall, CT 06753
$17.50, 100, Edward L. Ferman

Farmer's Market
Midwest Farmer's Market, Inc.
P.O. Box 1272
Calesburg, IL 61402
5, John E. Hughes

Fiction International
Department of English
San Diego State University
San Diego, CA 92182
$12, 25, Harold Jaffe, Larry McCaffrey

Fiction Network
P.O. Box 5651
San Francisco, CA 94101
Jay Schaefer

Fiddlehead
The Observatory
University of New Brunswick
Fredericton, New Brunswick
E3B 5A3 Canada
$15, 20, Kent Thompson

Five Fingers Review
100 Valencia Street
Suite 303
San Francisco, CA 94103
$8, 5, John Hish

Florida Review
Department of English
University of Central Florida
Orlando, FL 32816
$6, 16, Pat Rushina

Fm. Five (formerly Fiction Monthly)
P.O. Box 882108
San Francisco, CA 84188
$9, 15, Stephen Woodhams

Formations
University of Wisconsin Press
Journals Division
114 North Murray Street
Madison, WI 33715
$15, 4, Jonathan Brent, David Hayman

Four Quarters
LaSalle College
20th and Olney Avenues
Philadelphia, PA 19141
$8, 10, John Christopher Kleis

From Mt. San Angelo
Virginia Center for the Creative Arts
Sweet Briar, VA 24595
8, William Smart

Frontiers
Women's Studies Program
University of Colorado
Boulder, CO 80309
$14, Katni George

Gargoyle
Paycock Press
P.O. Box 3567
Washington, DC 20007
$10, 25, Richard Peabody, Gretchen Johnsen

Georgia Review
University of Georgia
Athens, GA 30602
$9, 15, Stanley W. Lindberg, Stephen Corey

Good Housekeeping
959 Eighth Avenue
New York, NY 10019
$14.97, 24, Naomi Lewis

Grain
Box 1154
Regina, Saskatchewan
S4P 3B4 Canada
$9, 15, Brenda Riches

Grand Street
50 Riverside Drive
New York, NY 10024
$20, 20, Ben Sonnenberg

Gray's Sporting Journal
205 Willow Street
South Hamilton, MA 01982
$23.50, 8, Edward E. Gray

Great River Review
211 West 7th
Winona, MN 55987
$7, 12, Orval Lunda

Greensboro Review
Department of English
University of North Carolina
Greensboro, NC 27412
$5, 16, Lee Zacharias

Harper's Magazine
2 Park Avenue
New York, NY 10016
$18, 15, Lewis Lapham

Hawaii Review
University of Hawaii
Department of English
1733 Donaghlo Road
Honolulu, HI 96822
$6, 12

Helicon Nine
P.O. Box 22412
Kansas City, MO 64113
$15, 6, Ann Slegman

Hoboken Terminal
P.O. Box 841
Hoboken, NJ 07030
$6, 15, C. H. Trowbridge, Jack Nestor

Hudson Review
684 Park Avenue
New York, NY 10021
$16, 8, Paula Deitz, Frederick Morgan

Indiana Review
316 North Jordan Avenue
Bloomington, IN 47405
$10, 20, Eric McGraw

Iowa Review
EPB 308
University of Iowa
Iowa City, IA 52242
$12, 10, David Hamilton

Isaac Asimov's Science Fiction
  Magazine
380 Lexington Avenue
New York, NY 10017
$19.50, 100, Gardner Dozois

Jewish Monthly
1640 Rhode Island Avenue NW
Washington, DC 20036
$8, 3, Marc Silver

Kansas Quarterly
Department of English
Denison Hall
Kansas State University
Manhattan, KS 66506
$12, 35, Harold Schneider, Ben Nyberg,
  John Rees

Karamu
English Department
Eastern Illinois University
Charleston, IL 61920
John Guzlowski

Kenyon Review
Kenyon College
Gambier, OH 43022
$15, 15, Philip D. Church, Galbraith M.
  Crump

Ladies' Home Journal
3 Park Avenue
New York, NY 10016
$20, 10, Constance Leisure

Latitude 30°18'
1124B Regan Terrace
Austin, TX 78704
$5.50, 5, Joseph Slate

Lilith
The Jewish Women's Magazine
250 West 57th Street
New York, NY 10019
$12, 5, Julia Wolf Mazow

Literary Review
Farleigh Dickinson University
Madison, NJ 07940
$12, 25, Walter Cummins

Little Magazine
Dragon Press
P.O. Box 78
Pleasantville, NY 10570
$16, 5

Mademoiselle
350 Madison Avenue
New York, NY 10017
$12, 14, Eileen Schnurr

Malahat Review
University of Victoria
Box 1700
Victoria, British Columbia
V8W 2Y2 Canada
$15, 25, Constance Rooke

Mark
2514 Student Union Building
University of Toledo
2801 West Brancroft Street
Toledo, OH 43606
$6, 10, Zona Gabe

Massachusetts Review
Memorial Hall
University of Massachusetts
Amherst, MA 01002
*$12, 15, Mary Heath, John Hicks, Fred
Robinson*

McCall's
230 Park Avenue
New York, NY 10169
$9.95, 20, Helen DelMonte

Michigan Quarterly Review
3032 Rackham Building
University of Michigan
Ann Arbor, MI 48109
$13, 10, Laurence Goldstein

Mid-American Review
106 Hanna Hall
Department of English
Bowling Green State University
Bowling Green, OH 48109
$6, 15, Robert Early

Minnesota Review
Department of English
State University of New York
Stony Brook, NY 11794
$7, Fred Pfeil

Mississippi Review
Southern Station
Box 5144
Hattiesburg, MS 39406-5144
$10, 25, Frederick Barthelme

Missouri Review
Department of English, 231 A&S
University of Missouri
Columbia, MO 65211
$10, 25, Speer Morgan, Greg Michalson

Mother Jones
1663 Mission Street
San Francisco, CA 94103
$12, 5, Deirdre English

Ms.
119 West 40th Street
New York, NY 10018
$14, 5, Patricia Carbine

MSS
Department of English
State University of New York
Binghamton, NY 13901
$10, 30, Liz Rosenberg

Nantucket Review
P.O. Box 1234
Nantucket, MA 02254
$6, 15, Richard Burns, Richard Cumbie

Nebraska Review
Writers' Workshop
ASH 215
University of Nebraska
Omaha, NE 68182
$5, 10, Art Homer, Richard Duggin

Negative Capability
6116 Timberly Road North
Mobile, AL 36609
$12, 15, Sue Walker, Ron Walker

New England Review and Bread Loaf
  Quarterly
Box 170
Hanover, NH 03755
$12, 10, Sydney Lea, Jim Schley

New Letters
University of Missouri
5310 Harrison
Kansas City, MO 64110
$15, 10, David Ray

New Mexico Humanities Review
Box A
New Mexico Tech
Socorro, NM 87801
$8, 15, John Rothfork

New Orleans Review
Loyola University
New Orleans, LA 70118
$20, 15, John Biguenet

New Quarterly
English Language Proficiency
  Programme
The University of Waterloo
Waterloo, Ontario
N2L 3G1 Canada
$10, 5, Linda Kenyon

New Renaissance
9 Heath Road
Arlington, MA 02174
*$10.50, 10, Louise T. Reynolds, Harry
  Jackel*

The New Yorker
25 West 43rd Street
New York, NY 10036
$32, 100

North American Review
1222 West 27th Street
Cedar Falls, IA 50614
$11, 35, Robley Wilson, Jr.

Northwest Review
369 PLC
University of Oregon
Eugene, OR 97403
$11, 10, Cecelia Hagen

Ohio Journal
Department of English
Ohio State University
164 West 17th Avenue
Columbus, OH 43210
$5, 4

Ohio Review
Ellis Hall
Ohio University
Athens, OH 45701
$12, 20, Wayne Dodd

Old Hickory Review
P.O. Box 1178
Jackson, TN 38301
$5, 5, Drew Brewer

Omni
1965 Broadway
New York, NY 10023-5965
$24, 36, Ellen Datlow

Ontario Review
9 Honey Brook Drive
Princeton, NJ 08540
$8, 8, Raymond J. Smith

Other Voices
820 Ridge Road
Highland Park, IL 60035
$15, 20, Delores Weinberg

Paris Review
541 East 72nd Street
New York, NY 10021
$16, 15, George Plimpton

Passages North
William Boniface Fine Arts Center
7th Street & 1st Avenue South
Escanaba, MI 49829
$2, 12, Elinor Benedict

Pequod
536 Hill Street
San Francisco, CA 94114
$9, 5, Mark Rudman

Piedmont Literary Review
The Piedmont Literary Society
P.O. Box 3656
Danville, VA 24543
$10, 10, David Craig

Plainswoman
P.O. Box 8027
Grand Forks, ND 58202
$10, 20, Emily Johnson

Playboy
919 North Michigan Avenue
Chicago, IL 60611
$22, 20, Alice K. Turner, Teresa Grosch

Playgirl
3420 Ocean Park Boulevard
Suite 3000
Santa Monica, CA 90405
$20, 15, Mary Ellen Strote

Ploughshares
Emerson College
100 Beacon Street
Boston, MA
$14, 25, DeWitt Henry

Poetry East
Star Route 1
Earlysville, VA 22936
$10, 5, Richard Jones

Prairie Schooner
201 Andrews Hall
University of Nebraska
Lincoln, NE 68588
$11, 20, Hugh Luke

Present Tense
165 East 56th Street
New York, NY 10022
$14, 5, Leonard Krigel

Primavera
Ida Noyes Hall
University of Chicago
1212 East 59th Street
Chicago, IL 60637
$5, 10, Ann Gearen

Prism International
University of British Columbia
Vancouver, British Columbia
V6T 1W5 Canada
$10, 12, John Schoutsen

Quarry Magazine
P.O. Box 1061
Kingston, Ontario
K7L 4Y5 Canada
$16, 10, Bob Hilderly

Quarry West
Porter College
University of California
Santa Cruz, CA 95060

Quarterly West
312 Olpin Union
University of Utah
Salt Lake City, UT 84112
$6.50, 10, Wyn Cooper

RE:AL
Stephen F. Austin State University
Nacogdoches, TX 75962
$4, 5, Neal B. Houston

Redbook
959 Eighth Avenue
New York, NY 10019
$11.97, 35, Kathy Sagan

Richmond Quarterly
P.O. Box 12263
Richmond, VA 23241
$10, 20, William S. Simpson, Jr.

River City Review
P.O. Box 34275
Louisville, KY 40232
$5, 10, Richard L. Neumayer

River Styx
Big River Association
7420 Cornell
St. Louis, MO 63130
Jan Castro

A Room of One's Own
P.O. Box 46160
Station G
Vancouver, British Columbia
V6R 4G5 Canada
$10, 12

Rubicon
McGill University
853 rue Sherbrooke ouest
Montreal, Quebec
H3A 2T6 Canada
$8, 10, Peter O'Brien

Salmagundi Magazine
Skidmore College
Saratoga Springs, NY 12866
$10, 2, Robert and Peggy Boyers

San Jose Studies
San Jose State University
San Jose, CA 95192
$12, 5, Selma R. Burkom

Saturday Night
70 Bond Street
Suite 500
Toronto, Ontario
M5B 2J3 Canada
Robert Fulford

Seattle Review
Padelford Hall
GN-30
University of Washington
Seattle, WA 98195
$6, 10, Charles Johnson

Seventeen
830 Third Avenue
New York, NY 10022
$13.95, 12, Bonni Price

Sewanee Review
University of the South
Sewanee, TN 37375
$12, 10, George Core

Shenandoah
Box 722
Lexington, VA 24450
$8, 10, James Boatwright

Sinister Wisdom
P.O. Box 1023
Rockland, ME 04841
$14, Melanie Kaye/Kantrowitz

South Carolina Review
Department of English
Clemson University
Clemson, SC 29631
$5, Richard J. Calhoun, Robert W. Hill

South Dakota Review
University of South Dakota
Box 111 University Exchange
Vermillion, SD 57069
$10, 25, John R. Milton

Southern Review
43 Allen Hall
University Station
Baton Rouge, LA 70893
$9, 20, Lewis P. Simpson, James Olney

Southwest Review
Southern Methodist University
Box 4374
Dallas, TX 75275
$10, 15, Willard Spiegelman

Sou'wester
Department of English
Southern Illinois University
Edwardsville, IL 62026
$4, 10, Joanne Brew Callander

St. Andrews Review
St. Andrews Presbyterian College
Laurinburg, NC 28352
$12, 10, Dr. Robbie Rankin

Stories
14 Beacon Street
Boston, MA 02108
$20, 30, Amy R. Kaufman

Story Quarterly
P.O. Box 1416
Northbrook, IL 60062
$12, 20, Anne Brashler

Telescope
15201 Wheeler Lane
Sparks, MD 21152
Julia Wendell, Jack Stephens

Tendril
Box 512
Green Harbor, MA 02041
$12, 12, George E. Murphy, Jr.

Texas Review
English Department
Sam Houston State University
Huntsville, TX 77341
$4.20, 15, Paul Ruffin

Threepenny Review
P.O. Box 9131
Berkeley, CA 94709
$8, 10, Wendy Lesser

Toronto South Asian Review
P.O. Box 6986
Station A
Toronto, Ontario
M5W 1X7 Canada
M. G. Vassanji

TriQuarterly
1735 Benson Avenue
Northwestern University
Evanston, IL 60201
$16, 30, Reginald Gibbons

Twilight Zone Magazine
800 Second Avenue
New York, NY 10017
$11.97, 45, John Bensink

U.S. Catholic
221 West Madison Street
Chicago, IL 60606
The Rev. Mark J. Brummel, CMF

University of Windsor Review
Department of English
University of Windsor
Windsor, Ontario
N9B 3P4 Canada
$10, 40, Eugene McNamara

Virginia Quarterly Review
One West Range
Charlottesville, VA 22903
$10, 12, Staige D. Blackford

Wascana Review
English Department
University of Regina
Regina, Saskatchewan
S4S 0A2 Canada
$5, 10, Joan Givner

Waves
79 Denham Drive
Richmond Hill, Ontario
L4C 6H9 Canada
$8, 20, Bernice Lever

Webster Review
Webster University
Webster Groves, MO 63119
$5, 5, Nancy Schapiro

West Branch
Department of English
Bucknell University
Lewisburg, PA 17837
$5, 10, Karl Patten, Robert Taylor

Western Humanities Review
University of Utah
Salt Lake City, UT 84112
$15, 10, Jack Carlington

William and Mary Review
College of William and Mary
Williamsburg, VA 23186
$3, 5, rotating editorship

Wind/Literary Review
RFD #1
Box 809K
Pikeville, KY 51501
$6, 20, Quentin R. Howard

Writers Forum
University of Colorado
P.O. Box 7150
Colorado Springs, CO 80933
$8.95, 15, Alexander Blackburn

Yale Review
250 Church Street
1902A Yale Station
New Haven, CT 06520
$14, 12, Kai Erikson

Yankee
Yankee, Inc.
Dublin, NH 03444
$15, 10, Judson D. Hale, Sr.